The Little Village Library

Helen Rolfe writes contemporary women's fiction and enjoys weaving stories about family, friendship, secrets, and community. Characters often face challenges and must fight to overcome them, but above all, Helen's stories always have a happy ending.

You can visit Helen online at www.helenjrolfe. com, on Facebook @helenjrolfewriter and on Twitter @HJRolfe

The Little Village Library

Helen Rolfe

ORION

First published in Great Britain in 2020 by Orion Books,
an imprint of The Orion Publishing Group Ltd
Carmelite House, 50 Victoria Embankment,
London EC4Y 0DZ

An Hachette UK company

1 3 5 7 9 10 8 6 4 2

A CIP catalogue record for this book is
available from the British Library.

ISBN (Mass Market Paperback) 978 1 4091 9137 7
ISBN (eBook) 978 1 4091 9138 4

Typeset by Input Data Services Ltd, Somerset

Printed and bound in Great Britain by Clays Ltd, Elcograf S.p.A.

www.orionbooks.co.uk

Thank you to all the libraries out there . . . may you continue to be a wealth of information, a source of escapism with the wonderful stories that line your shelves, and bring people together for many years to come

Prologue

I never thought I'd get this far. I never thought I'd be able to share what happened to me. I thought if I buried it deep enough it would all go away . . . that I could run from the pain.

I move a little to the left so that the winter sun bouncing off one of the cars parked outside doesn't pierce my eyes and make this any harder, although not being able to see the faces looking up at me expectantly could be a help – as could a very strong drink, or a hefty dose of courage. I don't actually need the lectern. I don't have notes; what I'm going to say will come from deep inside of me.

A gamut of emotions hit me as I place my diary on the lectern and rest my hands on top of it. The physical prop is going some way to steady my nerves, but for so long I've been frightened. I've been embarrassed about what happened; anxious people would discover the truth and think of me differently. For years I have lived with this secret, too scared to do anything about it. Sometimes I've been angry with myself for letting it get so out of hand and not putting a stop to it sooner, but the self-loathing has to stop. I never asked for any of it to happen to me. I didn't deserve it.

There are five rows of chairs with some thirty, possibly forty, faces looking right at me. Some look sceptical, and some look apprehensive as though they're not going to like what I have to say. Others who are here already know my pain and are anxious for me. All I hope is that what I'm about to say will reach at least one of these people who might be facing the same dilemmas as I once did and help them to know they're not alone. I hope that what I have to share lets them know it's OK to admit there's a problem . . . that it's OK to take action to change your own life . . . OK to face the cold hard facts.

A latecomer catches me off guard as they sneak into the last remaining seat. Funny how it only takes a tiny thing to make me want to run. But I've been running away long enough and as the room falls into a hushed silence and my heart begins to pound, my mouth turns dry. It's time. It's time for me to share my story.

Because, behind closed doors, only you can really know the truth.

Three Months Earlier . . .

I

Adam

'This place is so cool.' Zac – nine years old and as inquisitive as most boys of his age – flipped through the comics in the stand at the front of Cloverdale Library before he lost interest and dashed up and down the orderly aisles in search of more meaty material.

'I don't know why we have to come in here,' Zoe huffed. Adam's fourteen-year-old daughter wasn't as low maintenance as Zac. The teen hormones had kicked in and he knew he had a battle on his hands to manage the minefield of changes about to come his way. Plenty already had, and Adam knew he could handle more. He had his kids, and nothing was going to get in the way of him giving them the life they deserved.

'Make the effort, Zoe,' he told her, 'it's not that bad. Who knows . . . if you actually look, you might find something you'd like to read.'

'Doubt it.'

A chubby woman dressed in a long, floaty yellow cotton dress came bustling over. 'If you're looking for teen fiction, we have plenty to choose from.' The woman led Zoe over to the shelves against the wall and Adam hoped she'd have better luck convincing Zoe there might be something here for her. Anything he said these days was wrong.

He followed Zac, who'd found a David Walliams book and the full set of Harry Potters he already had at home. But Adam's eye was drawn to some bright yellow doors across the car park out the back of the library. They were bi-folds, concertinaed open at one end; someone was milling about inside.

'That's the Library of Shared Things,' the woman who'd taken Zoe to the teenage section told him. 'It's a new initiative for Cloverdale, opening any day now.'

'What's a library of shared things?'

'Oh, it's wonderful. Jennifer – she's the woman in charge . . . I must introduce you – well, she has set it up and negotiated suppliers to provide lots of different products from bread makers – I already have my eye on that – to pasta machines, a lawn mower, garden rakes, a badminton set . . .' She thought hard. 'I can't remember too many more off the top of my head, but locals can borrow items for a few pounds each, use them for as long as we need, and then give them back. You know, I almost bought a bread maker last month, but when Jennifer told me I could borrow one and test it out, I thought, why not? Knowing me, I'll get bored of it soon enough anyway and then be in trouble with my husband for wasting money.' Her laughter was enough to make Zoe pull a face from behind the book she was actually making some effort to look at.

'I'm Elaine,' the woman went on, at last taking a breath from her spiel. 'And you are?'

'I'm Adam.' He held out a hand. 'And this is my daughter Zoe. My son Zac is around here somewhere.' He knew he had to make an effort. It was why they'd come to Cloverdale. They'd moved to London from Australia, but life in the big city wasn't what he'd had in mind. The anonymity was good, but the kids deserved a bit of space, and he could never afford to buy there, at least not if he wanted to get a home for all three of them where they weren't living on top of each other. And so when he'd started looking at villages closer to his work with good schools, affordable housing and which would take away his strenuous daily commute by train, he'd leapt at the chance to buy in Cloverdale. And now, here they were.

'Oh, what a lovely accent, Adam. Where are you from?'

'England.'

'No, that's a New Zealand accent if ever I heard one.'

'It's Australian, and it's only a slight twang. I was born in this country.' Come on, kids, he thought to himself, make your selections, and let's get out of here.

'So what brings you back? Family?'

'Something like that.' Thankfully Zac timed it perfectly and piped up, asking to join the library.

Elaine reeled off everything they'd need to bring with them as proof of address and to head off any further questions he said he'd come back another time.

'Well, it was good to meet you,' Elaine called after him.

He raised a hand in return and left, glad of the summer breeze outside and to escape her look of interest. A local busybody was all he needed.

Adam was shattered. He'd been in Cloverdale for twenty-four hours, the cottage was a tip with boxes everywhere, the kids had been fighting and the carpet in Zac's room had taken a soaking when Zac spilt a full glass of Ribena over it after knocking it off the windowsill. He'd rushed out to buy cleaning supplies, scrubbed at the carpet and left it to dry. He'd dragged Zac's mattress into Zoe's bedroom, much to her intense displeasure, and now he had the joy of lying here on the sofa listening to them bicker. He didn't understand why they couldn't face one more night with each other; they'd been sharing a bedroom at the home they'd rented in London for the last three years. But then they'd been kids of eleven and six when they'd left Australia, and both had clung together. Now Zoe was a teen he should've known it wouldn't last.

When he tripped over a box in the hallway he swore through gritted teeth, and, using his foot, shoved it out of the way, then the next box and the next, kicking each one to vent the frustration and resentment at everything that had gone on in this family.

When he was done he took a moment in the kitchen to gather himself, calm down, take deep breaths, before he went upstairs to sort out the kids.

He must've trodden so quietly in his tired state that his soft footsteps didn't alert either of them, and, before he opened the door to what was Zoe's bedroom now, he stopped and listened. He smiled; they were playing a game where one knocked on the wall to tap out a tune from a TV series and the other one had to guess. He listened to two rounds of it – Zoe had done the *Neighbours* theme tune, which Zac guessed straight away; Zac did *Star Wars* and Zoe had no idea but berated him for choosing something too boyish that she didn't have a hope of guessing. He was about to go in and say goodnight when he heard the next topic of conversation.

'Zoe, do you think this is our home now?'

'Of course it is, Dumbo; Dad bought it.'

'Don't call me Dumbo.'

'Sorry.'

She must be tired if she was apologising, Adam thought. Mostly Zoe tolerated Zac but occasionally she mothered him and looked out for her little brother, and it was lovely to witness. He wondered whether this latest move would trigger so many emotions in Zac that he started to wet the bed again like he had when they first left Australia. Hardly surprising after the shock departure, and it had continued on and off for the last three years. At one point Adam had tried to get Zac to wear night-time pull-ups again, but Zac had screamed and yelled and refused; he didn't want to be a baby. And so Adam had faced night after night of washing sheets, and the duvet when it got wrapped around his little body and bore the brunt. Zac hadn't wet the bed in almost three months and Adam crossed his fingers that tonight wouldn't be a setback.

'No talking in your sleep,' Zac instructed and Adam had to smile. He loved hovering and eavesdropping on them. They talked like kids when there was nobody else around, no one to judge them, and they didn't have to put on a front.

'I don't talk in my sleep!'

'You do too!'

'Be quiet, Zac. I'm tired.' Zoe hadn't escaped the emotional turmoil either. She hadn't wet the bed but she'd had nightmares when they first left Australia. She'd wake up crying out. He'd raced in more than once and hugged her tight, rocking her to sleep each time. Thankfully Zoe had quickly fallen back to sleep after each time it happened, hadn't asked many questions, and the nightmares had eventually stopped. Or maybe they hadn't. Perhaps Zoe still had dreams, and she just didn't tell him about them anymore.

'Zoe . . .'

'Zac, go to sleep.'

'Zo-Zo . . .'

'Don't ever call me that!' Oh dear, Adam had tried to use her childhood name once too and got a similar response. Poor Zac. He was probably hyped up from all the excitement of the move and wanted to settle his mind down in the only way he knew how, by talking to his sister. Adam felt sure Zoe sometimes forgot he was only nine. But then she was only fourteen, not too much older for what they'd had to handle so far.

'Why doesn't Mum want us, Zoe?'

'Zac, I don't know.' Her voice wobbled but Adam could tell she was trying to stay brave for her brother.

'Doesn't she love us anymore?'

'I don't know.'

'You don't know anything!'

'Goodnight, Zac.'

But Zac didn't answer. And somehow Adam suspected he might be changing bed sheets again tonight.

A week later and the sunshine streaming into the windows of Lilliput Cottage woke Adam from the heaviest sleep he'd had since they'd moved in. Moving house was hard, but buying this place, finally having a sense of permanency or at least the prospect of it, must've helped. And Zoe hadn't woken up screaming once, and Zac's bedding and mattress had been dry every morning. They were settling in just fine. And he knew he owed it to them to try to do the same.

For the last few days he'd taken time off work and got the kids organised. Their days had been jam-packed. There'd been school uniform to buy, equipment – everything from pencils and pens to protractors, calculators and new pencil cases – and they'd done some reconnaissance about the best ways to get to school by car and on foot. The kids had made some friends too. They'd all gone back to join the library where Zoe had got chatting with another girl, Ava, and immediately formed a tight friendship, and Zac had met a boy called Archie in the playground. It turned out that Archie's mum was Jennifer, the woman in charge of the Library of Shared Things, and in the park it had taken her all of a second to enlist his help with starting the venture up.

He'd been in to the outbuilding to show-off his DIY skills by assembling a few hutch wall units to store the items on, and he'd helped haul a desk inside as the boys played ball in the car park. Later today it was the opening ceremony and he'd volunteered his help after Jennifer's persuasion, because it was about time he started to become a part of the community here in Cloverdale and make a life for himself. And taking himself for a lonely pint up at the pub really didn't count.

In London Adam had enjoyed the fact that nobody asked questions; they went about their lives and never expected the Parker family to explain themselves. He'd always known a village would run completely different-ly, but as long as people here kept their noses out of his business then everything would be fine. He'd give Elaine a wide berth for a while as he knew the questions were bubbling away beneath the surface and she was bound to ask them sooner or later.

And that couldn't happen. Because he never wanted anyone here to find out what he'd done.

2

Jennifer

Jennifer unlocked the first yellow door and, with the sun out in full force and not a rain cloud in sight, she folded back the concertina sections until they were against the far wall. As part of the remodelling of these outbuildings – once a row of four derelict and unused garages lining the rear of the car park behind Cloverdale's main library and handful of shops – high windows had been installed all round to generate the extra light that flooded in now.

The project to launch the Library of Shared Things was something for Jennifer to throw her energy into. After the ordeal she'd put everyone through eight years ago, she'd settled back into her role as a stay-at-home mum of three children. But lately, she'd become desperate for a lifeline, and last year, while visiting a friend near Crystal Palace, she'd found one. Her friend had spilt wine on the carpet, dragged Jennifer around the corner to an actual library, and within those doors she'd discovered the Library of Things. The founder, Rebecca, had just finished a presentation to others who might be interested in adopting the concept in their local community, and, while her friend borrowed a carpet steamer,

Jennifer booked herself on the next tour, and the idea had been born.

She'd left the Library of Things not only a little bit merry after her wine but enthralled by the idea that she could offer something similar to Cloverdale. Two weeks later and she had more information; she also had the determination that this was going to work. Because what Cloverdale really needed was to regain that sense of community her mum had always raved about. Somewhere along the line, with modernisation and busy lives, it had been lost and Jennifer longed to bring it back to the village with its expansive green, the duck pond surrounded by the white picket fence, its wood-beamed pub and chocolate-box houses in a mishmash of sizes and colours. There was a small bakery, a post office she'd hate to see disappear, and a playground on part of the green. And it was home.

After her second meeting with Rebecca, Jennifer approached the owners of Buddleia Farm. On the outskirts of Cloverdale, it was a sprawling, beautiful place with a walled garden, fountains, lush trees and a splendid lake bordered by oak trees. The farm had been in the same family for generations and the family were well known for their philanthropic work, supporting a number of major charities. And so Jennifer had seen an opportunity, got them on board, liaised with the local council, and it had been all systems go.

Now, behind the bright yellow doors, the Library of Shared Things was about to become one hundred per cent real with the opening ceremony outside beneath the sunshine a chance for locals to see what it was all about.

Items filled the hutches against the walls, with

everything from a lawn mower and hedge trimmer to a wallpaper stripper, a nail gun and a tea urn. Most items were brand new, secured on heavy discounts or given to them by generous retail outlets after she approached them and told them all about the venture. A few items had drifted in from locals in Cloverdale, some wanted, others not so much. When she'd begun to tell people this was what she had planned and why she was painting the doors of the outbuilding in preparation, she'd had donations of old lampshades, board games and jigsaws with missing pieces, a broken projector and a food processor that was so old it was dangerous to use. Jennifer had no intention of putting anyone's safety at risk and had had to politely decline some items due to their unsuitability. What had come in useful was the brand-new sewing machine donated by Belinda, local and a fellow mum at the kids' school. She was a dressmaker by trade and had got one at a bargain price. Local carpenter, Wesley, had brought in a power drill he'd got for Christmas from his dad – he'd bought the exact same one for himself and hadn't had the heart to tell his dad who was so chuffed at his choice – and Danny who ran the pub along with Melody had donated a set of loppers after seeing them on sale at a hardware shop, needing them only once himself. He'd told Jennifer there was no point him keeping them; he wouldn't need to cut back the tree in the beer garden for at least another year, and when the time came, he was happy to part with a small sum to borrow them again.

'Good afternoon.' Adam was first to appear at the doors as she unlocked the remaining sections and began to fold them all back to reveal the Library of Shared Things in all its glory.

'Here, let me.' He took over the task like a true gentleman.

'Thank you, Adam.' She looked outside where people were beginning to mill. A vintage ice cream truck was parked up and had already drawn a crowd. Multi-coloured bunting was draped between the posts at either side of the car park and swaying in the breeze, and the barbecue was ready to go. 'Are you still happy to man the hot dog stall?' She'd asked him as a way of helping him to become a part of Cloverdale, get to know others, and what perfect way than serving food to the masses? Moving somewhere new was always hard; her son Archie was already good friends with Adam's Zac, and Jennifer hoped Adam could settle easily and the family would be here to stay.

'I sure am. And I'm paying Zac and Archie a tenner each to be my assistants; they can put the sausages in rolls, hand out serviettes, manage the queue between them while I cook. Zoe and Ava – for a price, of course – will handle the money and wipe down the tables.'

When Adam called for Zac and Archie to come and help him take out the rolls, the sausages and all the other paraphernalia, Jennifer tidied the desk for the umpteenth time, brushing at little specks of dust, and then, with a deep breath, ventured outside. This was it, the project she'd worked so hard on, and now it was time to introduce it to the rest of Cloverdale and prove how good it would be for everyone.

Jennifer addressed the crowd on a makeshift podium – a small set of kitchen steps – and started at the beginning. She told them all about the first library of things she'd seen, how it had worked, what her vision was for this village. She kept it brief – she knew people wanted to come inside and take a look for themselves – and with the sausages already beginning to sizzle away on the barbecue and the aroma snaking its way around the car park, kids were fidgety and anxious to get in the queue and not miss out.

'Well, this is marvellous.' Local man Bill was the first to go inside the Library of Shared Things as Jennifer led the way, the first to pick up an item. He'd gone for the leaf blower, which had been a birthday gift for Jennifer's dad, brand new three years ago. Her dad had died soon after and the leaf blower had never been used. Before now it might have made Jennifer sad to offer it to anyone else, but her dad would've lent it out in a heartbeat. He was like that, always willing to think of others and be a part of the village. 'And now what do I do with it?' Bill asked, already checking the poster Jennifer had put up on a wall behind the desk, listing their items and the prices.

As part of the talk Jennifer had explained briefly how the library worked and had done her best to point at the hutch shelves as she talked her audience through the system, but she knew for a while that it would be a learn-as-you-go process. 'You've picked the leaf blower, so rest it against the wall and I'll show you what we do on the computer. You can use the website from home to reserve an item, or you can come in here and I'll do it for you.' She asked how many days he wanted it, they made the booking and he took it off home, assuring her he'd be back for a sausage before they all sold out.

Elaine borrowed the bread maker she'd earmarked already, almost tripping over her own feet to get to it when she saw local mum, Ruth, lingering near the item. Fiona from the corner shop borrowed the badminton set, and newly-wed Erin paid to have the waffle maker for three days. Adam was going to take the steam cleaner when he left so he could give his son's carpet another go with a proper tool this time; he'd scrubbed at it, but it had left a clean patch on an otherwise dirty carpet.

Adam had the kids doing a great job with the barbecue when Jennifer looked over. Luckily he'd rounded up helpers today at Jennifer's request. Her younger sister Isla had originally said she'd help, but, as usual, Isla thought about one person and one person only. Herself. She'd already sent two texts this morning, apologising that she was covering a yoga class eleven miles away for a teacher who'd come down with a tummy bug, explaining it was impractical to get to Jennifer in time given her reliance on public transport.

Whatever. Jennifer wasn't going to let her sister's unreliability ruin anything, not today. The Library of Shared Things was launching successfully with or without Isla's help, and she supposed her sister was helping someone else today. It was just that the someone else wasn't her own flesh and blood.

She refused to let her sister's shortcomings get her down, shook off the frustration, and instead smiled over to where Adam was outside making his volunteers laugh. He had the girls eating out of his hand, the boys joking about.

Everything was coming together. Her idea really was going to work.

*

A fortnight later and the Library of Shared Things had already become not only a place where people came to borrow items but also somewhere to share snippets of their lives and find companionship. It was exactly what Jennifer had intended.

'Good morning, Jennifer.' Recently widowed, Bill had leapt on board with this new venture well before the yellow paint on the doors had even dried. He was on the local council and she suspected he'd put his weight behind pushing the planning permission through so this place could begin operating quickly.

'What do you have there?' She nodded to the large box he'd already set down on the table she used to check returns before they were slotted away into their allocated sections of the wall hutches.

'Ronnie's sewing machine.'

'Are you coming along to the sewing workshop?' At Cloverdale's Library of Shared Things, Jennifer wanted to run workshops for locals to learn or improve new skills, to bring them together in a different way. And already she had a couple of ideas on the timetable, starting with the sewing skills workshop tonight.

'I don't want to sound mean-spirited but it's not really my thing. I thought I'd bring the sewing machine by though, to help.'

'You're very kind. Just remember, you're never too old to learn a new skill. You could use Ronnie's machine yourself. Others are bringing their own if they have one.'

'Ronnie would turn in her grave if she knew I was using her sewing machine,' he chuckled. 'I think I'll give it a miss. But I do need to sign up to the beginners' drill session. I've gone and bought myself some fancy drill and can't make head nor tail of the instructions.'

With the computer on, Jennifer found the online calendar, the workshop in two days' time, and booked Bill onto it. 'Adam Parker's running this one.' They didn't charge much for workshops, but a small contribution from attendees would go towards upkeep in the library – cleaning fluids, spare parts when items broke, maintaining the small kitchenette out the back.

'I don't know what to make of that family.'

'The Parkers? They're nice.'

'I'm sure they are, but they seem a bit cagey.'

'In what way?'

'Well, we don't know anything about them. Is Adam divorced? Separated? Widowed? Gay?'

'Bill, I don't think we should gossip about them.'

'You're quite right, of course. But I've seen him in the pub a couple of times, sitting right in the corner, avoiding eye contact with anyone and looking as though he's got the weight of the world on his shoulders.'

'I'm trying to get him involved as much as I can. Maybe he'll come out of his shell a bit when he gets to know more people in the village.'

'I guess so. And he seems like a good man; he'll do a good job with the drill workshop. We won't let him hide away from us forever.'

She laughed. 'No, I guess we won't.'

'You're a sweetheart, you know that? What you've done, introducing this Library of Shared Things? It's been an outlet a lot of people needed, including me.'

Jennifer reached out and gave his hand a squeeze. 'I'm so glad.'

'I wasn't bad at DIY myself, once upon a time,' he said, momentarily snapping out of anything bordering on emotional. 'But Ronnie's clutter put paid to that.'

Bill's wife had been a hoarder in the truest sense of the word, and, when she'd died, Bill had nearly killed himself clearing that place out on his own. After Ronnie had passed away, Jennifer had noticed a new skip outside his house three days in a row, each time only Bill doing the journey with an armful of things between the front door and the dumping ground, and she'd struck up a conversation. She'd thought he might be redecorating but he'd soon confided the pain he'd been through over the last four years with nobody but his wife to talk to, no kids to help, nobody to hear his problems or hers. Bill had been almost as enthusiastic about Jennifer's new community project as she'd been herself, and had donated several new, boxed items to the library – a set of screwdrivers, a sandwich maker, a collection of novelty cake tins – which Ronnie had bought, kept and never used – and Jennifer knew his focus on something different had helped to lift him out of some dark days.

'You're most welcome to come along to the sewing workshop, if you change your mind,' Jennifer told him now. 'Belinda is running the show but if you don't make it tonight, there'll be other opportunities in the coming weeks.'

'Maybe next time then.' His brow creased. 'I could use some new curtains. Maybe it's time to put up the new ones that sat in a packet for years.'

Jennifer sat against the desk. This was what people came here for, to offload, to share as much as to borrow. 'Did you keep many of your wife's things?'

'You saw the skips outside the house. But there were a few items I didn't let go to waste and the curtains – brand new and in their packet – well, they're mighty fine.

Velvet, extra long, the right width for the sitting room window.'

'Then the sewing basics workshop would be ideal for you.'

He winked. 'I might take you up on it eventually.' And maybe he would.

'Kids back at school yet?' Bill pulled on his tweed cap ready to go.

'Two more days. I'll miss them when they go back, especially Archie who's young enough to still cuddle his mum.' She suspected time was running out for that particular luxury. He was nine, the twins Amelia and Katie had already turned sixteen. Everything was beginning to change.

'They grow up too fast, don't they?' He tipped his cap to bid her goodbye.

'Think about the sewing workshop,' she called after him.

She sat down at the desk in front of the computer ready to go through bookings and see what she was up against, pleased to be busy. Some days she needed this place more than anyone else. 'It's good to have a hobby,' had been Jennifer's husband David's response when she'd told him about this initiative. He may as well have patted her on the back for good measure. As a pharmaceutical sales rep he rarely switched off from his work, but every time she felt like moaning about it, she told herself how good a husband he was, a provider, rock solid; he hadn't walked away when she messed up. There were worse ways to be. Yet, when had they reached the point where they no longer saw each other for who they were?

When Jennifer had first met David, she'd been a career

woman working for a top hairdresser in Exeter, with dreams of starting her own business. David had been a surfer dude who she'd met on the beach in Cornwall. He'd been studying at the same time and quickly landed his first job in the pharmaceutical industry. He'd never made any secret of wanting to work his way up the career ladder and for a while they'd been on that ladder together. Their shared ambition had been like a magnet, drawing them along at the same pace. But after they'd married and the twins arrived, something had to give. Her career went on hold and she lost a part of herself that she'd never really managed to get back. She'd tried once but it had been a total disaster and she'd nearly ruined so many lives with one mistake.

Jennifer spent the next hour ensuring items booked to go out today were ready. She thought about what Bill had said about the Parker family. They didn't give much away, and he was right: sometimes Adam was cagey if you made a remark or asked a question about his life before Cloverdale. But surely over time he'd reveal more about himself. He was becoming a friend already, someone to listen to her when she needed to offload. As he'd built the hutch shelves, he'd listened to her whinge about her teenagers' attitudes and lack of appreciation. They'd laughed about the boys' teacher this academic year: strict and a bit harsh for a primary school environment, although perhaps it would help the boys to knuckle down. It was that kind of banter Jennifer missed by not having a workplace or a close friend nearby, and she was happy the family had come to the village, whatever their background.

She checked the pasta maker and ran through its list of parts to ensure everything was included. Freda Livingstone was borrowing this for three days. Her daughter had a desire to become a chef, pasta her latest obsession. 'I don't want to fork out for a machine if she'll lose interest in a few days,' Freda had told Jennifer when she popped in to ask what kitchen equipment was available. A decent pasta machine cost at least thirty pounds but, here, Freda would get it for less than a fiver for a few days, and after that she would know if it was an item they wanted to invest in for themselves. She'd also booked a set of pasta bowls decorated in bright colours so her daughter could feel she was putting on a dinner party when she served her meals up to the rest of the family.

Twenty-one-year-old Mason was next in the door carrying a box filled with wine glasses.

'How was the party?' she asked.

'It rocked.'

'Glad to hear it.'

'Should I wait while you check them? I didn't break a single one and they're all washed and dried.'

A handful of the younger crowd in Cloverdale had borrowed items and she hoped it was the start of a pattern that they could carry on for years to come. 'I'm sure everything is fine; you can go.'

He thanked her and went on his way, and, as Jennifer checked through the box, satisfied it was ready to be put away ready for the next time it went out on loan, her phone pinged with a text to remind her that Isla was on her way to pick up the spotlight she'd reserved.

The sisters were different in more ways than one. Jennifer had their mum's luscious ebony locks that were fighting her approach to forty next year and still held their colour; Isla had their dad's auburn hair, which would probably fade gradually over the years. Jennifer had sacrificed career and dreams for a family of her own, whereas Isla was young, free and single, and had danced and travelled all over the world. In fact, the phrase 'the world is your oyster' was seemingly written with her in mind. Another difference was that Jennifer had been there for both their parents when the time had come that they needed looking after rather than the other way round. And Isla had been nowhere to be seen.

But now, she was back. They'd lost their mum in the spring and globetrotting Isla had finally come home to Cloverdale for more than a fleeting visit. The cottage their parents had lived in for decades, and the place that was once their childhood home, was in both of their names now and they'd soon have to work out what to do with it. The first part of the plan was for Isla to live in the cottage and do it up with a view to selling once the current property market picked up. When it did, they'd have it valued and start to make some firm decisions.

Isla came in to the Library of Shared Things not long after her text had arrived, collected the spotlight, and paid for it. 'What do you want it for anyway?' Jennifer asked. Heaven forbid she told Isla her feelings about her flighty, unreliable nature. She might do another runner, and if there was one thing their parents had always wanted, it was for the sisters to be friends for life. And after what Jennifer had put them both through, honouring their wishes was the least she could do. That's why she had to try to bite her tongue and be nice.

'Are you thinking of dancing again?' Jennifer asked. Once upon a time, when Isla had only dreamed of a dance career, she'd loved to set up a stage and perform for other people using table lamps to do the job of lighting rather than a proper spotlight.

Jennifer didn't expect to hit a nerve by hinting at Isla's dance career, which she'd suddenly left behind, but, by Isla's stilted reaction, she clearly had. Maybe she should've just kept quiet instead of trying to make conversation.

'I need to get up in the loft and I've tried using my torch app on my phone but it's not enough,' Isla explained, in the manner that suggested Jennifer was asking the most ridiculous question ever. 'This spotlight on the other hand should give a whole new perspective.'

'Not teaching today?' Maybe she'd avoid any questions that could cause a fiery Isla to lose her cool. She wasn't in the mood for a showdown.

'Not today, no.'

'How's it all going?' Isla had quickly made contacts, more of an astute businessperson than Jennifer would've ever given her credit for, and now had a schedule of yoga classes to teach at a handful of different venues as well as private classes that brought in more money. She'd even talked about setting up a permanent studio in or near the village, plans that seemed at odds with the Isla Jennifer knew who couldn't stay put for five minutes.

'If this is another dig about me not helping out at the opening—'

'It's not.' This wasn't going well. 'Hang on a minute, I thought Mum had cleared the loft out a long time ago.'

'Do you remember us building a cubby house in the old coal scuttle in Mum and Dad's back garden?'

Jennifer felt a pang of sadness that neither of their parents were with them anymore. 'How could I forget? That was disgusting . . . I can't believe I agreed to it. And I can't believe you picked up all the snails and creepy crawlies in there.'

'Well, Mum may have said the loft was empty, but given the dust behind the wardrobe, beneath the bed and lurking at the back of the larder, I'm not taking any chances. Although I am hoping for no snails.' She winked, bringing the old, happy-go-lucky Isla back to the fore. 'I'm starting top to bottom. I figure that way, dirt will fall down and I won't have to clean up twice before I can start with the fun part. Decorating.'

'I'm not sure the cord will be long enough on the spotlight. Let me grab the extension reel for you. Take it now, and if you don't need it you can return free of charge, or it'll be two pounds for the day.'

'Jennifer, I think I can spare two quid.' She pulled out a fiver from her pocket and bundled the extension lead into the same container as the spotlight so she only had the one box to carry. 'Have a good day.' And off she went with a smile and a spring in her step.

Isla, youngest of the family, wayward, wild, flighty, and now . . . back in Cloverdale. The question was, would Isla really stick around this time? And what was it that had made her run in the first place?

3

Adam

Adam pulled the front door to the house shut and ran over to the car. Amazing how school hadn't been in session for six weeks and today, the first day at new schools for both kids, they were still running late. They had all the uniform and equipment, gear for sports in case their first day involved PE, their shoes had that telltale new-term shine that wouldn't exist again unless he took charge of polishing, but underestimating the time it would take them all to get ready, breakfast had been rushed, there'd been a very loud and spiteful bickering between Zoe and Zac for time in the only bathroom, and, to top it off, Adam couldn't find his keys when it was time to go. Even though they'd moved twice in quick succession, they'd still brought clutter along with them to Lilliput Cottage and Adam must've put his car keys on top of an unpacked box when he came in yesterday from taking Zac to meet his teacher in preparation for today. He'd almost been ready to run them to school on foot when he'd kicked the box by accident and the jangle of the keys gave the game away that they'd slid inside.

'I thought I was done with being ferried to school,' Zoe whined the second they'd all piled into the car. She sat in the passenger seat, looking out the window with a face as grey as the morning. Not a good start.

'Hey, I seem to remember you moaning about walking in the rain at the end of last term. And it's your first day, I'm working from home, so I thought I'd do you a favour. Glad I bothered.' Sometimes he found himself reacting like a disgruntled teenager himself, but it was hard to be a model parent when there was only one of you.

She harrumphed. Round one to Dad. He was fast learning that teens only thought about themselves, didn't factor in others, and didn't always think about consequences. Had he ever been that bad? He supposed he must've been.

When they'd first arrived in Cloverdale, Adam had panicked that it wouldn't be quite right for them with its chocolate-box houses and windy lanes, he'd wondered whether the kids would find it far too small. Lilliput Cottage was on the road that ran like a ribbon from one end of the village to the other before the road sprouted off in different directions connecting other towns, hamlets and villages, and now the summer had brought the daisies and lavender out at the front of their cottage and in bursts around the village he felt a sense of place, and, he hoped, a feeling of permanency.

He turned left past the pub, which showed off its entrance with hanging baskets filled with a riot of colour, he drove cautiously along the narrow lane, wary of oncoming traffic semi-obscured by the thick, lush hedgerows lining the way over a small stream. Cow parsley still peppered roadside verges, brimming with frothy white flowers after a warmer than usual summer. It wouldn't be long before the nights drew in, the leaves and flowers shrivelled up at the end of another season, and the village would put on its winter coat with frosty footpaths and spectacular glistening frosts.

As they drove on, he resisted the urge to ask Zoe whether she had her insulin kit. He knew the reaction he'd get: the eye roll that would accompany the insistence she wasn't a baby. Zoe had been diagnosed as a Type 1, insulin-dependent diabetic two years ago and their whole world as a family had completely changed yet again. But today he knew he'd have to be content fussing from a distance.

'I could jump out here, get some fresh air,' said Zoe as they drove past crowds of school kids all flowing in the same direction.

'I'm not stopping now.'

'I'm a teenager . . . air and exercise are important for my mental wellbeing.'

Backchat and last wording weren't on the list of his favourite perks when it came to parenting. Zac wasn't quite there yet, and Adam was hoping Zoe would be well past this stage before he had another kid mentally exhausting him.

'Maybe it'll make you less moody,' Zac quipped from the back seat, much to his sister's annoyance.

'Shut it, you.'

'Zoe, don't talk to your brother like that.' Don't talk to anyone like that, Adam thought, and felt his forehead creasing into a deep frown as he indicated and pulled out from a T-junction. Or should that be a deep-er frown? When he'd hit forty he'd realised he was showing signs that came with age – his brown hair had faded, a few greys appeared at his temples between haircuts, and he realised life would pass him by if he'd let it.

'Sorry, Dad.' Zoe managed to look his way and smiled.

'Are you going to talk to Ava's mum soon, about decorating my room?'

Ah, she wanted something. A sure way to get a teen talking. 'I'm doing my first stint at the Library of Shared Things this evening so if Viola's around I'll mention it.' He hadn't quite worked Viola out; she seemed the more highly strung of the two mums he'd got to know through his kids, but she was easy enough to talk to and she kept a tight rein on Ava, which wasn't necessarily a bad thing.

'Ava says she has a whole portfolio on Instagram.' Zoe was chatty now it was a topic on her terms, talking about her friend's mum who was a Human Resources Manager but had a flair and passion for interior design and decorating. 'Not that I have Instagram, of course, which reminds me: have you decided whether I'm old enough to use it yet?'

'Sarcasm isn't your best quality, Zoe.'

'Worth a try,' she muttered. 'I am fourteen, remember?'

Ignoring the dig, he told her, 'I'll have a talk with Viola, see what we can do.' Fourteen sure came with a whole lot of attitude serving as a constant reminder that the placid toddler he'd wowed with his ridiculous jokes, or the girl who was happy to snuggle next to him on the sofa and read a book, only existed in his memories. Zoe was battling her teen years and well on her way to womanhood. She no longer wanted to throw her energies into dancing, drama club or swimming; instead she only wanted to hang out with friends and overnight he'd become the antagonist as well as the taxi driver.

'Not long till I'm in that seat, Zoe,' Zac riled his sister from his position behind her as they joined the snaking line of traffic that would lead up to the primary school.

Adam wouldn't be surprised if he put his knee into the back of her seat to add to his teasing.

'Have you got everything?' he asked Zoe.

'If you mean do I have my insulin kit, then yes, Dad, I have it.'

He opened his mouth to argue but he'd been caught red-handed so there was little point protesting.

As soon as he pulled up, Zoe's seatbelt was off. She murmured a goodbye and jumped out. Adam waved over at Ava who must've been waiting so they could walk past the primary school, down the lane and to the high school. He got a hug from Zac, which he savoured. It wouldn't be long before he bolted the second the car pulled up too.

He drove away with a tinge of sadness that Zoe and Zac were back to the routine as of today. They'd had a wonderful summer, plenty of outdoor time with England keeping up its end of the bargain and giving them not only a good dose of sunshine but week after week of dry days. He'd taken the kids camping in the Chilterns and in the Area of Outstanding Beauty stretching for miles, they'd got back to basics, playing card games by torch-light at night, cooking dinners on the miniature camping stove, playing frisbee together, rolling down the hills and racing one another back up to the top, the sort of fun that was easily forgotten in the days of technology.

And it was valuable time with Zoe too, who seemed to be moving so far away from him he'd never be able to catch up. Since being diagnosed as a diabetic, she'd gone through a gamut of emotions; anger, resentment, blame. All of her feelings were very normal, according to the diabetes educator they'd spoken with, and Adam was only thankful Zoe had soon progressed to acceptance and had mastered self-care. He'd wondered whether part of the difficulty had been Zoe wanting to keep a part of herself separate from him much like she wanted to do with everything else these days, but as long as whatever she did worked, he didn't care. All he wanted was for her to be safe and happy.

Sometimes he wished kids came with a manual for single dads like him. Zoe and Zac didn't ask too much about their mum, Susan – at least not yet – but he knew he couldn't avoid it forever. Zoe had so much attitude bottled up, especially surrounding his lack of trust when it came to social media. But he wasn't doing it to be controlling or because he thought her immature; he was doing it so he could keep the truth from them. A truth that could rip them apart, because if he was honest with them, he was worried they would see him as the bad guy, and he could lose them for good.

Adam drove home and spent the day working at his laptop on the round table in the dining room of their cottage. He kept the window open with the fresh breeze licking around to keep it cool, still missing the ease of flicking on an air conditioner when the heat inside got too much. This cottage would be great in the winter – it stayed cosy and snug – but in the warmer months it seemed to cling onto the heat for dear life.

He loved his job as a landscape architect, the interactions with clients and colleagues, but days like this were gold when he could focus and finish drawing up cost estimates and go over fresh designs for a new project, and he finished up much quicker than he would've done in the office. By early afternoon he was at a loose end. He'd offered to collect the kids from school but they'd both wanted to walk with friends and he knew he had to relinquish control at some point. He didn't like it, but today he'd let it happen.

After fixing himself a snack he set off for the Library of Shared Things to make sure everything was set up for tonight.

When he'd been asked to help out at the opening, he hadn't let on, but his first reaction to Jennifer's project had been That'll Never Work, and What a Waste of Time. But maybe that was his own negativity speaking, because it all seemed to be going very well so far and he certainly heard plenty of talk about it when he was walking in Cloverdale, enjoying a pint at the local pub, or even when he'd picked up the regional newspaper, which had given some coverage.

Jennifer had confided in him that she wanted the community of Cloverdale to evolve into something different. She hoped people would gradually start to take the time to stop and talk to one another a little bit more and she'd gone out of her way to get him involved. She'd asked him to help with a workshop tonight and although he'd wanted to say no at first, he liked Jennifer. And so he'd decided he had a choice. He could join in with a bit of enthusiasm or he could turn into a sad individual doing little else apart from work and parenting.

Jennifer's smile reached her kind, deep brown eyes when she greeted him today but didn't give him the answer he needed. 'Viola isn't here but she'll be around tomorrow.'

'I'll try to catch her then instead.' He'd have to or Zoe would never stop going on about it.

'I'm glad you're a part of all this,' said Jennifer, her hair twisted up and piled on top of her head to keep her cool. Like her, he'd favoured jeans and a T-shirt today, making the most of the September days before they gave way to autumn. 'You'll get to meet more people, as well as helping me out.'

'Here's hoping. And I had a pint with Bill last night; he wasn't happy I was sitting there alone. He laughed when he saw how wet my trainers were after I misjudged how deep the puddle was outside the bakery. It only rained for half an hour, but the water even got my socks too. Bill told me I'd soon learn.'

'It's a shocker. Every time it rains, someone forgets how deep the puddle goes. Who knows, maybe the road will get fixed one day.'

'I don't know, kind of a quirk for the village, isn't it?'

'I guess so.'

'Bill was also talking about learning how to take up curtains.'

She grinned and explained the sewing workshop.

'Think I'll stick to drills for now.'

'Then let's get everything ready.' She led him through the internal space behind the yellow bifold doors, two of which were open to allow the air to circulate. At the end was a table and he counted seven drills, all slightly different, but all functional at closer inspection. She discussed what would be expected of him, all very straightforward, told him to have a break for tea and biscuits halfway through tonight's workshop, but apart from that it was really up to him.

'This is here for you to make use of.' She pointed to a crate filled with wood, metal and pieces of brick.

'You should come along, give it a go.'

'I don't think it's for me, but thanks for the offer. Now, are you bringing your own drill?'

'I will be. I had to buy one in London to fix up a few things in our rental, which I'm sure I would've been charged for, so I'll bring it with me.'

He was grateful she didn't pry more into his personal life, even though he and the kids were probably the most mysterious family to land in these parts for decades.

'How many people are coming tonight?' he asked.

'Seven, including my sister, Isla.'

'Good for her. It must be nice to have her back.' He'd heard Jennifer's sister had been travelling for a long while before returning to Cloverdale.

'It's a little odd. To be honest I don't see what Cloverdale really has for her. It's too quiet around here. And Isla likes excitement.'

'I'd hazard a guess that she wants to be near you.' It seemed she wanted someone to listen to her, so he perched his bottom on the table as Jennifer rechecked the drills and ensured each one was clean and had its instructions. 'I only have one brother and he lives in Western Australia. Take it from me, life can get lonely.'

'That's what this place is for.' She smiled.

'Some evenings I'd give anything to go to the pub and have a beer with him.' Maybe tell him everything too, the reasons he'd had to leave the country and start over.

'It must be hard for you.'

He shrugged the suggestion away. He didn't mind talking about his family. His wife was a no-go area, but his brother, his parents, distant cousins, aunts and uncles he could cope with. 'We both went over there a long time ago, so I had a few years where we were at least in the same hemisphere. Hopefully he'll come to visit soon. Where was your sister before here?'

'She's been all over. She worked in a café in Amsterdam, a bookshop in France, as a waitress in Italy, I've no idea what she did in New Zealand, and she worked as a lifeguard in Queensland, then took up yoga and did some teaching in a place called Byron Bay after that. She's held so many jobs I can't actually remember them all.' She smiled over at Archie and Zac when they came in.

'Hey, boys.' Adam was happy for them to walk together. It was safety in numbers and they didn't have to walk the way he drove; there was a shortcut with hordes of other kids and parents all going the same way. 'How was your day?' If enthusiasm could be demonstrated by word count, the boys had a fantastic day as their voices competed to tell him the best parts. He hoped Zoe's had gone just as well. 'Why don't I take you both for an ice cream, my treat?'

Jennifer ruffled Archie's hair. 'That sounds lovely.'

Beneath the afternoon sun, Adam felt a sense of contentment that didn't always come his way, when the simple things gave you a metaphorical kick to remind you how good you had it – the generosity of friendship he'd found here in the village, his son's smiling face as he and a friend – tummies filled with ice cream – played at the park racing up the climbing frame, standing on the swings, pulling themselves up the fireman's pole and sliding down it, leaping off at the end before their feet touched the ground. But his biggest sense of peace lately had come from the blessing that Zoe was OK, and her text now – to say she was home at the cottage after school

– was a simple measure that meant his heart could settle down and he could stop worrying.

As long as what had happened stayed a secret from his kids and everyone in Cloverdale, they had a real shot at making their new life work.

That evening, at the Library of Shared Things, it didn't take long for the room to be filled with chatter. Isla bustled in late, apologising profusely. 'Don't tell Jennifer,' she whispered to him as she rolled up her sleeves. 'She disapproves of tardiness and being disorganised.'

Adam made his way around the room once he'd made introductions and got everyone started. Phillip, the only male attendee, seemed more nervous than anyone, coming here tonight so he could learn how to put together a flat-packed computer desk rather than having to ask his dad. Elin, who'd just got married and was determined to do her share of the practical tasks along with her husband as they renovated their new property, swore loudly when she dropped a bit of metal on her foot. Although at least she had closed shoes on or it could've been way worse. Cassandra who worked some shifts at the local pub was here so she could stick one finger up at her ex-husband who thought she'd never survive without him, and Isla soon got busy drilling holes along a piece of wood and fixing screws in place.

'How's it going?' He stopped in front of Isla.

Sea-blue eyes looked briefly up at him. 'I think I'm getting the hang of it.'

'Nice drill.' It was grape-coloured and so clean he knew it hadn't been used before now.

'Bet you say that to all the girls.'

He laughed then. 'Do you have any particular projects in mind?'

'Too many to mention. Our parents' cottage comes with old wallpaper, crappy light fittings, rickety bannisters, tatty carpets and a serious lack of shelving. I don't even have any bookshelves. Mum didn't like reading.'

'Sshhh ... the Cloverdale Library might hear you.' Cassandra sashayed past to grab a few screws and have a go herself.

At the end of the session Adam made sure everything was neat and tidy, the crumbs from the rich tea biscuits that had done the rounds were swept away, all lights were off and the big yellow doors were locked up for another day. He scooted home, checked on the kids, and with Zoe ensconced in the lounge diligently doing homework and Zac already in his pyjamas, he put Zac to bed, read a few pages of the first Harry Potter book to him, and grabbed his car keys.

'Won't be long, just dropping the keys back with Jennifer,' he told Zoe.

He drove the short distance to Jennifer's, along a winding country lane that led the way to a large home with a gravel driveway and a five-bar farm gate.

She kept her voice low and ushered him into the lounge when she eventually answered the door. 'If Archic knows you're here he'll be up and about again. I think the excitement of the first day back, then ice cream and the park was all a bit much and he's buzzing.'

'All my fault.'

'He had a lovely time. How did the workshop go?'

He filled her in and – when he eyed the glass of red wine waiting on the low oak coffee table coordinated with the rest of the room in soft beige, creams and chocolate brown – he said, 'You took my advice.'

'It's been a long day. Actually, it's been a long week. David's away, again, and the twins are driving me mad. Sixteen, far too independent, and neither of them realising the importance of their GCSEs that are just around the corner.'

'Relax, it's day one of a new term; it'll all settle down.'

'Can I offer you a glass of wine? I know you're driving, but how about a small one?'

'Go on then.' He perused the bookshelves in here while she went out to the kitchen, and, running his finger along the spines of the books, came to one titled *The Teenage Brain*. 'I might need to borrow this soon,' he told her when she returned and handed him a glass of red.

'Zoe giving you trouble?' She sat at one end of the soft, beige sofa and he took the other.

'Just the usual teen behaviour. Moaning about not having the social media apps she wants.'

'Well, she's at that age, and if Zoe is anything like Katie and Amelia, her phone is her lifeline. It's the way teens communicate.'

His protectiveness probably seemed like overkill but he couldn't share the real reason he didn't want his kids out there in the big wide world where they could make discoveries, have contact with people who could tell them everything. His kids were his priority; he didn't want the past to follow them.

They talked about the return to school, the homework load that had started already, the boys' passion for football.

'Zac wants to take up karate,' Adam admitted. 'I think

we'll get through this term at school before we start anything in addition to football.'

'Martial arts always look so rough.'

'It'll do him good; it'll mean he can stand up for himself with a bit of confidence.' She didn't seem convinced.
'God help us all! He tried to karate chop me this morning and it really hurt. He needs to know the proper moves
and when it's appropriate to do them.'

'I bet if Zac signs up, Archie will want to as well. They're
very good mates already. And your Zoe is friends with
Ava; they both seemed to have found their place in the
village quite quickly.'

It was true. His family was settling in fast in Cloverdale,
and in the eyes of everyone else, the Parkers were just another ordinary family.

And that suited him just fine.

4

Viola

Viola crammed at least five days' work into four in her job as a Human Resources Manager so she could take every Friday off and channel her energies into anything else that kept her sane. Because despite her success and bravado at work, dealing with everything from recruitment and training to policy recommendations and team-building exercises, she needed a regular break.

Usually Viola turned to her love of interior design, whether it was managing her website or lining up another room makeover, but today she'd be spending her Friday helping at the Library of Shared Things.

Once upon a time she and Jennifer had been the best of friends, but after what Viola had done, they hadn't had any contact for years until they both ended up living back here in Cloverdale. Viola suspected Jennifer could use all the help she could get when it came to this new venture of hers, and besides, her former friend hated confrontation so Viola had volunteered in front of Elaine to put Jennifer in a position where it would have been hard to refuse.

After what happened, Jennifer hadn't seen or heard

from Viola for years, until she showed up in Cloverdale. Now, Jennifer merely tried to keep the peace; she didn't want everyone to know their business, so around Viola she adopted an air of civility. And mostly it worked.

'I might borrow this myself you know.' At the library Viola took out the ice cream maker that had been returned that morning. Jennifer had explained she needed to check it had all the requisite pieces, ensure its instructions were inside, see that it was clean and ready to shelve until the next borrow. 'It's already got a few recipes on the notebook inside.'

That piqued Jennifer's interest before she climbed up the stepladder to clean the inside of the uppermost windows. 'Really? Like what?'

'Carmel from the bakery has laminated a recipe for cinnamon crunch ice cream, Melody from the pub has written down how to make dreamy apple pie flavour and Hattie has popped in a recipe for butter pecan.'

Jennifer talked as she cleaned the glass. 'I borrowed it last month; first time I've used one.'

Viola took the two-way conversation as a good sign. This was the most they'd spoken since the day they'd bumped into each other at the bakery when Jennifer went in to buy a Marmite loaf but Viola had bought the last one. It hadn't helped the tension between them in the slightest. 'And what was the verdict?'

'It's dangerous.' A hint of a smile reminded Viola of how close they'd once been.

'In an electrical sense, or because it makes highly calorific treats?' Viola examined the paddles, already dreaming up flavours she'd enjoy.

'The latter.' Jennifer stepped down from her position, moved this way and that at ground level to check for no smudges on the glass and came over. 'I made the best rum and raisin ice cream.'

'Now that sounds delicious. I'd do mint choc chip, Isaac's favourite.' She picked up the machine and stowed it in its container. 'I'd better put it away before I put on weight just by looking at it.' Not that she needed to worry. She'd been blessed with her dad's height and her mum's slim build and with her work ethic, she didn't have much time to sit still and gorge herself. She'd also inherited her dad's curls and she readjusted the ponytail that tamed the thick, blonde tresses to keep them out of her way.

The hutches in the Library of Shared Things were organised in sections, electronics to the left, then it was toys, next came garden equipment some of which required bigger sections and some items weren't in a storage container but left out with covers over them. Viola pushed the ice cream maker back into the appropriate section of the hutch where the kitchen equipment was housed at the far end. 'This shelf needs strengthening.' It had bowed and didn't look like it would last much longer.

'I know; Adam noticed it too. He also volunteered to build a bigger cupboard right at the end past the last of the kitchen items.' She pointed to the far wall that didn't have any units against it. 'We can use it for the lawnmower, garden rakes and forks, camping equipment.'

'I thought you weren't supplying camping equipment because it's too hard to maintain and clean.'

'We only have the one two-man tent at the moment,

so we'll see how it goes. I got a bargain in the sales after Easter and it's been borrowed seven times already. It seems to be doing well. I got David and Archie to camp out in the back garden.'

'You didn't?'

'I did. It was bonding time. David has been away with work so much lately; Archie really misses him.'

Viola had heard it mentioned that David worked away a lot and Jennifer was often left to run the home and the family. And although Jennifer's marriage was strong, Viola had her suspicions that all this working away was taking its toll. Jennifer looked tired. She seemed to have too much on her mind, although that could be her own presence rather than anything to do with her marriage. And Viola couldn't step in and ask questions or give advice; their relationship was so brittle she was afraid to tread too heavily and have it snap right in two. But today, at least, Jennifer was talking in more than short, sharp sentences. It was progress.

Between them, Jennifer and Viola worked efficiently alongside each other, checking returns. They slotted items back into their hutches, chatted with locals as they came and went, some collecting, others returning, a few who simply stopped by on their way to the bakery, the post office or to the library.

Harrison Pemberley, who owned the fruit shop near the bakery, came in next, armed with a big punnet of bright red strawberries. He lived up to his name, Harrison, as in Harrison Ford. He had hair greying at the temples, a year-round tan, was very handsome and charming. 'On the house,' he told Jennifer before she had a chance to escape for lunch.

'You shouldn't do that; you have a business to run.'

'It's bribery. I need help. I'm after a cake tin.'

'I'll help you with that, Harrison.' Viola ushered Jennifer on her way and took over the task to find the perfect tin to make a cake for Harrison's four-year-old granddaughter who was visiting next month.

'All I know is she can't stop talking about princesses,' he told Viola as she led him over to the kitchen section and they looked at what was there.

'Are you making it yourself?'

'I am. I'm a bit heavy-handed though, so I need a shape to help me,' he explained as she took out tins, one at a time, to find what she was looking for. 'Then I can plonk all the ingredients inside and have a hope that it'll be something to make Giselle smile about rather than cry.'

'I expect she'd appreciate whatever you made as long as it was covered in pretty pink icing and sweets. Girls are very forgiving when it comes to cake. Now what about this?' She took out the tin shaped like a Disney castle.

'I can't make that.'

Viola pulled out the additional leaflets that came with the tin, the recipe suggestion from another borrower, a photograph of the same borrower's finished cake. 'She'll love this. It has turrets, a drawbridge at the front, and if you take all this additional information you can copy the way Ruth decorated it.'

'She did do a good job.'

Ruth was a local mum of four who lived in one of the larger houses overlooking the village green. 'I know she doesn't bake often – she's a working mum – but she impressed even herself with the finished result. I bet if you asked, she'd help you, if you needed it.'

'It feels like I'd be cheating, but go on then. How much do I owe you?'

'Two pounds for the day.'

'Cheap at half the price . . . I looked to buy a new tin when I was out shopping last week, but given next year Giselle might be into ponies rather than princesses, or she could be a total tomboy and want a car cake, I don't want to fork out the money.'

'That's what we're here for. Makes life easier to share things around.'

'Makes life cheaper too,' he replied.

When Jennifer returned she was laughing and chatting. When Viola looked up, expecting to see her with David, new man to town, Adam, was the person she walked in with instead. They seemed to be getting friendly quickly, which wasn't a problem in itself, but Viola hadn't missed the way her friend acted around him. She'd heard Jennifer had gone out of her way to get Adam involved in the Library of Shared Things; Viola had seen him right at home as he manned the barbecue at the opening cere- mony, and he'd run a workshop for Jennifer the other night. Locals had been raving about what a charming man he was, how friendly, how likeable. But there was something odd about him and Viola couldn't quite put her finger on it.

And now he was heading over to her, smiling away. Never trust a man who smiled so much. 'Hey, are you looking for something?'

'You.' Still smiling. 'Zoe has been on at me to mention it to you, but she . . . we . . . would like to ask about a spot of decorating.'

'Right.'

'Is that OK?'

'Sorry, Adam.' Her mind had been on her friend's marriage; she wasn't sure whether to trust Adam's jaunty attitude. 'Decorating. Yes. I can help you. Zoe and Ava were chatting about it the other day and I'd be happy to take a look.' Viola liked Zoe. She seemed to be a good influence on Ava and vice versa.

'I meant to do it myself, but I think what she needs is female input. Not that I'm being sexist, but, well, she doesn't seem to want me too involved.'

'I'll pop over for a chat late afternoon, say around four, work out a direction and price up a makeover for you. I won't get things moving until you give the go-ahead. How does that sound?'

'Perfect.'

Viola didn't miss Adam's gentle touch to Jennifer's arm to bid her goodbye. It was only a slight tactile gesture, one plenty of people probably did without anyone reading something more into it.

Maybe she was imagining a connection that was totally innocent. And she knew better than to say anything. If past mistakes were anything to go by, she'd learnt her lesson.

'I'm sorry I'm a bit later than I thought,' Viola apologised when she arrived at Adam's. 'I had to go home and get a few things, check on the girls. Hazel was beavering away but as usual Ava was taking a break when she should be doing homework *and* piano practice. We have a timetable to make it easier, but she tries to get out of it all the time.'

'Can I offer you a tea, coffee, something cold?' Adam offered.

'A coffee would be lovely, thank you.' He probably thought she was a neurotic mess with her kids, ranting on about them the second she arrived, but she needed to stay on top of what they were doing; they'd thank her for it in the long run.

When she slipped off her shoes, he said, 'Oh, there's no need to do that here.'

'We're a shoes-off household; Zoe's new bedroom will be too,' she insisted and followed him into the kitchen. 'Sorry, I'm being bossy already. I'll try to rein it in when I'm here.' She took in the interior of Lilliput Cottage, a home she'd never been into. On the local grapevine she'd heard that Lilliput Cottage was once owned by Nancy and Bert who'd lived here for forty years before retiring to Cardiff to be near family. Until Adam bought it, the cottage had gone through four or five rounds of renting, each one inflicting wear and tear that Viola could see now in its drab wallpaper, dull carpets, and paintwork in desperate need of a facelift. Already she was itching to suggest some shelving in the tiny kitchen to get clutter off the worktops, perhaps lighting beneath the shelves to bathe the kitchen in a soft glow, but that wasn't what she was here for.

'Is Zoe looking forward to getting going with our project?' she asked, a little uneasy with a man she barely knew. The girls had become firm friends overnight and she'd been glad Adam asked for her help with doing Zoe's room because it meant she could get to know a bit about the household Ava spent so much time in.

'She's pretty excited. She's finishing her homework; I

did call up but she mustn't have heard me.'

'If she's anything like Ava, she'll have her earphones pushed in hard and it'll take a freight train to get her attention.'

He found some coffee capsules from the cupboard and looked at the labels. 'This one's fairly strong, will that suit?'

'Sounds good to me.'

'Not much room in this kitchen, but always room for a coffee machine.' He dropped a pod into the top of the contraption, put a cup beneath and switched it on to make it hiss and pour out the liquid that sent a rich, heady aroma circulating in the air.

'Well, I'm impressed with the café-like service.' She added a splash of milk to her coffee.

'Coffee is a huge thing in Australia, especially Melbourne. I found it difficult to find anywhere that did a good one when we got back to England, although I was spoilt for choice in London.' He tapped the top of the coffee machine. 'This was a moving-in treat for myself.'

'Good for you.' Nobody had delved too much into his reasons for coming here, why he was a single dad. He didn't wear a wedding ring and Viola had often wondered what the story really was, whether she'd get anything from Zoe via Ava, but so far, nothing.

Zoe made an appearance and pulled out her earphones as soon as she saw Viola. 'I didn't hear you arrive.' She smiled, so much more than Ava managed these days. At least Hazel, Ava's younger sister – who was the same age as Jennifer's son Archie and Adam's son Zac – still had a little reliance on Mum and Dad.

'That's because of these.' Adam briefly knocked the earbuds hanging on their wires and dangling from his daughter's hand. 'You'll damage your ears.' His remark met with the same eye roll Ava seemed to have perfected.

Viola and Ava got straight down to business, upstairs in the bedroom where Viola took the oversized bag she'd brought with her, containing everything she'd need to get going with the design phase.

'Pretty drab, isn't it?' Zoe perched on the edge of her bed looking around the space.

Viola found a scrap of paper to use as a coaster before setting her coffee cup down on the windowsill. 'You need to think of it as a blank canvas, which, might I add, is my favourite kind of room. So much potential.'

'Really?'

It felt good talking to a teen who, at least with her, wasn't programmed to be aloof, rude or just plain incommunicado. 'My worst nightmare is when someone wants me to redesign a room but tells me this can't go, that can't go. I don't mind working around some things, but a complete do-over is so much easier and fun.' She wished her own daughter had been so open to her suggestions, but when Ava had turned thirteen and wanted a more grown-up bedroom, she'd almost done the exact opposite of anything Viola suggested.

Zoe's bedroom was typical in a house that had been bought with 'room to improve' on the estate agent's listing. Pale green wallpaper lined the walls with sections that had faded in sunlight, a tatty border ran around the top in a paler green, or it could possibly be yellow, the light fitting was nothing special and had one of those paper spheres in an off-white, although the colour may well have been determined by years of grime. Zoe had added some colour where she could with peppermint-striped bedding, a green cushion on the stool at her desk, a small cream sheepskin rug. On the plus side there were wooden floorboards rather than carpet, the windows were double-glazed and let in plenty of light, and Zoe's furniture was unscathed, white and plain. What this bedroom really cried out for was a good injection of personality.

'Do you mind if I take some pictures?'

'Sure.'

She hadn't been allowed to linger in Ava's room for years, let alone take photographs. 'I can look at the shots when I'm at home.' She stood by the window to snapshot the perspective from there. 'Ideas come to me at the strangest of times and these pictures will jolt my memory and help me think. Are you still happy with all the bedroom furniture? It's in very good condition.'

'I am. I chose white at the last house so it would go with whatever colour I chose, or ended up with if we moved again.'

She wondered how many times these kids had been shunted around from place to place, their lives upended, a change of schools, another circle of friends, and for what reason? But she'd learnt as a parent to steer clear of conflict if you possibly could and so she asked, 'Any thoughts on colour?'

'Part of me wants bold and unique, the other part wants something soft.'

'Have you seen some of my posts on Instagram? It's

where I add pictures of other home makeovers I've played a part in.'

'Ava showed me.'

She grabbed her iPad. 'Great, let's go through some of my previous examples and see if anything grabs you, then work from there.'

They ploughed through pages of examples, hopping over to appropriate websites as they saw fit. They agreed the floorboards, which were in surprisingly good condition, would be cleaned and polished rather than having carpet, and they'd add a large rug to give warmth, colour and cosiness. They went through examples of colours, wall accessories, new linens and lighting, and after an hour or so Viola was ready to go away and do some pricing up.

She poked her head around the door to the lounge where Adam was reading about Voldemort and Hogwarts with little Zac, the spitting image of his dad with his light brown hair and deep caramel eyes that looked up from beneath a fringe that needed attention. There was a boxing match on the muted television, a strange choice of background wallpaper as far as Viola was concerned, and not wholly appropriate for a nine-year-old to see men smash each other's faces in. 'I'll get back to you with costs and some sketches of designs.'

He thanked her and she went on her way, out of Lilliput Cottage with her bag and a head filled with ideas. Zoe waved from the top window as Viola turned to flip the latch of the little gate, wobbly on its hinges and in desperate need of a repaint, at the end of the path, and after she waved back and got into her car she wondered what the story was with the Parker family. They seemed nice enough, but there had to be more to them than the rest of Cloverdale got to see. Perhaps she should ask, find out more the next time she was round there.

Or maybe she should learn to mind her own business for once and simply keep the peace.

5

Jennifer

Jennifer opened the Library of Shared Things three days a week, which seemed to cater for local demand, although some days when she was at home sorting out bills, keeping on top of the laundry and the kids' school emails, invoices and various newsletters, she wished it was full-time. On the odd day David was around but working in his study, she'd found herself coming in here and cleaning up, or contacting local suppliers to see if she could negotiate a donation or a hefty discount for new items. The Library of Shared Things had become a distraction from her problems, not least because she got to talk to other people rather than be surrounded by silence at home.

Jennifer had a steady stream of visitors and now she finished her day by washing up the tea cups used by the local WI who'd stopped by to arrange a booking for the gazebo and tea urn, she vacuumed the floor, and took return of the lawnmower from a local, Pete.

'It runs like a dream,' Pete told her, 'but there's rust on the blades.'

'I'll make a note and get it looked at when we have a maintenance session. Wesley should be able to help get rid of it.' Jennifer had a list of reliable volunteers willing to donate their time once a month on a rotational basis to come in and repair items or give them a thorough clean. She was grateful for the enthusiasm and support the venture had met with so far.

Hattie was in next. She rented a flat above the local pub and today she'd come in to borrow the waffle maker. Dressed in an outfit befitting an art student, with red trousers, a white puffy-sleeved linen blouse, and boho bangles made partly of leather, she was a chirpy girl once you got to know her.

'Are you making waffles for yourself or having a friend over?' Jennifer enquired.

Hattie blushed, long curly chestnut hair tumbling freely across her shoulders. 'My boyfriend Martin is home from university for an extra-long weekend and I want to make his favourite, waffles topped with blueberries and Greek yogurt.'

'Do you have the fruit?'

'I bought four punnets from Pemberley's.'

'He'll never let you go if you keep him this happy.' Jennifer winked as she found the waffle maker from the hutch and went through the checkout process on the computer.

Hattie went on her way, waffle maker in her arms, excited about seeing her boyfriend, a huge smile on her face to match the sun outside.

Jennifer's heart longed for those heady, early days with David, when everything was so exciting and they couldn't keep their hands off one another. Perhaps their marriage was like any other and had normalised into something else. But she felt like such a failure. She and David were drifting apart and she didn't know how to get them back on course.

After they'd married and she fell pregnant with the twins, she and David had discussed their five-year plan. She'd stay home at first, then return to her career, juggling childcare and school drop-offs between them. They'd make it work. They could do anything. How hard could it be? But as with all plans, they were only as concrete as the world around them, which turned out to be as changeable as it was unpredictable. Katie gave them endless, sleepless nights. Amelia wasn't so bad but what she lacked in night-waking she made up for with countless rounds of ear infections, back-to-back colds, impetigo and, at one point, diarrhoea and vomiting that lasted five whole days. Jennifer was left permanently shattered and so work outside the home was soon forgotten in an effort to simply get from one end of the day to the other, and David became the one and only breadwinner. When Archie turned one, it was a different story. She was ready. She needed to return to hairdressing, and she wanted to go back all guns blazing. She wanted to open that salon she'd dreamed off. She was thinking big, dreaming big, but the risks had been huge, the fall from grace even bigger. The Library of Shared Things was fulfilling its potential now by getting the people of Cloverdale talking to each other more, but it still wasn't enough for Jennifer, and sooner or later she knew she was going to have to look at getting back to work once again. But after what happened before, was it really worth rocking the boat of her delicate marriage all over again?

When she got back to the house after she finished up

at the library, Jennifer took her sunglasses from their position nestled in her ebony hair and set them on the table in the hall, calling out to see who was home. But she got no answer. It was too early in the day for the girls to be around and definitely not a time she ever saw David during the week, so she went upstairs and took a long shower to wash off the day and the feeling that she still wanted more.

The house came to life when the door went, less than an hour later as Katie and Amelia arrived home and not too long after that Archie was dropped off by Adam after a trip to the playground with Zac. Jennifer waved a thank you to Adam from the front door and wrapped Archie in her arms. 'Did you have fun at the swings?'

'We spent the whole time on the fireman's pole.' He mimed the action, jumping his little feet up and across the hallway, school uniform still on and mud on the bottom of his trousers.

'How about a hot chocolate?' With September came a sunshine that did its best to warm the days, but there was a definite chill in the air even by early evening and it made her long for autumn when she could cosy up, the leaves would fall, and eventually the fireplace would be operating in the lead-up to the end of the year.

While Archie slipped off his shoes and socks, Jennifer leaned her head around the door to the den, the second lounge commandeered by one of her teenagers who wasted no time heading there the second they came home, and repeated the offer of hot chocolate.

Amelia, who had the same colouring as Jennifer but with the slight dimple in her right cheek like her dad, removed an earbud and almost sat up from her reclined spot on the sofa. 'Only if you're using those one hundred per cent cocoa drops.'

'Yes, please.' Katie, the more placid of her twins, and the one who looked more like a mini version of Jennifer, appeared behind her, ears tuned in from wherever she was in the house to listen for anything good. And hot chocolate fell under that heading.

Jennifer ruffled Archie's hair as he passed her in the doorway on her way out, no doubt to plead with his older sisters to hurry up and vacate the den so he could play on his Xbox. He was addicted to Minecraft, and Jennifer had no interest in what it involved, although she did hover now and again to make sure it looked appropriate for her nine-year-old. She'd already been warned by other parents that he'd soon be begging for Fortnite. She wasn't looking forward to that transition. Archie was the youngest of her three, her baby, and she was savouring every moment until he too broke away and grew up and beyond her reach. Viola was going through the same with her youngest, Hazel, and if they were as close as they'd once been, Jennifer would have been able to talk to her about it, but polite exchanges were about as deep as their friendship ran these days.

In the kitchen she took out the milk and the cocoa drops and mixed the hot chocolate in a pan. She'd put out some of her homemade lemon drizzle cake too, which all the kids loved and which would have the power to keep them at the table longer. When the twins were little life had been crazy, there'd been no baking or serving up velvety hot chocolates then. Back in those days, an hour or two to herself was bliss, the biggest treat in the world, but now she craved those manic days of chaos when she'd been on the go from the moment she got out of bed until the second her or the kids' heads hit the pillow at night. The time had gone too quickly and although she loved her family with all her heart, a tiny piece of her mourned for the fourth child they'd never brought into the world. She'd carried the twins to thirty-six weeks with no troubles at all. She'd struggled to get pregnant with Archie, and a couple of years after he was born, once the fallout from her mistake had given way to a calmer life for all of them, she'd tried to fall pregnant again. She had done, three times, but each of those times she'd miscarried.

The fact her body couldn't do what she wanted made no sense at all to Jennifer, but David had never understood why they needed to add to the brood once they'd had Archie. He'd been supportive at first, because she'd been so desperate for another baby, but with every miscarriage came the grief, her devastation, each time inflicting itself on every member of the family until after their third try David told her enough was enough. He wasn't willing to put any of them through it again and she agreed it was time to stop.

But even though she'd said the words out loud, believing them was another thing entirely. And she knew it wasn't all down to wanting another child. Part of it was the fear that once her kids grew older and no longer relied on her so much, she'd be lost. Every way she tried to turn met with a wall that prevented her from doing what she wanted, and she felt selfish, spoiled for not being happy with what she had in life. Plenty of women would be. She lived in a stunning property they'd sympathetically renovated with a porch at the front that stretched all the way across and housed a table and chairs for long summer days. The gardens were immaculately tended by a gardener and again there was a seating area, this time with a fire pit for the colder months when they could entertain friends and sit outside beneath blankets. And here she was standing in an all-white, sleek, contemporary kitchen in their home with its Georgian characteristics and proportions. She had so much, others had so little, her family were all healthy, some families battled illnesses and financial strife. So why couldn't she be happy with her lot in life?

She tilted her neck to the left and then to the right when she realised she'd been clenching her jaw, holding on to so much tension, and as Katie, Amelia and Archie emerged to her call of 'Hot chocolate's ready!', she disguised her doubts that her life was anything less than perfect with a jolly voice.

Their kitchen was well organised and Jennifer's favourite part was its island in the middle. Square-shaped, it had two edges that, beneath, had space for legs so they could all sit up here as a family for mealtimes, which made a relaxed change to sitting at the table. 'Lemon drizzle?' she asked all three of them after she'd handed out mugs filled to the brim with rich, decadent hot chocolate, a little bit of sugar already added to sweeten. At their nods of agreement, she distributed slices all round. This was where the kitchen came into its own, a place where they could all gather, no matter the crumbs or the splashes of hot chocolate left behind by an over-zealous Archie, they had time together and that really was all that mattered. Her parents had made sacrifices for her; she made sacrifices for her kids. That was the way it worked.

That was life.

*

When David came home as Jennifer was slotting a lamb tagine into the oven for dinner, he didn't say much before he disappeared upstairs for a shower. He was always so tired these days, much like she'd been in the early days of parenting, except this time they weren't in it together. Instead, they went through the daily motions snatching small moments with each other that never seemed to be enough.

'Did you book Cornwall for Easter?' she asked when he came downstairs, hair still wet from the overhead rainfall shower and reminding her of how he'd looked back in his surfing days when he'd emerged from the sea and splashed cold water over her as she lay on the sands waiting for him.

'Not yet, I've been busy.' She resisted the urge to tell him not to eat too much before dinner, when he pulled open the fridge.

'We're all busy.' She hated the way she sounded, but she'd also begun to resent the isolation she felt too often when she was at home so much.

'I'll get to it. Promise.' He leaned in to kiss her, his zesty shower gel carried on the air with him.

She softened, picked up the iPad and sat on the stool next to him so she could find a website with photographs of Cornwall to give them both inspiration. They usually went away at Easter when the weather was starting to turn for the better, when beaches weren't as crazy as in the summer months. 'How about Crooklets Beach, along the coast from Bude?' She turned the iPad so he could see photographs. 'You could take your surfboard, get the kids into it.'

'I'm not the same surfer dude I once was. I'm not even sure I could squeeze into my wetsuit.'

'Of course you could, and your surfboard is in the garage; it only needs the cobwebs dusted off. What do you think?'

'About surfing or Cornwall?'

'Both. Cornwall is beautiful; we've been to St Ives, so this is somewhere different for us all. Archie is super keen; remember how he saw your surfboard at the start of the summer holidays?' And how they hadn't gone anywhere to use it, much as their son had begged.

'I'm up for that.'

In moments like these Jennifer's doubts about their marriage dissipated, but as soon as they were over, the bad thoughts crept back in. 'The twins could learn to sail; we could go to see the Eden Project.'

'I expect the twins will be happy with us at the beach if they're anything like their mother.'

When he gave her the same grin that had won her over all those years ago, she said, 'Maybe a surf spot isn't such a good idea.'

'Come on, they're sixteen. Boyfriends are inevitable.'

He was right, she couldn't keep them young forever. 'I don't think Katie and Amelia will want to holiday with us for much longer.'

'That depends where we go. I couldn't see them turning down a nice resort in Europe or further afield if that was where we were heading.' He took the iPad for a closer look at the accommodation she'd found. 'Looks a bit remote for our girls.'

'We should ban devices on the holiday, really go back to basics.'

His laughter echoed around the kitchen. 'If you do that, they'll definitely not come away with us again.' He read snippets out loud. 'Tucked away . . . five minutes from the beach . . . ten minutes' walk to the pub . . .' And with a few more clicks he only went and booked it.

A huge smile spread across Jennifer's face and she wrapped her arms around him, leaned in to his familiar smell, the feel of his almost-smooth jaw that saw the sharp side of a razor every morning except when he was on holiday. 'It'll do us good to all be together.'

'We're together now.'

'You know what I mean.'

'Just think, once the girls head to uni or work, they'll go on holidays with their own friends. It'll save us a fortune.'

'We've got a while for that yet. And you do realise we'll be paying out for our kids forever, don't you?'

He ran a hand across the back of his neck. 'Then I'd better get into the study, put in another half-hour or so before dinner.'

Her heart sank. She knew she should be grateful for his work ethic, this beautiful house they lived in, the fact they could afford holidays a couple of times a year, not to mention his part in helping her out of the big hole of trouble she'd managed to dig for herself eight years ago. But the last fifteen minutes had been a nice reminder of who they could be when they weren't so busy. When Archie was a baby they'd curled up on the sofa together the second he was down and the twins were tucked up in their beds reading. They'd watched television, chatted, made the most of each other before the whole routine started again the next day.

She looped her arms around his shoulders and rested

her face against his neck. 'Surely it can wait until Monday. We could go for a walk while the dinner cooks.'

'Unfortunately that won't pay the bills or for country cottages in Cornwall.' He let himself relax in her arms a bit longer, then pulled away. 'I need to stay on top of my workload; I've got an important conference call tomorrow.' He kissed her on the lips and lingered a moment longer than usual. 'I love you.' He said it as though wondering if he'd done wrong.

'Love you too.' They said it often, kind of like a habit. Over the years the words had replaced other gestures they'd both made to show their appreciation of one another rather than vocalise it. Like when he'd run her a bath with candles along the tub and rose petals floating in the water. More than once he'd taken the kids out for the day so she could have time out, and, back then, she'd relished it. When he'd had a particularly stressful restructure at work and had had to reapply for his own job, she'd had her mum watch the kids and taken him off to Gleneagles where they'd dined in luxury and she'd caddied as he played golf. They'd revelled in one another's time, wanting nothing more than the precious moments that were so easy to take for granted. Back then they'd talked to each other, they'd known when to give each other space, they'd read each other's signals in a way they didn't seem to be able to do anymore.

With dinner taking care of itself and filling the kitchen with a fruity aroma, Jennifer leaned against the kitchen bench thinking about Cornwall and how good it would be for all of them. She twirled her hair around her fingers, a habit her mum used to tell her off for once upon a time, a behaviour David had said drove him crazy, in a good way, at the start of their relationship. Inspecting the ends she knew it needed a trim and with her iPad, she made an appointment with her favourite hairdresser whose salon was out of town, but who, with every visit, reminded Jennifer of the world she'd once loved but left behind. The dream she'd given up.

Amelia came in to ask when dinner would be ready. Where she put that cake and hot chocolate was anyone's guess. She played a lot of sport at school, probably where her appetite came from, and already she'd opened the oven to inspect what was on offer.

'Bit longer,' said Jennifer.

'What are you up to?' Amelia shuffled her bottom onto the stool next to her.

'Booking a haircut.'

Amelia stood on the wooden rails at the bottom of the stool so she could see the top of her mum's head. 'Nope, no greys in there.'

'I'm lucky, I take after your gran; she told me she didn't spot her first grey hair until she was fifty-three.'

'I miss her.'

'Me too.' Since she'd died, Jennifer had gone to lift up the phone for a chat more times than she could remember. What she'd give now for one more chat, ask her mum's advice about marriage.

'Auntie Isla doesn't have any grey either. I can't imagine her getting old.'

'But you can imagine me?' She poked Amelia gently in the ribs.

'You know what I mean. Auntie Isla is unattached, free.'

'Whereas I'm haggard and shackled to you guys.'

'Stop putting words in my mouth.' She ran her fingers

through her dark hair. Longer than Jennifer's, it had that thickness and glossy appearance that came with youth, and something you only valued when it was gone. Jennifer crossed her fingers that her daughter would never hack off her beautiful hair. Katie had already begun talking about experimenting. She was the same blonde as her father, and she'd been talking about cool blonde, ice blonde, highlights and lowlights. But that was where her interest in hair stopped. Katie was all about trying things out, but Amelia was the one who was inquisitive, planning to follow in her mum's footsteps when she left school. And Jennifer loved it when they talked shop, discussed colouring, cutting techniques, blow-drying methods.

'Will you get your roots done when you go grey?' Amelia did have a way of getting to the point. 'Lots of people are embracing the grey nowadays. Lots of younger people; it's on trend you know.'

Just because she wasn't working in the industry didn't mean she wasn't interested and didn't pick things up along the way, but sometimes she tried to block out the information, as though if it wasn't there she wouldn't think about what she was missing. 'Who'd have thought?' She hugged her daughter. 'I'm not sure I'm on board with it.'

'I think it can look cool.'

'Some girls look stunning with grey colours, but I always wonder why you'd do it when you'll have no choice in decades to come. I say make the most of the colour you have.'

'I'm intending to.'

'Good. Oh, and we booked the holiday.'

A smile spread across Amelia's face and she pushed both

palms together in prayer. 'Please say somewhere exotic.'

'Cornwall.'

She made a face but then said, 'Cornwall rocks. Everyone says so. And it could be worse . . . Natalie's family booked them on a week's walking holiday in Scotland.'

'She's into walking?'

'Her parents are. She isn't.'

'Then I think we've done well.'

'How did you pin Dad down long enough to book something?'

'I think he saw the possibility of surfing and went for it.'

Amelia covered her eyes and peeked out from behind her fingers. 'Dad . . . in a wetsuit.'

'Heard that!' he hollered from the study.

'Have you got much school work?' Jennifer asked Amelia, the twin who'd been born second, seventeen minutes after Katie, and who ever since had been the more laid-back of the two.

'Quite a lot, I'll get to it soon.'

'I know you will.' She reached out to steal a hug. Although she was set on a career in hairdressing and could leave school at the end of this academic year, Amelia was measured in her decisions and had decided to ensure she had plenty of options. She'd shown flair for mathematics and business studies and so, with parents willing to fund her education further, she'd decided to get a business degree, then do a hairdressing course. She'd told Jennifer it would stand her in good stead if she wanted to open her own business and when she'd said those words, Jennifer couldn't have been more proud. She'd also felt, although she'd never admit it, jealous of her daughter who was going to do the very thing she'd wanted to do but never had.

'What were the hair trends when you first started out in a salon?' Amelia wanted to know. She may work hard at school, she may be going to university, but the underlying passion for her career choice couldn't be held back, and right now Jennifer knew she was stalling before she had to do her homework.

'We're going back years.' Jennifer thought hard, back a couple of decades to when she'd been doing her apprenticeship and was full of ambition. 'I lost count of how many people wanted a Rachel cut.'

'Oh yes, the dreaded *Friends* phenomenon.'

'Hey! It was hugely popular back then; still is.'

'I know, you guys used to make references to it all the time.'

They had, but Jennifer had forgotten. They'd often annoyed their kids with their little in-jokes, *Friends* references, and it had been their thing. But along the way that had got lost too.

'We also got a lot of requests for the Meg Ryan pixie cut,' Jennifer went on. 'It was sassy, edgy. I think perms were on the way out, but I loved the changes.'

'Do you ever wish you'd gone back to hairdressing or got your own salon?'

Without Jennifer noticing, it had begun to rain as they'd sat there in their quiet kitchen and the drops pattered the window panes along the side wall of the house. 'I always wanted a family, so I chose to stop.'

'But still . . .'

'I will never regret it.'

'We are pretty awesome.'

'And modest.'

'But you were good, weren't you? Dad always said you were.'

Warmth flowed through her at the thought of David talking about her in that way. 'I wasn't bad. I trained and did an apprenticeship. I worked really hard, I got a good job and moved up to senior stylist. I never intended to stop, but life kind of had other plans.' Her kids would be disappointed in her for what she did, if they knew, especially the trouble she made for their Gran and Grandad who the girls had always been close to. She gave her standard response if ever people asked her why she'd not returned to work once the kids started school, which was to tell them having a parent at home was the easiest option, followed by a nonchalant laugh as though her life was so much better now and she hadn't given her career a moment's thought since. 'I've been out of the business for years,' she said matter-of-factly.

'Doesn't mean you can't go back.'

She shrugged away the thought as the rain turned diagonal, and they both pulled a face at each other at the unexpected turn in the weather. 'I like being here for you all. What would you do without me?'

'Mum, I'm sixteen. I won't be here forever.'

'I remember when you used to say to me you'd never move out of home, you got quite upset when I suggested that one day you'd probably want to.' She looked fondly at her daughter, such a reminder of herself at that age. 'How did my little girl get so grown-up all of a sudden?'

'You raised me to be like this.'

'Then I did something right.' She hugged Amelia tightly and kissed the top of her head. 'I'm proud of you.'

And before she left the room when her sister yelled out to come and check out some ridiculous meme she'd been sent by a friend, she added, 'Mum, just because you chose to raise a family doesn't mean you can't want something for yourself ever again.'

Jennifer sat watching the rain as it hit the windows, the stream trickling down the left side, and wondered whether her daughter was right. Having her own business was a desire that had consumed her before she'd met David. She'd put in the long hours; she'd made plans on pieces of paper about what her own salon would look like one day. It had been all she'd ever wanted. And she'd almost done it once Archie turned one. But it wasn't meant to be.

She was still sitting in quiet contemplation when David came in having finished work for now. 'When did that happen?' He nodded outside the window.

'It was beautiful earlier.'

What Amelia had said a moment ago was still turning over in her mind when the oven timer pinged. She couldn't deny she hadn't thought about resurrecting her career, especially since Archie's school years seemed to skip by at a rate of knots, but having the confirmation from one of the kids was the type of encouragement that took her from contemplation to wanting action.

She set the oven dish down on the cooktop and took out plates ready for serving. 'David, I've been thinking –'

'That's always dangerous.'

She pushed his hand away as he reached for the serving spoon to try the tagine before she dished up. 'I've been thinking a lot lately about my old job.'

'What's brought this on all of a sudden?'

Should she tell him it was anything but sudden, a

burning desire that had been smouldering away for a while now? Then again, he'd remember what happened before, the pain she'd put everyone through and that would tarnish everything.

'Nothing, it's just—'

David's phone in the back pocket of his jeans began its familiar, repetitive buzz. 'I have to get this. Sorry, it's about my next work trip. I'll make it short; I know dinner's ready.' He kissed her cheek, assuming she'd be annoyed if he didn't sit down for dinner on time, and she felt dismissed like a secretary at his work who'd taken the minutes but was no longer needed.

She dished up the tagine and set the oven dish into the sink to fill with water so the remnants didn't dry hard as they ate, but her own phone soon demanded her attention. It appeared that phones had more clout than actual people when it came to your social life.

When she saw Adam's name she clicked on to his message about a missing trainer. Zac had come home with three in the bottom of his PE bag. They'd swapped numbers with the boys seeing each other so much and being at each other's houses, and after she checked Archie's kit and explained to him the importance of taking responsibility for his own belongings, she texted Adam back to thank him and ask Zac to bring it to school Monday morning.

Her phone bleeped quickly again and as she tore up the Moroccan bread for dipping in the tagine, she read and responded to each message.

Adam: I'll be at the Library of Shared Things on Monday to fix up that shelf you mentioned.

Jennifer: Thanks! It needs doing before it collapses.

Adam: Happy to be of service. Will you be there?

Jennifer: Of course.

Adam: I heard Elaine talking about collecting something. Don't want to be rude, but that woman looks like she wants to eat me alive!

Jennifer laughed out loud. Elaine was very lovely, but very bossy, very vocal, and she seemed to have an eye for Adam ever since she'd met him in the library when he first arrived in the village. Like any other community effort, Elaine had leapt on board with the Library of Shared Things, bought and donated a couple of items, regularly borrowed things. She also volunteered up at the local primary school and she was always in the pub having a good gossip. She was married to Tony, plumber, and one of the quietest men Jennifer knew. Maybe he shunted her off to all these voluntary positions to give himself a break.

At the opening for the Library of Shared Things, Jennifer had overheard Elaine telling Adam the best foods to barbecue when it turned out he'd bought a barbecue for himself and was cooking the kids' dinner that evening. It seemed to have gone right over her head that Adam was a single parent and probably knew a thing or two about cooking. Jennifer had overheard her recommendations for kebabs that incorporated meat and vegetables, patties that were tasty yet nutritious, the best sorts of salads kids would actually touch rather than turn their nose up at. She had three robust children who took after her with their stocky build and no doubt she wanted everyone to have the wisdom of her years child-rearing. When Adam had asked, 'What's wrong with a few snags and chook wings?', reminding them all of his stint in Australia, Jennifer had tried to keep a straight face, Elaine must've given up all hope with him and left with a look of horror on her face.

Jennifer continued their conversation after she'd taken the cutlery out of the drawer:

Jennifer: She'll be volunteering at school that day. So don't worry, you're safe. I expect someone else will pick the item up or she'll come at the end of the day.

Adam: I might be safe, not sure about those poor kids!

Jennifer: They'll be safe soon. I've heard she's quitting the library to return to work in a month.

As their texts continued about Elaine and her return to her job as a nurse, jokes batting back and forth about whether she'd scare patients away with her advice or whether they'd find it reassuring, Jennifer found herself typing out a question for Adam:

Jennifer: How old do you think is 'too old' when it comes to returning to work? Asking for a friend. . .

Adam: Why, are you thinking of going back?

Jennifer: Is that totally crazy?

Adam: No! What is 'work'? What did you do before you
       were a mum?

Jennifer: I was once a hairdresser. The dream was to get
          my own salon, but think the time has passed. I'd
          settle for a part-time job in a salon.

Adam: You shouldn't settle . . . reach for the stars!

Jennifer: So you think I could do it?

Adam: If anyone can, you can.

She was still holding her phone when David came in
and hollered to the kids that dinner was ready.

'What are you smiling about? Can't be the weather.'
He looked out again at the murky skies and hovering
clouds beyond the window and across the surrounding
countryside.

She put her phone face down on the table when the kids
bundled in and took their seats, wasting no time diving in
for bread. 'Nothing, I'm only daydreaming.' Once upon
a time he might have asked what she was daydreaming
about, maybe made a suggestive remark, they might have
ended up running off to the bedroom to make love. But
he was in his own head, probably still in work mode and
she'd tried, yet failed, to talk to him earlier. She wondered
whether, had she got the words out, David would have
had the same enthusiasm for her idea that Adam, this
stranger who'd quickly become a confidant, had?

The man she seemed to talk to more than her husband

these days had encouraged her not to give up on herself. And as she tucked into another family dinner, she couldn't feel guilty about it.

Because it felt good.

6

Adam

Both Zoe and Zac only had smartphones on the understanding that their dad was always kept informed of the password. Zac didn't much care – he was a boy and young enough – but Zoe minded a lot, and Adam hated having to insist, but he felt justified when he heard other parents did the same. He knew Viola even went so far as to track Ava's phone so she could see where she was at any minute of the day.

Standing in the kitchen he scrolled through the history on Zoe's phone, happy to see it was all harmless enough: articles about eyebrow shaping, another about the going rate of pocket money and what kids should expect, an endless number of websites with images for teenage bedrooms. He checked through her text messages but tried not to pry too much as long as names were those he recognised from her friendships in London, or others she'd mentioned here in Cloverdale, and after he'd replaced her phone before she made it down the stairs ready to head off for school, he did a search on his own laptop to make sure she hadn't opened up any random social media accounts he wasn't aware of. He checked for any presence on social media and when he found nothing, a familiar relief flooded his body.

He wondered how many years he'd have to do this for. They'd come to England to start a new life and, as far as the kids knew, their mother didn't want any contact. But how long could the pretence go on? Every day he dreaded social media connecting the members of his family in a way that could destroy them. Because that's what would happen. They'd blame him, they'd know what he'd done, and it would finish him.

He went back to his laptop. His skills as a landscape architect were varied, given his years in the field and his wide-reaching experience in two continents. His latest project was for a mixed-use development of residential, retail and commercial premises, and he'd gathered enough information to draw up a proposal. Design brought together thinking in many different realms, whether it was the buildings themselves or the spaces connecting them, and part of his enjoyment was collaborating with a team of professionals. He was, however, grateful he had freedom to work from home on occasion and he'd already been up working for a couple of hours before the kids surfaced today.

After the kids set off for school he finished up the email he was composing and headed over to the Library of Shared Things, armed with a spare piece of wood he'd salvaged from the shed at the foot of his garden. It would do to reinforce the shelf Jennifer had texted him about, before it gave up under the weight of kitchen equipment.

'You look away with the fairies,' said Elaine, when he turned up in front of the yellow doors.

He tried not to let disappointment show. He'd thought

Jennifer would be there, an ally, even though he wondered whether she'd even want to know him if the truth he'd been hiding from the whole of Cloverdale should ever come out.

'Good morning, Elaine. I wasn't expecting to see you.' The sun definitely didn't match the bright yellow bifolds this morning, and he shivered against the wind and a temperature that told him he should've put a long-sleeved top on today rather than a T-shirt.

'I need to get going to the school but I was hoping Jennifer would be here by now. I wanted to pick up the pressure washer.'

'I'm sure she won't be long.'

'How's Zoe?' Elaine still had the same head tilt he'd become all too familiar with ever since she'd seen Zoe injecting insulin at the opening ceremony. He hated the way this woman felt sorry for his daughter, and he knew Zoe couldn't stand being thought of in that way.

'She's good, thanks.'

'And is she managing?'

Zoe had been managing her diabetes like a pro for a long time. He'd never expected it, especially at first when she'd been so angry. He'd read all the literature he could, grasped at facts about eating a healthy and balanced diet, doing enough exercise. It was the same advice given to everyone really, but there was more urgency in Zoe's case now she had to maintain that delicate balance with her food, activity and insulin. But once she'd accepted it, she'd read as much as he had, she'd taken control and got on with it. She usually made sure she had plenty of snacks and glucose tablets at hand, she tested her blood glucose levels before it was a problem, but occasionally she slipped up.

He'd had no friends or neighbours to call on when Zoe was carted off in an ambulance in the middle of the night, nobody to confide in about how terrified he was that he'd lose her. Zac had needed reassurance, not a panicking father, so Adam had had to rein in his feelings. He'd had nobody to help when Zoe had a hypo in the street near their house earlier this year either, but luckily he'd arrived home from work at the right time. He'd found his daughter trembling, sweaty and incoherent, and had quickly given her jelly babies to boost her blood sugar levels. She'd been embarrassed and angry with him when she came round properly. But after it had happened he'd got to thinking about making one more change, one more move for him and the kids to give them the best life possible. And that meant leaving the city and heading towards the country. And now he was here in the village he knew he had to make the effort to interact with the people of Cloverdale and be a part of something. But mingling with Elaine wasn't quite what he'd had in mind.

He knew full well what Elaine had meant by her question now, but chose to pretend otherwise. He'd got better at reading women over the years. 'She does her homework on time, seems to understand it all and that GCSEs are just around the corner; she's a normal kid like her brother.'

Jennifer arrived full of apologies for being late, and Adam helped Elaine put the pressure washer in the boot of her car.

'Sorry,' Jennifer said the second Elaine went on her way. 'Was she unbearable?'

'She's a good sort really. She means well.'

'So she was unbearable.'

'No comment.' As Jennifer switched on the computer

he got straight to work fixing up the shelf. He couldn't be away from his own work for too long – he had plenty to do – but doing favours for locals was part of making themselves at home here in the village and he liked Jennifer enough not to mind.

He borrowed the saw and out in the car park he cut the piece of wood to size. Jennifer took returns – the lawnmower from Mason who'd mowed the grass verge outside the pub to earn himself extra pocket money after Melody, who ran the pub with her husband Danny, elected to outsource the job given they were so busy, the Thermomix from Margaret who lived up near the school.

'Yes!' Jennifer called out from the desk at the opposite end to where he'd hammered in the nails of the wooden support.

'Sounds like good news.' He returned the saw he'd used and the hammer, and picked up a piece of sandpaper to smooth the edges.

'Sorry, I got a bit excited there. A garden centre has kindly donated a hedge trimmer to us, to add to our collection. It's been a requested item from a few people and I was happy with a good discount, but this is even better.' She reeled off a list of locals, some he'd heard of, some he hadn't, who wanted to borrow the item.

'I'd better get in soon . . . wouldn't mind doing my hedges at the end of the back garden.'

'I'll let you know when it's available.' She came over to inspect his handiwork. 'Perfect, thanks again for doing this.' Between them they had the items loaded back onto the shelf in minutes and sat down with a cup of tea each, at Jennifer's insistence.

'What made you late today? I hope everything's OK at

home.' He sipped the tea, grateful for the moment's respite before he headed back to the cottage to work.

'Archie wasn't well; he's been up in the night with a temperature. David had to go into the office, so I had to get a babysitter to come over.'

When she scraped her hair away from her face it was the first time he realised she looked tired. But he wasn't going to say that, not to a lady. 'You should've said. Left this place closed for the day or at least the morning.'

She shook her head. 'People rely on me, people like Elaine.' She laughed when he pulled a face.

'How's Archie now?'

'Better. Hopefully he'll be back at school in a couple of days.' She sipped her tea. 'So how was Elaine really?'

'Her intentions are good. But she can be a bit much. Am I the only one she takes an interest in?'

'Yes.'

'Does she do it because she feels sorry for me?'

'Yes.' She bunched her hair up at the back, twirled it round her fingers and pushed a clip into it.

'Is it because she saw Zoe injecting herself in the car park?' He put himself into a pose as though he was a druggie getting a fix.

Jennifer laughed. 'Yes.'

'Well, I wish she'd forget she saw it and move on.' There were other things lurking in the past he wished would go away too. Pity there wasn't a magic eraser to get rid of the bits of your life you didn't want, keep the memories that you did. Life would be a whole lot easier.

'How are things with Zoe?'

'She's still being a normal teen; she's got the stroppiness down pat. But I'm glad she's got a friend like Ava; it's as though they've known one another for years rather than weeks.'

'Ava is lovely. And so is Zoe, for that matter. Hang in there, parenting is tough, you're winning, you're surviving.'

The yellow door folded back and in came Isla.

'What brings you here?' Jennifer asked.

She didn't sound as friendly as she usually did. Perhaps the tiredness he'd noticed wasn't helping. Or maybe it was something else. When she'd texted him and asked what he thought about her returning to work, he'd encouraged her. If anyone could do it, Jennifer could. The way she'd launched and now ran the Library of Shared Things said plenty about her work ethic and organisational skills. But it was as though she didn't think she could have more. Her role as a mum was well established but what was stopping her grabbing on to a piece of life for herself? He'd wanted to ask but didn't feel he could when they hadn't known each other that long, so he'd let it be. For now.

Isla didn't bristle at her sister's less than enthusiastic greeting. Instead, her delicate blue eyes fell on Adam. 'I wanted to thank Adam for the drill lesson the other night and when I knocked at the cottage, Elaine saw me and told me he was in here.'

There was something enticing about Isla, maybe her eyes, or her smile and the way her lips weren't sure whether to show much emotion right now in front of her sister. 'It was my pleasure,' he said.

'I also wanted to show you my handiwork.'

'Great!' He took her phone from her outstretched hand. This woman had all of Jennifer's warmth but an added confidence and bubbly demeanour he could really get on board with. She'd taken pictures of everything she'd done since the class. 'You put up the light fittings? Nice. And the shelving, good too. And it all went without a hitch?'

'Of course. I can handle a drill.'

They smiled at each other like a couple of lovestruck teens until he remembered they weren't alone. 'It must've been my exemplary teaching skills.'

'Something like that.' She grinned. 'Perhaps I can return the favour.'

'Yeah? What do you have in mind?' He was enjoying the flirting. It had been a long time since any woman had taken notice of him, unless it was in a work capacity, or maybe he'd always been so stressed and busy that he'd never noticed. 'What can you teach me that I don't already know?'

Jennifer's hunched shoulders said she wasn't appreciating the exchange as much as either of them.

'I teach yoga at the village hall,' said Isla cheekily.

Now he laughed. 'Learning to use a drill is easy in comparison. It's a long time since my body has bent in any weird fashion.'

'Really,' she quipped.

He cleared his throat, conscious of Jennifer's cool reaction to their banter. 'Maybe something else other than yoga.' Dinner, a drink, a walk in the countryside? He'd leap at anything, although he tried to dial down his enthusiasm in front of Jennifer who perhaps wouldn't want her sister involved with a man none of them really knew well enough and who came with a whole heap of mystery baggage.

'Isla, I don't think yoga is Adam's thing,' Jennifer put in. She started fussing around the kitchen equipment, checking the Thermomix that had come back that day, although Adam was pretty sure she'd already done that.

'I'm sure Adam can speak for himself.' Isla stood her ground.

It didn't seem to take much for these two to push each other's buttons. He picked up his phone, ready to scarper and get some work done.

When he said his goodbyes, neither woman spoke and all he got was a tentative smile from Isla before she turned on Jennifer. 'Have you ever thought maybe I can have a conversation on my own? That I don't always need your input?'

'I get it: you don't need me.'

'Now you're twisting my words. Are you still annoyed I didn't make it for the opening?' Her silence must've been all the answer Isla needed. 'I was teaching, it was work.'

'Oh, and I wouldn't know because I don't work, is that it?'

'There you go again, twisting what I say. I couldn't make the opening, but I'd like to come and help out if you'll let me.' Silence. 'But I'm not going to beg.'

'Why would you want to come in here? It's dull, your life has been one journey of excitement.'

'And for some reason you resent me for it.'

'I do not!'

'Well, if you don't resent me, then you're jealous or being judgemental, because I'm not like you with your cosy family.'

Ouch, he didn't know Isla well but she'd never come across as bitchy before. He suspected there was a lot he didn't know and when she stormed past him he said to Jennifer, 'I'll see you around.' And he escaped the escalation of female drama himself.

'Zoe, Zac, dinner!' he hollered up the stairs later that evening. For all that this house was small, it still amazed him how loud he had to shout for them to respond.

'Could you please set the table?' he asked Zoe, who was first through the kitchen door for the chicken curry he'd cooked in the slow cooker, with the smell torturing him as he worked. He'd only had toast for lunch and he was starving. 'Zoe.' His eyes went to the cutlery when she eventually looked at him. 'Set the table, please.'

The harrumph she made had him questioning whether he'd asked her to put some cutlery into position or if he'd asked her to give him one of her kidneys. Honestly, it was hardly a big deal.

'And what's *he* doing?' she asked when Zac came in and sat down.

'He can do it tomorrow.' He set down a bowl of curry with rice for each of his kids and then another for himself. 'So what's been happening? How was school?'

'All right,' Zac offered.

'Dull,' said Zoe.

'What lessons did you have today?' he asked of his son first.

'Maths, PE . . .' He screwed his face up, thinking. 'Assembly.'

'Not a lesson,' came Zoe's most helpful sisterly response.

'And what did you have, Zoe?'

'It was school. Now I'm home. Can we not discuss it?'

'You start a topic then.'

'I'd rather just eat.'

He let it go because sometimes conceding was the only way to stay sane. He at least got compliments from Zac about the curry, and both kids cleared their bowls so he assumed it had gone down well. The only way he managed to evoke some kind of enthusiasm from Zoe was when he asked Zac to take the dishes over to the sink and he changed the topic of discussion to her bedroom. They talked about colour schemes, how the current furniture would work, how Viola had recommended keeping the beautiful floorboards and adding a rug.

'Viola's added loads of images to Instagram,' said Zoe.

'Has she now.'

'Apparently. But I haven't seen them yet, of course.'

He sighed. 'We'll talk about you and social media another time.'

'See that?' She pointed out of the window.

He looked but, now the light had faded, all he could see was the steeple of the church across the fields behind their house. The clocks would go back next month and the long summer days would be a distant memory. 'I don't see anything.'

'Yes, you do.' He didn't miss the note of sarcasm in her voice. 'It was a pig; I think it was flying.'

He felt anger boiling up inside of him. 'There's no need to be rude.'

'I'm not being rude, I'm being honest.'

'You're being rude!' He wondered if the neighbours heard him yell. He was certainly loud enough; he'd seen Zac shudder in his seat. 'Go to your room if you can't be nice.'

'Fine.' Her chair scraped against the kitchen floor, she stomped up the stairs and then an almighty slam of her bedroom door brought her departure to its conclusion.

'Dad.' Zac finished his dinner and looked up at him

with a face so serious Adam had to adopt the same expression. 'Why won't you give her that app she wants? All the girls use it.' He lowered his voice as though someone could have their ear up to the window, listening in. 'Some girls as young as me talk about it.'

'Then that really is worrying.'

'We learn all about social media at school, you know.'

'Already?'

Zac nodded his head at the offer of a chocolate biscuit as pudding.

'We talk about keeping ourselves safe when we use the internet. We have to tell an adult if we see things we don't like. We don't share passwords. We *always* ask a parent's permission if we want to download new things, and we *never* post any photographs we wouldn't want to see on the front page of a newspaper.'

If it wasn't so serious, Adam would've laughed. This whole move across the other side of the world would've been much easier twenty years ago, before technology made it almost impossible to keep anything a secret. And kids were the worst offenders, flippant with the information they shared, blasé about their lives being out there for all to see.

When he excused Zac to go and watch television after they loaded the dishwasher – it was Zoe's turn but he couldn't face getting an angry teen downstairs right now – he thought back to when Zoe had first been diagnosed with diabetes. All three of them had been scared witless when she was lying in that hospital bed going through all kinds of tests, and when she came home, all she wanted was to get back to normal. She wanted to fit in. Be like every other kid in her class. Maybe if he agreed to let her be like her peers and have this wretched social media app they all seemed so obsessed about, then it would be a step forward. He'd messed up his kids' lives enough already, he owed them. And as long as their mum didn't ever find out where they were, his kids' belief and trust in him would remain intact.

But if they ever found out the truth, there'd be no coming back from that. The lies would be exposed, the truth about what he'd done would become local knowledge, gossip for people he passed in the street, people like Elaine who seemed to hover and wait for you to slip up.

He'd have to make sure that never happened.

He wiped down the sink and then grabbed the bag of rubbish to take outside to the wheelie bin he'd manoeuvred round to the front for collection tomorrow.

'I'd forgotten it was bin day so thanks for the reminder.' The warmth of Isla's voice stopped him as she walked past the cottage.

'Hello again.' He was more than pleased to see her smiling face. 'Are you heading to the pub?'

'I'm having a drink with Hattie.'

'She's nice, you're quite similar.'

'Non-conformists, you mean?'

'I didn't mean that.' Isla wasn't your average thirty-six-year-old; she was young and free, and, by Cloverdale standards, that was out of the ordinary. 'I meant . . . well, she's single, loves art, you know you could talk to her about doing your place up. Or there's Viola, she does interior design. What, why are you smiling?'

'You're trying to dig yourself out of a hole and probably making it worse.'

He leaned against the gatepost. 'I apologise.'

'Don't worry, I know I'm completely different to Jennifer. I think that's what you're getting at.'

'It's not a bad thing. Not that there's anything wrong with Jennifer. What I mean is . . .' He scraped a hand across his face and she giggled. 'Your sister seems to want to look out for you, it's kind of nice.'

'Yeah, well, sometimes I wish she wouldn't.'

'You don't mean that.'

'Daaaaaaaaaaaaaaaaaaaad!' a voice hollered from inside.

'Would you like to come in for a tea, or coffee?'

He was pleased to see her smile grow wider when she said, 'Go on, then. I'm actually a bit early anyway.'

They went inside and Adam saw the disaster – the batteries had run out in the remote control – so he found some more from the utility room, popped them in and Zac went back to watching cartoons.

Out in the kitchen, Isla sat at the table and Adam ran through the choice of coffee pods he had on offer. 'This one has the description full and balanced.' He held up a pod, then another. 'Or this one is intense and syrupy.'

'The second one sounds like me, let's go for that. Full and balanced sounds far too Jennifer.'

He couldn't help but laugh, and felt guilty. Jennifer was the first to really welcome him and the kids to Cloverdale and he respected that. 'Your sister isn't quite the ogre you make her out to be, you know.'

She looked like she was going to disagree until she said, 'I know, but I wish she'd trust me to manage my own life like I've been doing for years.'

He made two coffees and set them down on the table. 'So what have you been doing with your life? I'm assuming it's nothing too catastrophic like spending time in jail or going around committing crimes.'

'I'm not that wild. Although I did do a pole dancing class earlier.'

'Yeah?'

She explained some moves, had him wondering how on earth anyone could hold themselves in those positions. He blew across the top of his coffee as she carried on. Listening to her was an unexpected pleasure this evening.

'I went travelling for a long time, hopped from job to job. Along the way I started to do a lot of yoga and ended up loving it, so much so that I thought I'd try my hand at teaching. I'd like to build up my business as a yoga instructor, but it might take a while. I trained while I was travelling, first in New York, a little in Portugal, more in London. For the last couple of years, I've worked for other people, filling in for teachers when they can't take their usual class, that sort of thing.'

'Sounds ideal.'

'It is, and I love the escapism. I'm not sure I've ever been cut out for working at a desk. Yoga is something I didn't know I needed until I did it, if that makes sense.'

'It does.' Her auburn hair hung loose this evening rather than being tied back and out of the way like it often was and it made her seem more relaxed. 'Did you enjoy your time in Australia?' He offered her one of the chocolate digestives he and Zac had enjoyed earlier.

She took a biscuit and smiled over at him, her blue eyes giving away her youth. 'I loved it. So much sunshine, the ocean, the space.'

'It's a wonderful country.'

'You were there for a while, I hear.'

'Amazing part of the world.' He didn't elaborate on how much he'd adored Melbourne, had felt at home there. It wasn't the place he'd fallen out with, quite the opposite, and rather than wanting to leave, he'd had little choice.

'I spent time in New Zealand,' she went on, 'skied, did the crazy adrenalin sports for a time.'

He finished his last bit of biscuit. 'Bit different to yoga. Are we talking skydives and bungee jumps?'

'We are.'

'Yeah? Never had the guts myself. I had friends who did but even watching it was a bit too much for me.' He made a quiet growling sound at the back of his throat. 'I don't sound like much of a man, do I?' If there was one thing he hated, it was feeling emasculated.

'Well, put it this way, I'd never do a bungee ever again. Bloody terrifying.'

'So why do it in the first place?'

Before she could reply, Zoe schlepped into the kitchen and only stopped scowling and stood up straight when she saw they had a guest, a female who was on the trendy side, especially compared to her dad. Adam had already spotted the small tattoo of an anchor with some tiny wording he hadn't quite been able to read on Isla's ankle and as the girls chatted, he found himself wondering whether she had any anywhere else.

'She's a nice girl,' said Isla when Zoe disappeared back upstairs.

'She can be.'

'How are they both settling in, here in Cloverdale?'

'We've been here long enough for them to have made some good friends, which I'm grateful for.'

'Zac is friends with Jennifer's Archie, is that right?'

'They're very good buddies, yes. And Zoe's got a good friend in Viola's Ava.'

'I don't know Ava too well but Viola is OK.'

'She and Jennifer knew each other a long time ago, right?'

'That's right. They're similar in a lot of ways, nice enough, both a little uptight.' She put a hand across her mouth. 'Me and my big gob, I shouldn't say things about women who are obviously your friends. This is probably why Jennifer worries about me getting into trouble.'

'It's not a problem, I agree with you. But Viola's heart seems to be in the right place. I've only known her five minutes but she was more than willing to come and talk about doing a makeover for Zoe's bedroom, Zac's eventually, at least I hope so. Saves me a job.'

'Girls are fussy about their space; she'll love it when it's done.'

'I hope it makes her a bit happier.'

'Giving you grief, is she?' She shrugged. 'That's teens for you.'

'I suppose it is.'

'If you need to talk . . . I might be able to help. As her mum's not around, I mean . . .'

He told her all about Zoe pushing the boundaries, not accepting his role as the parent and his prerogative to say no to some things. 'Social media is the latest battle,' he said. 'I don't want them on it, Zoe thinks she's plenty old enough.'

Isla shook her head at the offer of another biscuit. 'I can understand why you'd be worried. There's a lot of bullying these days, especially with girls. Those little cows hide behind their phones sending nasty messages, taking horrid pictures. It's sickening.'

'Zoe doesn't actually have any social media accounts at all.'

'What, none?'

He began to laugh. 'Your reaction is as though I haven't let her have any life outside of this house.' He could never tell her the real reasons why he was so social media averse.

'It's the way they communicate now. Speaking as a girl, Zoe probably misses out on a lot. There'll be conversations on there, group chats she's not a part of.' When she hesitated he urged her to go on. 'I'm not a parent, but I do know a bit about the female mind. I remember being a teen and earning my parents' trust was a biggie. When you have it, it makes you feel more grown-up, you begin to mature and it's all part of learning to make your own decisions, not to mention making your own mistakes. As long as you don't abuse the trust, you get to keep your freedom. As a kid, for me, it was being able to walk to the shops on my own down the country lanes. If I did that and I was honest about who I was meeting, came back on time and behaved myself, then my parents were happy.'

'You're probably right.'

'Are you on Instagram yourself?'

'I'm not.'

'Can I make a suggestion?'

'Anything.'

'Perhaps instead of teaching you yoga, I could give you a crash course in Instagram before you give it to Zoe. That way you'll have a head start and know what to look for when she's using it, then you'll be keeping her safe.'

He wasn't stupid. He could work out a bit of technology

himself and the only reason he wasn't much of a social media user was for the same reasons he didn't want the kids using it. They needed to stay incognito.

'You'd do that?' So what if he could work it out himself. Having a gorgeous woman teaching him would be a lot more fun.

'Hey, you show me drilling, I show you Insta.'

'Well I have to say it does sound a much better idea than yoga. You're on.'

'Great. Although bear in mind that I once offered Jennifer advice about the twins and I got the old, "you're not a mum, how would you know", so you might not want to listen to me at all.'

He smiled across at her. He enjoyed having her here and wished she didn't have to go to the pub because he could sit and chat like this all evening. 'Can I offer you a bit of advice?'

'I guess so, I've been doling out enough of it to you.'

'Maybe you and Jennifer both need some time to be in the same village, to live close by in a way you haven't done in years.'

'She thinks I'm the irresponsible little sister, the one whose life is all over the place. Should've seen her face when I mentioned the pole dancing.'

He grinned, his mind all over the place thinking of Isla and that kind of dancing. 'Whatever has gone on between you two, and I'm not asking you to tell me, perhaps you need to rebuild your relationship again.'

'Well it'll have to work both ways. I don't go around telling her she was wrong to get married, have children, give up her hairdressing career. So she shouldn't . . .' She swished a hand in front of her face. 'I'll shut up. You two are friends, I really shouldn't moan about her.'

'Go on; we're on a moaning streak tonight. Get it all out there.'

'She doesn't approve of my lifestyle choices.'

'No?'

She began to count things off on her fingers and he realised he'd opened a real can of worms. 'One, my job choices, none of which are reliable enough, apparently, and that ties in with number two, which is that I get bored too easily and move on to the next best thing. I prefer to think of it as being free, but Jennifer doesn't see it that way.'

'Well, that's only two things. That's not so bad.'

She lifted up her hair and pointed to the top of her ear where a small sparkling stone was almost imperceptible beneath the fold of skin. 'I get piercings in bad places, that's number three . . . well, actually it's also number four,' she said and pointed to where her belly button was beneath her clothing. '"Pierced ears are for the lobe, no other part should be mutilated." I think those were her exact words.'

'Oh dear.'

'She made sure she told me in front of Katie and Amelia so I think a lot of it was for their benefit rather than mine. And lastly, the piece de resistance . . .' She lifted her leg so her ankle was facing him, pulled up her jeans to expose honey-coloured skin still kissed from summer sunshine, to reveal the anchor tattoo he'd caught a glimpse of before and the words over the top in an arc that read 'Refuse to Sink'. 'She nearly had a fit when I told her I had a tattoo. Mum really liked it. She said, "that's my brave girl."'

He hadn't missed her eyes clouding over and wondered

96

what was behind the words, Refuse to Sink. People often had tattoos as permanent reminders of someone or something. A mate of his had his wife's name tattooed on his arm because they were soul mates, he said – all well and good until the wife upped and ran off with his cousin.

'She's angry with me for something else too.'

'I'm not here to judge, you can tell me.'

'When our mum was dying, Jennifer nursed her, she was there any time day or night for months. And I wasn't.'

'Where were you?'

'I was in Bali at first, then Canada.'

'Working?'

'I was. But Jennifer thinks I should've come back here. I did, I came three times in the nine months Mum was sick, for two weeks at a time. Then again for the funeral.'

'And she thinks you should've been here more?' When she shrugged he asked, 'Why didn't you come home for longer if you knew she was dying?'

But she shook her head and swiped a tear from her cheek. 'I've said too much already, and now' – she looked at her watch – 'I'm five minutes *late* for Hattie.'

He led her along the hallway to show her out of the front door, and, when he opened the door to a cool evening breeze, she said, 'How about next Thursday after work?' Her soft floral fragrance floated his way as it had so many times tonight.

He stood on the front doorstep of Lilliput Cottage. 'For what?'

'Insta training,' she whispered, and tapped the side of her nose conspiratorially, all trace of upset gone now as though they hadn't even discussed her relationship with her sister. 'I'll be flat out working on the cottage for the rest of this week and I have a few classes to teach, but next week would work for me.'

'Sounds good to me.' More than good. 'I'll be home by seven.'

'I teach at the village hall until half past seven, so I'll stop by after that.' With a little wave she went on her way and he hovered at the door for a moment watching her go down the street towards the pub.

As he shut the door he hoped his friendship with Isla wasn't going to be a problem for Jennifer.

He'd come here for a peaceful life, not more trouble.

7

Viola

Viola admired the jukebox standing in the far corner of the Library of Shared Things. 'It looks good here, should be great to listen to during the workshops, I guess, or during the day if you need to rev things up a bit.'

Ricky, son of the owner of the pub in the next village, had been asking around and found his way to the library this morning. He'd obviously been rehearsing his sales pitch and both Viola and Jennifer had taken pity on him as he was trying so hard. It was tough times for many pubs in the area and they were obviously selling off whatever they could. He'd thought the Library of Shared Things could rent out the jukebox for parties and Jennifer told him it was a lovely idea, but had exchanged a look with Viola that said she'd be doing no such thing. It wasn't exactly an item that could be moved to and fro on a regular basis. But still, she'd said yes to Ricky, he'd gone and got some help, and now here it was.

'Thank you for having Ricky plug it in and show me how to work it,' said Jennifer.

'I didn't do it so he could show you how it worked. I wanted to check he wasn't giving you something broken, you know, to get rid of it.'

'I hardly think . . . actually, you're right, people do that. Luckily Ricky has some scruples. And . . . thank you.' The words didn't come easy but at least they tripped off Jennifer's tongue.

'He's a decent kid. Talking of decent . . .' She nodded over to the bright yellow doors cheering up the overcast day when Isla walked in.

'I popped in to see if the carpet cleaner is available.' Isla directed her request to Viola.

It was bad enough tiptoeing around Jennifer when it was only the two of them, but add Isla to the mix and whatever angst these two had going on made it even more uncomfortable for Viola. 'Let me check the computer and see if it's free. Do you want it today?'

'If possible.'

'What carpets are you cleaning?' Jennifer at least kept it polite as she opened some of the mail that had been slid beneath the doors this morning.

'The lounge carpet and the bedroom.' Isla was civil in return.

'It's available,' Viola advised. 'How long would you like it for?'

'Today should be enough.'

Viola got the item from its place in the hutch. 'Take it now, bring it back any time tomorrow. And let me give you some cleaning tablets. Four are included in the price, will that be enough?'

'Should be.'

Viola popped four tablets into a small bag and left it on the front desk ready for Isla to take. 'The carpet cleaner's pretty heavy, do you need a lift home?' She may as well offer, anything to break the air of hostility that politeness did its best to hover above.

'No need. I hired a car so I could do a big food shop and come here for this, and tomorrow I'm going out to a big DIY store to buy more paint.'

'I don't blame you. Borrowing a car is far cheaper and you never have to clean one.'

'Another positive.' Isla smiled, but not as much as when her gaze drifted over to the new addition in the room. 'When did you get the jukebox?'

'It was a donation, believe it or not.' Viola watched her go over to the smooth, black and aluminium machine.

'It's beautiful. It's a modern take on the vintage, if that makes sense.' She couldn't take her eyes away from it. 'Can we play something?'

'Sure.' She was going to plug it in but Jennifer had already done the honours and with a few CDs loaded Isla made a selection and the modern turntable spun a CD as though it were yesteryear and it was on vinyl. LED lights changed colour, the sound was clear and pleasant as it filled the Library of Shared Things.

Isla pressed her hand against the glass as though connecting herself to the music, her body swaying to the rhythm. 'I'd have one of these at home if I could.'

'Isla used to dance,' Jennifer put in, a throwaway comment that Viola expected to induce some sort of follow-up but all it did was break Isla away from the moment.

'Can I take the carpet cleaner now?' she asked.

'Oh, sure.' Viola didn't miss Jennifer's frown, nor Isla's impatience as though she couldn't get out of here quickly enough.

Isla waddled out of the door with the heavy load, over to a pristine white car. It wouldn't stay clean for long on the country lanes around here, Viola had fought that particular losing battle with her own car.

She braved asking Jennifer the question. 'Is everything OK between you both?' Any fool could see that it wasn't, but Viola trod lightly. 'She didn't seem too keen to talk about her dancing, did she?'

'No.' Jennifer went back to sifting through the mail, back to being aloof.

'Was she a professional?' Perhaps if she pushed, Jennifer might at last treat her as the friend she'd once been.

'She was. She toured, she performed in the West End, and then . . .'

'And then?'

Jennifer looked up partway through prising open an envelope. 'And then I really don't know. She went travelling, maybe she was bored and it was time to move on to the next best thing. She's fleeting; once upon a time she wanted to be a star, then she intended to open a dance school, then she went through a series of different jobs, and now it's yoga.' She shook her head as though she really didn't understand her younger sibling.

Viola decided she'd pushed it enough and the safest thing to do was to change the subject. They talked about what CDs to bring in from home to load into the jukebox, they contacted regulars and organised the next mending meet-up.

When Viola checked her Find Friends app on her phone Jennifer asked what she was up to. 'It's great for keeping an eye on Ava,' Viola explained, 'and I can see whether Isaac is stuck in traffic, or still at the squash club.'

'I've never bothered using it for the twins, it feels a bit Big Brother.'

'It's about safety. I like to know where they all are. And when Hazel is old enough to get out and about without me, I'll do the same with her.'

'Does Ava mind? And Isaac?'

'Isaac sees the practicalities, and I'm not doing it to please Ava.'

'Ava's a sensible girl, maybe trust her a little . . .'

Viola was about to tell her friend that she was parenting, she wasn't trying to be her daughter's best friend, when Isla made a reappearance. Probably a good job; she didn't want to retaliate over Jennifer's comment and find anything more to widen the rift between them.

'I forgot to take the cleaning tablets with me.' Impatient, Isla twirled her car keys around her fingers, this time not looking at the jukebox she'd fallen in love with earlier, even though music still played softly in the background.

'That's because you left in such a rush.' Jennifer looked at her as though challenging her to share more than she wanted to.

Viola handed the bag of tablets to Isla. 'How's it going over at the cottage, you enjoying a bit of DIY?' She had to say something. The atmosphere in here was even worse than earlier.

'I never thought it would be my thing, but I feel inspired, especially after the drilling workshop. Even Adam was impressed when I showed him photos of what I've managed to do.' She sure knew how to rile her sister. Viola daren't look at Jennifer; she didn't need to to know she was fuming. 'I'm going to give him a crash course in Instagram.'

Jennifer adopted a stance Viola recognised only too well. Hands on her hips, chin jutted a little forward, she'd looked the very same the day she'd told Viola to get out of her life and stay out of it. 'He's in his forties, Isla, not his nineties. I'm sure he can work it out for himself.'

Isla simply shrugged, the perfect accelerant to fuel Jennifer's annoyance. 'I'd better go.' She'd thrown in the grenade and now she was off.

Anything resembling conflict where Jennifer was concerned didn't exactly help Viola make progress with repairing the damage she'd done to their friendship, and, sure enough, it wasn't long after Isla left that Jennifer made it known she didn't need any more help for the rest of the day.

Viola left wondering why Jennifer had such a problem with her sister and, more importantly, why she was so opposed to Isla spending time with Adam. They were both free agents; Jennifer wasn't.

If Jennifer was getting closer to Adam and having feelings for him, it could ruin her marriage, and the last person she was going to listen to would be Viola.

8

Jennifer

Jennifer finished arranging cheeses on a board – brie, camembert, vintage cheddar – and added an assortment of crackers to a plate and a small bowl of chutney to a tray before taking everything in to the lounge. Since she and Isla had clashed at the Library of Shared Things, her mum's words had been at the forefront of her mind. 'Be friends for life,' she'd said, her hand over Jennifer's as she spoke on a breath that was none to easy to get out in her final weeks. 'Be there for one another. Always.' And so Jennifer had texted her sister and invited her over tonight to make peace.

Isla came in out of the drizzle and shook her umbrella off beneath the porch.

'Not too pleasant out there, is it?' said Jennifer. 'I'll get David to run you home later.'

'I'm quite capable of negotiating a few country roads, Jennifer.'

'I know you are.'

'Then stop fussing.' She seemed to pick up on the point of the evening pretty quickly when she said, 'But thank you. A lift home would be great.'

'Right then.'

'Is he still at work?'

'Unfortunately.' Jennifer watched her sister whose blue eyes sparkled and as she turned she caught a flash of the shining earring at the top of her ear and wondered why Isla's choices wound her up so much. Isla was a grown woman, capable of running her own life, making her own mistakes. She wasn't one of Jennifer's offspring who needed guidance to find their way.

'Worth it for this place though.' Isla stood in the vast hallway with its espresso oak wooden floors and a staircase that curved all the way up to the landing. There was nothing cluttering up the floor, the only thing in sight a side table with an enormous vase filled with bright orange gerberas.

'Are you warm enough?' Jennifer hung Isla's coat on one of the hooks behind the door and gestured for her sister to go through to the lounge.

'Your house is way warmer than mine.' Isla flipped her lustrous auburn hair over her shoulder and plonked herself down on the sofa. She always looked so much younger than Jennifer, even though their age difference wasn't vast. It was probably the yoga, or the lack of kids in her life, or maybe it was how she dressed, in jeans with embroidered flowers snaking up one leg and a loose-fitting bat-wing jumper that skimmed the top of her jeans and showed off her taut figure. 'I've had the windows open to get rid of the paint fumes so I've come here to warm up.' She smiled.

'I'm itching to pop the fire on, make it cosy, that's all.'

'Won't be long, sis.'

Phrases like that one always reminded Jennifer how much her mum had wanted her and Isla to stay close, and it was why Jennifer was determined to keep on trying with her sister. She hoped Isla felt the same way, despite their differences.

'Have you been teaching today?' Jennifer handed Isla a small plate so she could go ahead and help herself to the cheese and crackers.

'Early class this morning, and guess who I bumped into?'

'Who?'

'Audrey from school.'

'That must've been nice. You were besties once, weren't you?'

'We were. And we're catching up tomorrow, heading down to the south coast.'

'A day by the sea . . . that'll be lovely.'

'We're abseiling down the Emirates Spinnaker Tower.'

Jennifer almost choked on her cheese and cracker. 'Are you serious?'

'Why not? I've not done anything much since I was in New Zealand. What? Why are you shaking your head?'

'No reason.' This was why she knew spending time at the Library of Shared Things wasn't Isla's bag. How her parents had coped knowing she did all these crazy, irresponsible things was beyond her. She wasn't sure how she'd manage if one of her kids announced they were going to do anything as reckless.

'Red wine OK for you?' Jennifer asked.

'Red sounds perfect, and knowing you it'll be a decent one, not something I'd buy for a couple of quid. Wait, is that why you insisted I didn't bring anything along tonight?'

'It's because you're a guest.' She was about to get more

defensive when she realised Isla was winding her up. 'Oh, you're teasing me.'

'Couldn't resist.'

She went to fetch a couple of glasses and a bottle of Cabernet Sauvignon. She didn't mind a bit of sisterly banter, and she wondered whether Isla had done it to distract her from voicing her opinions about the latest escapade down some crazy high tower. Her sister was rash, her life was all over the place, and, although different personalities and traits were what made the world go round, Jennifer couldn't forget that Isla had once left her high and dry in her hour of need, most likely doing something just as stupid as abseiling down a bloody building.

She took a deep breath, blew it out and went back with a smile on her face to pour the wine. 'So you're handy with a drill now?' she ventured.

'I'm not half bad.' Isla had her side plate right beneath her chin when the cracker snapped and the cheese tumbled off. She finished the pieces and took out her phone to scroll through the pictures Adam had already seen but her own sister hadn't. If Jennifer hadn't been so bloody-minded the other day she'd have looked at the same time as him, but she'd been jealous, affronted at her sister's bond with a man who was her friend.

She took in the shots of kitchen shelves, sturdy and straight, hooks on the kitchen wall ready to hang saucepans, the set of bookshelves Isla had put up in the sitting room. 'It looks like you know what you're doing.'

'I'm no longer the useless little sister.'

Jennifer ignored the subtle dig. Best to move on from anything that could generate an argument. 'Are you going to fill those bookshelves?'

'Too right. I didn't buy many paperbacks when I was travelling around. I can't wait to fill it with some great titles, kind of like my own library.'

'The ghastly wallpaper has gone at last.' Instead of the murky green, mustard and off-white wallpaper, Isla had washed the walls in a soft white. 'Mind you, flower power wallpaper is back in fashion, you could've probably got away with it.'

'I was tempted, but there were tears, stains, it wasn't worth it. I'll probably do a feature wall but not yet, I want to get more of a feel for the place and with small rooms, I don't want to feel boxed in.'

They talked about how long it had taken, the arduous task of taking off all that wallpaper, which had been made easier after Isla borrowed the wallpaper steamer from the Library of Shared Things. And when Jennifer topped up both wine glasses, glad Isla agreed to the suggestion that David take her home later so she could relax and enjoy a drink now, she realised how much she missed this. Sisters. Sisters who could chat about anything and everything without petty bickering, little digs, jealousy getting in the way. This is what she'd really needed when she'd been taking care of their mum day in day out, and she took a big gulp of wine to stop the resentment ruining the evening.

'I bumped into Elaine yesterday when I was at the fruit and veg shop,' said Isla. 'She asks a lot of questions. I'd forgotten what she was like. She wanted to know how many rooms I was doing, what colour the paper was now, was I intending to make any major changes because I'd need to notify council if that were the case, not to mention local residents as a courtesy, and she was very curious as to how I could afford to take on such a financial challenge without a husband and no steady job.'

'She said all that? Nosy woman.'

Isla topped another cracker with chutney and a generous wedge of camembert. 'If she gave me a grilling, whatever would she have made of Adam when he moved in to the village? I mean, he arrives from nowhere, with two kids and no wife – that must send her mind whirling. What is his story, do you think?'

'How would I know?'

'You're good friends.'

'I try not to ask too many questions, I get the impression there's more to his story than he lets on, but I figure if he wants to talk, he will.'

'It must be hard going looking after two children on your own, but both Zoe and Zac seem like nice kids, don't you think?'

Jennifer nodded, her mouth full. She liked having Adam to talk to and she didn't want Isla to stomp all over his feelings when she eventually got bored. 'They're both lovely; Archie and Zac are a duo for life, I think.'

'He seems a bit lost with a teenage daughter.'

'He's finding his way, like we all are.'

Conversation dried up until Jennifer changed the subject to talking about Isla's passion for yoga, the classes she was teaching, how she'd got into it when she was away travelling.

'Mum loved seeing all your photos,' Jennifer told her sister.

'She always said she did.'

'She showed me all the time; it looked wonderful. I was

pretty envious being stuck here, and you discovering new things every day.'

'Don't start, Jennifer.'

'I'm not. I mean it. It looked like you had the time of your life.'

Isla cosied back on the sofa, leaving the cheese for now, perhaps reminded there was more to come when Archie came through and asked for a snack only to be told that no, he could wait for dinner. 'Were you really envious? Of me?'

Whether it was the wine or her mum's words in her head, Jennifer didn't know, but she was the most relaxed she'd been around Isla since her sister's return to the village. 'While you were sunning yourself in the Great Barrier Reef, leaping off bridges in Queenstown, doing yoga on the beach or drinking beer from enormous glass vessels in Bruges, I was trying to keep my head above water raising three kids.'

'Do you wish you'd travelled before you settled down?'

'I had my career, I loved it, but I began to enjoy my daily routine and kept travel for the holidays.'

'Mum and Dad never expected you to stay so close to them.'

'Well, I did.'

'I miss them both.'

'Me too.'

'You know they never blamed you for what happened, Jennifer. We all make mistakes.'

'Yeah, well . . . I'm in Cloverdale because I want to be, no other reason.' And she really didn't want to talk about it now. 'Wouldn't mind a couple more holidays though. Some of yours looked amazing. There were times when

I would've given anything to be whisked away to one of those white sandy beaches in the photos you sent Mum. I admired you, you know.'

Isla began to smile. 'In all the years you've been watching over me, waiting for me to fuck up, I never once thought you admired what I was doing.'

'I wasn't waiting for you to fuck up, Isla.'

'Except I did, didn't I?'

Not now, Jennifer thought. She didn't want to get into this tonight. 'We all do.'

'You could always go off travelling when the kids are older, see what else is out there.'

'I feel wrong for wanting more. Wondering what else is out there for me. Does that make me a terrible person?'

'It makes you human.'

'So you like the jukebox at the library?'

'If I had the money or the space at the cottage, I'd get one myself.'

'Actually, I wanted to run something by you.'

'Go for it.'

'We've got that beautiful jukebox and it's wonderful for background music, but I was thinking we could run some dance classes for the village.'

'Don't tell me, you want me to run them.'

'No pressure, have a think about it. You'd be doing me a favour. The whole point of the Library of Shared Things is to get the community together and it's starting to work, but events do so much more. And who knows, it might even be fun.' Perhaps it could also be a way to spend more time with Isla, become a part of each other's lives again as their parents, especially their mum, had wanted.

'I'm not sure. Do you really think anyone would be

interested? I'm more of a yoga instructor these days. It's been a while since I took to the dance floor.'

'I think it'd be really popular. We could put a gazebo in the area in front of the Library of Shared Things, open up the bifolds of the final section to give us a nice big dance area. We wouldn't charge a huge amount but the costs could go towards buying more items.'

'I don't know; I've got quite a lot of classes to teach already.'

'We'll fit it around those.' Her sister still looked unsure. 'Imagine it. The jukebox would light up, we'd string fairy lights across doorways, around the gazebo poles, it could be really magical. You must miss dancing, you were so good at it.'

Isla knocked back the remains of her glass and filled it up again from the open bottle on the coffee table. 'I could do a pole dance class, that'd go down well. Elaine would be up for it.'

Jennifer burst out laughing. 'Can you imagine?'

'Her husband might appreciate it.'

'I'm sure he would.' She watched Isla carefully. 'Why did you stop dancing? You and Carlos were good together, you won plenty of competitions, electrified the stage according to the write-ups.'

'You read them?'

'Mum made sure I did, but I would've read them anyway.'

'Well, that was then.' Isla slumped back against the sofa.

'Wasn't the plan to open a dance school?' Jennifer wanted to get her talking. 'But now it's yoga. And tomorrow it's abseiling.'

'What are you trying to say?'

'Nothing, but you seem to change your mind all the time.'

'Didn't you once want to open a hair salon?' she batted back. 'I don't see you doing that. At least not after what went down before.'

Jennifer put her wine glass down too roughly and slopped some on the table.

Isla leaned forward and wiped it up with a napkin. 'I'm sorry, that was uncalled for. I shouldn't have said it.'

'Don't worry about it.' She took over the task of wiping up to make sure she didn't miss a drop.

When David came through the door, it at least eased the tension between her and Isla with another person to talk to, as Jennifer took care of the final dinner preparations. They all slid into a sense of familiar chatter about all sorts from school, to weather, to work, the Library of Shared Things and the upcoming holiday to Cornwall. And when Isla got Jennifer on her own again as she took an ice cube tray from the freezer, she agreed to do the dance classes. Perhaps as an apology for her comment earlier.

'You'll enjoy it,' Jennifer assured her.

'Well, I'll give it a go, but no promises.'

Jennifer liked having guests over for dinner not only for the extra conversation but also because her children became impeccably behaved, cleared up the dishes voluntarily, talked with everyone and were far more social than when it was only the five of them. And after dinner she left Isla with David while she got Archie off to bed. By the time she returned they were having an in-depth discussion about his work, career paths, the way Isla was already building up her yoga business. Jennifer had once spent a long time having similar discussions with her husband when he came home, but nowadays it was as though neither of them could be bothered, as though it would be a repetitive dialogue that neither of them was much interested in.

Talk turned to the Library of Shared Things when Isla reeled off a list of the items she'd used already. 'I wouldn't want to pay out for all of those things, and I definitely wouldn't have the room to store them all at the cottage. Jennifer is a superstar for introducing that place.'

David's gaze fell on his wife. 'She's very organised, very caring.' The look they exchanged reminded her of their strengths rather than their weaknesses and as they discussed their own experiences scraping off the layers of wallpaper in this home when they hadn't had access to a wallpaper steamer to do it all for them, Jennifer enjoyed unmasking the side of her husband she rarely saw these days. He was either at work or preoccupied with it in his study, or else so knackered he fell asleep in front of the television. Perhaps now when she had two people here, both on her side, she should broach the subject of her own career. Just because it fell flat on its face once before didn't mean it had to again.

But when David and Isla pored over the photographs of Isla's renovations in progress, Jennifer lost her nerve and then they were onto something else.

'I still call it Mum's house,' Isla admitted. 'Taking the wallpaper off, redoing floors, putting in new fixtures, doesn't change the fact that she loved that cottage and spent the last of her days in it. I miss her.'

'What will you do with the garden?' David asked.

'It's a mess right now, overgrown, weeds sprouting up everywhere. I'm not exactly green-fingered; I wish Dad was here. He'd have helped.'

Jennifer could imagine that if he was still with them he'd have perched on a garden chair in among the leaves that blew bronze, red and golden in every direction as autumn well and truly set in, as he told Isla what to do. She would've protested at his bossiness, but they'd both be grinning from ear to ear as they spent time with each other. Isla had left them all to go on her adventures but their parents had never once tried to hold her back. Even in her mum's last days, it had been Jennifer's bugbear not hers. They'd embraced the adventure, living vicariously through their youngest daughter's photographs and anecdotes, snatched conversations via phone or text. The daughter who hadn't let them down so badly and hadn't felt the need to make it up to them over and over.

'I picked a few of the purple flowers Mum loved so much from the garden and put them on the windowsill,' said Isla.

'Crocuses,' Jennifer clarified. 'I saw them when I last went to the cottage.' The flowers were the only colour left in the neglected garden aside from the odd dandelion that sprouted up near the fence, a cluster of snowdrops that came every spring like clockwork.

'The bookshelves look good.' David was still scrolling through photographs on Isla's phone. 'Who helped you?'

'Cheeky.' Isla punched his arm playfully. 'All my own work after Adam's drill workshop.'

'Ah, the infamous Adam.' Jennifer's heart skipped a

beat at the odd expression. 'What's his story anyway?' He handed back the phone and looked to Jennifer. 'We don't know much about him, do we? He could be an axe murderer for all we know.'

Isla laughed. 'Hardly. He seems nice.'

'Which reminds me,' said Jennifer as she busied herself serving coffee to end the evening, 'he's dropping Zac over at half past seven tomorrow morning; he has a business meeting that couldn't be rescheduled.'

'I thought Zac was coming over after school.'

'He is, for a proper playdate. But I'm helping out in the morning too.'

David held up both hands in defence. 'I'm not criticising. And anyway, it won't affect me, I'll be out of the house first thing and won't be back until late.'

'But you've worked so late tonight.'

'Lots of work on at the moment. You know that, Jennifer. Please don't nag.'

Isla must've sensed the tension because she took over the task of making the coffee.

'You're a guest,' Jennifer scolded, 'you don't have to help.'

'I'm family and it's only coffee.'

Jennifer wiped down the table instead, pissed off David had portrayed her as a nagging wife when she felt she was quite restrained these days, always being left to run the household and the family and keep her own desires firmly locked inside her head.

They drank coffee and talked more about the cottage and possible ideas for the garden, and when Isla put on her coat ready to leave, she thanked Jennifer again. 'It was a lovely meal. I have a microwave and a toaster but have been too knackered to even try using the new cooker that came last week.'

'You're welcome any time.' She didn't look at her husband when she reminded him, 'Would you please run Isla home?'

David grabbed his keys, conversation entertaining without the inclusion of a henpecking wife, and as they left the house Jennifer slumped on the sofa with another glass of wine. Sod the fact she'd already had too many; she was past caring.

Why couldn't things go back to normal with David? And why couldn't he be as relaxed as he was tonight when it was only the two of them?

Perhaps then she'd be able to talk to him about how she was really feeling. Or maybe she shouldn't. If he was still angry about her mistake all these years later, perhaps she should avoid going down that path ever again.

9

Adam

'Thanks so much for doing this, Jennifer.' Adam had already said goodbye to Zac and now he was chatting with Jennifer at her front door. 'And you're sure about the sleepover tonight?'

'Of course I am. It's lovely for Archie to have some company and I'll be strict with bedtime seeing as it's a school night.'

'It's great to see him so happy these days.' He hadn't realised but his gaze had drifted up the stairs as the sounds of the boys' laughter bathed him in a glow that reassured him this move across the other side of the world had been for the best. All he wanted was for his kids to be happy and safe. For them to see him in the same way as they always had.

'Have you time for a coffee?'

'Yes, but don't let me stay more than fifteen minutes, or I'll be late.'

'Perfect.'

He followed her into the kitchen, always impressed by the space and how well it was kept. Green and cream gingham curtains hung at mullioned windows, windowsills didn't have clutter on them like his did but rather delicate pot plants or ornaments such as the chubby chef figurine on the sill behind the sink. A utensils pot, a mug tree, toaster and kettle were the only other things on the worktop that stretched along one wall, and of course everything was clean, whereas sometimes he felt he should check before he sat down in his own kitchen.

He sniffed the sweet-scented air. 'Something smells good.'

'I cooked pancakes for the twins before they left for an extra study session before school. I'll make the boys some next. You're welcome to join us.'

'I'll pass. If I turn up late to my meeting and they smell pancakes on me, I'll never get away with it.'

She had a coffee machine built in alongside the wall oven and made two lattes to bring over to the kitchen bench.

'Have you given any more thought to getting back in the game?'

'The game?' She sat down and looked at him over the top of her mug.

'Going back to work.'

'I have.'

'And what's the plan?' Her look told him she'd done a lot of dreaming but not taken any action, and he got the feeling he'd have to prise details out of her. 'Don't feel guilty for wanting something for yourself. You'd be showing your kids that mums can work, they can provide, and that you and your husband are equals. It's a great endorsement for a family.' Better than his own relationship had been at any rate. He wondered whether her husband preferred her being at home, especially given how good she was at managing the family. 'What does David think?'

'I haven't mentioned it to him. And anyway, if I go back to work I might not have enough time for the Library of Shared Things, the family . . . it might be stressful.'

He took a mouthful of coffee so he could think about his response. She really was being far too tough on herself. 'I think it's worth talking it through with your husband.'

'Maybe.'

'Start small, get a job one day a week somewhere. Or you could think about mobile hairdressing.'

'I suppose that's pretty risk-free.'

'How is hairdressing a risk? Unless you stab someone with scissors, I suppose. I tell you what: Zoe and Zac will be your first clients.'

'If Zoe is anything like Amelia and Katie, she won't want me anywhere near her hair!'

'Fair enough. So start with Zac and me. Nothing fancy. Short back and sides. He's nine, won't give a toss if you give him tramlines through his hair by accident – although the school may have a problem with that – come on, what do you say? I'm desperate.' He touched a hand to the sides of his light brown hair. He'd once been told he was a dead ringer for Josh Duhamel but lately he could make no such claims. He'd found himself hooking his hair over his ears yesterday, so any effort with scissors could only be a good thing. 'What's the worst that could happen?'

'I'll think about it.'

Both Archie and Zac came bundling into the kitchen, and he downed the rest of his coffee. 'Make sure you do. I'd better be off. Thanks for the coffee, and for having Zac.'

'Any time. And good luck with the Instagram lesson.'

'Thanks for the reminder. I would've got carried away

today at work with Zac staying over here and not having to race home, and I'd hate to stand Isla up.'

His comment didn't seem to sit very well with Jennifer, so he said his goodbyes. Perhaps it was natural for Jennifer to be concerned at her sister spending time with a man who could be anyone. He knew she'd be even more worried if she ever discovered the whole truth about him.

'You're looking smart.' Isla stepped inside Lilliput Cottage when Adam answered the front door still wearing his suit.

'I've only just got in from work; give me a minute and I'll get changed. I hate wearing a tie any longer than I have to.' Isla, on the other hand, looked relaxed in slim-fitting jeans turned up at the bottoms to show off her ankles and the anchor tattoo, white lace-up Converse and a loose silky sheer black top. 'Make yourself comfortable in the kitchen; I won't be long.'

He was downstairs within a couple of minutes, scraping a hand through his hair to at least give it half a chance of looking neat. 'Right, first things first. Coffee?'

She opened up her bag and pulled out a bottle. 'I was thinking wine could be better? Or is that terribly irresponsible, given you're a dad trying to be a role model for your kids?'

Smiling, he told her, 'The kids are out.' He put back the coffee pods he'd taken from the cupboard and instead found two wine glasses. 'And after the day I've had, it'll be good to relax.'

She poured the wine, they clinked the glasses against each other but laughed when they realised they had no idea as to what they were toasting.

'We could toast to spying on your children,' he

suggested, 'or being an Instagram sensation.'

'Hey, I'm all for showing you how to use it, but I don't have the secrets to take you that far.'

He picked up his phone from the kitchen bench and opened up the app he'd installed earlier. He'd already signed up and got himself an account but he hadn't bothered doing anything else. He rather wanted to get up close and personal to Isla, have her show him, and so for the next half an hour she ran through adding photos, hashtags, popular filters, direct messaging, tagging others and following people. He played it dumb; he loved the way she explained it all so patiently.

'You could have Zoe's account hanging off yours. Viola does it with Ava apparently. She sees everything on Ava's feed, any messages she sends or receives.'

'I don't think that'd go down very well. This is all about giving Zoe some trust.'

'It's a judgement call, and only one you can make.'

He sat back in his chair. With every day that went by, the kids grew older, and with age came curiosity, curiosity that had so many risks he couldn't even fathom what might happen if they delved too deep. As far as the kids knew, their mum had had a breakdown and didn't want to be a parent anymore. He'd done what he felt he had to do to keep them with him, to give them the life he knew they deserved and a life he wanted, but if they found out the whole truth, would they see it the same way? Or would they see him as the baddie for his role in all of this?

'Let's leave the stalking for now,' he said. 'I'll see how she goes.'

'Good idea.'

Hungry after cutting it fine getting home from work in time to meet Isla, Adam suggested they get a takeaway and they placed an order at the local Chinese. As they'd chatted they'd already managed to polish off the wine Isla had brought with her, so he opened up a top cupboard in the kitchen and pulled out a lonely bottle. 'Another glass?'

'Go on then. I can be good tomorrow.' Her cheeky smile captivated him. Waves of auburn hair tumbled across her shoulders; he tried not to stare and instead laughed when he realised he'd only gone and bought a bottle with a cork.

'Please tell me you have a corkscrew.'

'Somewhere.' He didn't miss the goosebumps that snaked up his bare forearm when she helped him rifle through the same wide drawer and their hands met at the back. His hand moved and settled on the familiar object. 'Found it.'

'Thank goodness for that.' Her breathing changed as though she was as nervous as he was.

'Hey.' A voice came from behind them.

'Zoe.' He jumped as though he'd been caught going through her private things in her bedroom rather than searching in his own kitchen. 'I didn't hear you come in. Is it that time already?' A quick glance at his watch told him time had galloped by as he'd sat here with Isla and he wished he could've put it in slow motion and made it last longer.

'That's because I'm so quiet.' With Isla being so easygoing and likeable, Zoe didn't seem to mind one little bit that her dad had company – female company. Since he'd left Susan he hadn't been involved with any woman.

There'd been an office party where he'd flirted and kissed a co-worker, but that had come to nothing, and other than that his sole focus had been restoring his life and putting his kids first.

Isla and Zoe lapsed into friendly conversation about some band he'd never heard of. With her free attitude and youthful aura, Isla came across as far younger than she was, and, more importantly to Zoe, far cooler.

'What does it mean?' Zoe asked, pointing to Isla's ankle tattoo.

Refuse to Sink. He didn't need to look to know what the design looked like, the phrase permanently etched on her skin.

'Long story,' Isla replied, and he sensed she wasn't entirely comfortable because despite the blasé reply, the smile on her mouth couldn't disguise the hint of trepidation on her face.

'Are you hungry?' he asked his daughter to take the focus away from Isla. 'There'll be plenty of Chinese if you're interested.'

'Viola made lasagne and I had ice cream at Ava's too.'

'So that's a no then?'

'A definite no, Dad.' She looked at him like his words had been the most ludicrous statement ever. Teens could be judgemental but he was slowly learning to at least try to see the funny side. The other week he, Jennifer and Viola had chatted at the Library of Shared Things about how teens had a knack of telling the truth, not mincing their words. Jennifer's daughters had both, that morning, told her the colour of her top – a very respectable turquoise – did nothing for her. Viola's Ava had suggested her mum might like to colour in her eyebrows, which were sparse given her fair colouring and blonde hair, to which Viola had told her under no circumstances did she want to look like the trendy girls nowadays who all appeared to have big fat slugs crawling above their eyes. And for Adam that day . . . well, Zac had told him to stop dancing in public after he walked past the pub, heard a favourite tune, and tried to get his son to join in.

'Zoe, before you go, I need to talk to you.'

'What have I done now?' She pursed her lips.

'Hear him out.' Isla nudged Zoe like a friend rather than someone of a generation below and it seemed to do the trick.

'If you give me your phone, I'll install Instagram for you.'

He barely got to the end of his sentence before she flew at him. Was there anything more satisfying and special than your kid running up and wrapping their arms around you? Especially when they were fourteen and the last time you were permitted to invade their personal space in such a way was back when they were in a hospital bed, frightened and trying to adjust to a different way of life. He didn't get much out of his daughter these days. Snippets, grunts, he took what he could, when he could. The biggest conversation he'd had with her lately was when she offloaded her feelings about the maths they were doing at school, asking when on earth she was going to use this knowledge in real life. He'd let her go on, he enjoyed listening to her voice, usually only heard when she talked with friends or moaned at him that her life was so unfair. As she'd got older he'd learnt to appreciate any piece of verbal communication on offer, and he did the same now with the physical contact, hugging her back, relishing the moment, knowing he wouldn't get another for a long while.

'Do you mean it, Dad?'

'I do. But . . .' He held up a finger of warning. 'There will be some conditions.'

Zoe looked less pleased. 'Don't tell me you're going to do what Viola does with Ava and stalk her every minute of the day.'

'I don't think it's stalking.'

'It is, Dad. Sometimes Ava gets messages that her mum reads before she does. She even responded to one from Luca, a boy at school who asked Ava out on a date. She told him that, no, fourteen was far too young for a boyfriend. It made Ava the laughing stock for a while until Tilly Roger's mum did the school run in her pyjamas and got out the car when Tilly forgot her PE kit.'

Adam winced. 'That would've been mortifying.'

'It was. Someone took a photo and posted it on Instagram. Tilly Rogers is still working to live that one down.'

If he looked at Isla now, he knew he wouldn't be able to keep a straight face. They could laugh about it later but for now Zoe needed to understand the repercussions if she broke his trust. He was taking a huge risk letting her have something with the potential to reveal everything he'd been doing his best to hide. 'I'm not going to have your account on my phone. But I do have my own account.' He ignored the corners of her mouth that twitched in amusement. 'You will follow me; I will follow you so I can see your posts. But for now, that's enough.'

'I promise I'll use it properly.'

'No inappropriate photographs, no dodgy messages, and you tell me the second strangers try to make contact,' he went on. 'You need to think of your privacy. And this is a learning curve for me.'

She pulled a face as though he was treating her like a baby, but knowing Zoe she'd sense she couldn't rock the boat and risk not getting something she'd so desperately wanted for a long time. 'I won't let you down, Dad.'

'Right then. Now, go and do your homework.'

And with a big grin she gave him the second treat of the evening, another hug, and he clung hold of her a little longer than he needed to.

The Chinese food arrived, and Adam and Isla laughed and chatted their way through chicken chow mein, honey king prawn, stir-fried mixed vegetables and fluffy white rice, all the while with a happy teen ensconced upstairs. The vibe in the house was positive, and it had been a long time since Adam had been able to say that.

And even more, it was good to share the company of a beautiful woman he wanted to get to know better.

IO

Viola

Viola liked nothing better than to keep an orderly house. She'd always been that way, and – after ensuring Hazel was practising piano, Ava was doing her homework and the slow cooker with the beef bourguignon had been on for as long as expected – she went into the bedroom, pulled on her favourite Diesel jeans and a black chenille jumper, and padded through to the study. She'd been helping Jennifer at the Library of Shared Things this afternoon, supervising the Mending Meetup whereby locals brought clothes along that needed mending either by hand or on the machines. And the frosty reception Viola had endured from Jennifer for so long had given way to something better. They actually talked more these days; sometimes Jennifer even smiled.

An enormous antique oak banking desk, which Viola insisted they keep clear, flanked one wall of the study, with everything tucked neatly away in drawers or the shelved cupboard in the corner of the room, and so Viola had plenty of space to look at her sketches for Zoe's bedroom. After their initial chat, she already had a good idea of Zoe's tastes when it came to the soft furnishings, she knew the colour scheme – they'd settled on shades of lavender and white – and she fired up the computer, the only item on the desk, and made a mood board to send to Zoe.

Viola enjoyed her time with Zoe and perhaps once the teen years had passed, she and Ava would get back to being on such good terms, when she was seen as more than a useful resource to cook and clean, to put a roof over her head and food on the table. And as they'd spent time in Zoe's room, in her personal space, she'd found herself wondering more about Zoe's mother too. There were no photographs around the home or in Zoe's bedroom, at least none she'd seen, and nobody ever said a word about her. At first Viola had wondered whether Adam's wife had died, but over the short time he'd been in the village, she suspected that wasn't the case. Not having photographs around kind of confirmed it, at least in Viola's mind.

The timer on the rice cooker snatched her focus and she saved her document, checked Isaac's location on her phone to see that he was almost home, and went to dish up the dinner.

'Have you washed your hands?' She emptied out the remaining water from the steamer when her kids appeared in the kitchen.

'I'm not a baby,' came Ava's retort. 'Yes, of course.'

'Me too. Do you want to smell them?' Hazel inhaled from the palms of her hands. 'They smell of lemons.'

Viola smiled over at her as she set their plates and cutlery in front of them. 'I don't need to, but thank you anyway.' She kissed the top of Hazel's head, something she wouldn't get away with with Ava.

'Did you hear Zoe's dad is giving her Instagram?' Ava

said when they'd all sat down.

'Really? I thought he was dead set against it.' Viola scooped up some rice onto her fork.

'He's not even linking her account to his.'

'Don't start, Ava.' She could feel a headache coming on. The good mood as she'd created the document for Zoe's bedroom seemed to have been left behind in the study.

'Just saying. It's all about trust, Mum.'

'Let me be the judge of that,' she said as the front door went and Isaac's footsteps announced his homecoming.

'Sorry, sorry, sorry.' He came into the kitchen, still sweaty from his game. 'You know David, he got me talking at the end.'

According to Jennifer, David didn't talk much at all these days. She hadn't gone into detail but she'd made a remark one day, perhaps forgetting they weren't as close as they used to be, and if he wasn't making time for his wife it seemed pretty unfair he was playing squash for hours. But Viola would never say anything; she couldn't interfere. 'Go and shower. I'll cover your dinner until you're ready.'

'I'll eat first, I'm starving.' He sat at the long pine table.

'You're all sweaty.' Her look told him she'd most likely go on about it if he didn't relent.

'Fine.' But he still leaned in and planted a kiss on her lips.

'Get off, go and wash!' But she was laughing. He'd always had the knack and she knew she was lucky they still had the same spark that had drawn them together in the first place.

They'd met at Ascot shortly after Viola had disgraced

herself at Jennifer's wedding. She hadn't drunk alcohol since that day and only had moderate amounts at the races despite the rate at which the champagne was flowing. Viola had begun to believe she'd never fall in love – she was too hard, too uptight – and then Isaac had pushed in the queue in front of her at the bar without realising and apologised so much, insisting he made it up to her, and his smooth-talking had got her to agree on going on a date with him. And they'd been happy ever since, even when Jennifer refused to come to their wedding.

'Ava, I forgot to mention: I've had a word with my colleagues and I've arranged a week's work experience for you in the next school holiday.'

Ava's mouth fell open. 'You what?'

'Darling, mouth closed at dinner, please.'

Ava did as she was told, chewed and tried again. 'I've no interest in Human Resources, you know that.'

'You're interested in marketing. Any office experience, practising your interpersonal skills, attending meetings and being in the real world, will all count.'

'I know it will, which is why I said to you that I wanted to get a part-time job over the summer. I'd get paid then, and it'd be something I've done myself.'

'We give you everything you need; you don't need extra money.'

'It's not about the money, it's about . . . it's about my own life.'

Viola bristled. 'You won't be working with me, if it's any consolation.'

'You don't listen to me.' Ava went back to her dinner

and, as far as she was concerned, the conversation was over.

'We'll talk about it when you've calmed down.'

But Ava ignored her, finished her dinner and asked to be excused to carry on with her homework.

Relieved to be left with the easiest of her two daughters, she asked Hazel about her day. 'Did Nessa listen to your violin practice?' Nessa was the nanny who did school drop-off and pickup a few days a week, and hung around until Viola or Isaac came home from the office.

'She says I'm a whizz at my scales. I did it without any mistakes,' Hazel announced proudly.

She put a hand out across the table to high-five her daughter with her tight blonde curls and soft blue eyes. Why couldn't your kids stay this easy forever?

'What's all this?' Isaac returned, smelling a lot better, and took a seat at the table.

'I did D minor, twice, with no mistakes.' Hazel told him as he uncovered his dinner and tucked straight in.

'My daughter the violinist. You'll be joining a music quartet next. I'll be first to buy a ticket to your concert.' Hazel had also inherited Viola's porcelain skin, and blushed at her dad's praise. Isaac, dark-haired with chocolatey eyes, had passed his colouring onto their older daughter and Ava had the same olive skin as he did. It was as though their daughters had each taken on the characteristics of one parent to make it fair.

'Where are you rushing off to?' he asked when Hazel took her empty plate over to the sink.

'I need to practice some more.'

'But you practised with Nessa already.'

'Go and do another fifteen, honey,' Viola encouraged. 'It'll be worth it come exam time.'

When Hazel went off quite happily, Isaac forked up another mouthful of beef bourguignon and rice. 'You push her too hard; you push both of them too hard. They're kids.'

Usually he didn't do confrontation at dinner time and she wished he wouldn't now. 'I want the best for them.'

'And so do I.'

'She enjoys her violin.'

He didn't answer.

'I'm in the bad books with Ava.'

'Why?'

'I arranged a week's work experience for her at my office and she's not too happy about it.'

He harrumphed. 'I warned you about that.'

'You agreed that experience on a resume was key, that it would set her apart from others when her time came to apply for a job.'

'I also suggested you let her find something herself. Perhaps even a part-time job rather than working for free.'

'There's no need; we fund everything and are happy to. It lets her focus on her school work. And a part-time job means she'll end up in a local café, or a fast food joint. It won't exactly broaden her horizons.'

'You worked in a fast food joint for three years, I seem to remember.' His defensive mood over his daughters went on pause. 'I loved the little white lacy apron you wore over that mini skirt. I'd come in and sit at the same table and wonder how long I could stay there without getting kicked out. I'd order everything singularly. I'd have a burger, which I'd eat slowly, then I'd order fries and take my own sweet time. I'd run great distances every night to burn off all those calories and go back for more the next day.'

'My boss didn't like you much, but she was happy to take your money.'

'You were always so relaxed back then, cruising along, not worrying about things.'

'Doesn't seem possible now.'

'You can't control everything, Viola.' He set down his cutlery now he'd finished and put a hand to the back of her neck before pulling her in for a kiss. 'You don't need to be so perfect, nobody does. And I hate seeing you beating yourself up trying to be nice with Jennifer.'

'I wish I could take back what I did.'

'We all make mistakes; I wish she'd realise that. I bet she's made some of her own somewhere along the way.'

Viola harrumphed. 'I doubt it, she's far too together.'

'I'll bet there's something, you mark my words; nobody goes through life without messing up occasionally.' He kissed her full on the lips. 'And you're already as near to perfect as you ever need to be.'

'You have to say that, you're my husband.'

When Isaac took over the clearing up, Viola thought about the behaviours she'd had ingrained since she was a kid herself, brought up to only expect the highest standards of herself and others. Her parents had seen her win awards at school, she'd been on the winning team in athletics year after year, achieved high distinctions in every single one of her piano exams. But nothing she'd ever really done seemed to get her noticed by two worka-holic parents, not unless you included Jennifer's wedding that was. She'd got plenty of attention then.

What her upbringing had done was make Viola vow never to be that type of parent. She wanted her kids to do well, she pushed them to achieve, but she also tried to be a part of their lives the way her parents never had. It was as though they'd held back their love and affection, plough-ing their energies into their careers and leaving little room for anything else, and when her own children were born Viola had showered them with love. Maybe to the point of suffocation. Ava had told her that once and Isaac was right to tell her now, in his wonderfully subtle, kind way, to back off a bit.

She only hoped she could achieve the balance before her kids were pushed so far they never came back to her.

The following week, bright and early on Saturday morn-ing, Viola went to Adam's to get started on Zoe's bedroom. He'd come straight back to her after she sent all the in-formation and confirmed he was happy with the quote, and he'd hired the wallpaper steamer, which he'd already put to good use at Lilliput Cottage, insisting he help out.

'Zoe's moved to the box room so all the furniture is out of the way,' he told her once she was inside the house with all her paraphernalia. He led the way up to Zoe's bed-room. 'And you're sure you don't want Zoe here to help you?'

'Definitely not. I was glad when Ava told me they were

going roller skating; it gives me a chance to do the boring bit.' She looked around the vacated space. 'It looks like you've made a good start for me.' There wasn't a trace of wallpaper left on the walls and already it had opened up the room.

He put a hand to one of the bare walls. 'I know you said not to bother, but I thought I'd at least do this part for you. And the wallpaper steamer was a god-send. Came off in no time. Isla had told me how great it was for home renovation projects. And I bought some sugar soap for you to use to clean the walls; I'll dig it out for you.'

'Thanks.' She set down her bag containing her designs although she didn't really need them today, and another bag with some new sponges ready to clean the walls, a small toolkit and a couple of dusters to give the surfaces a once-over. She rolled up the sleeves of one of Isaac's old shirts, a little worn around the collar, the button holes partially frayed. 'I can put in the next few Saturdays to get this done.'

'However long it takes; I'm not pinning you to a time-line. As long as Zoe's happy, that's the main thing.'

'I think she'll love it by the time we're finished.'

'Coffee?' He clapped his hands together decisively. 'Come on, you've got time, then I'll leave you to it.'

She accepted the invitation and followed him back down the stairs and into the kitchen. 'I can pop over a couple of times during the week too if I'm able. Would that suit you better?'

'I'll leave it up to you. Send me a text whenever.'

'You're not having one?' He'd only taken out one mug, one coffee pod.

'Zac and I are venturing out for the day. I'm taking him on a long walk, followed by hot chocolates at the end. And we're taking his kite too.'

'Ah, so you've bribed him with hot chocolate, and the kite is a distraction when his legs begin to tire and the whinging starts?'

'Got it in one.' He made the coffee and handed her the mug. 'We'll be out of your hair in twenty minutes.'

She'd appreciate it. She didn't know Adam all that well and it was kind of awkward even though they were both grown-ups. And with nobody else around it meant she could hum or sing away as she worked and not have to be embarrassed about her atrocious voice. Last year she'd repainted the den for a friend who lived near Cloverdale and she'd had all the windows open, headphones on, and got so involved in the task that by the time the owner walked through the door she realised she'd treated most of the neighbourhood to her most likely very off-key rendition of 'I Will Survive'.

Adam took the stepladder and vacuum up to Zoe's room, along with a bucket for when she was ready to wipe down walls.

'Put the shelves, brackets and anything else to be thrown out on the landing at the side and I'll sort it later,' he told her, grinning her way.

'What's so amusing?'

'Nothing, it's just . . . well, I've never seen this side of you. Getting your hands dirty.'

'I suppose we never really know a person till we dig a little deeper,' she said, unimpressed at his observation.

But he didn't reply. He turned and clomped back down the stairs and after a few minutes Viola heard the front door close behind him and Zac and she was left to her own devices. She lifted the existing shelves from their brackets, then undid the vertical braces and set the pieces with the shelves. She removed the ancient light fitting from the ceiling trying not to think about how many cobwebs it housed, and she removed two posters of Chris Hemsworth from the wall nearest the door. She'd carefully rolled each of those up. Last year she'd torn down one of Ava's posters and replaced it with a beautiful print and, while Ava had loved the print, she'd been furious the posters had been thrown out.

Now that all the walls were clear of shelves, wallpaper and posters, she started on the dusting. She made her way around every surface of the room, focusing too on the smaller crevices, the little rim on top of the skirting boards, the cornices. She looked behind the bucket for the sugar soap but couldn't find it, she looked out on the cramped landing and behind her bag near the door in case Adam had left it there, but he must've forgotten. She couldn't move on without it so she went downstairs and into the kitchen to see if he'd left it there instead, but no sign. There was really only one place it was likely to be and that was the utility room so she went in, scanned the benchtops and still found nothing. She opened up a couple of cupboards, but no luck. If he'd bought it recently, surely it would be somewhere visible, she wouldn't need to snoop, which was exactly what it felt like she was doing. She moved the airer but couldn't find what she was looking for there either, and it was only when she stood back and looked up that she was pretty sure a bottle of sugar soap lurked at the top. Why on earth he'd shove it on the uppermost shelf she had no idea.

She looked around, saw a set of kitchen steps and opened them out. Once she'd climbed to the top she got onto the cabinet and leaned round to reach the bottle, careful not to lean out too much and fall. Huffing and puffing with effort she made one more attempt and managed to get the bottle this time, coax it to the edge of the shelf and make a grab for it. The sugar soap must have been on top of something else and a book fell to the tiled floor with a thud.

She tutted, because without even pouring anything from this bottle of sugar soap she could tell by its weight that it was practically empty and wouldn't be enough to use for one wall let alone the entire bedroom. She climbed down. Adam must have bought more unless he thought this bottle would suffice, but when she noticed the old-fashioned price ticket from a shop that had closed down years ago Viola realised this bottle had probably been in the house since before Adam even bought it. She'd have to text him.

She picked up the book that had fallen and when she turned it over, she smiled at the pretty flowers on the front. She opened it up, perhaps it was a diary, maybe it had someone's name inside, because if it had been stashed up there with the sugar soap, then perhaps it belonged to the previous owners or one of the renters and they might well want it back. When Viola and Isaac had moved into the house they lived in now, they'd found a diamond ring beneath the floorboards in the bedroom and returned it to very grateful former owners who'd thought it long gone. But somehow, a diary was even more personal, far more intriguing.

She opened it up but shut it quickly enough when she

didn't see a name. It felt intrusive. Maybe she'd leave it with the sugar soap and tell Adam and he could deal with both. Perhaps whoever this diary belonged to was missing it and would love to have it back, but it was none of her business.

She climbed up the steps again and went to put the diary back where it had been, but in doing so, something fell out and drifted to the floor.

'Damn it.' She climbed down, picked up a photograph to slot back in, but when she turned it over she saw Adam, a woman, Zoe and Zac. The kids were much younger and by her reckoning this picture was at least three years old, possibly four. The woman had to be Adam's wife. Or an ex-wife. But the thought niggled her; why did Adam never mention her?

She tucked the photograph inside the book back where it had been, climbed down the steps and scuttled through the utility room, up the stairs and back to the bedroom. It was then that she spotted three bottles lined up against the door of the box room. In such a dim light they'd been in the shadows earlier and she'd missed them.

She laughed to herself as she picked up a bottle. Adam definitely didn't have much of a clue about decorating. She'd only need one bottle, not three. But they'd come in useful if he ever wanted to do the rest of this place. She took the bucket, used the tap over the bath to fill it up, squirted some of the sugar soap into the water and got started on the ceiling, the hardest part to do given the angle you needed to stay at to get it clean. She used an abrasive cloth for a couple of stubborn marks over by the window and wiped all the suds off with a soft cloth, and by the time she was done it was almost lunchtime so she ate the sandwich she'd brought with her and made another cup of coffee.

She'd made good headway with the bedroom and so she stood in the kitchen enjoying the rush of caffeine as she looked out at the compact square lawn that sat behind Lilliput Cottage. The Parkers were a nice family; they'd settled in Cloverdale without much of a backwards glance, but what did anyone really know about them? Not much. She thought about the photograph she'd found, and the notebook it was hidden inside. Could it tell her something more about this family who kept their story close to their chests?

She shook the thought away, rinsed her mug, popped it in the dishwasher and went back upstairs. She carried on wiping down the wall surrounding the window, plus the windowsill itself, but her mind wouldn't stop drifting to that diary, and when she went to the kitchen to get a cold drink less than thirty minutes later she found herself hovering by the utility room door, longing to take a look. But she couldn't do it, she couldn't snoop, and justifying it as parental concern didn't make it any easier. She'd just ask Adam when he got home.

She went back up the stairs but only reached halfway when she thought of Adam's reaction earlier, when she'd said you never really knew a person unless you dug a little deeper. At the time it hadn't registered as anything unusual, but he'd avoided any conversation after that, and it reminded her that Isaac said he'd seen Adam in the pub a few days ago, sitting in a corner drinking on his own, looking into his pint and avoiding all eye contact as though his whole world was about to implode. 'He's fighting some demons, you mark my words,' Isaac had said. And yesterday when Viola bumped into Elaine outside the library, Elaine had asked her what she made of the newcomers to Cloverdale. Viola had thought it was a case of Elaine and her usual gossiping, but the woman usually made her own judgements, she rarely needed opinions from the masses.

But it was Ava's involvement with this family that propelled Viola back to the utility room. All she needed to do was look at that book, diary, or whatever it was, make sure her daughter wasn't being pulled into some weird family, an environment that could do her harm or a bizarre cult to lead her astray, and then she'd put it back and forget she'd ever seen it.

She climbed up the kitchen steps, heart pounding as though she was sneaking into Ava's bedroom checking her diary, which she did on a regular basis. You read such things about young girls these days, bullied without their parents knowing, going on to commit suicide in some of the more tragic cases. It was terrible. She couldn't leave her family wide open to hurt like that. Isaac would see it as overstepping, but she didn't.

The book safely in her hands she told herself she'd read a few pages to make sure they were a normal family, nobody was at risk, and then she'd put it back without reading any more. She took the diary in to the lounge where she perched against the back of the sofa so she could look out to the street and see if Adam came back.

She read the first page, then the second, and on and on, absorbing what she was finding out. There wasn't a name to give ownership to these thoughts on paper but Zoe's name told her they needed to look no further than the Parkers for who this belonged to. And as much as she wanted to believe Adam was kind and good, friendly and loyal, reading this, she wasn't so sure she could ever trust him again.

The diary started off harmless enough with a recap of a wedding day, the arrival of baby Zoe, but from there it turned into something else. Viola's eyes took in descriptive words, passages that talked about violence, belittling, ridicule. It was an account of a world she'd never had to experience. The author of the diary talked about their fear, despair, hopelessness living a life that had been so far from the dream existence we have when we marry the person we thought we'd share the rest of our life with.

Viola's heart leapt when she heard a car pull up outside and seeing it was Adam and Zac she quickly ran through to the utility room, climbed the steps, deposited the diary back where she'd found it, positioned the old sugar soap container on top of it exactly as it was before and without enough time to run back upstairs she filled another glass of water from the tap to make her excuse for being in this part of the house.

When Adam saw her as he came through she tried to play it cool, launching straight in to an explanation of her progress so far. She was gabbling along, but, if he noticed anything was amiss, he didn't mention it.

It wasn't long before she excused herself to go and clear up. She couldn't be in this house a moment longer; she needed to get away, regroup, think about all of this and decide what to do next. Her kids were the most prized part of her life and her heart ached for Zoe and Zac and what else was in that diary, because from what she'd seen, it hadn't painted a rosy picture at all.

And now she knew she wouldn't stop until she knew

absolutely everything about this man who had come to Cloverdale thinking he could keep the truth from everyone. No wonder he'd flinched at her earlier remark that you never really knew a person until you dug a little deeper.

It seemed her digging had revealed a lot more about the Parker family than they had ever intended to share.

II

Jennifer

Jennifer had spent her morning doing the laundry, cleaning the kitchen floor and waiting for the sports outlet to deliver two new badminton sets for the Library of Shared Things. They already had one but she'd negotiated a substantial discount for more because they'd been in such demand over the summer that she wanted to be ready for next season before it went clean out of her mind.

Since her conversation with Adam last week, she'd not only begun to think more seriously about a return to hairdressing, she'd agreed to cut his hair, and although plans had been firmly in her head up until now, with a few minutes to spare before Adam came over to be her first hairdressing client – she'd confessed she'd rather not do Zac yet because she didn't want him to tell Archie – and, with Isla manning the Library of Shared Things so she could set up the outside ready for her dance class this evening, she took out the new notepad she'd treated herself to yesterday when she was at the shops.

She wrote Home Hairdressing by Jenn at the top of the page and drew a circle around it. It didn't have to keep its name, but it was a start and she allowed herself a little smile, her inner being urging her not to stop now. She wanted to make a plan before she even thought about telling David; they'd been here once before and it hadn't gone well. She needed to keep a level head, not let her dreams pull her in the wrong direction.

She began to make a list of the equipment she'd need. She already had a few of the basics as she still cut Archie's hair and the other day when she'd passed by a supplies store she'd picked up a feather styling razor ready to do Adam's. Grown-ups needed that bit extra, although she was sure Archie would be asking for the same treatment soon enough. On her iPad she trawled through information on the other equipment she'd need if she was going to do this, noting down items on her list, although she could've made a list off the top of her head anyway: salon grade high-quality scissors, combs, hairdryer and straighteners, a curling iron, bleach-resistant towels, chemicals for bleaching, dying and colours and a good supplier who could deliver quickly if a client wanted something a little different.

She started a new list of everything else she had to think about. She'd need to take charge of her own accounts, she'd need insurance, she'd want to adopt an advertising plan and set up a Facebook page to build her client base. It was all online these days, you had to have a presence. Viola seemed to be good at it, perhaps she could ask for a bit of advice. Since their falling-out years ago, she missed her friend, even though she was the one keeping her at a distance. Once upon a time she would've been able to confide in Viola and tell her how worried she was about her marriage and whether she and David were going to go the distance, confess to Viola that she was turning to Adam more and more, jealous of her own sister who was a free agent in the same way he was. And Viola had no idea of the mistakes Jennifer had made along the way. How could she tell her when she'd made Viola pay time after time for what she'd done wrong? It would serve her right if all Viola saw was sheer hypocrisy and never spoke to her again.

When there was a knock at the door she stowed the notebook in the study filing cabinet where she kept household bills, receipts, manuals for everything in the kitchen. David never went in that drawer so she could keep this little piece of herself until she was ready.

The first thing she said to Adam when she opened the door, was, 'I'm nervous.'

'Good, because that makes two of us.' He breathed with relief. 'It's weird though, I mean, it's a haircut and it's not like I'm giving Zac the scissors.'

'Well, I appreciate you being my guinea pig.'

He shut the front door behind him. 'If you make me look like a guinea pig I might not be your friend anymore.'

With a laugh she offered tea or coffee, he went for the latter, and as she sipped hers she tried to quell her nerves. She'd never had a problem with male clients at the salon she'd worked in for years; it had to be the gap between then and now that was causing her anxiety to skyrocket. 'How did the steamer work out for you?' That's what they needed, normal conversation. And he'd borrowed the wallpaper steamer from the Library of Shared Things in preparation for Viola's makeover of Zoe's bedroom, so asking him about it would ease her into that client relationship she used to have without even thinking.

'Fantastic. Quick and very easy. I'll never use a standard scraper again.'

'You're going to do more decorating?'

'It won't be long before Zac wants something done to his room, especially once Zoe's is finished.'

'And it's going well with Viola?' She'd wondered how it would go without anyone else as a buffer.

'She's different when she's not in helicopter parent mode.' He pulled a face. 'Sorry, I shouldn't say that. It's judgemental.'

'It's a tiny bit true though,' she whispered as though the walls could hear. 'But I'm glad it's going well.'

'So how's this going to work?' he asked as the moment hovered between them.

She pulled one of the kitchen stools to the centre of the room where she'd already laid down a large ground sheet she'd found in the garage. 'When did you last wash your hair?' She'd meant to tell him to do it before he came over, save the awkwardness of him bending over the bathtub while she tried to do it for him.

'This morning.'

'Great. In the salon I'd usually wash it for you but you having done it already makes it far easier. I'll go and grab some towels and my kit, and we'll make a start.'

'See, you have a kit. You already sound like a professional.' When he smiled the warmth in his brown eyes did little to ease her trepidation, and she found her skin prickling as she thought how attractive he looked with the slight stubble to his jaw, the grey T-shirt he had on beneath the hoodie he'd removed and laid over one of the other stools.

She escaped from the kitchen, grabbed the things she needed and took a deep breath before she went back in. What was happening? She was married. She had a family, a life, but there was an inexplicable pull towards this man.

'What's up?' He was watching her, hesitating at getting started.

'I don't have a mirror for you.'

'Do *you* need one?'

'I don't suppose I do. But I'll go grab a hand-held-mirror so you can at least see the final cut when we're done. I don't want you to be unhappy with it.' She went off to the bathroom, found the little mirror and back in the kitchen she set the mirror down on the bench top. Over the last week or so she'd been trying not to get carried away, tried not to imagine a boutique hairdressing salon all of her very own in Cloverdale or a village nearby, done her best not to imagine going to her place of work every day and having to pinch herself that it was all hers.

One step at a time.

She put a towel around his shoulders and fixed it with a clip at the front. 'Sorry about the pink towel and clip; it's what I usually use on Archie and he doesn't care about the girlie colour.'

'You should've said. Zac has a Batman cape I could've borrowed.'

'Damn.' She smiled. 'Next time maybe.'

His hair did look in need of a trim so she'd try to focus on that, not the fluttery feeling in her tummy that reminded her of the early days with David, when she'd watched him zip himself in and out of a wetsuit on the beach when he went surfing. 'I think we're ready to start.'

'Great. I mean, what's the worst you can do?'

'You're not helping steady my nerves.'

'I apologise. I'll stop messing with you. Let's talk as though I'm a client in a salon.'

For the next half an hour Jennifer soon found herself relaxing into her role as hairdresser, talking with her client as she worked. She used the plastic spray gun to wet the hair down, combed the hair through as they talked about what else she'd need to purchase if she were to go for mobile hairdressing as a start. She cut the hair over the tops of the ears touching his ear lightly each time to pull it out of the way as they moved on to a discussion about perhaps renting a chair at a salon and getting back into hairdressing that way. She textured the hair on the top using the feather styling razor to create a softer finish rather than a blunt cut as his soft brown hair lightened back to its original shade now that it was drying.

She snipped a few extra bits here and there, giving it a tousled look on top that he favoured and she shared her dream of one day owning her own salon. She was really starting to believe in herself again. And Adam's support helped her to do that. He was funny, good company, a pleasure to talk to. All the things she should think about her husband, who was becoming increasingly aloof and harder to spend time with when he worked such long hours, and she was too afraid to share this with him for fear he'd worry history was going to repeat itself.

'Back to work after this?' she asked.

'Yeah. We've been looking at a new apartment development.' He told her about the responsibility of ensuring the design of public spaces was right, how they'd need to be multi-use for both residents and office workers.

'It sounds as though you enjoy your job.'

'I like working with so many different people, keeps the day interesting.'

She put a little bit of product through his hair to finish and, holding her scissors, she checked the hair over the ears once again, not wanting to miss any. She was so close she caught a hint of aftershave, something fresh but not too overpowering, enough to make its presence known.

'Jennifer . . .'

She was checking the other side and absent-mindedly said, 'Hmm?'

'Jennifer . . . I think you're done, stop worrying.'

She held up her hands. 'You're right, I am obsessing. Well?' She grabbed the mirror and passed it to him.

'You've done a brilliant job. Thank you.'

'My first happy client.' She beamed, taking the clip from the towel and removing it from his shoulders.

He turned and clasped both of her upper arms in his hands. 'Now where's your sweeping brush and I'll clear up.'

His touch caught her off-guard. 'It's in the utility room.'

While he fetched the broom she wiped down the stool and put it back, and with the dustpan and brush cleared up the big pile of hair he swept up. 'Can I interest you in another drink before you go?'

'A glass of water please. Then I'd really better be off before I'm described as one of those people who "works from home".' He put the phrase in air quotes.

She filled a glass of water. 'I miss the social side of hairdressing,' she admitted when they sat at the bench again. 'Meeting so many new people or those who return after a couple of months, talking through concerns, happy and sad events in their lives, good and bad issues, it made me feel . . . valued, like I had a purpose. Does that sound silly?'

'No, but you're forgetting all the ways you're already valued. Here, for example, in the home.'

'I know, but it's different.'

'I'm guessing you feel like everyone takes you for granted, that sometimes they forget you're a person too and need your own life.'

She looked down at her hands, her fingers grasping together in her lap. 'I feel terrible thinking it. It's kind of ungrateful.'

'I had a stint where I was at home with the kids and not working. I nearly went crazy.'

'Was that when you first came to the UK?'

'Yup. But I got a job soon enough and it was good to be back in the adult world. Kids have a way of taking all your energy and, although you love them to bits, most of us need something else going on. And I'll bet most of us feel as guilty as you do now, if we say anything.'

'Have you always been in the same line of work?'

'I've been a landscape architect for a while and worked for a similar company as I do now – got the opportunity to work on plenty of different projects. And before that I was a humble gardener.'

She smiled. 'How come I never knew that about you?'

'There's a lot you don't know, Jennifer.' He seemed to catch himself. 'And I'm sure it's the case vice versa.'

'Was it hard to change your career?' He didn't seem to mind the question. She wondered whether he could sense their friendship deepening in the same way she could.

'It took a lot of work and study to go from being a gardener to something a little different, but the gardening was a good foundation.' His eyes levelled with hers. 'It's why I know you can do whatever you want to do, much like I did. You have the passion, the drive and, now I've seen my hair I have to say, the talent.'

'I appreciate your confidence in me.'

'Have you mentioned it to David yet?'

'No. I want to get everything lined up, be confident of what I'm talking about.'

'He's not your bank manager.'

No, but he'd bailed her out once before when she'd brought so much trouble their way they'd wondered if it would ever end. 'We get so very little time together let alone time to talk deeply about something like this, so I want to be able to show him I can do it.' Show him she wasn't going to mess up.

'Well, now you can tick your first client off your list. Your first *satisfied* client.' He pulled out his wallet from his back pocket. 'How much for today?'

'No way! I'm not taking money; it was a favour.'

'Your business won't get far with that attitude.'

'I'll charge you the going rate next time. Is that fair?'

'Then I'll buy you a drink at the pub some time, although not tonight, I'll be dancing.'

'You're going to the dance class?'

'Isla was trying to round up a few men to go and so I thought, why not?'

Jennifer couldn't help it, but jealously reared its ugly head again, as well as the panic that Isla could flit off elsewhere when she got bored and ruin her friendship with Adam. Maybe it was best not to talk about the dancing or Isla right now. Things had been good the other night when her sister came over for dinner; she'd trusted her to look after the library, which she knew spoke volumes for Isla when it came to their relationship, and Jennifer wanted to hold on to that. But if her sister hurt this man, she wasn't sure she could ever forgive her.

'How's Zoe going with the whole new freedom on social media?' she asked him to change tack.

'She follows me, I follow her, I promised not to comment on her pictures but to linger in the background. To be honest most of it is way too girly for me, all about contouring in make-up, whatever that is, and pictures of girls pouting at the camera. What's that all about?'

'I've no idea. David thinks it makes girls look like constipated ducks.'

His laughter bounced off the kitchen walls. 'That's a great visual.'

'Katie and Amelia do a bit of it but thankfully they don't take themselves too seriously. Did Isla show you everything you need to know?' OK, so she hadn't managed to steer clear of the Isla subject for long. What she really wanted to know was every little detail of the evening they'd shared. Jennifer had heard from Isla that there'd been wine, Chinese food. But was that all?

'I seem to know what I'm doing.' His turn to change the subject now. 'What's the next step for you, now your first cut is out of the way?'

'I'm thinking I'll start with mobile hairdressing, then progress to renting a chair in a salon.'

'Have you thought more about advertising?'

'I'll start by getting a website up and running, a Facebook page, some business cards, do some good old-fashioned leaflets. I think initially most of my clients will be local but that's fine. I have my family commitments

. . . the Library of Shared Things to see to.'

'I could help you with some of the start-up activities, point you in the direction of someone to do the business cards. You really need to tell David.'

Her heart sank. 'I know.' She smiled. 'I will.'

'Good, he seems like a decent man. Not all men are.'

He was right. David was a good man. But these days it was Adam she turned to when she needed to talk.

12

Adam

Adam had been about to text Isla and tell her he couldn't make tonight's dance session when Zoe came into the kitchen far more perky than she'd been an hour ago. 'Dad, it's OK if Viola comes over, isn't it?'

'It's getting a bit late; surely she doesn't want to do your bedroom tonight. I hope you're not badgering her.'

'Of course I'm not. She said she wanted to keep going with it.'

'And you're feeling better?'

'Yes, Dad. I'm fine. Chill. So what should I tell her?' Zoe prompted.

Perhaps this was a blessing. He'd been about to cancel with Isla because Zoe had come home from school not feeling well. She'd had a headache bad enough to go to bed for a while, a delicate tummy, and he'd checked on her every hour or so. But it seemed a sleep had helped as he watched her now, back to her old self. He worried far too much according to Zoe but he always would. That was the deal when you became a parent.

'Is that a no then?' Hands on hips, Zoe blocked the doorway, but Zac squeezed past and into the kitchen to get himself a drink.

157

'Actually it's a yes. But don't be tempted to help, you need to rest.'

'But I helped yesterday.'

'That's the deal, take it or leave it.'

She smiled, knowing she was defeated. 'I'll take it.' But the smiled faded. 'Don't tell her I've been unwell.'

'Everyone gets sick now and again; you don't need to be embarrassed.'

'But I've been sick more than most, haven't I?'

'She's a mum, she'll get it.'

'Dad, I'm fed up with not being normal. People look at me differently or start to panic if I'm not well, you know they do. My PE teacher at my last school was permanently freaked out from the hypo I had after netball that time. He really needed to strap on a pair.'

'Don't talk about your teacher like that.' Where did she pick up these phrases?

'Just let me enjoy tonight without someone else thinking they need to look out for me all the time.'

When Zoe disappeared back upstairs Adam turned to his son who'd been eyeing up the chocolate biscuits on the bench top. 'Can you keep a secret, mate?'

'Of course.'

'Your sister will kill me if she knows I've asked, but can you keep an eye on her for me tonight? Text me if she's looking unwell, or get Viola to run over to me at the Library of Shared Things if you have to.'

Zac sighed long and hard. 'It's gonna cost ya.'

'Really. How much?'

He held up his thumb and index finger. 'Two chocolate hobnobs.'

'Deal.'

Zac enthusiastically grabbed the biscuits and Adam headed out to the hallway to call up the stairs and ask Zoe what time to expect Viola, but the knock at the door gave him his answer.

'Viola, come in.' Now it was chillier in the evenings he closed the door quickly behind her. 'Can I get you a drink?'

'I'm good, thank you. I'll go and get started.' She made no comment at his smart appearance.

'You do know I'm out tonight, at the dance class.'

'I know.' She smiled tentatively, which made him wonder whether he'd done something to offend her.

'I can cancel, stay here to look after the kids.' Maybe that was it; she thought he was using her as makeshift babysitter.

'It's fine, really.' A woman of few words, and when Zoe came downstairs Viola went straight up to the bedroom with her.

Zac appeared in the hallway beside him. 'Dad,' he said all seriously, 'if you learn any new moves tonight could you do me a favour?'

'Of course, I can teach you anything, you know that.'

'No, I was going to say, could you promise me you won't ever do them when we're out with other people.'

Adam ruffled his hair. 'You're on.' And with a laugh he left the house to set off for a rare night out.

He'd done a lot of things wrong over the years, but having Zoe and Zac . . . well, those were two things he'd bloody well got right.

When he arrived at the Library of Shared Things, fairy lights had been strung up outside along the front of the outbuilding, a gazebo covered a large area in front of the section furthest to the right. The jukebox on the wall at the back showed off its array of colours and an instrumental tune he wasn't sure the name of played into the evening air as a couple of outdoor heaters offered their warmth. There were a few people milling about inside and he spotted Isla at the desk. Her silky-smooth auburn hair was wound up into a bun, and she looked quite the professional with black bottoms fitted at the waist, a soft cream vest top beneath a floppy black cardigan that kept falling off one shoulder, and she was busy laying out safety pins and name tags when she saw him arrive.

'It feels like you're running some kind of speed dating event,' he said.

'Don't panic.' She wrote his name on one of the pieces of white card, pushed a safety pin into it. 'May I?' Her hands reached up to his shirt.

'Thanks.' He tried not to register her closeness, the eyelashes that delicately shadowed the skin beneath her eyes and fluttered naturally. 'Will I do? You said to wear comfortable clothing.' He turned around on the spot for her inspection of the pair of khakis and navy polo shirt he was wearing.

'You'll do just fine.'

He looked around him. 'You've got this place looking really good. Many coming?'

'I assume what you're really asking is whether you're the only man.'

'Busted.' So far, he could only see women, including Elaine. 'So am I?' he ventured.

She laughed. 'Danny is coming over from the pub,

Harrison's coming, Bill said he'd join us and Hattie has persuaded her boyfriend Martin.'

'Thank goodness for that.'

She spoke quietly when she asked, 'Are you worried Elaine will pounce?'

'Honestly?' He got close enough that only she'd hear his reply. 'Yes.'

'Don't worry. What I wanted was enough people to have them dance in pairs, but we'll swap partners regularly so nobody gets fed up. And there are more women than men so sometimes women will dance with women. That's OK when you're learning; all part of the fun.'

'I'm not sure how I'd feel if you made me dance up close with another bloke.'

'I'm not asking you to press your body parts against his.'

'I'm glad you think it's funny.' He nudged her, enjoying the flirting.

By the time they got started he guessed there were around twenty participants. It had cost a fiver each for tonight, all of the profits going towards new items for the Library of Shared Things. Isla wasn't getting paid and he sensed she wanted to do this as a special favour for Jennifer as much as for the village. Whatever was going on between the sisters he could see their fondness for each other even though they sometimes managed to hide it.

Isla connected up her phone to the vintage-look juke-box and before the music started she introduced herself to those who might not know her, recalled a bit of her dance background, which Adam found himself fascinated with. He wanted to hear more, talk late into the night with her like they had over wine and Chinese food, but for now, he had to focus on the lesson and not making a total idiot of himself.

They started with the waltz, all of them listening attentively to the beat as Isla counted out loud. Some of the men were scratching their heads, quite literally, as though it could make them think harder, and Adam noticed some of the women looking just as unsure. Isla taught them the basic steps, had them repeat the footwork over and over until they began to get it. Adam thought he had to concentrate at work, but this was something else. His mind was totally focused; he had one aim, and that was to not make a fool of himself in front of Isla.

He smiled across at Danny from the pub, who looked like he wanted to do a runner, although Melody seemed to be keeping a close eye on him, Elaine and another lady seemed to be getting the hang of the rhythm, and Martin looked like he'd rather be anywhere else but here.

Harrison piped up. 'I had lessons, a long time ago.' He held out his arms in a shape that Adam swore he'd seen on movies when a couple danced, and Isla stepped into them as he added, 'I wanted to waltz with my new bride, not be a laughing stock.'

'Perfect. We can demo.' Stupid, but right now Adam was jealous of Harrison Pemberley even though he was way too old for Isla. He wished he was holding her in his arms, moving her around the dance floor as she counted out loud for the onlookers to learn and hopefully repeat themselves.

'You make it look too easy, Isla.' Melody took off her

cardigan as the warmth from the outdoor heaters moved around them.

'Everyone find a space,' Isla instructed, standing back by the jukebox. 'We'll do the moves individually again, really feel the rhythm.' She'd obviously got a whole play-list made up of tunes they could waltz to, so, without having to touch the jukebox, she indicated for everyone to make a start while she demonstrated at the same time at the front of the group. Adam could've watched her all night.

Adam moved cautiously, lost the timing to the music on several occasions, but after a few minutes seemed to have the pattern ingrained in his mind. He was counting out loud, as many of the others were, looking at his feet trying to get it right.

'That's it, good work.' It was Isla making her way round helping people, demonstrating again if they needed guidance. 'Try to anticipate the first beat. So rather than beginning to move on beat one, lift the foot so you're ready.'

He looked at her. 'I've no idea what you mean.'

'Watch.' She demonstrated, starting the move on beat one. 'See how it was rigid, didn't flow. Now watch if my foot begins before the beat.' She counted out loud, getting to three a couple of times and then right before the first beat he saw her foot lift so it glided down smoothly for beat one, and, as she kept the demonstration going, he got it and repeated her actions.

She clapped her hands together. 'Brilliant, you're doing it. You're a natural.' She moved on to help someone else. They had to look like a bunch of village idiots out here in the evening, dancing away on their own, arms cocked as though an imaginary friend were there too. Isla paired him up with Hilary who he recognised as one of the teachers from Zac's school and apart from smacking foreheads when he insisted on looking down at his feet, they did a good job. And at the end of the lesson he realised that, apart from having a bit of a workout and some adult time, what had really happened was that he'd enjoyed himself. This was the most fun he'd had in a long time, and he'd even switched off from worrying so much about Zoe.

'Don't you have to get back home to the kids?' Isla asked when he insisted on helping clear up. They'd had a break midway through with sausage rolls and cups of tea and inevitably flaky crumbs had found their way to the floor, so he stayed behind to sweep up. 'You took the gazebo down for me, that's more than enough.'

'Don't be daft, I don't mind at all.'

'I'm glad you came.' With all the jobs finished, Isla flopped into one of the chairs with a cup of tea. She'd taken off her cardigan, and now beads of perspiration ran across the top of her chest, and a glow to her cheeks displayed her exertion.

'You were in your element tonight,' he remarked before she caught him staring. He put his name tag into the container with the others and stashed it in the drawer she indicated, ready for another class next week. Who would've thought he'd ever take to dancing? Although the teacher had a hell of a lot to do with his enthusiasm for it.

'I forget everything when I dance.'

He wondered what she needed to forget. 'I'm pretty

sure I still have two left feet after one lesson.'

'That's crazy, you did well, and we'll do the waltz again next week.'

'So you're definitely sticking around?'

'Why wouldn't I?' Her face fell at the realisation. 'Jennifer has been talking about me. She thinks I never stick to anything.'

'She cares. And she talks about you because you're her sister.'

'For my sins.'

'Not that bad is it?' He leaned against the desk.

'No, I don't suppose it is. But our relationship is delicate and I know she's still angry I wasn't here for her when Mum got sick. I get that. But Jennifer needs to learn not to hold a grudge. Lord knows other people have given *her* the benefit of the doubt enough times; she's been allowed to make mistakes without paying for them for the rest of her life.'

'Like what?'

Isla must've realised she'd been spouting off when she probably shouldn't. 'Doesn't matter now, but sometimes she's hypocritical, and she doesn't always want to listen to someone else's side of the story.'

'And what makes her think you won't hang around in Cloverdale?'

'I've moved around a lot and I guess she got used to me being that way. But I'm finally at a point where I want to put down roots.'

He knew exactly what that was like. He felt old when he said it but all he craved was stability, a run-of-the-mill existence. Was it too much to ask for?

'I have a track record; I guess that's what makes her

doubt me. Although she did tell me she'd been envious of my adventures.'

'Yeah?'

She recapped their dinner the other night. 'Evenings like that remind me how much I love her, but when she's telling people her doubts about me . . . well, it winds me up, that's all. I'd far rather she said them to my face, or perhaps asked me the reasons why I've done the things I have.'

'If you need to talk, I'm not a bad listener.' He thought about the tattoo on her ankle, he wanted to ask what the words meant. 'And I'm glad you're sticking around.' Had he really said that out loud?

'Me too.' She looked as uneasy as him before she changed tack and asked, 'How's Zoe getting on with her new-found freedom on Instagram?'

'I'm surprised she hasn't followed you yet.'

'She has.' Isla grinned. 'And don't worry, all my posts are appropriate.'

'I know; I followed you when we set up the account.'

'You need to post some pictures.'

'Not really my thing.'

'You might find it a bit of fun.'

'What am I going to post?'

'Surely you can think of something. How about a photograph of you at your first dance lesson?'

'Luckily all my potential partners have gone home.'

'There's always me.'

He'd love nothing more. 'We don't have anyone to take the shot.'

She held a finger up in the air and then disappeared out the back and returned with a stepladder.

'What's that for?'

'You'll see.' She climbed up the steps and positioned her phone. 'Stand outside, over there where you were before,' she urged.

'You're crazy.' But he did it anyway. He suspected he'd do anything she asked of him. He'd gone all teenager again, over a girl. It was absurd!

'More to the centre,' she advised, and he moved. 'It's still light enough with the lights from inside.'

'You're going to take a photo of me dancing like a lunatic in the middle of an abandoned car park without another soul in sight? I don't think that'll make a good first photograph. And Zoe might disown me.'

'Bear with me. Put your arms up like you're dancing and now imagine you have a partner.'

He felt like a complete tosser. 'This is a bad idea.' But she came to his side before he could throw in the towel.

'You're in the right position.' She stepped into his arms and he drew his breath inward when he realised she was going to dance with him. He could feel the thud of her heart against his ribs, or was he imagining it?

'I can't do it without music.' He was desperate for a moment to gather himself. Isla was beautiful, stunning in her own unique way. He loved that she was unconventional, had her own mind but had a gentleness too.

Her eyes glistened in the light snatched from inside the Library of Shared Things, the winking stars up above them. 'We should do a video rather than a photo.'

'I don't know . . .'

'Come on, live a little. I think out here, with the soft lighting, you might see you're actually a bit of a natural mover.'

'I doubt that.'

'We'll look at the video afterwards and we can scrap it if you're that uncomfortable. Then you can do what so many other people do and put up a photograph of your breakfast or something.'

At the jukebox she selected 'Moon River' and the soft strains of violin accompanied by piano had his nerves jumping around as though this were a date, not an extension of dance practice where she was the teacher and he was the pupil.

They had a quick practice before she started the video and all the while she told him to relax. But how could he, when they were so close he could smell a citrusy shampoo, his hands were against her silky skin and their bodies were touching in the way he'd only been able to imagine until now?

'Eyes on me,' she said again, and he dragged them from the floor upwards, hardly daring to breathe. 'It'll make it easier, honestly. You'll get a feel for the rhythm.'

As they moved he did his best to focus on the beat. One-two-three, then four-five-six in the other direction.

'Ready?'

'Let's do this. Although I'm still not sure I want it plastered all over the internet.'

She set the camera at the top of the stepladder to film, then came back and slotted into his arms as though she were made for them. And with a nod to start the beat they were off, gliding around the concrete area as though it were a ballroom dance floor, the twinkly lights reflecting in her eyes and the music carrying them along against the night sky, their rhythm good, conversation lulled in their involvement in the dance.

He made mistakes but they laughed, carried on, and everything else melted around them, until a voice said, 'I'm not interrupting, am I?' Jennifer stood at the doors to the Library of Shared Things, and, although she was smiling, Adam could tell she wasn't happy. Maybe there was a rule that said no involvement with friends' sisters, but Isla was the first woman who'd turned his head in a long time and she was hard to ignore.

When Isla went over to the jukebox and turned the music off, Adam felt exposed in a way that made him uncomfortable and frustrated. 'Isla insisted on getting me started with Instagram and sharing a video no less,' he told Jennifer, going over to talk to her as Isla took the stepladder back inside. 'I enjoyed the lesson tonight a lot more than I thought I would.'

'I'm glad.' She hadn't said a word to Isla yet, and Isla seemed to be avoiding eye contact with her sister. 'I came to make sure everything was switched off, locked up.'

Neither sister said anything so it left him to break the silence and he talked about the dancing classes, how they'd all managed to look less moronic than when they'd first arrived and were all over the place. And all the while he talked, Isla finished clearing up and gathered her things.

'Why don't you come along next week,' he suggested to Jennifer.

'I'll think about it.'

Isla looked at her sister briefly. 'I've locked up the back room, everything is swept and tidy.'

Jennifer didn't say anything else and as she found the switch for one row of lights, Adam found another and Isla found the last. Adam pulled across the bifold and with them all inside, bolted it shut and they went to the single panel opened at the other end, shutting the yellow door behind them.

Jennifer locked up as Adam turned to Isla, 'You don't want to walk home alone, how about I walk with you up the lane?'

Isla smiled and was about to reply but Jennifer got there first. 'I have my car. I'll take Isla; you don't want to be walking down the country lanes at night. Drivers won't see you.'

'Shame, I could've done with a walk,' Adam did his best not to stare at Isla. There was a spark he wanted to explore and he could tell she felt it too. But he didn't want to piss Jennifer off. He'd had enough grief in his life, especially when it came to women.

'Another time.' Isla smiled his way as she followed Jennifer who was already heading over to her car.

'Next week maybe,' he called after her hopefully before he set off for home feeling pretty good. Dancing had magical uplifting powers, or maybe it was Isla who did.

Zac came downstairs the second he opened the door to Lilliput Cottage. 'I thought you'd be asleep by now.' Judging by the laughter coming from upstairs, Viola was still here and was it any wonder the kid didn't want to settle?

Zac beckoned for him to bend down to his level. 'Zoe is fine. Still annoying. Still loud. Still bossy. I wanted to show her some karate moves and she told me she was too busy.'

'Want me to watch?'

Zac dragged him into the lounge and showed him his best side kick.

'Whoa, that's a big kick, you nearly got me!' Adam fell back laughing onto the sofa.

'I could crush your throat.' Zac put on a voice as though he were in an action movie. 'It would take seconds to die,' he added with an accompanying roar.

Adam pulled him down onto the sofa making him giggle. 'You, my boy, need to leave the karate and get some sleep. School in the morning.'

'I can't sleep with those two up there, it's too loud.'

They looked at one another and both shook their heads as they said, 'Women.'

Adam called up the stairs and, after the fourth attempt to get a response from Zoe, when he thought he was going to have to go up himself, she appeared. 'It's a school night, remember.'

'But it's going really well.'

All he wanted to do was relax and his anger mounted at her response. 'Zoe, call it a night, please.'

'Fine.'

'Sorry!' came Viola's voice. 'Almost done.'

He couldn't get too angry when they had a guest so he sent Zac upstairs and went through to the kitchen to make a cup of tea and when Viola came down moments later he was relieved the house would soon be quiet. He needed some time to process tonight. Since his marriage had spectacularly and dramatically fallen apart with the remaining loose end the divorce he'd have to eventually see to, he hadn't entertained the thought of getting involved again. But the second he'd laid eyes on Isla, that had all changed. And he wanted to tread carefully, make sure he didn't mess anything up.

'I'll be off.' It was Viola at the bottom of the stairs,

slipping her Skechers on her feet.

He glugged a mouthful of tea. 'Thanks, Viola. I appreciate it, but I need to get Zoe to go to bed or she'll be a zombie at school tomorrow.'

'No worries.' She didn't meet his eye until she had her bags looped over her arms.

'Everything all right?'

'Of course.' She seemed flustered, much like a person who very much wasn't all right but wasn't about to share the details with anyone. 'We're making good progress. Goodnight, Adam.'

When he heard Zoe go into the bathroom upstairs and run a shower, it gave him enough time to check her phone and make sure she was keeping up her end of the bargain by being sensible, and, relieved she was, he flopped down on the sofa. For now at least, the truth about the Parker family seemed to be intact.

With that in mind, he flicked through the television channels laughing when he came across an episode of *Strictly*. He'd need a lot of training before he looked like any of those contenders. And when Isla sent him the dance video they'd made tonight, he watched it over and over again. Perhaps they'd go viral on Instagram, him for being the worst dancer over forty, her for being . . . for being beautiful. He couldn't take his eyes off her, the way she moved, the way her body looked against his.

But after texting Isla to say he was happy for her to upload the video, his mind went somewhere else, because the way Viola had looked at him tonight niggled him, made him feel as though his world could one day unravel and all of this, his life in Cloverdale, the relationship he was hoping for with Isla, would be destroyed.

Maybe he was just tired. Tiredness brought out worries, paranoia. And so he switched his thoughts back to Isla and the good things he had in his life these days, not the memories he wanted to bury under a ton of rubble for good.

13

Viola

Viola had excelled in high school. She was part of the debate team who won awards against other schools, she could voice an opinion and argue her case, but when it came to being the whistle blower on anyone, friend or foe, she had this inexplicable way of clamming up.

In her first year as a junior Human Resources officer she knew full well her manager had been claiming a lot of sick leave but in reality she was in the throes of setting up a party planning side business that she had every intention of leaving the job for. Word had gradually got around to this woman's superiors and they started asking questions of everyone. When it got to Viola's turn, she'd darted off to the bathrooms before she was cornered. Breaking out in a sweat she'd opened a top window relishing the cold and the smell of the rain as it brought a freshness to clear the fug in her mind. She'd wondered how she could lie yet still be the woman who valued honesty and transparency at home and in the workplace above everything else. She worked hard and did everything to the best of her ability, she didn't want to be the person to cause trouble for someone else. She'd done that to Jennifer once before, and look how that had turned out.

And now she faced the same kind of problem, except on a far bigger magnitude. She knew things – bad things – and she desperately wanted to tell someone else to get it off her chest. She had this information and not any idea if or how she should use it. People deserved to know the truth about Adam, his kids certainly did, but would they see it that way? And would Jennifer thank her for blowing the Parkers' world apart by revealing the truth? If their history was anything to go by, probably not.

Viola pulled in to her allocated space in the office car park, and, in a navy pinstripe suit and a crisp white shirt, her blonde curls tugged into a low side ponytail, she turned back to being Human Resources Viola. The woman who didn't let much bother her at all. Who got down to business and kept a level head at all times.

On her way home that evening she stopped at the Library of Shared Things to pick up the bread maker. She'd almost bought one for herself last week – she used it often enough – but this way she was supporting Jennifer's idea for the community, and she'd do anything to put their friendship back on an even keel. She knew it would take time; she was determined to get there, and if baby steps were what it took then so be it.

'You look like you've got a lot on your mind.' Viola watched Jennifer and wondered, did she know the contents of that diary too? Had she got close enough to Adam that he'd admitted everything to her?

'It's been a busy day.'

'Well, that's good, isn't it?' Maybe she was reading too much into Jennifer's tiredness, hoping she wouldn't have to be the one to unveil the secret.

'Of course, I'm not complaining, but I had three

overdue items so chased those up, I managed to drop a cup in the kitchen, and of course it was full and went everywhere, and Archie was up three times in the night with a tummy ache so he's off school today.'

'Poor kid, he's been unwell a lot lately. Who's with him?'

'David's working from home. Between you and me, I think Archie is missing his dad and saw an opportunity.'

'Naughty, but understandable.' This was progress from the tight-lipped Jennifer she'd met when they'd first bumped into each other after all this time. She was talking, but Viola wished they could talk to each other more. Viola could see Jennifer's marriage had run into a stumbling block, but her friend was bottling everything up inside, something she wasn't immune to herself and it had certainly been the root cause of all the trouble between her and Jennifer before. Being open and honest had a lot going for it, and if she'd done that, they may never have fallen out in the first place.

'I'd better put this away.' Jennifer indicated the tea urn she'd been inspecting. 'It was borrowed for a fiftieth wedding anniversary. I might borrow it come bonfire night, put mulled wine in there.'

'That sounds good.' She let Jennifer slot it away and retrieve the bread maker. 'I've got my parents over for dinner tonight so I'm going to wow them with freshly baked dinner rolls. Last time I had them over it was lunch so it was a fresh loaf with homemade soup.' She reeled off her menu choices, the slow-cooked lamb, the glazed honey carrots, a dessert of pavlova she'd managed to perfect over the years. She was rambling but all she kept thinking was, should I tell her about the Parker family? Does she already know? Will she hate me for saying anything?

'It all sounds amazing, say hello to both of them from me.'

'I will do.' She caught sight of the poster on the wall by the desk advertising Isla's dance classes. 'Adam seemed to enjoy the dancing the other night.'

Jennifer's head snapped up. 'Why, what did he say?'

'Nothing, I bumped into Elaine and she told me he was in his element, one of the naturals.' Was it the dancing that was a sore subject? Or Adam?

'Isla had them all eating out of her hand I'm sure.'

When Jennifer made a funny sound, she asked, 'Is anything wrong? Between you and Isla, I mean.'

'No more than usual.'

Viola left the bread maker where it was on the desk, and took a seat opposite Jennifer. She didn't say anything; in fact it was Jennifer who spoke first.

'I worry about her getting involved with Adam.'

'Why are you worried?' Did she know something?

'She's flighty, and I'm concerned she'll get bored and leave Cloverdale.'

So nothing to do with the truth then. And Viola hadn't missed the way Jennifer acted around Adam. She suspected her friend's feelings ran deeper than they should. 'They're both adults, and for what it's worth, Isla seems to be settling in.' She hesitated before asking, 'Are you worried Isla will hurt Adam and at the same time ruin your friendship?'

It took Jennifer a while to say anything at all but when she did she admitted, 'I'm worried she'll lead him on and then when she's had enough I'll be left to pick up the pieces. He's a friend, a good one.'

'And you're sure that's all it is?'

Jennifer snapped into defensive mode. 'Of course. What are you trying to say?'

But their conversation was cut short when Zoe came in.

'I've come to borrow something called loppers.' She pulled a face and made them both laugh.

'And you have no idea what they are,' Jennifer concluded as she went to grab them.

Viola explained. 'They're kind of like a big pair of scissors to reach tree branches that are high up, or far away, or tough and need something more than the smaller pruning instruments.'

'Makes sense. Dad wants to get rid of hanging branches that are getting in the way of us shutting the back door. He says if we leave it until next summer it'll take over.'

'Good thinking. Actually, I was going to text your dad to see if I can come over early evening on Friday.'

'I'll be home from netball around half past four.'

'Great.' Zoe seemed to enjoy her company, and now Viola knew more about the family, her motherly protective instincts had shot up.

'You're putting in the hours at Lilliput Cottage,' said Jennifer when Zoe went on her way. 'Zoe seems to like you.'

'She's a great kid.' Who'd most likely been through a time tougher than anyone in Cloverdale would realise. Since she'd read those words in the diary she'd been desperate to get hold of it again and read the entire thing. Perhaps getting the whole story might help her know what to do.

'They're a lovely family.'

'Sure, but how much do we really know about them?'

'I'm sure they've got their baggage, haven't we all? But I hope Adam sticks around.'

'You mean the family . . . you hope the family sticks around.'

'Same thing.' Irritated, Jennifer turned her focus back to the computer screen.

Viola took the finality of their conversation as a warning to keep her nose out and her cue to leave. And when she left with the bread maker she held on to the worry that her friend was getting closer to Adam than she should be. And she couldn't rid the thought from her mind as she prepared for her parents' visit, a tense occasion at the best of times.

Her parents' visit was civil enough, but Viola spent the entire time stressing whether the carrots were overcooked, the bread rolls tasted fresh enough, was the lamb tender or a little on the overdone side? Was the wine to their liking? Halfway through the meal Isaac sneaked a hand beneath the table and held her knee steady and until he'd done that she hadn't realised how worked up she was. She was constantly waiting for them to criticise something and breathed a huge sigh of relief when they left having not complained at all.

'They're older now,' Isaac said as they went up the stairs to bed. 'They've mellowed.'

'Perhaps.' She had a throbbing headache. She still felt like a child in their presence, expecting approval, being disappointed if she didn't get it. They'd set high standards for her growing up and now she was doing the same with her own children, but at least she was hands-on and involved in her kids' lives. She'd been left to her own devices and it still hurt all these years later.

'Did you tell your office not to expect Ava for work experience?' Isaac, down to his boxer shorts, climbed beneath the duvet, leaving her side of the bedding peeled back.

'No, of course not. It's a good position, she'll learn a lot.'

He sighed. 'You need to allow her some independence.'

'It'll be really hard to find something. I'm doing her a favour. She wouldn't even let me help her with her CV when I'm in Human Resources, for Christ's sake!'

When she climbed into bed, Isaac lay a hand over hers. 'Leave her, Viola. Let her do it. If she doesn't find anything, then we can jump in. Please.'

She was about to argue but didn't have the energy. She picked up the hardback she'd bought weeks ago and still hadn't read and tried to get into it but after five pages she realised she hadn't taken in a single word. Her mind was full, but this time it wasn't with her own kids but with the two who lived not too far from here. Zoe and Zac had a mum out there somewhere, a woman who'd been so very wronged at the hands of her husband. And the only reason she wasn't stepping in to keep those kids safe was because Adam seemed to dote on them both and they all seemed happy.

For now, she'd bide her time. She needed to read the rest of that diary and figure out what to do about the man Jennifer was getting closer to, the person Jennifer's sister was so taken with, and she needed this to not be something else that came between her and Jennifer, the friend she missed being so close to.

But if she ever got a whiff of Adam harming either of those kids, all bets would be off. She'd make the contents of that diary public knowledge and Adam Parker would have to pay for what he'd done.

Friday came and Viola spent the day at the Library of Shared Things, although all she wanted was for the hands on the clock to keep on turning so she could get over to the Parkers' cottage. In the morning, she chatted with Bill who hadn't come to borrow anything but he'd wanted to ask about winter berries and what would be best to use in a crumble if he were to try to make one. He also waxed lyrical about the sewing basics workshop he'd attended last week after finally getting up the nerve to join in. He told Viola all about the plush curtains he'd taken up by himself that now hung at his sitting room window. By mid-afternoon a few locals had passed by to say hello, although they were really looking for Jennifer who wouldn't be in until it was time to close for the day. Viola had booked the waffle maker out on the system for Freda Livingstone who'd really come in for a chin-wag, but didn't linger when Viola's short answers proved she wasn't really in the mood. A dull ache from last night's horrendous headache that had sent her down to the kitchen for paracetamol in the early hours, still pressed at her temples; thoughts still evaded her mind like poison ivy, multiplying.

When 4 p.m. finally came around, Viola drove over to Adam's, a ridiculously short distance from the Library of Shared Things, but she'd filled her car with everything she needed for the bedroom renovation.

Before she knocked on the door, she took a deep breath.

She was finding it increasingly difficult to be in Adam's company given what she knew, and what she had yet to find out . . . her suspicions that Jennifer was getting too close.

'Viola, come in.' He'd opened the door with his usual smile.

She was tempted to mutter, 'I know what you did, I know the type of man you are,' but resisted the urge, especially when Zoe came smiling along the hallway, a glass of milk in one hand, a slice of toast in the other.

'Zoe, I told you to use a plate,' Adam said gruffly and Viola wondered, was this it? Was this when he was going to lose his rag in front of her, over something as trivial as a few crumbs? But he didn't. He was clearly well versed in the game of pretence; he grabbed a plate from the kitchen and gave it to Zoe.

Viola supposed she had to give the man some credit. He treated his kids very well. Zoe's only real complaint about him had been that he was too protective. Not necessarily a bad thing. When Viola was Zoe's age, her parents hadn't been around like Adam was now, talking about the merits and pitfalls of multigrain bread with its bits that got stuck in his teeth. There'd been no idle chit-chat for Viola growing up. There'd been a clinically clean house when she'd come home after school, nutritionally sound foods filling the cupboards, and the only conversations they'd really had were about Viola's grades, whether she'd practised the piano enough to perfect her pieces before her music exam, and how many hours of homework she'd done. It had been all work and no play, and probably why their relationship now was so stilted and challenging.

'What's that you're holding?' Zoe finished her last crust and eyed the enormous bag Viola was carrying.

Viola set it down, her arms feeling the strain, and lifted out a framed print. 'I found it last week when I was passing a little gallery near work. I forgot to bring it last time. I think it'll fit in your bedroom and if you'd prefer not to have it, I'll keep it.'

Zoe gave her empty plate to her dad, having already devoured her toast, and picked up the picture. 'I love it.' Inside the white frame was a print of a heart made up of different flowers. When Viola had seen it, it had been a toss-up of whether Zoe would see it as an ancient relic or very on trend. Luckily it seemed to be the latter.

'I think the colours will go well with your bedroom.' She was aware of Adam watching their exchange and felt uncomfortable beneath his scrutiny. 'We're only putting colour on one wall so this will add a little something extra. How about we work out where to put it now? And no extra charge; it's all in the budget.'

Adam went back into the kitchen and a sense of relief washed over her. She took a special tool out of her bag. 'It's a cable detector,' she explained to an inquisitive teen, 'so I don't drill a hole through wires, metal or studs.'

'Sounds like a good idea to me,' Adam called out to them, eavesdropping. 'I don't fancy the electricity going, not now we're coming into winter.'

When he emerged from the kitchen, Viola said, 'You'll be feeling the cold after all that time in Australia.' Her voice almost challenged him to give extra details about his life before London, before Cloverdale.

'I found it freeeeeeeeeeeezing last year.' Zac scuttled past them in the hallway, skidded through the kitchen in his socks and the sound of rustling suggested he was looking for something to eat too.

Zoe took the picture upstairs and when Viola took off her shoes, ready to follow, Adam was still hovering. 'What else is in there?' He indicated her bag.

'Everything a DIY person needs . . . a screwdriver set, hooks, nails, brushes, varnish. I think this evening we'll concentrate on getting that picture in the right place, maybe see if I can do the shelving.' She was prattling on but didn't meet his eye, instead rummaging in her plastic caddy where she kept all her bits and bobs for things like this.

He leaned against the bottom bannister, relaxed but with an edge of nervousness about him. 'Is everything OK?'

'Of course. I'm tired, that's all.'

Would he lose it with her if he knew she'd read that diary?

Probably.

'Then take a break. Zoe is fine in the box room for a while longer.'

'I like to see a job through.' And with that she waited for him to move aside and disappeared off up the stairs.

Viola scanned the bedroom walls thinking about where best to put the picture and settled on the area next to where the door opened. 'This way it'll be visible from the bed, and also when you enter the room.' She admired the picture again. 'It's a great injection of our lavender colour.'

'Can I use the cable detector to check?'

Viola loved how involved Zoe was. She wanted to keep this girl close until she knew what to do with the knowledge she'd gained. She gave Zoe a brief overview of the handheld tool and Zoe ran it flat across the wall they were interested in. It turned red near the light switch, she ran it further along and more red, some amber, but towards the centre she came to an area of green and Viola took out her pencil to mark the spot.

'Won't we paint over it?' Zoe was still having fun detecting metal, cables or any stud work behind the walls in the rest of the bedroom regardless of whether they needed to or not.

'I'll drill the hole before I paint. Actually, talking about painting, would you mind if I got started tomorrow morning? Are you guys around?'

'I'll be here; Dad is taking Zac to soccer practice.'

Perfect. She'd be able to talk to Zoe without Adam there, and perhaps even snatch a look at the diary she was desperate to get her hands on again. 'Nine o'clock all right with you?' She knew soccer practice wasn't too long after that; she'd heard Jennifer talking about it because Archie went too, and Jennifer had kissed goodbye to a restful weekend because one of the twins went to gymnastics on a Sunday.

'Bit early but yeah.' She pulled a face and Viola was reminded of Ava although Ava probably would've muttered under her breath and then said 'fine' with a lot more venom.

'Right, time to get another coat of white on these other walls.'

'Let's do it.' Zoe already had on an oversized shirt, one of Adam's old ones Viola presumed, and looked quite the part with a rag-like tie around her delicate strawberry-blonde hair.

Viola knew from the photograph that Zoe's mum

had blonde hair. Adam's was light brown and she wondered which parent had passed down the red gene. Maybe they'd passed down other genes too, genes far more worrying than hair colour. 'You do the second coat on this wall here where your desk will go, I'll do the second coat on the wall with the window. Unless you'd like to.'

'No way. With the big wall I get to use the roller.'

Viola opened the tin of paint, poured some into a tray for Zoe, more into a tray for herself. As a rule, her clients didn't help with the decorating, that was her department. But this was a special case. And if Adam was out tomorrow morning, all she needed to do was get Zoe busy doing something and she'd be able to look at the diary again. She'd been tempted to grab it and take it away but didn't want to risk it in case Adam went looking for it. Who knew whether he checked its presence every day out of habit, and she didn't want wind of him knowing she'd found it. What if he took the kids in the middle of the night and left? Maybe he'd done the same thing in London; perhaps that was why he was in Cloverdale in the first place. Had someone else discovered his guilty secret?

As Viola got down on her knees and used a brush and a steady hand, Zoe hummed away to Queen's 'Bohemian Rhapsody' – the girls had been to see the movie last week – and shunted the roller up and down the large wall, this way and that. 'Not too much paint, remember.' If Ava could see this she'd be shocked at how much control Viola was letting Zoe have. As a parent Viola hovered, not so much over Hazel, but definitely over Ava – homework, cooking, changing her bedroom furniture around – who was at such an impressionable age. Isaac had warned Viola about it more than once, saying she'd alienate her kids if she kept it up, but she couldn't stop herself. It was almost like she was repeating her parents' behaviour but trying to lavish love on her kids at the same time, and it was becoming a disaster. The recipe for perfect parenting definitely wasn't something she had any idea how to mix. It was as though she'd thrown a whole heap of baking powder into a cake recipe, which rose more and more with every passing day, and eventually the entire mixture that was her family would explode in her face.

Viola almost laughed at her own crazy analogy, but channelled her energies into the decorating, chatting away, moving about the space, treading carefully over the old sheets that covered a pretty perfect wooden floor. When it was eventually uncovered it was going to set off the new walls beautifully once she gave it a wet clean then a proper going over with special polish to give it a lift and fill in the micro scratches.

'Don't get me in the photographs!' Viola looked up to find Zoe snapping away. 'I've got a reputation to uphold.'

Zoe turned the phone her way. 'What do you think?'

Viola scrolled through a few. 'I'm surprised, they're not bad, probably because I wasn't aware of you taking them.'

'Sorry.'

'Don't be, natural shots are often the best. The picture of me painting beneath the windowsill is good; you've captured the debris in the room, the sheets on the floor. It'll make a brilliant part of the "before" collage I can put together and use on my website.'

'Really?'

'If you're happy for me to do it. It's not like I'll put your address on there.'

'Will it be OK for me to show people at school?'

'Of course.'

'You might get a lot more girls my age wanting your services.'

'Sounds like a win-win situation.' Even though she'd tied her hair back, tendrils had a habit of escaping and she tucked a blonde curl behind her ear. She'd loathed her curly hair as a youngster, and hated the way it got so knotty. She'd longed for straight hair but had learnt to embrace what she'd been given as she got older.

'I don't know why Ava moans about you so much, you're pretty relaxed.' As soon as Zoe uttered the words, she caught herself. 'I mean . . . well . . .'

'It's all right. She's my daughter, and mums and daughters rarely see eye to eye in the teenage years. I certainly didn't with mine.' Or in adulthood for that matter. And now she'd put her foot in it because, although Zoe smiled back at her, her face fell, the disappointment evident that she couldn't draw such a comparison.

Adam's voice came up the stairs to tell them he was going out for milk and would be back in twenty minutes. After he'd left and Viola was rinsing her paintbrush off in the jar of water safely tucked by the windowsill so neither of them kicked it over, she told Zoe, 'You can talk about your mum . . . you know, if you'd like to.' It was a risk, mentioning her, but one she was willing to take.

Zoe didn't say anything for a while and just when Viola was about to take the roller and paint tray downstairs for cleaning, she said simply, 'I miss her.' She sat down on one of the closed paint tins.

Viola sat on the floor next to Zoe. 'Don't you have any contact with her at all?' This was dangerous ground. How much should she push it?

'Dad won't like me talking about it.' She'd reverted to a sheepish teenager, unsure of sharing her feelings.

'There's no harm in talking and what we discuss in this room won't go any further, I promise. I won't tell Ava, not your dad, not a soul.'

It took Zoe a while to weigh up whether talking was a good idea. Eyes downcast, picking at her thumbnail on one hand, she said, 'I haven't seen Mum for more than three years. Not since we left Australia.'

'Three years is an awfully long time.'

'She had some kind of breakdown.'

'I'm sorry, I didn't realise.' From what Viola had read, she wasn't surprised.

'She didn't want to be a parent anymore. She told us. I still remember that day.' Tears spilled from her eyes. 'I wasn't good enough for her to want me.'

'I doubt that's true.'

'Whenever I try to ask Dad about her, he changes the subject, says she was sick. He must mean in the head.'

'He can't ignore your questions forever.' As Zoe got older she'd have more rights and be able to find out the truth herself, but when you were a teen, adulthood seemed a long way off. She remembered when she'd been this age and wanted to get out into the big wide world, get a job, prove herself.

'Aren't you going to tell me that my dad wants the best for me?'

'Well . . .'

'I knew it. That's what all adults say.'

'I really don't know your dad well enough to understand why he doesn't want to talk to you about your mum.' Although she knew more than most people around here and possibly more than Zoe did. 'But I can say, honestly, that he is a good dad.' That much was clear. The kids were loved, they were well looked after; it was the secrets hidden beneath that would do the most damage when they came to light. 'Does Zac ask about your mum?'

'Not really. Maybe because he's a boy or because he was a lot younger when we left. I doubt he'd remember her like I do.'

'And what do you remember about her?'

'Not as much as I'd like.'

'There must be something.' Oh, how she wished Ava would open up to her like this, treat her as a sounding board when she needed it, have an in-depth discussion about anything.

Zoe sniffed away her tears. 'I do remember how she liked to surprise us. One time, she picked me and Zac up from school but we didn't drive home to the house and when we asked where we were going she kept saying it was a secret. We ended up at the beach, and even though it was winter we were allowed to take our shoes and socks off and tiptoe through the surf. Our feet were covered in sand.' Her eyes lit up, her smile brightened the room more than the sunshine filtering through the glass devoid of any window covering. 'Zac got it all in the footwell of the car and Mum joked that he could build another sandcastle with the amount he'd collected. We stopped for ice creams on the way home, I had rum and raisin, and thought I was so grown-up with an alcoholic flavour.'

'See, and I bet you'll remember so much more about your mum if you try really hard.'

'I looked for her, you know.' Zoe didn't meet her gaze. 'I think that's why Dad didn't want me using social media, in case I found her.' She looked as though she was waiting for Viola to berate her for abusing the trust she'd begged to have. 'I searched for her name.' She bit on the side of her bottom lip.

'What did you find?' She tried to sound nonchalant, but her heart was thudding; she was desperate to know more.

'Nothing. I mean, she probably doesn't even use it. It's not every adult's thing. It's not Dad's; he's rubbish at it.' She allowed a giggle to escape and her demeanour told Viola that whatever else Adam had done, he hadn't hurt his kids. At least not physically. 'He's put up a video clip of him dancing with Isla.' She covered her face as she said it, as though to hide the embarrassment.

This girl loved her dad, which was what made the truth so hard to fathom. It would crush Zoe to find out what Viola had discovered. What sort of man kept his kids from their own mother? Viola couldn't process it at all. Every girl needed their mother, didn't they? As much as her own kids pushed her away the best they could, she knew even they'd admit they needed her.

Zoe turned serious again. 'I felt terrible looking for her. Like I was betraying Dad.' They both heard the door go downstairs as Adam returned with the milk and Zoe went straight back to decorating. 'I can't wait for this to all be finished.' Just like that she'd withdrawn from the conversation in typical teen fashion. But it was a start. She was talking, and Viola knew eventually she'd get to the bottom of all this and unravel the mystery about the Parker family.

Until then she'd snatch glances at the diary whenever she could and she'd be the safety net for Zoe and Zac if everything fell apart. She'd be there for Jennifer too, who would eventually have to find out the truth.

Because no matter how much you tried to hide it, secrets always had a way of coming out.

14

Jennifer

In the Library of Shared Things, Jennifer kept the yellow doors well and truly shut as the autumn winds whipped around the car park, leaves skittering. Today, she was wearing a cosy roll-neck jumper, jeans, and boots, but she had a scarf on the back of her chair in case she needed it and she'd also pulled out the portable oil radiator for a bit of extra heat.

A text came through from Adam and she wheeled the radiator closer to her legs to warm up as she read his text.

Adam: How's operation Jennifer's hair?

His texts were a little flirty, or was she reading too much into it? Whatever; she was enjoying herself. It was a relief from thinking about her strained relationship at home with David, how she still hadn't broached the subject of starting up her hairdressing again. It wasn't like he was a 1950's husband thinking she should be chained to the kitchen sink, but he'd be worried, she knew that. And why wouldn't he be after the mess she'd made before?

Jennifer: You make it sound like I'm trying to think of a new style for myself, like a teenager getting ready for a party.

Adam: Your style is fine as it is.

Jennifer: Fine? Now my Auntie Dotty has 'fine' hair, and Elaine has a 'fine' style when she comes in here after her regular weekly cut and blow dry. I'm offended!

Adam: Don't be! I wouldn't change a thing . . . rather than fine, I meant fabulous, wonderful, stylish. Am I making it worse?

She laughed out loud until Viola poked her head around the door and Jennifer dropped her phone on the desk like a hot potato.

'Not interrupting, am I?' Viola quickly shut the door behind her. She blew into her hands, rubbed them together, and came closer to the heater. 'When did autumn get here?'

Jennifer switched her phone to silent when it bleeped again to indicate another text from Adam. Viola had come to pick up the drill so she found the item and handed over the container. 'What do you need it for today?'

'Zoe's bedroom.'

'Oh, but Adam's at football today.'

'I know. I'll get far more done with people out of the way.' She handed Jennifer the payment. 'How's Archie? Elaine told me she was helping at the school and he'd been in a fight.'

'Typical, and I bet she made it sound worse than it was.'

'What happened?'

'Another child pushed Archie over in the playground and Zac came to the rescue, but all three of them ended up in a fist fight. For little boys!'

'Did you tell David?'

'I did but all he said was boys will be boys and it was better than the bitchiness with girls; we had plenty of that when the twins were younger.'

'I guess he's got a point. But it's still serious.'

'I know. Adam understood. We talked to the boys together and explained behaviours, expectations. Although Adam admitted after they'd gone upstairs to play that he wanted to teach Zac how to punch properly so he could stand up for himself.'

'I'm not sure that's the answer.'

Viola had one of her disapproving looks on again so Jennifer turned to file away the papers left in the in-tray on top of the desk. 'I'd better get on.'

'Sure. Oh, I saw Adam's video on Instagram. He's quite the dancer. The lessons you're running here must be working wonders.'

Jennifer tried not to let it show she was bothered about her sister and her good friend getting up close and personal.

'They look good together, don't you think?'

'Isla's a good teacher.' Maybe they did look good together, but friends and family getting involved always got messy, and she didn't want to have to pick up the pieces when Isla moved on to the next person, place or thing that caught her eye.

When Jennifer gave her nothing else in the way of gossip about Adam or Isla, Viola told her she'd bring the drill back later on and she left the Library of Shared Things, shutting the door on the blustery day once again.

Jennifer busied herself running the place. She sent a reminder to Fiona from the corner shop, who'd forgotten to return the bread maker, she replied to the email from a local garden centre to confirm the discount they'd secured on another gazebo after their existing one had begun to show signs of wear and tear now that it was being used so frequently. As well as the dance classes, it had been loaned out yesterday for an eighteenth birthday party and got caught in the wind, leaving the canopy marked on top of its cream finish.

Fiona didn't take long to return the bread maker, apologising profusely that she'd not brought it in yesterday but her husband thought she was taking care of it and vice versa. Items came and went, people gathered for chatter and Jennifer offered tea and biscuits to anyone who popped in.

Isla poked her head around the yellow door. 'Wow, it smells good in here.'

'That'll be Carmen's cinnamon loaf cake.' Don't think about Adam, don't think about the dancing, don't think full stop.

Isla was carrying a container and resting it on the top of an uplifted knee; she shut the door behind her. 'Any left?'

'Sorry, her son hoovered up any leftovers when her back was turned.'

'I'll time it better next time.' She handed the container

to Jennifer. 'I saw Zoe outside and said I'd return this on behalf of Viola.'

Jennifer checked everything was clean and intact, and returned the drill to its rightful slot in the hutch against the wall.

'Is everything all right?' Isla asked as Jennifer updated the item as returned on the computer system.

'Of course.' Isla reminded Jennifer of the way she'd been as a little girl when she'd asked her the question. Usually it was after she'd gone into her bedroom without permission and borrowed some make-up or when she'd been home late and got in trouble with their parents and Jennifer had only been able to cast disapproving looks her way.

'You look like something's bothering you.'

Where would she start if she had to make a list of everything that had got under her skin lately? It was best to simply change the subject. 'It's nothing. How's your house coming along?'

She accepted the change of subject readily. 'Great, and it's cosy now the log burner is in to replace the ugly heater.'

'I'm glad. And well done with your dance classes; they've been really popular. Feedback has been very positive.'

'Adam seems to enjoy them.'

Jennifer picked up her mug from the table. Time for another cup of tea perhaps.

'You don't seem keen on me being friends with him.' Isla's voice followed her out to the kitchen where she flicked on the kettle.

'You're both free agents.'

'You're not denying it.'

'It's none of my business who you spend time with.'

'But you'd rather I didn't. Is it because you're worried I'm going to skip town as soon as I can?'

She'd bitten her tongue until now, but she was tired of doing so. 'You'll get bored. I know you will and you'll move on again, like you always do.'

'Why do you always assume the worst of me? We all make mistakes.'

Jennifer bristled because she knew exactly what Isla was getting at.

When Phil, Jennifer's neighbour, interrupted them to borrow the projector in time for a family get together tonight, Jennifer forgot about making tea and carried on, business as usual, checking out the item and making polite conversation.

'This isn't about you,' Jennifer assured Isla once Phil had left them to it. 'It's about Adam. I saw you dancing together, you know.'

'So what. We're both single. I don't see the problem.'

'He's a friend; he hasn't been in Cloverdale all that long and I don't want to lose the friendship. The boys get on well; in fact Archie has never had such a close friend as he has with Zac. I don't want to see anyone in the family hurt.'

'So you're more worried about them than your own sister?'

'You know I always put family first.'

Isla shook her head in disbelief. 'And there it is, yet another dig, another way to point out that I never do.'

'Don't be so paranoid.'

Isla opened her mouth to say something else but instead said, 'You know, Mum and Dad always wanted us to stay close to each other. I wish we didn't fight so much.'

'You started it.' But she smiled, and it jolted Jennifer's

memory back to their childhood again and arguing in front of their parents, how their dad had said he wanted to knock their heads together sometimes.

'I thought we were getting back to some kind of normal after I came for dinner at yours.'

'We were,' said Jennifer. 'We *are*.'

'I really like him, Jennifer.'

Jennifer swallowed hard. 'Adam is a kind, gentle man, but, Isla, he has two kids.'

'And . . . ?'

'You don't like kids. What I mean is, you don't want your own.'

'Right, so based on the fact that I'm not married at thirty-six and don't have any kids, you're concluding that I don't like them and never wanted them?'

'You seem suited to a life with no ties, no permanency.' She put her hand on her sister's arm before she could get up and leave. 'I don't mean to sound bitchy or condescending, but I've always thought you enjoyed the free and single life. You never once said you wanted to settle; that's why I keep questioning it.' She let go of her sister's arm when Isla relaxed into her chair once again. 'Why didn't you come home when Mum was sick? You left it all up to me.'

'You said at the time that there was no point me coming back here too. You said you had it all in hand. I felt as though I'd be in the way.'

'What? That's a load of rubbish and you know it.'

'Is it? I'd come home for a visit and each time wondered should I stay longer, but you made it pretty clear you had everything in hand. And to be honest, I felt suffocated by your perfection!'

'Isla, you're being ridiculous.'

'I came home a lot during that time, I helped as much as I could, but my life wasn't here then. And there are things you don't know about me, Jennifer.'

'Then tell me. Because your life has always seemed so exciting to me. Why would you want to return to Cloverdale and live the same way as I do, why the sudden interest in a family man like Adam? Is it because you don't want to be alone?' Jennifer could tell that as soon as she finished her spiel, she'd lost Isla. She hadn't meant to sound quite so accusatory but the words were out before she had a chance to dilute them or filter them into something not quite so venomous.

Face like thunder, Isla stood up. 'You think I'm desperate and clinging to anyone who comes my way, is that it?'

'Of course not.'

'You always were jealous of me. Sod envious, it's out and out jealousy.'

'What? That's ridiculous.' Jennifer stood to meet her match.

'You've always been the same way. And you're hardly perfect yourself!'

'I don't claim to be, and the mistakes I made were a long time ago. Stop bringing it up; we've all moved on.'

'Have you? I mean, you've never let Viola forget what happened between the two of you.'

'That has nothing to do with this.'

'It has everything to do with this. You expect perfection from others, want them all to do what you think is the right thing. And if they don't, then they must be wrong, they must be up to no good.'

'I think you'd better leave.'

She didn't make a move. 'You should have a think about your friendship with Adam.'

'What the hell is that supposed to mean?'

'You're jealous of me and Adam. I saw it in your eyes the other night when we were dancing. At first I thought you were being protective and not wanting me to hurt him, but now I think your feelings run beyond friendship.'

'Isla, you need to go.'

'Hit a nerve, have I?'

'Go!' Her heart thumped at her chest, her voice sounded like it hadn't come from her at all.

'I'm going, don't worry.'

Isla's words echoed around the walls long after she walked away. She was right. And Jennifer had been kidding herself that her feelings weren't beginning to stray beyond the boundaries of friendship. She was getting out of her depth.

But she wasn't a cheater. She never had been. Since she'd married David she'd never contemplated the thought of anyone else and somehow her feelings about Adam had crept up on her when she wasn't looking.

And what that meant for her marriage, she had no idea.

An emotional affair could be as damaging as a physical one. That was the gist from what Jennifer had read. As soon as she got home she'd felt so confused that she'd ended up looking online for advice, cautionary tales from other women who had found themselves in the same situation as she was, good friends with a man they weren't married to, and turning to him for support, the bond and often a dependency growing stronger and creeping up on them unexpectedly.

Isla's accusations had got to her and when Adam texted to ask if he could keep Archie a while longer because he and Zac were having fun playing in the park, she replied that of course it was fine, and then she shut herself in the bathroom for a long soak. Adam had asked whether everything was OK when she returned texts with one-word answers or two or three at best. Usually she would've made the conversation last longer, made a joke, but now it all felt so confusing, so wrong. An innocent friendship had morphed into something else without any warning and she hadn't put a stop to it.

She lay soaking in the bath thinking about some of the articles she'd found online. There were phrases that resonated far too closely. How emotional distance with a spouse could increase the more a relationship with some-one else developed. How channelling energy whether physical or emotional into someone other than your spouse could be detrimental, how a connection between two people didn't have to be physical to be strong, pow-erful and ultimately damaging. The stories had been told by ordinary women, wives, mothers, women just like her.

The heat of the water finally exhausted her and she climbed out of the bath, wrapped herself in the fluffy soft-grey towel.

When David came into the bathroom, surprised to see her, he asked where Archie was.

'He's still with Zac.' She watched him root around in the top drawer of the vanity unit.

'I thought football was this morning.'

'It was, but you know what they're like. They're at the park now. What are you looking for?'

He pulled out a razor and then collected up his tooth-brush, a new tube of toothpaste stashed in the cupboard beneath, his wash bag. 'I've got to go up to Nottingham tonight.'

'But it's a weekend.'

When he looked at her, she could see tiredness in him too. How had she thought it was only her? He had the hint of bags forming beneath his eyes – he'd never had those before – and his shoulders slumped as though the weight of their lives had found him as well.

'I'm sorry, I got the email on my way back from the office.' He'd already been in catching up on paperwork and meeting with a colleague to discuss the way forward at another important meeting next week. Jennifer used to ask all about it but these days she'd lost interest. 'I'll be back Monday night if that helps.' He'd shoved everything into his wash bag and set it down on the edge of the bath. 'We're OK, aren't we?'

'Huh?'

'Us, Jennifer. Are we OK?' He reached out a hand to toy with the wet strands of her hair, causing a shiver to cascade its way down over her body.

'Of course we are. You're away too much, that's all.'

He took his hand away and turned to leave. 'Please don't have a go at me again.'

'Since when do I have a go at you?' She followed him into the bedroom and wondered, was his mind on some-one else just as hers had been? Or worse, was he involved with someone? The question was out before she could stop herself. 'Are you telling me everything?'

'What are you on about?' He'd taken two fresh shirts out from the wardrobe and laid them on the bed before selecting a couple of ties from the special hanger she'd bought him years ago when they first moved in here.

'It seems odd you're working at a weekend.'

'I don't do it all the time.' He began loading things into his overnight holdall, another thing she'd sought and given him, ever eager to keep her family organised and happy, not thinking of herself and what she needed. 'Hang on, what do you mean, have I told you everything?'

'Who are you going with?'

'The usual . . . Max, Brian, maybe a couple of others. Wait . . . are you asking what I think you're asking?'

'Ignore me.' She was letting her own behaviour influence her questioning of her husband, the man who'd never betrayed her.

'No, Jennifer. I won't ignore you.' He'd followed her back into the bathroom where she rinsed the bath using the shower attachment to rid it of the oil. 'This is exactly why I'm asking whether we're OK, because lately I don't think that we are.'

It hit her like a bullet, realising he might be as unhappy as she was, carrying the same element of doubt. She put the shower attachment back in its holder. 'I miss you, that's all.'

With a sigh he drew her into his arms. 'I miss you too. But my job is the reason we're so comfortable, the kids get to do their activities, you get to stay at home, you get to concentrate on the Library project. You've done a great job there. I'm proud of you.' He took her by the hand, through to the bedroom and they sat on the bed.

Now was her moment, the time to tell him she wanted to get her own career started up again. 'I loved staying at home when the kids were young,' she began.

'I know you did. Where are the twins anyway?'

'They're out shopping; they'll be back for dinner.'

'We have the house to ourselves.'

'We do.'

Neither of them said anything until he turned to her, a smile that left no doubt as to what he was thinking, because not only did they not talk enough these days, they weren't intimate either, and when they were it was usually rushed, done with one eye on the door in case the kids came in.

'Archie could be dropped back here any second,' she protested, although her body had already begun to betray her as he kissed her neck delicately at first until she moaned and made it obvious how welcome this was.

He tugged at the knot at the top of her towel, using his weight to ease her back on the bed, his cooler skin meeting hers, still warm from the bath. Talk would have to wait because this felt good, better than it had in a long time.

'I'm going to show you how much I'll miss you when I'm away.' He trailed kisses along her collar bone, further down, across her tummy and around her belly button, lower, and for the time being she forgot about anyone or anything outside of her marriage.

So she had a friend who was male . . . it didn't mean anything, especially not when she and her husband were making love and David was touching her in all the places he'd discovered and come to know so well over the years.

Isla was wrong. This was what she wanted. David. Not

Adam. And she wanted a marriage, with all its good and bad parts.

She was happily married and intended to keep it that way, no matter what anyone else thought.

15

Viola

'Right, where were we?' Viola pushed open the door to Zoe's bedroom. She'd been for a much-needed bathroom break and as she went into the room Zoe was pricking her finger with a little device. 'Everything all right?' She held up her hands in defence. 'I'm not fussing, just asking, that's all.'

'I'm checking my levels. You don't need to worry about me, I've been doing it a while now.' She put her blood testing kit away and zipped up the case.

'I'm not worried that you don't know what you're doing; I'm worried I'm taking advantage and making you do too much.'

'I'm not an invalid.'

'Then I apologise for mentioning it.' She began using the masking tape to run along the top of the skirting board to protect it from the lavender paint they were about to put on the wall. 'I've never had a right-hand man – or woman – when I've worked before. Usually I'm in my own little world as I decorate and whoever it's for is usually only interested in the final outcome.'

'Am I in the way?'

The panicked look on Zoe's face had Viola striding over

to her, the roll of tape dangling from her fingers. She put an arm around her and hugged her tight like she'd do with Ava if she'd only let her. 'It's amazing to have the help and the constant input. I don't mind one bit, you hear me?'

Zoe nodded and, convinced, she helped Viola tape the rest of the skirting board. 'I'm looking forward to seeing the lavender on the wall.'

'Doing the one wall will be a powerful contrast with the white and still make the room feel spacious.' The other walls were looking good already, but even Viola was excited about adding in a bit of colour now.

'Thanks again for the painting.' Zoe looked up at the hole drilled in the wall. 'It's going to look so cool in here. I'll have to persuade Dad to buy me some new bedding.'

'No need. Soft furnishings were included in my price.' Her comment got a beam of a smile. 'Right, I think we're ready to start.'

'I'll need to eat first.'

'No worries.'

'Would you like lunch?'

Viola smiled. Zoe sounded so grown-up acting the hostess. 'I actually didn't bring anything today, I thought I could power on through, but I am a little hungry.'

Zoe's phone pinged. 'Let me check this; it's from Dad.' She read and then recounted the message. 'He's taken the boys to a park and they're having lunch out, says there isn't anything here for us but I can go to the bakery and he'll pay me back.' She rolled her eyes. 'He's not really on top of the supermarket shop every week. I could go buy some bread and make beans and cheese on toast.' She thought for a moment. 'I might need to go to the corner shop for the cheese and beans though.'

'It sounds wonderful.' And when Viola's tummy growled, they both laughed.

'You go and make a cup of tea and I'll be, like, twenty minutes.'

'I'll carry on.'

'Not without me; I want to see the colour when it first goes on.'

'Then I'll put my feet up, but don't tell your dad.' She wondered what he might do if she put a foot wrong. When Jennifer told her the other day that Adam had wanted to teach his son to punch properly after a scuffle in the playground, Viola had thought how typical of him to turn to violence and try to pass on tips to Zac.

Zoe trotted down the stairs and after another couple of minutes Viola heard the front door slam and she knew she had her chance.

She went downstairs, ensured the front door was shut and Zoe was definitely gone, and, heart thumping inside her chest, went into the utility room, grabbed the steps, climbed up and pulled out the diary. She took it into the lounge so she'd be able to see when Zoe came back, or Adam for that matter. And she flipped the pages to find the last place she'd left it. But after reading two sentences she knew what to do. She ran back upstairs, grabbed her phone and snapped photographs of each and every page of this distressing read she didn't want to process but knew she had to.

She finished, checked the photos and that she could zoom in and still read the writing well enough and then returned the diary to its hiding place. Back in the kitchen she flicked on the kettle to make it look as though she'd been relaxing with a cup of tea all along rather than snooping into the Parker family's private business.

'I'm back!' Zoe hollered when she came through the door a few minutes later. She came into the kitchen and plonked two carrier bags on the benchtop. 'Did you have a bit of time to relax?'

'I did.' Relax? She was so far away from being chilled out. She felt as though all the fibres of her being had been scrunched up into one big ball and it was an effort to force a smile, to give this girl a sense of equilibrium she very much needed. Because Viola hadn't only taken the photographs, she'd glimpsed some of the words in the entries, and what she'd found hadn't been nice at all.

'I'll just run up to the bathroom and then take my insulin, then we'll cook,' Zoe gushed, operating at full speed ahead like most teens.

She left Viola drinking her cuppa and unpacking the contents of the carrier bag.

'I know it's not gourmet,' said Zoe when she came back, 'but beans are kind of nice, especially with melted cheese on top.'

'What can I do?'

Zoe patted the top of a big fat bloomer loaf. 'Slice this for toast?'

Viola took charge of the breadknife and when she went to cut the bread, Zoe kept insisting she go bigger, then bigger still. They toasted the enormous doorsteps and added butter then put them beneath the heat again and with the cheese grated, the beans warmed, they sat down to a lunch that was more about the process of pulling it all together between them than its gourmet rating.

As they ate, Viola found herself having to remember

this was her daughter's best friend. She wondered, did Ava get on with other people's mothers? Why did teens prefer other parents to their own? She'd always vowed to be the parent her kids wanted to be seen with, wanted to talk to, but maybe it was one of life's cruel jokes that it was an impossible feat and she should give up now.

Viola wished her own parents had done this with her. They never had. They'd both worked long hours, and she and her brother had been given independence early on with the emphasis on not abusing it or messing up. They'd been model kids, but she'd missed the simplicity of having something as easy as beans on toast for lunch, laughing at the size of the bread, not caring that a messy pan with tomato sauce dripping down the side was on the cooker and making a mess of that too. There'd been no mess in her house growing up and she'd been programmed to stay that way as an adult.

Viola finished her meal, full from the bread that was probably four times the usual portion she'd eat. And as she took her plate to the sink she caught sight of a photo pinned to the fridge. It was a black and white print of Adam, the top of his light brown hair blowing in a breeze, his arms around both kids' shoulders. Zac and Zoe were grinning, Zac missing his two front teeth, which had been replaced now so that you'd never know. 'Where was the picture taken?' she asked.

Zoe took her own plate to the sink. 'That was our first weekend in London. We went on the London Eye, saw the Houses of Parliament, walked beside the Thames. We're laughing in the photo because Zac told us he liked England because when he woke in the mornings there was a "nice fresh breeze".'

Viola laughed out loud. 'It would be a bit of a contrast to Australian weather, for sure.'

'Melbourne did get quite cold in the winter. I had a winter coat, gloves, scarf.'

'I can't imagine it. My impression of Australia is all surfing, beaches and sun.' She contemplated whether to ask the next question and decided to go for it. 'Is your mum from Melbourne?'

'Mum was born in Melbourne. Dad loved it there. We all did.' She hesitated. 'I still don't understand why we had to leave.'

'Life can be complicated, I suppose. Come on, let's go and get on with the room.'

That seemed to put a smile back on Zoe's face.

Back upstairs Zoe opened the lavender paint and stirred it with the stick. She picked up the roller. 'Can I start?'

Seeing Zoe go from helplessness whenever they brought up the subject of her mum to joy when she was up here was enough. 'Go for it.' She ran her hand over some of the cracks and holes she'd filled with Polyfilla and sanded over, to check they were as good as could be. 'Not too much paint on the roller remember.'

Viola watched Zoe load up the roller, reiterated the need to not cover too big a space and to do her best to overlap wet paint each time so they didn't end up with marks. She was tempted more than once to say 'give it here, my turn', but she could see and hear how much Zoe was enjoying this, she was humming away to a tune Viola recognised as blaring from her own daughter's room although she couldn't identify the band playing. She used a brush and followed Zoe, getting the sections the roller didn't quite reach. They made quite a team, both in men's old shirts, covered in paint splotches.

'We'll do the other coat on Monday night if you're around,' said Viola as they made progress.

'I can't wait.'

Zoe concentrated on the task, still humming away, Viola touched up edges carefully and neither of them noticed time marching on or that Adam had come home and into the room. Not until Zoe looked over Viola's shoulder and said, 'Hey, Dad.'

'Ladies.'

'Hi, Adam. What do you think of the colour?' Keep it polite, keep it normal.

'Bit feminine for me, but perfect for my Zoe.' He winked in her direction and Viola was amazed to see Zoe smile back at him. If she or Isaac had done that to Ava in front of someone else, Ava would've freaked and most likely told them how inappropriate they were being. Ava was a normal teen. Zoe wasn't. But then Ava came from a stable home where she knew what was what.

'I was suggesting to Zoe that I come back on Monday to do the second coat.' Viola, brush in hand, was following Zoe's work to ensure the paint didn't have time to start drying before she blended the roller areas with the brush areas.

'That suits us. I'll be home around seven.'

'Perfect.'

When he went downstairs Viola stood back after touching up the last section and, alongside Zoe with the roller still in her hand, they admired their handiwork. 'It looks great. The colour is perfect. We'll do the second coat and then later this week we'll do the coving.'

Zoe put down the roller in the tray and then turned around on the spot.

'What are you up to?'

'Imagining it all finished.'

'Not coping in the box room?'

'It's cramped. But it'll make me really appreciate in here. Ava's coming for a sleepover as soon as I'm in.' They'd agreed to buy a trundle for below her bed complete with extra mattress so she could have friends over.

'I'm sure she'll be looking forward to it.'

Zoe took out her phone and snapped a few more photographs. 'I'll put these on Insta, it's progress. Can I tag you?'

'Of course you can. It's all good business for me. Who knows, maybe one day I'll give up the office job and do this full-time.'

'Really?' Zoe slid her phone back into the rear pocket of her jeans.

'Why so surprised?'

She shrugged. 'Ava said you love work, and that you do lots of hours, that's all.'

'I think Ava sometimes forgets how much I'm at home.' She'd always made a point of not repeating her own parents' behaviour and, despite her respectable job with a handsome salary and her interior decorating work, she made herself available as much as she could, shuttling Ava and Hazel to their activities, being on hand for homework help, at the ready for cuddle time although that was something only Hazel went for these days.

'I'm sure she appreciates you.'

Viola wasn't so sure, given a lot of the communication was delivered in a series of grunts, but still, it was nice to be popular with someone. 'I'm sure she does.'

'I tell her she's lucky. You're strict but it's only because you care. Dad . . .'

Viola pushed the bedroom door closed after ensuring the only other people in the house were downstairs – she could hear Zac and Adam chatting in the kitchen, Zac declaring his hatred of all types of beans. 'Is your dad strict?'

'He can be. Like with the social media stuff.'

'Every parent has different rules.'

'I know, but I'm relieved I could have Instagram like my friends; I felt really left out.'

'I'm glad too. And your bedroom makeover has a lot of likes already.'

'It's going to look brilliant.' Zoe grinned.

'Who's Noah Brammers? He liked one of your photos earlier today.'

Zoe blushed. 'A boy in our year.'

'Nice?' OK, one probing question too far. 'And who's Stacey Reed? She's commented with an awful lot of exclamation marks. It's like she's shouting.'

'She's very creative, wins awards with her artwork. She's OK.'

'And who's Deedee Dwight?'

'She's new in our year. I thought she hated me. She was one of those people who stared when I was doing my insulin one day. I think she thought I was a druggie.'

'I don't think people assume that, do they?'

'You'd be surprised. One of the supply teachers came scurrying over to me last week when I was doing it. All flustered he was, spluttering questions. Didn't help that Noah Brammers had had a word in his ear and told him there was a girl shooting up in the playground.'

'The little troublemaker.'

'He's hardly little; he's almost six foot. And I suppose it was a little bit funny.'

She suspected Zoe had an enormous crush on this boy, but she wasn't going to pry. She put the lid on the tin of paint and sat on the floorboards with Zoe sitting in front of her, cross-legged.

'I hated being asked about my diabetes when I was first diagnosed. I tried to hide it. I wanted to be like everyone else and it made me different yet again. Do you know I'm the only one in my class whose parents don't live together?'

'There are plenty of girls your age whose parents have separated.'

'Not in my class. And I've got an Aussie accent, even though it's fading. Being different sucks sometimes.'

'It'd be a pretty boring world if we were all the same.'

Zoe toyed with the stick Viola had used to stir the paint. 'That's a parent comment designed to make me feel better.'

'Is everything OK at school? I know girls can be awful to one another at your age.'

'It's not too bad. It was nice to know Ava before my first day.'

'I'm glad.'

'There are a couple of not-so-nice girls in our year, but we stay away from people like Lucinda Hall.'

'Well she's been a bully since Ava started primary school. And I expect she always will be. She'll end up with no friends, that one. I'd steer clear if I were you.' She shuddered. 'Come on, we'd better get these things cleaned up ready for another day.' She got busy taking the brushes down to the utility room to give them a thorough wash through while Zoe got a bag to throw away the rubbish – offcuts of masking tape, the cellophane from a new paint brush, newspaper that was sodden after too many splashes from the jar of water used to rinse brushes right after painting.

Downstairs Adam was helping Zac with some home-work so conversation was minimal and after Viola shook the brushes dry she gave them a quick smile as she passed by and went back upstairs where she lay the brushes on a piece of newspaper in the bedroom.

'What's with the face?' She noticed Zoe wasn't smiling much anymore. Instead she was staring at her phone.

'Someone has liked my post on Instagram and followed me, but I don't know them.'

Viola's parent instincts cranked up a notch. 'You do have your account set to private, don't you?'

'Of course.'

'Zoe.' Not only did she have a built-in alert for some-thing amiss, she also had a pretty good radar when it came to lying. Isaac called it her bullshit detector, and said even he, a grown man, would never get away with telling fibs.

'I did, when I first set the account up.'

'You changed it.' She could tell from Zoe's face that yes, that was the case. 'Why? You do know that anyone can see your photos, learn about your life, get information, con-tact you. You're at risk of—'

Zoe cut her off. 'I did it in case my mum tried to get in touch.'

'Oh.' How should she handle this? 'But if it's been public for a while, why the surprise that someone new has liked your post? You must get plenty of random people doing so. It's a dangerous game.'

Zoe was staring at her phone. 'This person's name on Instagram is Suzie.' She looked up at Viola. 'Mum's name is Susan. What if it's her?'

Viola tried not to let it show but her heart was pumping overtime, her mouth dry. 'Do you think it could be?'

'I guess. But I never heard her called Suzie.'

'Is there a photo?' Viola could remember enough about the woman in the photograph that had fallen from the diary to know whether Zoe was on the right track.

'No. It's a kid's drawing.'

'Then it could be anyone.' And most likely was. If her mum wanted to get in touch she'd probably do something more than like a photograph and have a picture that didn't tell Zoe who she was. Maybe this was someone who wanted some interior design work done and had seen the progress shown in Zoe's photographs. She'd uploaded enough of them and added a whole series of hashtags to give the post more visibility.

'Click on their profile,' Viola suggested. 'Does it tell you anything?'

'It's set to private.' Zoe's finger hovered over the 'follow back' icon. 'What should I do?'

'I think you should be careful. Not having your account set to private . . . it's risky, Zoe.'

All of a sudden Zoe burst into tears and Viola pulled her into a hug. 'Come on, what's all this? Is it because you think you're in trouble for fiddling with your account? Because you think I'll tell your dad?' She felt hot tears land against the collar of her shirt and held Zoe, listened to the murmurs of a distressed teen.

'No, it's not that.' She clung onto Viola for dear life. 'I miss her. I miss her so much. I want my mum.'

It was all Viola could do not to take her home with her there and then.

At home Viola poured herself a generous glass of wine as Isaac finished making his cup of coffee and came over to kiss her on the cheek. She leaned against his warmth.

'You look tired,' he said.

'Thanks.'

'I mean it in the nicest possibly way.'

She looked up at him. Her husband, loyal to a fault, loving and devoted, was right there and she very nearly told him everything, about the man in Cloverdale who hid a past nobody would approve of, how she'd nearly offered Zoe and Zac a safe place to stay to get them away from a man none of them should trust.

But she couldn't. She wanted to bide her time. Keep her friends close and her enemy closer. And she wasn't only thinking about the Parkers. She was thinking about Jennifer and how she'd once interfered and made a total mess of things.

She wouldn't ever make the same mistake again.

16

Adam

Zoe had been quieter than usual this morning on the drive to school and was reluctant to share much with Adam at all, let alone give him any hints as to why Viola might be acting weird around him. There was definitely something a little off, but he had no time to obsess about it once he reached the office and found himself conducting an interview he'd totally forgotten about.

In the interview his mind turned to challenging design boundaries, 3D visualisation, how design was multifaceted taking in architecture, product design, landscape and a whole host more. But he found it hard to focus a hundred per cent. Despite the candidate's superb appropriateness for the job, his mind instead wondering how it was so straightforward to find people who suited your work culture, yet finding a partner for life out of the office was so damn hard. Neither of you could fire the other for doing wrong, or, when you didn't like what they brought to the table, it was way more complicated than that, and sometimes it took one hell of a fight to end up with a family design you were remotely happy with.

When he'd first met Susan she'd blown him away. She had this confidence about her, a shock of long blonde hair, striking blue eyes the colour of morning glory. He knew that because his first client had wanted the flowers featured in her garden and when he'd seen the first signs of the sky-blue hue peeping out from its green bud and lighter colour bottom petals, he'd been so happy. He'd taken a ton of photographs of the morning glory flowers, the pond he'd put in, the privet hedges he'd planted at the borders, a paved path that zigzagged its way down to the potting shed. It had been his first big project and those flowers had stayed in his mind ever since. The second he looked into Susan's eyes he'd immediately thought of morning glory; he'd told her as much, and she'd thought him a hopeless romantic. They'd met in September right after those first flowers came into bloom; by October Susan had accidentally fallen pregnant and in December he'd proposed.

The rest of his day flew by he was so busy, and before he left the office – on time because he had a dance session at the Library of Shared Things to look forward to to-night – Adam fired off a text to the kids to let them know he was on the way. Zac dutifully replied and told him about the cartoon he was watching; Zoe messaged a quick response that she and Viola were putting up her new bed-room light. After that, he texted Jennifer. She was being weird with him too, and the only thing he could think of was that it was because he was getting closer to her sister and it was freaking her out. He guessed being overprotect-ive was natural; he didn't know what it was like to have a sister, but he'd invited her along to the dance session to-night to try to get things back to normal.

Jennifer didn't reply to his text. He wouldn't have an-swered it while he was driving but he'd still been waiting for a telltale ping of his phone, and it hadn't come.

When he got home he fixed the kids dinner and had a brief exchange with Viola who couldn't seem to leave the house fast enough.

'What time will you be home?' Zac was ensconced on the sofa in his pyjamas when Adam came downstairs after he'd showered and got himself ready. Charlotte, a babysitter recommended to him by Jennifer, was setting up Connect 4 on the coffee table and Zoe was hidden away upstairs.

'Late. You'll be asleep.'

'I'll make sure he is,' Charlotte clarified. 'We're playing a few games, then it'll be teeth and bed. I've brought my college work along with me so it'll be nice and quiet down here; I won't disturb anyone. What time should I tell Zoe? Or is she too old for that stuff?'

'She's not too old.' Although he knew she wished she was. 'But I do insist on devices being kept in the kitchen overnight. She'll need to bring her phone down by eight o'clock. I'll go and remind her. She won't play up for you.'

When Charlotte shot him an appreciative glance and Zac slipped off the sofa onto his knees in front of the coffee table to slot his first red disc into the plastic struc-ture to start a row, Adam went back upstairs and knocked on the door of the box room. When he heard nothing, he went in.

'Dad.' She shot up in bed as though caught doing something untoward. 'You made me jump.'

'Well, I knew you wouldn't hear me if I yelled up the stairs.' He reiterated the rules about devices.

'I'll make sure I bring it down.'

'Everything OK?'

'Just listening to music and relaxing.'

He knew she'd had a big essay to hand in today so this was one of those times to take a step back and leave her to it. 'I'll see you later then.' He hated how careful he had to be with his behaviour sometimes, how lightly he had to tread around her in case one comment or look could detonate a bad response. Occasionally he'd worry she'd inherited a terrible temper and a not-so-nice streak, that the bad had been passed down as well as the good, but watching other teens and hearing other parents' discussions Zoe didn't seem any different to them. And that, after all, was what he wanted. What they all wanted. To fit in, and for life to run as smoothly as possible.

Adam walked across to the Library of Shared Things, the cool evening air a hint that October was passing by rapidly. The streets were dark, the streetlamps casting ominous shadows as he crossed to take the pedestrian path down the side of the library and towards the lights coming from the yellow-doored outbuilding where Isla was waiting. Already the music from her video clip, the memory of their dancing, the feel of her body pressed close to his, invaded his mind and made his mouth go dry.

She seemed as happy for him to be there as he was. 'You're just in time to help.' She indicated the gazebo, opened out and ready to be assembled.

'Right you are. I'll start with the heavy stuff.' He hauled the sandbags collected in the far corner outside to put them in position ready for the poles of the gazebo. He often missed manual labour – part of what he'd really enjoyed about gardening before he'd furthered his studies and career – and having a physical release for his energies and any pent-up frustration. Being completely active all day, every day, washed your body with a tiredness that was rewarded with a heavy night's sleep. Last week he'd heard a man thank Isla for the class, telling her if he hadn't come along then his butt would still be spread out on the sofa getting bigger by the second. Adam had heard a wobble in her voice as she'd tried not to giggle at the animated description. After that, Adam had found himself wanting to tell Jennifer how much her sister was fitting in, but lately he'd got the impression that the topic of her sister was off-limits.

He tried to ignore the flash of cleavage he got when Isla bent down to help lift the gazebo cover outside. They secured each of the four poles, the little silver buttons poking through the appropriate holes to click into place.

Isla stood up straight after fixing one of the sandbags with the Velcro straps to the pole where she was standing. 'I'm glad you came tonight.'

'Yeah?'

'You're nice and tall. I can use the stepladder to get the canopy on top but I need someone with a bit of height to help because I'll only have the step stool.'

'Using me for my height.' He shook his head.

'I'm hoping the dancing is enough of a repayment.' She brought the step stool round for him before positioning the stepladder by the pole opposite where he stood, on a diagonal.

It would only be enough repayment if he got to dance with her, but Adam didn't voice that out loud. Instead he lifted the weighty material from the ground and edged backwards, guiding them both to where they needed to be before they lifted and manoeuvred all of the material into place.

With the gazebo up and ready, they retreated inside. 'Thank goodness it's not raining.' Isla looked out at the dry evening they'd been gifted.

'I don't know, we could've all worked on a performance of *Singing in the Rain*.'

'Maybe it's something to add to the list.' She grinned. 'The outdoor heaters should at least keep everyone warm enough tonight.'

His first winter back in this country had a rude awakening for him, and the kids hadn't known what hit them. Melbourne could get cold, but the temperatures in London had plummeted well below zero and he knew the kids had been as shocked as he was. He'd lived in Australia long enough to forget. Perhaps he could live in England long enough to forget everything that had happened over there. Or maybe not. Perhaps some things haunted you forever. He wasn't proud of what had gone on, but if he could wipe out some of the memories, he'd be a much happier man.

People gradually began to drift in, and, after Isla took return of the leaf blower from Harrison, she took centre stage and welcomed everyone, and it was time for Adam to get his dancing shoes on, or something like that.

An hour later and they were done. The music had carried them all, laughing and smiling, into the evening air as they'd danced. If someone had told Adam a couple of months back that he'd ever take dance lessons, let alone enjoy them and wish they didn't have to come to an end, he would've laughed hard. And as he grabbed a glass of water he realised what his feelings resembled . . . happiness. He'd once driven in the red centre in Australia, travelling from Kings Canyon to Ayers Rock where the roads were barren, the surrounding earth red, with dry vegetation swaying in the hot, claustrophobic breeze. On that drive there had been nothing else around apart from the King of the Outback roads, the monster road trains which scared the crap out of you and snapped you back into the moment if your concentration dared to wander. Many a time on the long, straight road, he'd thought the end was in sight, then, half an hour later, he was still driving along the very same stretch of the highway as though the end could never be reached, and it was just a figment of his imagination. For such a long time, happiness had felt like a similar mirage, something he could never quite get to. Until now.

He looked over at Isla chatting animatedly with Elaine, then Harrison, Martin, Belinda. Everyone loved her. She was a real hit. But he'd have to tread carefully himself, earn her trust, her respect, her friendship. Because when she learnt the truth about him she might feel differently altogether.

The jukebox was still belting out Simply Red's 'If You Don't Know Me By Now', a tune he and Isla had both been singing along to, the younger members of the crowd pulling faces at the ancient band they had never even heard of. Adam poured himself a tea from the urn set up on a table in the corner. 'I suggested to Jennifer a couple of times that she bring David along tonight,' he told Isla. He spied the collection of orange poppy seed muffins Carmel had brought along for the hungry attendees and told her, 'Dance teacher's privilege to have two, surely.'

'No way, you have it.' Sweat still glistened across her collar bones but she pulled on a long cardigan and wrapped it around herself. 'I've had one. I need to steer clear of the bakery or I'd buy everything.'

'One of Cloverdale's institutions, I'd say.'

'Was my sister interested?'

'Sorry, the muffins totally sidetracked me.' He pulled his phone from his back pocket. 'She still hasn't replied.' Odd, she was usually quick to respond, very sharp when it came to anything requiring an answer. 'I think she and David could do with some quality time together. She seems to have a lot on her mind at the moment.'

The look Isla gave him told Adam he wasn't the only one with concerns. 'I'm not sure my sister would want to be here with me. But you're right, they do need to take some time for themselves. David is always crazy busy with work.'

'Has it always been the same way?'

'I guess it has. And my sister runs the home like clock-work, but they never do much together.'

'Wait a minute, wind back. Why wouldn't your sister want to be here with you?'

'You know what they say . . . family, can't live with them, can't live without them.'

He was about to ask more but she was commandeered by a girl around her age who wanted to know about different dances they'd progress to learning, the time for next week's class, whether she should practise before then. Someone else wanted details of Isla's yoga classes and she handed them a business card. So Adam, along with a couple of the other men, dealt with the gazebo, and soon had it down and the canopy folded then put the outdoor heaters back in the outbuilding where they lived.

'Where should I stash this?' He directed his question to

Isla, the folded canopy in his arms.

She helped him over to the table beside the desk. 'We'll leave it here; I've told Jennifer I'll come in first thing to give it a clean. I'll open it up outside in the car park.'

'You do know it's forecast for rain and gale-force winds tomorrow, don't you?'

'Looks like I'll have to take it home and clean it there.'

'You're going to take it home on the back of your bike?'

She smiled. 'I'm walking.'

'Not down those country lanes in the dark.'

'You sound like Jennifer.'

'Well, I have to take sides on this one. Your sister is right. And with a canopy in your arms, now that's asking for trouble.'

'I don't know, I could throw it over an unlikely attacker, they'll be far too busy trying to escape to care about me while I make a run for it.'

'I'll take you home. We'll walk over to mine, I'll grab my car keys and Charlotte will be only too glad to rack up the pounds as she stays on a bit longer.'

At Isla's cottage, they opened up the canopy between them, in a room that was empty apart from paint tins lined up beneath the windowsill on the far wall.

Adam cupped his hands so he could peer out of the window into the darkness. He could just about make out the garden stretching around the cottage. When he looked back he asked, 'What's this room going to be?'

'It was always the dining room, I'll keep it the same.' The walls were bare, wallpaper stripped and gone, little white patches where she'd filled holes, cobwebs still around the light fitting with one smashed globe in a piece shaped like a flower. 'You know, neither of my parents could ever understand anyone eating a meal in front of the television. It's what I do now though. It's either that or stare at a wall.'

'If I didn't want to set an example for the kids I'd probably eat from a tray on my lap. But it's the only time I get their undivided attention and pretty much the only time Zoe is forced to talk to me.'

'I'm pretty sure you're not alone. All teenagers go through the same.' She stepped over the canopy and led them out of the room and into another. 'This is the lounge.'

'The shelves.' He smiled; she'd already shown him the photographs of her handiwork following his drill workshop. 'They're still up.'

'Don't be cheeky; of course they are.'

'And the wood burner looks new.'

'It is. Much nicer than the ugly heater that used to be there.' She picked up a magazine and flipped the pages until she settled on one with a photograph of a sofa with chesterfield-style deep-buttoned arms, in a red wine colour, patched with beige. 'I'm also getting a wing-backed chair' – she flipped another couple of pages and showed him – 'plus a large button footstool to go with it. It should add a bit of character in here.'

They talked more about the shade she'd chosen for the walls – something called silver thaw for one, a soft white for the others, her preference to add colour with soft furnishings. They moved to the hallway where he admired the intricate bannisters and suggested that with a good varnish they would look like new and from there they went into the kitchen where she'd done some DIY already and had new appliances, but tiling and painting were still to come.

'Cup of tea or coffee?' She plucked two mugs from the mug tree on the shiny stone benchtop that ran along beneath one of the windows. The other was at a right angle looking out the back, he presumed, again confirmed by pressing his face close to the glass to see what was out there.

'Sure, thanks.'

'Earl Grey?'

'Fine by me.' The room wasn't big enough for a table, nor an island, but it was functional enough with a sleek red retro fridge freezer in one corner, a farmhouse gas cooker, and a butler sink that slotted comfortably into the space next to the back door. 'You must be almost done.'

'I'm getting there. It's been a labour of love, that's for sure.'

'Has your sister seen the place?' He didn't miss the way her shoulders hunched the second he brought up Jennifer.

'She has but she never lingers. She's dropped me off, picked me up, but is always in such a rush getting the kids here and there.' She handed him a mug of steaming tea and he leaned against the sink, while she settled against the benchtop.

'I think you should get Jennifer round to have a better look.'

'Maybe. I could do a cheese and wine night perhaps.'

'That's the spirit.' He sipped his tea. 'It might show her you're serious about staying.'

'She and I had a bit of a row the other day.'

'What about?'

'Long story.'

He sighed and found himself pouring out his own concerns. 'I don't understand women at the best of times. Jennifer sometimes tells me things, we get on well, but she's been a bit off with me lately. So has Viola, for that matter.'

'In what way?'

He recounted the times she'd visited his house to do Zoe's bedroom, the initial conversations and ease of working with her, and how all of a sudden she seemed to shut down and act as though he'd done something to offend her. 'I don't get it. She and Zoe seem to get on like a house on fire and up until a few weeks ago I thought I was on good terms with Viola. I mean I've never been on exactly the same wavelength as her but we've always been friendly, never exchanged a cross word.' He wondered if the kids had acted up but that couldn't be it, because Viola and Zoe were behaving as if they were in cahoots about something, as though they were two girlfriends and he was the fretting parent. The situation had an uneasiness about it, but he was sure he was being paranoid.

Isla took her cardigan off as the tea warmed her. He tried to drag his focus from her bare shoulders, the dancer's body he admired . . . the body he'd been up close to. He followed the tail of her tattoo on her ankle poking out from the end of her leggings, the racy hot-pink polish she'd painted her toenails with. And then he gulped back the rest of his tea and set the cup in the sink to break the train of thought in case she'd picked up on it. She was looking at him oddly, not saying anything, and reading women seemed to be a degree-level subject he had no hope of passing.

'What's wrong?' He came straight out with it and asked

her, usually the best way. He hated mind games, detested them. His past had seen to that.

She set her own cup in the sink and, standing close to him, looked out of the window. He could see her top teeth gently biting down on her bottom lip and it almost drove him to distraction. He wanted to get closer and almost did but perhaps it was time he left. She'd closed up, he had no idea why, but suddenly he felt like he was intruding.

The second he stepped away she clamped a hand around his wrist. 'Don't go, please.'

He fell back against the sink and this time she turned to face the same way, into the kitchen, the retro fridge buzzing in the corner, the old clock above the door hanging crooked but with hands that still managed to creep around full circle. She still had a hand on his wrist and slowly she moved it down until she was holding his hand. 'Did Jennifer tell you about her falling-out with Viola?'

Hand encasing hers, he looked down at her, doing his best not to let their skin-on-skin contact turn him into a bumbling fool who couldn't string a sentence together. 'They're still friends from what I can make out.'

'I don't mean recently. I'm talking about what happened a long time ago, back when Jennifer married David.'

'She hasn't said anything.'

'They were inseparable in high school. Viola had some weird home life. I don't really know the details; I don't know why she wasn't happy. Anyway, Jennifer was her best friend and Viola spent a lot of time at our house. They both kind of complemented each other. I used to be jealous.'

'Of their friendship?'

'They just got one another. I always felt a bit of a misfit, a non-conformist, growing up. Jennifer was the one who did well at school and never got into trouble. I barely scraped by in my exams; I never had the focus. Jennifer and Viola had this strong friendship where Jennifer supported Viola through whatever crap she was going through at home, and I know Viola pushed my sister on with her career, telling her she could do anything, being in her corner one hundred per cent. It was almost as though Jennifer was a project Viola could see from fruition to success.'

'What happened?'

'The trouble started on Jennifer's hen night.' She hesitated, clearly unsure whether she should be divulging any of this. 'Everyone was drunk, but Viola was the worst.'

'Can't imagine that; she's far too together.' Weird how holding hands with someone could begin to feel natural in a very short space of time. He no longer felt the nerves, instead he felt a sense of calm. Their skin still met; Isla hadn't let go and neither had he.

'Viola tried to warn Jennifer off marrying David.'

'You're kidding.'

'She told her he was boring. Said she could do much better. I was there, I heard it all. She was talking to my sister as though David was another project that could either succeed or fail. It was horrible and Jennifer was so upset. The next morning Viola apologised but I knew if it wasn't for the wedding Jennifer would've lost it and told her to go away.'

'She didn't?'

'No, but I wish she had. You know that bit in a wedding where the vicar asks if anyone objects to the wedding and tells them to speak now or forever hold their peace?'

'Oh no.'

'Yep, Viola must've been on the champagne that morning too, and swaying near the altar, tried to whisper – which totally didn't work – that Jennifer was settling. She could do better. She could have her pick of men. It was hideous. Our parents, aunts and uncles, cousins, friends, everyone witnessed it. Jennifer was humiliated. Viola realised she'd told the entire congregation and then she started laughing, she said she was joking and motioned for the vicar to please, carry on.'

'Shit.'

'My sister was fuming, but more than that, she was devastated. David was so calm, he was brilliant. They were, and still are, a match made in heaven.'

'What happened after the ceremony?'

'Every time Viola went near my sister, Jennifer ignored her, pretended she wasn't there. And I thought it had simmered down. Jennifer and David had their first dance as a married couple, it was beautiful, and then we heard a commotion coming from the edge of the dance floor.'

'Viola again?'

Isla nodded. 'She'd been shagging the best man in the coat cupboard. It wasn't the fact she'd had sex at the wedding – that was bad enough – but it was that she'd made it so blatantly obvious when she came out adjusting her dress, him tucking his shirt back into his trousers. They were shameless. It was the way it was done without giving a shit about the bride. It was Jennifer's day and Viola ruined it.'

He took a deep breath. 'Your sister must be very forgiving to ever speak to Viola again after that. I don't think I would. I wonder why Viola did it.'

'I think that's the only thing that made Jennifer keep her cool. Our parents told Viola to leave, Dad escorted her out to make sure she got in a taxi, and from that day Jennifer never mentioned it again. I know she didn't speak to Viola for years and then Jennifer settled back here in Cloverdale. Viola moved back to the area when her husband set up his practice, and with them in the same vicinity, Jennifer said she just wanted to forget everything that happened. She didn't want to hear another word about it. It was all water under the bridge.'

'And is it?'

Isla shook her head and this time dropped Adam's hand, and began rinsing out the mugs and slotted them into the dishwasher. 'I very much doubt it. I mean, you'd want to yell at the person at least, demand an explanation, you'd want them to grovel.'

'I wonder why she let it go.'

'I don't think Jennifer ever really did. They're on speaking terms, but those issues are still simmering deep beneath the surface.'

Adam shuddered. Because he had so many things bubbling away beneath the surface himself. And every once in a while, usually when he had a jolt of happiness, he felt another bolt of uneasiness go through him, just like the one he was getting now that said his time would come.

He wished she hadn't dropped his hand. He wanted that closeness back again. 'Tell me more about you, Isla. I want to hear more about your dancing days, how you enjoyed travelling around the world, why settle down in Cloverdale now?'

'I'm thinking that's more fourth date conversation' – she smiled – 'or fifth?'

'This is a date?'

'Do you want it to be?'

'I think you know I do.' He took her hand again, pulled her back to stand with him. 'I just wanted to find out more about you, I don't mean it to sound like an interrogation.'

She looked out into the darkness. 'I've had a lot of ups and downs, and I haven't always shared them with my sister.' Her arm touched his and she spoke as though the heat between them urged her on. 'I was a professional dancer for years. And I loved it. Every second of it.' He waited patiently while she disappeared into her own memories. 'I started training from the age of five and, to me, it wasn't hard work . . . don't get me wrong, it was rigorous, demanding, but I thrived on it. The way it used to make me feel learning dances, telling stories through dance and displaying such emotion. It's all I ever wanted.

'I got auditions, some came easy others not so much, I sailed through some, failed monumentally at others but always picked myself up and battled on. I starred in the West End, I performed whenever I could, my body responded to changes and demands to get my next gig. I earned a good enough salary to keep myself going. And I fell into a relationship with Carlos, choreographer and incredible dancer. We began ballroom dancing classes together in our local area, we had a jukebox not too dissimilar to the one now at the Library of Shared Things. Seeing that there was a reminder, a nice one at first, and then a stark symbol of everything I'd wanted but lost.

'Carlos was an incredible human being until I ruined things. We were together for eight months, going strong; we worked, we danced, we had a great life in London and were the envy of all our friends. I think my life was so far removed from the lives my family led that it was hard for them to understand me. Or at least that's what I assumed. They were wowed when they first met Carlos; he was like the first thing I'd done right. They thought him charming, gorgeous and a rock to steady me and my crazy ways.'

'What happened?'

'I dislocated my knee and it was the start of a string of injuries from my knee to my ankle and then it was my hip. I missed out on auditions, I got frustrated at having to rest and not practise; I began arguing with Carlos and most of what I threw at him wasn't fair.'

'He didn't stick around?'

'He did. He understood my frustrations; he'd seen it before. I can't fault him. But I fell pregnant, a surprise to us both, and what was more of a surprise was that I was actually excited. I was only in my mid-twenties and babies were something I hadn't considered. I didn't know whether I even wanted to be a parent; I was happy building a career and living a life I'd dreamed of. But all of a sudden I could see it. Girl or boy, I knew I'd teach them to dance' – she smiled – 'we both would. But the baby wasn't meant to be. I lost it at thirteen weeks.'

'I'm so sorry. That must have been hard.'

'After that I became obsessed with the idea of being a mum; it was all I wanted. Carlos was totally on board. But a second pregnancy went the same way, and after that . . . well everything fell apart. Carlos did his best, but, with my injuries that never healed, my body's rejection of motherhood, he had his work cut out trying to keep me going. He talked about the two of us setting up a dance school, funding me to go to university and study dance therapy, but I didn't want it. It didn't interest me.

I wanted to dance and that was that. And then my dad died and I could barely function. I kept myself together enough to come back to Cloverdale for the funeral and to support Mum and Jennifer, but I hadn't told them anything about what had gone on; I didn't want them to have to deal with my problems as well as their own. So back I went to Carlos. And we fought, we made up, we went into a cycle of doing the same over and over until he could no longer stand it.'

'He left you?'

'There was so much grief and resentment. I'd pushed him away until one day he had enough. After we split up I kept on running, pretended I was fine, that I'd chosen to leave dancing behind for something far more exciting. I shared my adventures with Mum, she loved hearing all my tales, hyped up with enthusiasm especially when she was sick. She didn't deserve a misery of a daughter to have to support when she was dying. I came to see her as much as I could manage without letting the façade slip in front of her or Jennifer. Much longer in Cloverdale and it would've done. I didn't want Mum's memories to be of her loser daughter who couldn't do the thing she was proud of. I couldn't dance, the career she boasted about to all her friends was a disaster. She had grandchildren from Jennifer to talk to everyone about. But me? I was a mess. So I gave her the fun Isla, the one she could get a buzz out of.'

Isla smiled at her memories. 'She really loved it, you know; she'd talk about me with anyone who'd listen according to people around here. I used adrenalin sports to forget my sad existence, my failure at the one thing I wanted. I went ice-climbing in Colorado, bungee jumping in New Zealand, white-water rafting, volcano boarding.'

'When did you get the tattoo?'

She smiled as she reiterated the words permanently etched on her body. 'Refuse to Sink. It was exactly the way I felt. Life kept throwing me curve balls, or more like grenades, and I wasn't going to go down without a fight. I saw the design, the words spoke to me, and that was that. Branded for life.'

'I think it's . . . kind of sexy.'

'Really?' The look they exchanged left him in no doubt as to her feelings. The energy in the room could've powered the whole of Cloverdale.

'I got so sad that I'd never again be able to tell Mum, or even Dad, the stories that would make them proud of me.'

'I'm sure they were proud anyway.'

'I hope so.'

'May I ask what changed?' He trod carefully. 'What made you finally decide to come back to Cloverdale longer term?'

'When Mum died, I thought about my life from a different perspective. I thought about what was really keeping me travelling, what I was getting out of it, and it had changed. I'd needed to do it after Carlos and I split but then it became more like a habit I no longer needed. I was working in bars to support myself, or fruit picking, working as a lifeguard, I had all manner of jobs but I had no home. And when Jennifer and I talked about how the cottage needed work before we could even think about selling it, I thought I'd take the job rather than paying someone else to do it. I knew it would give me time, space in my own home, to get a feel for whether coming back here was the right thing.'

'And is it?'

'I really think it might be.' She took his hand again. 'I was a mess, Adam. A total mess. And I wasn't just a little bit lonely; it was an aching, depleting hurt that came from the isolation that running away had made me feel. Nobody can run forever. The past is always there, lingering, and it's only when you stop and face up to it that your mind can start to process a way forward.'

He gulped at the harsh reality of her words. She'd never know how very applicable they were to him. He wanted to tell her, confide like she had done, but how could he? She wouldn't look at him in the same way, she might even run. And he couldn't bear the thought of losing her. He never wanted to let her go.

He wrapped an arm around her shoulders, squeezed her tight. 'Just one question . . .'

'Go on.'

'What the hell is volcano boarding?'

He felt laughter beneath his arm and she recounted the thrill of hiking up a volcano before zooming down on some sort of toboggan clocking speeds you'd do in your car.

'How did you stop?'

'I used my heels to brake and steer.'

'Now that's impressive.'

'I abseiled down the Emirates Spinnaker Tower a few weeks ago. And it was amazing. I was proud. I had the best day, but it was a bit of a reminder about the Isla who's lost herself somewhere along the line and the Isla who tried anything to make herself feel alive again.'

'So you're done with adrenalin sports.'

She grinned. 'I didn't say that, now, did I?'

'You're a brave woman.'

'Not really.'

'Isla, you are. And the bravest thing you did was to come back when you needed to.'

They stood side by side, the window pane behind them now, rattling in the wind, Adam's head tilted and lightly resting on top of Isla's until he said, 'I really have to go. Charlotte might call out a search party soon or else she'll call the police when I can't actually pay her because I don't have that much cash in my wallet.'

'I wish you didn't have to leave.'

'Me neither.'

'Thank you, for listening.'

He turned to face her, his eyes held hers. He thought about kissing her. He wanted to so much.

But she looked away. 'I need to tell you something else.'

'More tales of crazy pursuits? I don't think there's much left is there? You seem to have done everything.'

Her face said this wasn't a moment to joke. 'The way Jennifer is with you.'

'She's been a bit odd lately, but I think we're good.'

'You don't see it, do you?'

'See what?'

'My row with my sister was because she can see I have feelings for you.' When he began to move closer she held a hand up to stop him. 'But I'm not the only one.'

'I don't understand.'

'My sister, Adam.'

'Jennifer? We're friends. She's married.'

'She's getting attached to you. The way she talks about

241

you, the way she acts when you're around, and then when she thought I was getting too close. She didn't like it.'

He scraped a hand across his chin. Jennifer was beautiful, a stunning woman, but he'd never seen her as more than a friend.

Isla was in front of him now, holding both of his hands. 'I like you, Adam; I like you a lot.'

'I like you too.'

'I'm worried about Jennifer. And me being with you seems to be getting to her. It might not be right, but it's the way she feels and it's making her angry with me.'

'I don't get it. She's married; you and I are single.'

'She *is* married, but I think she's going through a really hard time and doesn't know where to turn.'

'And I've been there to talk to.'

'Has she said her and David are having problems?'

'No, but she turns to me about other things. I feel terrible for leading her on.'

'No, don't,' Isla insisted. 'You have been a friend, but Jennifer is confused. And there's a bit more to it than she's letting on. I can't tell you what, it's not my place, but I can understand why she's reluctant to talk to David. And I can't even give her advice, because I doubt she'll listen to her wayward sister. God, I feel really guilty talking about her like this.'

His fingers lifted her chin to look at him. 'You're doing it because you care.'

'She won't thank me for telling the truth about her and Viola either.'

'I don't want you to worry about it.' He kissed her lightly on the lips, enough for now. 'Thank you for telling me.'

He hoped whatever was going on between Jennifer and

her husband was something Jennifer saw before it was too late. He'd left behind one mess of a marriage, he didn't intend to be involved in the destruction of another.

17

Viola

Viola found it difficult to push away the image of Zoe clinging to her that day, telling her she wanted her mum. It had taken up her headspace in meetings at work, during family dinners ever since it had happened, and again last night as she zipped to the supermarket and managed to forget half of the items on her list, causing Isaac to run her a bubble bath, pour her a glass of wine and instruct her to chill out.

And now it was all she could think about, as she joined Jennifer at the Library of Shared Things. Her head had started to ache in the way it did when she got stressed. She'd been the same when she first started work, striving for success, not wanting to put a foot wrong, but these days she usually got a bit of perspective before she ran herself ragged worrying. She couldn't seem to reach that point this time; there were so many variables. There was Zoe, a vulnerable teen on the cusp of learning the truth about her dad, then there was her friend Jennifer who was getting close to Adam, not to mention Isla who seemed innocent enough to be taken in by this man and would probably end up the same way as his wife.

'You're away with the fairies today.' Jennifer was astute

at picking up on moods, good and bad, and Viola wished she'd been better at hiding her worries. She put the projector that had just been returned back into its space in the hutch. 'I asked you twice if you'd taken the return of the portable karaoke jukebox this morning. You didn't mark it as returned on the system.'

'I'm sorry. I must've forgotten.'

'Is everything all right?' Jennifer wasn't looking at her now but instead back to the computer, trying to keep everything running like clockwork.

'Of course it is,' Viola replied. Maybe she should be asking Jennifer the same question. Any fool could see she and David weren't working the way they once had, sharing time together, talking and laughing. He'd been in last week to grab a spare key for the house after forgetting his and where once they would've exchanged a kiss on the lips, there'd not even been a perfunctory kiss on the cheek for Jennifer. Viola suspected part of the problem stemmed from the fact Jennifer was turning to a friend rather than her husband when she needed emotional support, but she wasn't going to say anything. She only hoped Jennifer would see it for herself before it was too late.

Viola checked every piece of the party starter kit was there – the disco lights, a balloon pump, a remote for the lights, instructions, power leads. She ensured the lights still worked and then tidied it all into its container and lifted it to take over to the relevant slot and put it away.

The winds outside meant they kept the door to the Library of Shared Things closed for now, and next to battle inside was Isla. 'It's nasty out there.' Dressed in jeans and a jumper, her auburn hair lifted as she shut the door behind her, and then settled calmly around her shoulders. 'But it's good renovating weather.'

'How's it all going?' Viola asked.

'Good; I've come to collect the hand sander.'

'I'll get it for you,' said Jennifer, far too cordially when it was her sister not a stranger.

'I'm going to sand down the bannisters and revarnish,' Isla told Viola. 'I wasn't going to bother, but it was Adam's suggestion and I think he's right. They'll look impressive when I'm done.'

Viola didn't miss Jennifer's shoulders stiffen at the mention of Adam. And by the look on Isla's face she'd wanted to test the waters and mention his name but seemed wary now as she said to her sister, 'You'll have to come over one night for cheese and wine.'

Jennifer managed a smile. 'Of course, that'll be nice.'

'Right then.' Isla paid the fee, picked up the sander and hovered a moment longer to see if she could penetrate Jennifer's aloof exterior but when she had no luck she gave up. 'I'm off, see you later.'

When it was just the two of them again, Jennifer picked up the dustpan and brush and swept up the debris that sneaked in every time the door was opened.

'What's going on between you and Isla?' Viola couldn't let it go this time. If it was Adam, maybe they'd get talking about him, perhaps Jennifer had some secret doubts about him and she'd welcome Viola's insight in the form of what she'd found in the diary.

'Nothing.' Her frown could've been used to advertise the immediate need for Botox.

The look Jennifer had given Isla when she'd mentioned Adam reminded Viola of her own jealousy when Jennifer and David first got together. He'd become her friend's world overnight and Viola had faded into the background. Jennifer had been busy falling in love while Viola was still battling tension at home, the constant need to impress her parents, make her mark, gain their approval. Her parents hadn't shown her a whole lot of love, but she'd found a good friend in Jennifer and they'd been inseparable for a long time, much like Ava and Zoe were now. She became consumed with the fear she'd lose Jennifer, the ridiculous notion that she would get left behind in some kind of imaginary race in which she was coming last. It sounded so crazy now, but at the time she hadn't been able to see past the stability she'd created with her friendship and how it was all disintegrating in front of her eyes.

When the winds howled outside Viola looked out at the darkened sky. Jennifer was milling around looking miserable, there wasn't a soul in sight beyond the yellow doors, and Viola grabbed the key and locked up.

'What are you doing?'

'I know something is wrong. And I think you need someone to talk to.' She held her hands out in a I'm-all-you've-got kind of way.

But she wasn't prepared for what happened next because Jennifer burst into tears. Uncontrollable floods of tears. She slumped against the wall, then lowered herself to the floor.

Viola turned off the main lights and instead put on a small lamp. 'It'll look like we're not here, so hopefully we won't be disturbed.' And she sat down as she waited for the sobbing to subside. 'Now are you going to tell me what's going on?' She handed her a tissue from the box she'd pulled down from the desk. It had been a long time since she'd seen her friend this vulnerable, a long time since Jennifer had allowed herself to display much emotion in front of her.

'My marriage . . .' A tear-stained face looked at her, Jennifer's gorgeous dark hair stuck to one side of her face by the tears. 'It's a mess. I'm a mess.'

Using a tissue Viola gently wiped Jennifer's cheek and added the spent tissue to the pile. 'You're making a mountain there. Not very environmentally friendly.'

'I guess not.' At least that got her laughing, and she hadn't told Viola to leave her alone.

'You need to start from the beginning.'

For the next hour Viola listened to Jennifer tell her all about the problems she'd already seen for herself, from a distance. Viola didn't once say she knew, didn't for a single second consider throwing an accusation her friend's way.

'Somewhere along the line I stopped talking to David as a friend. He became the man of the house, the worker, the one who brought home the money for his family; I was the mother of his children, and our lives haven't met in the middle long enough for us to enjoy each other.' Viola waited patiently for her to go on. 'I turned to Adam when I had grievances with the school or a conundrum with the kids; he was always so willing to listen, and it was easier to do that than it was to talk to my own husband.'

'You turned to a friend.' Those words were hard to say given what she knew, but they were still true.

'I did, but I started to have feelings for Adam.' She looked down at her hands, guilty, in search of absolution. 'It was wrong to push David away. I didn't do it on purpose; it just kind of happened. I say I tried to talk to him about my return to work, but I don't think I tried hard enough.'

'Only you can know that.'

'I need to try again. Adam told me to, encouraged me.' She covered her face with her hands. 'He must think I'm such an idiot.'

'Adam?'

'Yes! He must see this little puppy dog following him around, lapping up attention.'

'I'm sure you've read that wrong.'

'I'm embarrassed; it makes me cringe to think how much I relied on him. It became exciting to get his texts; I got uncomfortable having my phone anywhere David could see.'

'But nothing happened, did it?'

'No.'

'Then you're putting a stop to it at the right time.'

'Adam and I often chat with text messages flying back and forth, sometimes late at night, often when David was away. At first I felt as though I was cheating, then I told myself Adam was a friend, but then, I don't know, over the last couple of months I've started to feel differently. I began to push David away more, turn to Adam especially when he was so supportive over my idea of returning to work.'

'Was there flirting?'

'Occasionally . . . at least I think so. Or maybe I imagined it.' Jennifer looked like she was beating herself up inside.

'Adam would've been no more than a friendly face had you and David not run into problems in your marriage.

But because you have, he's become something more, even if it's only in your head.'

'Maybe you're right.'

'I usually am.' Viola raised a smile. 'Can I ask you something?'

'Please do.'

'Are you jealous of Isla? She and Adam seem to be starting something.'

Looking at the floor beneath her and picking up a stray piece of lint that she balanced on her knee and toyed with, Jennifer said, 'I felt she was taking away an important friendship, but perhaps that wasn't all I was feeling. God, what kind of sister does that? What kind of person? I'm married!'

'The kind of person who is having problems themselves and is trying to find a way out. Like we all are.' Viola let the words settle on the air, with the scent of the cedar furniture polish she'd used to clean the desk, something done at the end of every day in here. 'David loves you unconditionally, you know he does. You two are made for each other.'

Jennifer pulled at the tissue between her fingers, almost decimated by now. 'He's always been there for me, in the background lately, but still there, still reliable.'

'Let me ask you this . . . do you love David? When you look at him, do you still have the feelings you once had? They might be buried, but are they there? Close your eyes, go on . . .' They were both giggling. 'Now think about him, not how it is because you're both busy, but think about shared moments over the last few years. See him as the man he is, not just the provider, or only as a father, but the person you fell for.'

Eyes shut, Jennifer stayed quiet until she began to smile. 'I do still love him, I really do. And I want us to work through this.'

'He's still the old David, the man you fell in love with. The same man who proposed on bended knee in the worst thunderstorm to hit the UK in years.'

Jennifer's face lit up with the memory. 'I miss the spontaneity we had at the start, how free we both were, watching him surf—'

'While freezing your bum off on the sand.' Viola laughed. 'You dragged me down there once trying to pair me off with his friend. What was his name?'

'Surfer dude, that was all I ever heard.'

'A right surfer dude; he had dreadlocks and everything. Could you imagine me with someone who doesn't wash their hair, and thinks its natural oils will take care of it?'

'I really can't. Isaac is far better for you.'

'He is. And he's laid-back, which stops me being so highly strung, but still serious enough that we work.' She hadn't met him until a few years after Jennifer married, but the second she did, she understood what her friend must've found with David and she'd also seen how hurt she would've been by what she'd done. 'I'm sorry, Jennifer.'

'For what?'

Viola's look said it all.

'No need to dredge that all up.'

'I think we need to. You haven't forgiven me and I miss you. I miss this. Us.'

Jennifer smiled. 'I do too. I've needed to talk to someone for a long time. Isla told me off recently, said I'd never let you forget what happened.'

'Then let me apologise properly. What I did at your

wedding was horrible. I'm lucky you talk to me at all.' She took a deep breath. 'I was jealous, so jealous of you. You were moving on with your life, and I was left behind.'

'But why be jealous? You had everything going for you – still do. Tall, leggy, gorgeous, all the men were after you. You had brains and a good career path being paved, your parents gave you everything you wanted. I was the jealous one. When they bought you a brand-new Mini for your eighteenth, and I was still getting the bus, I wished I could save up and get something half as nice. Or when you'd all go off on ski trips to Colorado every year and I was left behind in the dismal British winter, days like today, cold and wet and you were in the sun and snow having a grand time.'

'Except I wasn't. Well, I was; I loved to ski, and enjoyed the holidays. But you see, I always wanted to be part of a family like yours. Because you had so much more than me.' Her voice wobbled. 'My parents gave me a lot of things, they pushed me to do well, but I lived my life in a permanent state of fear that I'd fuck up. I wanted their approval so much, and even to this day I don't think I ever got it. My brother felt the same way and that's why he moved further away from them when he left home. He didn't want to be like them, neither of us did. I even tried to talk to Mum about the way she brought us up.'

'How did that go?'

'She pretty much dismissed it, said I was spoilt, and that was the problem. All I wanted was their time, but they were so busy working and making their way to the top, my brother and I had to get on with it. At least we had each other.'

'You should talk to your mum again.'

'I don't really want to. I talk to my brother; he listens to my frustrations. All I want is to not let history repeat itself.'

'It won't. You're a parent of two, nothing sways you and you shower those kids with love and attention.'

She harrumphed. 'Isaac says I do that a little bit too much.'

'Well . . .'

Viola managed a smile. 'I'm trying my best to back off a bit, especially with Ava. I don't want to lose her like Mum lost me. I want us to be friends when she's an adult, I want to be someone she wants to spend time with.'

'You will be. You've got the right attitude for a start, but I do agree with Isaac.' It was her turn to look wary of offering advice. 'Maybe back off a little.'

'I can't promise anything. Oh, now look at me.' A tear escaped her eye and she blotted it with a tissue so it didn't make her mascara run. 'I hope Ava knows she can talk to me. I never had that and I know you did with both of your parents. You know, I once told my parents about my love of interior design?'

'Recently?'

'Years ago when I was still at school. They told me I needed a proper job, not some arty-farty pretence of a career. I wouldn't have minded but they'd recently paid through the nose for someone to come and redo the formal sitting room at their place and had booked the same person to come back and do the dining room.'

'Didn't they see how ironic that was?'

'They were blinkered. But anyway, I've learnt to let my anger and frustrations about them go, at least a little.

They almost disowned me when they heard what I did at your wedding.'

Jennifer's voice came out small. 'They know about that?'

'Gossip made its way to our house, yes. I was told to fix it, apologise, to stop my partying ways this instant. To get a real job, move out and prove I wasn't the sort who went around getting drunk and having sex in a public place.'

Airing all of this after such a long time made both women take pause.

'For what I did,' Viola said eventually, 'I am truly, very sorry. I will never ever be able to make it up to you. But believe me when I say if I could change it I would.'

'Except you can't.'

'Except I can't.'

When Jennifer got up and threw all her tissues in the bin, Viola thought they were done. She'd given it a good go, but she couldn't force Jennifer's forgiveness.

Jennifer turned to look at her. 'You're not the only one who made mistakes.'

'I made some huge ones. I'm pretty sure nothing you've ever done came close.'

'You'd be surprised. I'm not as perfect as I'd like people to think.'

'Come on, have you ruined someone's wedding?'

'No, but I nearly ruined my family's lives.'

Viola studied Jennifer's face. 'You're serious. What the hell did you do?'

Jennifer pointed to the kitchenette. 'I've got a couple of bottles of wine out the back; Fiona bought them for me to apologise for returning the bread maker late. I think this conversation is going to need support in the form of a glass or two.'

Viola grinned. 'You get the glasses; I'll get the wine.'

They spread out a picnic blanket and settled on the floor, the bottle of red wine between them, their glasses full.

'I guess I'd better start at the beginning.' Jennifer took a big sip of wine for added confidence. 'Remember how I always wanted my own hairdressing salon?'

'It was all you ever talked about. And I always thought you'd do it.'

'I tried.' She took a deep breath. 'I wanted a family so much and I couldn't be happier when the twins were born, and then Archie. But when Archie turned one, something inside of me clicked. I wanted and needed to go back to work.'

'So what happened?'

'I made plans, so many plans. I got a part-time job with a hairdresser but I wanted my own salon so badly. I wanted to be my own boss, I wanted to take on the world.' She shook her head. 'I went to the bank with my business plan and tried to secure a loan. The perfect vacant premises came up, footfall would've been amazing, and there became an urgency to my plans. But the bank turned me down. The amount I wanted to borrow wasn't a risk they were willing to take and I wasn't keen on using the house as collateral either. But I could see it, my hairdressing salon, there on a high street, the place I made my business a roaring success.

She paused, took another sip of wine, and Viola waited patiently for more.

'I was gutted; I hadn't even told David much about it because he was under huge pressure at work with a re-structure looming. I'd wanted to go home and tell him I had the finance, tell him it would work, show him when I opened the salon.

'A couple of weeks later I was out at a restaurant with a friend who seemed to know everyone in the bar. That was fine; I was happy to chat with other people, as they were a nice crowd. I met a woman called Gail and at first we talked about her own cocktail bar down south, and when we started talking about my work and I admitted I wanted to open my own salon she was all ears. I was happy to have found another businesswoman who kind of got what it was all about, the effort I needed to put in, the rewards, the stress of starting out. And when I admitted the bank had turned me down for a loan and showed her the link to the premises I was interested in, she agreed it was prime real estate and she could totally see why I didn't want to miss out. We swapped numbers and a few days later she called me, she said she'd been thinking about my predicament. She asked me my projections, how much I thought I could earn and how fast I could pay back a loan, and then she said she might be able to help me. She made me feel special, like she really had my back and wanted me to succeed. She even said how excited she would be to come into the salon to get her hair done.

'Gail agreed to loan me some money. We drew up a repayment schedule, but nothing was official; there was no paper trail. I wanted to wait until the lease for the premises was agreed before I got the cash, but she insisted I have the capital so I was ready to go. She reiterated exactly what I was thinking, that I didn't want to miss out on that premises. Viola, I was so stupid.'

Viola set down her wine and covered Jennifer's hand with her own. 'Tell me the rest.'

'It was all going well, I trusted Gail, we went out for drinks together, she came to the house, she even hugged my kids. But then the lease fell through, it never happened. So I tried to give Gail all the money back, said I'd have to wait until something else came up. To be honest, I was relieved. I knew it was one hell of a risk borrowing money and I hadn't told David at that stage. But Gail wouldn't take it back. Well, she would, but for the short time I'd had the money in my account ready to buy equipment, pay the lease, set up the business, the amount I had to repay had gone up thirty per cent.'

'Oh my God.'

'I know, and I didn't have thirty per cent. I told her no, I'd pay her a little extra for the inconvenience, but I couldn't understand why she was being so unreasonable.'

'She was a loan shark.'

'One I didn't see circling. She started calling any time of the day and night, I had to make excuses to David about it being a friend in need. I'd paid all the capital back into her account but I didn't have the extra even if I'd wanted to give it to her. She turned up at the house again one day and told me she'd have to take what was owed to her. She had two heavies with her, they took our television, David's watch I'd bought him for our first wedding anniversary, they found the kids' pots of dreams and smashed each one of them.' Head in her hands she cried at the memory. 'Oh, Viola, it was horrid. And even then she wasn't happy. I told her I'd call the police and she made threats to me, about the kids. I finally told David, I had to when he came home right after they'd left and saw the mess I was in, the mess they'd made in the house.'

'What did he say?'

'He was upset, angry, he wanted to call the police straight away but these people were clever. I'd never been to Gail's house; I didn't have anything more than a mobile phone number that she never answered anymore. She contacted me, never the other way round. She'd covered her tracks. On top of it all David was stressed out at work; he thought he might lose his job, but he put in all the hours he could to ensure that didn't happen.'

'Did you eventually pay the crazy costs back?'

'I couldn't. They went up even more with every day that passed. That was when Gail targeted Mum and Dad. She went to the cottage with the heavies, took Mum's jewellery, anything else they could get their hands on. And they smashed the place up.' Her voice cracked. 'They were terrified. But Dad was the strongest I've ever seen anyone and he told me without question we'd be calling the police. The police came; they told us how hard it would be to prove anything about these people. Even though there was a banking transaction, it was my word against Gail's; I knew that. And Gail worked for a reputable employer, for goodness sake. That was the laugh of it. By day she wore tailored suits, her appearance was impeccable, I knew she'd say it was a loan between friends and she would deny any bullying or theft for the extra money they'd demanded.'

'Stupid bitch.'

'She really was. And the word "stupid" is an apt description because while we were wondering when the nightmare would end and she backed off as she somehow got wind we'd gone to the authorities, and she targeted someone else. This time the person recorded some of their conversations, got the police involved right at the start. Gail had been doing this for a while; her moonlighting profession funded the expensive clothes she wore and the townhouse she owned, she'd got away with it a dozen times but the police were onto her.'

Viola swigged her wine and topped up both their glasses. 'So you really aren't completely perfect,' she teased.

Jennifer laughed. 'Far from it.' She got up, retrieved another bottle of wine and topped up both glasses.

'I always had a lot of respect for your parents, but now? I'm in awe of how they handled it. How did you keep it all so quiet?'

'Dad was very together when we reported it. They'd been terrified when they were at home and the heavies wrecked their place. He was devastated they took Mum's jewellery. He was fuming underneath, but he never fell apart once. For me, he made sure it stayed our business and nobody else's. They only told Isla because they wanted her to watch out in case there were repercussions, but thankfully we never heard from Gail or the men she'd used to help her again.' She looked at Viola. 'This makes me a total hypocrite, you know. I made one hell of a mistake and my whole family suffered. But they forgave me, they moved on and looked forwards not backwards, whereas I never let you forget what you did.'

'I've been tiptoeing around you for a long time, hoping you'd eventually let me apologise properly.'

'And I kept you at arm's length because I wondered if you'd ever tell David what happened when we first got engaged.'

'I'm not sure I follow.'

'Hal.' Jennifer smiled.

'You mean Hal Dickenson, your high school sweetheart?'

'The very same. And I know you saw us together before my engagement party.'

Viola did remember, but she'd put it out of her mind, assuming Jennifer didn't know she'd seen them, thinking Jennifer had well and truly moved on.

'Why did you never say you'd seen me?'

'For years Hal wanted me to go to America with him and I was tempted but my home was here. That night you saw us kissing – or him kissing me – he asked me again, even though we'd broken up years before. He told me to ditch David, get back together with him. He'd gone from Wall Lane Comprehensive to Wall Street; he had an apartment in Greenwich Village, a house in Connecticut, and he told me he wanted a life with me.'

'Seeing you with him made me wonder whether you were settling with David, whether you could've had a more exciting life with Hal and you wanted it but didn't know how to say.'

'You always worried too much about me.'

'I should've kept my mouth shut. So what did you tell him? I mean obviously you turned down the offer.'

'Your comments at the wedding hit home because I'd been tempted. I'd never done anything so adventurous as to move to another country and here was the opportunity of a lifetime with a boy I'd known for years, now a man, who was asking me to share his life. We'd talked about it over and over when we were teenagers, we'd had plans, he'd gone off to university in America and then I'd met David. I was in love, but there's nothing like a blast from the past to rattle you and make you question whether you were doing the right thing.

'When you started putting the thought in my mind

that David wasn't the one for me, that I was settling . . . well, those comments got to me. I panicked. I wasn't the calm, collected bride everyone thought I was. I was the bride whose feet twitched at the altar when she thought about the email she'd had from her ex, Hal, saying, "Wish you were here."'

'I never realised. And I would've made it so much worse.'

'You knew me, Viola; you knew me so well. And part of me thought you were right but I had to protect myself, David, my family, my future. And once I was married I can honestly say I never looked back. Going with Hal would've been great for all of five seconds, but I'd changed into a different person. Hal and I had that young love that so many dream of, but it was nothing compared to what David and I built together. So when you came back into my life here in Cloverdale, I guess I worried you'd blab about seeing me with Hal, you'd tell David I'd had doubts about our marriage. You were a reminder that I wasn't anywhere near perfect.'

'None of us are.' Viola moved her engagement ring with her opposite hand, each rotation helping her think how to explain herself. 'I was also frightened I was losing you. You were moving so far ahead and I was left behind.'

'That's crazy, you were always the one so in control, you never failed at anything.'

'But you were the sister I never had, as dramatic as that sounds. I felt as though David became your world and I know it's the way it is when you meet someone, I got that once I met Isaac. But I was worried that our friendship would take such a back seat that I'd lose a little piece of myself.'

261

'I never would've dropped you.'

'I couldn't see that at the time. I wanted to carry on as we were, Viola and Jennifer, girls out for fun when I took myself way too seriously the rest of the time.'

Jennifer leaned her head against the wall as they let their conversation settle. And Viola, fuelled by half-decent wine, decided they needed cheering up.

'What do you have in mind?'

She went over to the jukebox, selected Abba and walked back to Jennifer as she moved with the music and broke into song. It was the release both of them needed and they belted out a couple of numbers before they sat back down exhausted but pumped with energy.

'So was the sex even good?' Jennifer ventured.

'What sex?'

'The sex with David's best man, at my reception.'

Viola covered her mouth as a giggle escaped. This was what she'd missed. A good friend, one who knew her, one she could laugh with. 'He was so drunk it took him a while to, you know . . .'

This time Viola rocked back and almost lost her balance with her laughter.

'You're my voice of reason when it comes to Adam,' Jennifer told her. 'I couldn't have confided in anyone else the way I have tonight with you. And let's face it, you could've done worse, you could've shagged the groom at my wedding. Now that would've been unforgivable.'

When 'Super Trouper' came on, Jennifer was up, loud and dancing, freely and the happiest Viola had seen her in a long time. They both were. They danced, they drank, they talked; and, although they hadn't touched too much on their own differences over the years, Viola knew that, somehow, in time, they would. Tonight was only the start. And they'd both made mistakes along the way.

But it was too soon to confide what she knew about Adam. She wanted to enjoy having her friend back, if only for a short while before she told her something that could throw her whole world into disarray once again. And she wanted to help her friend with her marriage troubles in any way she could.

18

Jennifer

Later that week, Jennifer and Viola borrowed the gazebo from the Library of Shared Things and Isaac helped them put it up in Viola's garden, a sprawling area that ran right the way round the entire house and where the gazebo would afford Jennifer and David complete privacy to talk without interruption.

'It's so bloody cold that nobody will come outside,' Viola assured her. 'I'll collect David from your house the minute he comes home from work and drop him here.'

Wrapped up in her winter coat and scarf, Jennifer moved the outdoor heaters into place. Viola had three of them, she often hosted parties here she said, and Jennifer had a pang of sadness that she'd never been to one. Although she hoped that when the next lot of invites went out, she would be on the list.

They opened up a low-rise picnic table beneath the gazebo as well as two of Viola's best outdoor chairs, which were so plush and comfy they resembled inside furniture. Two deep-grey snuggle blankets were housed on one of the chairs should they need them, and on top of the table sat a vintage picnic set they'd borrowed from the Library of Shared Things. The item had been donated by local woman Ruth last week. It had been in her family for years and while Jennifer didn't usually take items unless they were new or at least as new, this was different. Ruth had written a little card she'd slotted into the picnic basket, which told how this item had been passed down in her family and used when her dad proposed to her mum, then again when Ruth's husband proposed to her. And it was gorgeous. The wicker in the basket creaked in transit, as though reminding you of its age, the tan leather buckles were a little worn but still held the bottle-green plates in place, the small glasses in position, and the cutlery gleamed, wrapped in the same green, white and brown checked colours that lined the hamper.

'What did you make?' Jennifer had offered to cook but Viola had taken over that task and there were a few containers stored in the hamper as well as a big flask.

Viola put her hand on one tub. 'My speciality chilli.'

'You mean the same chilli you used to make back when we were at school?'

'The very same. The one I found in an old cookbook and have been making ever since.'

'Then I know I'll love it.'

Viola put a hand to another container before they both got too emotional. 'Garlic bread.' Then another. 'Cheese to sprinkle on top.'

'So it goes all gooey and stringy,' Jennifer finished for her, remembering the way they'd liked it.

'Exactly. And in the flask is mulled wine, loaded with cinnamon and spices. Neither of you will be driving home after that; I'll call you a taxi or drive you myself.'

'I really appreciate all this, Viola. I hope David does too.'

'He will. He's a good one, Jennifer. You picked a good one.'

She should've talked to Viola about Hal a long time ago; perhaps things never would've got so out of hand if she had.

Jennifer unravelled the twinkle lights and between them they looped them around the gazebo structure so that the entire thing was bathed in a soft glow.

Viola surveyed their work and put an arm across Jennifer's shoulders. 'We've done it; it looks really romantic. I might have to leave this all up and have an evening with Isaac.'

'You should. And you picked a good one too. Isaac, I mean. And I'm sorry I didn't come to your wedding.'

'Now, now.' Viola sniffed. 'You'll start me off again. And tonight isn't about me or us; it's about you and David.'

While Viola went to fetch David, Jennifer shook out one of the snuggle rugs, soft as a baby's blanket, and curled up on the chair beneath it. Viola had said she was welcome to go inside the house where it was warmer but she didn't want to. She could imagine the family would've been briefed to stay out of the way, not ask questions, but she wanted some headspace before David got here. And she and Viola had agreed this rendezvous had to be anywhere but at their own house, it needed to be somewhere they wouldn't be interrupted.

The sky was as dark as the bottle of ink that had once sat on her mum's writing desk at the cottage Isla now occupied. Her mum had great penmanship, one of the things she'd refused to give up. She had a phone to stay in touch with her daughters, but she insisted on writing to friends and family far and wide, and dug her heels in when it was suggested emails were easier, faster and cheaper. Even birthday cards had always arrived with her curlicued lettering, and Jennifer had kept a few of them so every now and again she could take them out, hold them against her heart and feel closer to the woman who had gone. Her mum had written to Isla too, the letters finding Jennifer's sister no matter where she was in the world, and Isla had written back many a time, something that had surprised Jennifer. For all the criticisms she had of her younger sister, there seemed to be a lot she still didn't know or understand.

Stars above punctuated the sky as she tilted her head back to feel the evening breeze on her cheeks, already a little too warm under the blanket, and when she heard Viola's car pull in to the driveway, her nerves fluttered up inside her, taunting her that this couldn't possibly work.

It wasn't long before David came around the house, walking determinedly across the grass towards the gazebo. He'd changed into jeans and a jumper and Jennifer could imagine his confusion when he'd arrived home to Viola in the house rather than her, to a barrage of instructions not to keep her waiting.

'I'm worried,' was the first thing he said. He'd picked a marl-grey fisherman's jumper and the jeans she knew were his favourite. They had a small tear at the back pocket and had begun to fray across the bottom, but he'd never let them go. His blond hair had gone darker over the years with a few greys, and he reminded Jennifer of the singer, Keith Urban. It was a thought that shook away her nerves as he sat down in the chair beside her.

'We need to talk.'

'I know. Are you leaving me?' He was looking at his hands.

Her own hand shot out and covered his. 'God, no!'

'Are you sick?'

'No, I promise you.'

'Then why all the cloak-and-dagger operation tonight?'

'I knew that if I tried to talk to you at the house, we'd both be busy, the kids would come in, we'd never get anywhere.'

He looked nervous and she squeezed his hand before she took hers away. 'Can I ask that you let me talk and don't say anything until I've finished?' He seemed a little put out but she needed to unleash all the things she'd been bottling up. 'Please, David.'

His stomach answered for him, with a growl. 'Hungry,' he clarified. 'Whatever's in that hamper isn't helping.'

'The smell must be seeping through the container. I promise food after we talk.'

'OK, go.'

'Now I feel like I'm facing a firing squad.'

'Then we do have problems. You're my wife; for you to feel that way when we're together isn't exactly a good sign. Talk, Jennifer, please.'

She smiled across at him. 'Marrying you was the best thing I ever did, and having a family was the icing on top. I love being a mum, I gave up my career and was happy for a long time. Even after I failed so badly when I tried to start my own hairdressing salon. And then I wanted to add to our family, but I couldn't even do that right.' She stopped him when he almost interrupted. She didn't need praise; she didn't need platitudes. 'I was happy at the time to give up my dreams of my own salon and I was only too happy my family didn't hold what happened against me. The silly risk I took, the mess I got into. I took it as a sign I should stay put, be the stay-at-home mum I was happy to be. But the kids . . . well, they're growing up so fast, and, to be honest, I've started to feel lost.'

He must've seen her shiver because he pulled the blanket further up her lap so it covered her better. She huddled it beneath her chin. 'I feel our lives have been running on separate tracks. You work hard, and I'm not criticising that, but I get lonely.' She almost mentioned her turning to Adam, but she and Viola had been over this as they put up the gazebo, laughing when their heights left them at a disadvantage and they had to enlist Isaac's help to get the canopy on top. They'd decided that there was nothing to gain by doing so, especially given her feelings stemmed from confusion rather than a real desire to go off with a man who wasn't her husband.

When he spoke this time, she didn't stop him. 'I was a mess after the loan shark came to our house. I was angry with you, Jennifer.'

'I know you were.'

'Angry but sympathetic, if that makes sense. You'd made a mistake, but it was a lot to deal with. And my firm was restructuring at the time, which added to my worry. I threw myself into work and it was my escape. And you pushed me away every time you had a miscarriage. I was as devastated as you were and seeing you in so much pain was unbearable. The depth of your grief was something I didn't seem able to reach, so I tried to carry on around you, tiptoeing, being kind, earning the money, keeping us going as we'd always done.'

'I did push you away.' Her admission took him by

surprise. 'I could see I was doing it, but I got selfish; I never imagined your pain could be anywhere near the same as mine. I know that seems terrible of me, but it's as though I couldn't admit to it being our problem rather than mine alone. I'd failed to do the one thing I could always do. Being a mother was my thing, working is yours, and I'd felt I'd let you down. Again. And once it was in my head, I couldn't change the way I thought. It's the same now, with Isla. I'm being stubborn and refusing to let go of the feelings I'm holding inside. I was always envious and jealous she got to go off and travel the world with no responsibilities, when I was here with our parents. Don't get me wrong, I love Cloverdale and I wanted to be here for them, but her having an entirely different life has always niggled and I've let it get in the way of our relationship, when she hasn't really done anything wrong. And I also stayed in Cloverdale because no matter what Mum and Dad told me, I felt I owed everything to them after what I put them through. I thought I deserved to be punished and so when Isla came to visit I never really let her help in the way I was. I always knew best for Dad and then Mum, especially Mum. I think if I hadn't been so bossy, so controlling, Isla probably would've hung around.'

'Your relationship with your sister is reparable,' David reassured her. Her David, supportive as always, but hiding in the wings lately.

'I've been thinking a lot about going back to work,' she admitted. 'But somehow, I've never managed to actually tell you. And after what happened the last time, I tried . . .'

'It's in the past, Jennifer, stop beating yourself up. And maybe you did try. Perhaps I didn't manage to listen.'

He looked heartbroken. He leaned so that his elbows rested on his knees, his hands rubbed his face, the stubble making a scratchy sound as it met with his palms.

'We got busy.'

'We did get busy. Too busy for each other.'

'Remember when all we had to worry about was which beach you'd surf at, where the best waves would be?'

He leaned back in his chair now, arms behind his head. 'Back in the day. It seems a lifetime ago. I can't even remember the last time I went surfing.'

'I can. It was in Cornwall, right before Archie was born.'

'That's right. Amelia had a beach ball, and said it looked the same size as the bump in your tummy.'

'And you wouldn't let me lift anything from the car to bring down to the sand, so it took you multiple trips and lots of swearing.'

Somewhere nearby an owl hooted into the night sky. 'That'd be right. Under my breath to avoid the kids hearing, but I can remember wishing they were a bit more helpful. They'd already run ahead, keen to get onto the sand. Remember that beach picnic we had in Newquay, pre-children?'

'How could I ever forget?' They'd enjoyed the picnic but ended up tearing one another's clothes off as soon as the sun went down, thinking they were all alone with only the moonlight for company.

'It was kind of romantic until we got busted by the dog walker.'

Her laughter mingled with his. 'I still remember him yelling at us as we tried to gather everything up and get away from him.'

'I wonder if we scarred him for life. Or whether he

ever went back to the same beach.' He moved his chair so it was right up against hers and put his arm around her shoulders. 'We need to make more time for us. Maybe ask the twins to look after Archie and we go away.'

'You're joking. It cost me forty quid for tonight; imagine what I'd have to pay for an entire night.'

'It'd be worth it.' His frown deepened. 'You know, when I found Viola at the house I thought she'd come to tell me something terrible had happened to you, and all those moments we've gone out the door separately, all those times we've been too tired to talk to each other, or when I've been in a lonely hotel room without you ... well, they all flashed in front of me, and, on the way over here I thought, what's life all about? I have to make a living, but does it have to cost me a marriage? I really thought ...'

'I'm still here, I'm not going anywhere.' They sat in silence, breathing in the still night air, feeling the coolness on their skin and embracing the kind of moment Jennifer had feared was gone. 'Archie misses you, you know.'

'I know.' He kissed the top of her head. 'I figured that's what was behind the days off school.'

'He needs his dad. So do the girls. So do I.'

'I'm glad we booked the holiday. It'll be good for us. And I'll see if I can get Archie going with surfing, maybe enrol him in a proper session with kids his own age first rather than his old dad.'

She smiled. 'You were listening when I suggested it.'

'Of course.' He hesitated before he asked, 'Did you start the Library of Shared Things because you were tired of our life at home?'

'I suppose I needed something, and I thought that

might be it. I got my fingers burned before, attempting to start my own business. I fell at the first hurdle. I thought the library might distract me from wanting to go back to work and risk throwing everyone's world upside down again. But no, I didn't do it because I was tired of us. I just missed doing something for myself. And I saw it as something good for Cloverdale.'

'Your mum was really excited about you doing it too.'

Her eyes misted as she thought of her mum. She'd have loved her to see how much the Library of Shared Things was bringing to Cloverdale with more items than they'd had at the start, the mornings where people stopped by for a cup of tea and a gossip, Isla back in the village and running dance lessons. 'It was Mum who got me thinking seriously about it.'

'I thought it was when you saw your friend in Crystal Palace. Didn't she spill wine and you borrowed a cleaner?'

'We did. But before that, I'd been chatting with Mum. She said that once upon a time, Cloverdale had been a friendlier place. I told her it still was but she told me how the bakery had once been a hub for locals. There was no library back then, the pub was mostly for the evenings, but people of all ages used the bakery before and after school or work, during the day or early in the evening, weekdays and weekends, and everybody knew each other. You couldn't pass a stranger in the street; if you did, you'd know they must be a visitor. Mum told me she missed those days, and it was a shame how people led their lives without knowing the people who lived one, two or three doors away.'

'And you wanted to get a little bit of that back. You've done a wonderful job with it and I loved seeing the passion in your eyes when the project got off the ground. I hadn't seen that kind of passion since we lost . . . since we lost our babies.'

'Our little angels.' She wiped a tear that tumbled from the corner of her eye.

'You've done an amazing job with the family we already have, and I should've told you so more often. I think seeing you throw yourself into a new project also helped me to feel less guilty.'

'Guilty?'

'About having my work, not being good enough to help you after you lost the babies. I couldn't do anything to bring back a smile to that face, light up those eyes.' He ran a hand across her chin and looked into the pools of deep brown. 'But the Library of Shared Things certainly has. And I understand the desire to go back to work, I really do.'

'I wish I'd talked to you sooner.'

'We've been busy.'

'Far too busy.' She moved and sat on his lap as the twinkly lights and stars mingled up above.

'You know what we've been too busy for tonight?'

'What's that?' She snuggled against him, inhaling the warm scent as she nestled her face against his neck.

'Food. I'm starving.'

'You're not just saying that to get me off your lap are you?'

'Of course not. We'll eat and you can get right back on.'

Between them they uncovered the chilli, the garlic bread, the cheese to sprinkle on top. Jennifer poured the mulled wine into the mugs rather than glasses so it would stay warmer. And for a while they enjoyed good food, the company of each other, so simple and so easy to neglect. They talked about hairdressing, her love that had never really gone away, her idea to start home hairdressing for a while, manage it around family commitments, build up a client list and see where it took her. He talked about scaling back a bit, being at home some more and learning to delegate if and when he could.

David's next comment took her by surprise. 'You know, I was beginning to wonder whether you and Adam were getting close.'

Her mouthful of chilli burned the back of her throat. 'In what way?'

'He always seems to be there for you, you talk to him, you're happy in his company. I watched you once outside the library and it was the happiest I'd seen you in a long while.'

'He's a good friend.' It wasn't a lie. It was the absolute truth. Adam was a good friend, a good man, and it was she who'd confused it in her mind with something more. And she'd forever be grateful she'd stopped the friendship in its tracks from becoming something it shouldn't. 'I enjoy his company. But that's it. You know you're the only man I love.' Hal had almost come between them a long time ago but she hadn't heard from him since she got married and she'd never regretted her decision. She'd made the right one.

'Hasn't Isla been seeing Adam?'

Tonight the topic didn't niggle at her the way it had up until now; her worries didn't bunch up inside her at the thought of her sister getting involved with her friend. 'She has; they seem to get on well. She invited me over to her place one evening too.'

'Well, that's good, I want to see you two be the sisters your mum wished you'd be.'

'She told you that?'

'Once or twice. And she made me promise I'd make sure you two never lost touch. I'm not sure how I'd have done that – you're both strong-willed – but I'm glad you want to make the effort.' He lifted another forkful of chilli and chewed contentedly.

They talked more about Adam, what brought him to Cloverdale, his single dad status and the fact that, even though they were friends, none of them had really asked for any details.

'I guess if he needs to talk, he will,' said David. 'Us men like to keep our private lives under wraps . . . can't say I told anyone about our problems of late.'

'Neither did I, until Viola.'

'She told me you'd talked things through. I'm glad you two are starting over.'

'Me too. Because she makes the best chilli.'

They finished their mulled wine tucked beneath one blanket, cuddling up together in the privacy of the idyllic spot her best friend had helped her set up. Jennifer texted Viola when they decided it was time to get going, thanked her and told her they didn't need a lift home. They'd walk together beneath the moonlight instead.

And when they did, they may have stopped along the secluded country lane to kiss in the same way they had back on the beach in Cornwall. They stopped short of going any further; after all they were a respectable married couple now. And they'd stay that way for years to come.

19

Zoe

Zoe lay on her bed waiting for Ava to come over to Lilliput Cottage. It had been the longest, best, most thrilling forty-eight hours of her life and she couldn't wait to tell her friend that her mum had been in touch. Her mum!

After showing the profile picture of her latest follower to Viola and accepting that it was most likely a random fan of interior design, Zoe had left it. But gradually she'd begun to think, what if it *was* her mum? What harm could it do to follow the profile and if it wasn't, she'd un-follow and block if the person turned out to be some kind of weirdo. She knew it happened. Tatiana in her class at school was followed by someone at the beginning of term and the person she thought was a thirteen-year-old girl, interested in talking about make-up, turned out to be a twenty-something male with an obsession for taking photographs of his bare chest and tattoos to send to girls much younger than him.

Zoe had followed Suzie on Instagram on Friday night but there was nothing on her profile or timeline to give Zoe any clues as to Suzie's identity, so she'd put her phone in the kitchen as usual. She hadn't been expecting it but

tears of disbelief that this was really happening – party balloons, a smiley face, hearts. And her mum had sent back a lovely message telling Zoe all about her home in Melbourne, how she still loved the beach.

Zoe: I remember! We used to go all the time.

Suzie: Do you ever go there with Zac?

Zoe: Bit cold here in England.

Suzie: I wish you weren't so far away.

Zoe: What's the profile pic you used on Insta?

Suzie: You don't recognise it? It's one of yours. You drew it after a day at the beach; it's your picture of me in a turquoise dress with my straw hat on.

Zoe had replied to that message through angry tears, frustration that they'd been kept apart for such a long time. Her mum had kept this picture she couldn't even remember drawing. All those wasted years neither of them could get back. And it was all her dad's fault. Her mum had had problems – she'd gone through a breakdown – but surely it didn't mean they had to leave her behind when she needed them the most.

They'd carried on texting the whole time her dad was at football, then again in the evening until it was time to leave phones in the kitchen, and Zoe had been back to it yesterday too. Ava was away for the weekend and she'd been dying to tell her everything but it was good to stay in her own little world with her mum for a while, although she'd had to leave her phone alone for a couple of hours yesterday when her dad started to ask questions about what she was doing. She made up some excuse about Candy Crush and thankfully Zac piped up with his support, dropping her in it, or so he thought, for working her way up the levels.

She'd wondered what her dad would say if he knew what she was really doing.

And now, on a Monday morning at Lilliput Cottage, it was time to tell her friend everything.

Ava lay alongside Zoe on her bed in the newly decorated bedroom as both girls tried to process what this all meant. Here, in Zoe's new haven, finished yesterday, with its brushed cotton lavender duvet with tiny white embroidered flowers, the lavender and white pillows that added a touch of comfort and bold colours asserting themselves throughout the room. A lavender velvet cushion sat on the desk chair, a lavender rug on the floor, while desk accessories added a splash of striking purple. However, even such calm surroundings couldn't cushion the real-life drama that was beginning to unfold.

'This is huge, Zoe.' Ava was still taking it all in.

'I couldn't wait to tell you.' She fiddled with one of the flowers on the duvet cover.

'I can't believe you found her after all this time. Your mum. How does it feel?'

Zoe turned from her tummy onto her back as Ava looked at the Instagram messages on her phone. She'd sent her mum photographs of her new room, loving the fact she could finally involve her in part of her life again. 'I don't know how to explain it.'

'Does *my* mum know?'

'She knows I had some contact from this person and I thought it might be mum, but since I found out it definitely was, I haven't told her. I kind of wanted to keep it to myself.'

'You and my mum got really close.' Ava turned onto her back too, both mirror images, lying there looking up at the ceiling, hands clasped across their tummies.

'She's all right, your mum.'

'She has her moments. She's never as relaxed with me as she is with you.'

'That's because you're her responsibility. I'm not.'

'I guess so.'

'All I ever wanted was to have a mum who cared, who was there. You're really lucky.'

'I've been really mean to her lately,' Ava admitted. 'Even meaner than usual.'

'Why?'

'Because I was jealous. I told her she loved you more than me.'

'You daft cow,' Zoe giggled.

'I know. But all she does is ask me about school; she's nosy about everything and she never lets up.'

'She cares. I wish I had someone who thought so much of me.'

'Your dad does.'

'I suppose.'

'Your mum seems kind of cool.'

'She does, doesn't she?' Zoe couldn't help the smile that formed.

'To be fair I think your dad is kind of cool; maybe you should talk to him about her.'

'No way! I've tried enough times. He refuses to tell me anything. Maybe her breakdown freaked him out or something and he thinks if we hear about it, we'll be psychologically damaged.'

'What do you think he'd do if he found out you were in contact with her?'

'Probably have a meltdown.'

Ava laughed. 'As bad as the time Mum saw me kissing Hugo Revella outside the school gates?'

'That was hilarious . . . at least looking back on it, it was. She met you every day for a fortnight after that.'

'Don't remind me. Anyone would think I'd had sex with him in the car park the way she'd reacted.'

'Your mum is cool in so many ways.'

'Yeah . . . but we're talking about your mum now.'

Zoe had zoomed through all kinds of emotions since Susan had first got in touch. She'd told Zoe how she'd been to hell and back when their dad took her kids away but she'd got the help she needed, she was better, and she wanted to make amends but was afraid Adam wouldn't give her a chance.

'I don't mind sharing my mum for this,' said Ava.

'What are you talking about?'

'Ask her what she'd do.'

Zoe shook her head. 'Your mum is another parent. There'll be some kind of parent code that means she has to tell Dad, and once he knows, he'll go back to policing my every move. He's only just started to let up a bit.'

'When's your dad coming back?'

'He's at work all day.' The girls' school had closed due to a burst water pipe and Zoe had been allowed to stay home alone with the proviso that she remained in the house and responded to his text messages.

Ava sat cross-legged on the rug, her back against the bed, Zoe opposite with her back against the wardrobe as they chugged the cans of Diet Coke Ava had brought round for them. 'Do you have any more photographs of your mum?'

'She posted something this morning with her picture.' Zoe found the image. 'Apart from the picture she sent in her message, this is her first post with herself in it; all the others seem to be of the beach. I think she's quite arty; there are a few of seashells.'

Ava took the phone to see for herself. 'She looks like you. Same blue eyes.'

'Do you think so?' The clear picture of her mum with windswept blonde hair and sunglasses propped on the top of her head looked back at them both. Zoe had analysed it over and over since it had appeared, wondering what her voice sounded like, her laugh, what it would feel like to hug her after all this time.

'For sure. And she looks fun.'

'She always was. Sometimes she'd surprise Zac and me and whisk us off somewhere exciting. I remember she pulled us out of school once for a family emergency – she took us to Luna Park.'

'What's that?'

'It's an amusement park with a pirate ship, a roller coaster, right near the beach.'

'The only way my mum would drag me out of school was if she thought I could get considerable educational benefit from an outing.'

'Another time she drove us up to the snow. She took us sledding. We fell off so much that day. My nose was pink and cold. Zac fell asleep on the way back home he was so tired.'

'She sounds pretty awesome.'

'She really does.' Yet she'd still let her kids go. But she'd been sick, hadn't she? And mental problems were often immeasurable, not like her diabetes where she could test herself and inject insulin as and when she needed to keep it under control.

'Has she asked to talk on the phone?'

'Neither of us have mentioned it.' Zoe felt resentment rise inside of her. 'I wish she'd tried to find us sooner.'

'Maybe she was worried your dad would put a stop to anything and then she'd be stuck.'

'Sometimes I hate him, you know.'

Ava put down her can. 'Hate's a strong word.'

'OK, so I don't really *hate* him, but I'm angry. What kind of parent doesn't give the other one a chance to put things right? She can't help the way her brain works, the problems she has or had. And he just left her. Isn't marriage about sticking with each other, through the good times and the bad? You have to agree on it, when you say all those words.'

'Vows.'

'Exactly.'

Zoe's voice wobbled with excitement . . . and nerves – she wasn't sure what emotion to pin on it. 'I'm so, so happy I've found her, Ava.'

Ava moved from her position and hugged her friend. 'Then don't give up. It's a shame she's so far away. If she was in England you could get her to come to the house, she could show your dad how together she is now, that she wants to be a part of your life. Does Zac know anything?'

'No, and I won't tell him. He'll get his hopes up and then it'll disappoint him if she goes away again. I don't know what to do to make this right. Am I going to have to wait until I'm eighteen to see her properly?'

They sat in contemplative silence, considering their options. With Susan all the way in Melbourne and them in England, what could they possibly do?

'Ask her,' Ava prompted.

'Ask her what?'

'Ask her to come.'

'To England? No, I can't do that.'

'Why not? She's your mum. Put the suggestion out there. She can only say no.'

'I don't know.'

Ava picked up Zoe's phone and handed it to her. 'You want to see her, don't you?'

Zoe bit down on her bottom lip. She wondered whether her mum did that when she was nervous too. She could remember some things, the way her mum's hands smelled after she'd put on silky-smooth hand cream, the softness of her cheek when she kissed her goodnight, the vacant look in her eyes the day she'd said goodbye as though she didn't really want to do it. But there was still so much to find out.

Before she could change her mind, Zoe tapped out a message. She said she missed her, she wanted to see her, and she asked her if she'd consider coming to England.

'She won't answer for a while,' said Zoe, desperately trying not to get her hopes up. 'It's getting on for midnight in Australia.' When her phone rang it made them both jump. 'Relax, it's only Dad,' Zoe managed.

She chatted as normally as she could, making a point of

asking him what they could have for lunch, keeping the conversation normal. But it was hard. And she was starting to miss her dad and their closeness, even though they were in the same house, shared mealtimes and talked on a daily basis. He frustrated her, nagged, he worried too much, but, as much as he'd kept her from her mum, she missed laughing with him, a cuddle at the end of the day when she was young enough for it not to be embarrassing or even when she wasn't and resisted, but secretly liked the fuss.

'You all right?' Ava must've noticed tears pricking her eyes when she hung up.

'Fine, yes. Cheese on toast for lunch?'

'I'm starving.'

'Then we'd better do some homework; Dad will ask what I've got done.'

'So will Mum.'

They made their snack, and got through some homework. Then they chatted on their phones with school mates, laughing at a meme someone had shared about rumbling stomachs in the middle of a school exam, and by two o'clock they were lazing up in her bedroom again.

'What you need are answers, Zo.' Ava fiddled with the reed sticks of the lavender infuser so the opposite ends could emit more scent. 'You need to know exactly what happened, why she let your dad take you and Zac all the way to another country. I mean, why couldn't he stay in Australia?'

Zoe stared at the ceiling. 'I don't know.'

'Then let's take action. Your dad is usually here, so make the most of it while he isn't.'

'And what, call Mum and talk to her?'

Ava considered it. 'No, he'll see it on the home phone bill or as extra charges on yours. But haven't you ever nosed around looking for answers?'

'Of course I have. I didn't find anything though.'

'Then you didn't look hard enough.'

'I did. I looked in his wardrobe, under the bed, his bed-side cabinet, through all the papers he has in a cardboard box filled with rental agreements, bills, boring stuff.'

'Do you have a loft?'

'Yes, but no ladder. He's never used it.'

'What about the cabinets downstairs?' She got to her feet. 'Come on. What time is your brother coming home?'

'Not until Dad collects him from Jennifer's house around six.'

'Then that gives us a few hours. We're going to search this place from top to bottom.'

They started downstairs in the lounge, looking under sofas, Ava picking up cushions to see what was there, glee-ful at finding a pound she handed to Zoe who put it in the swear jar her dad had bought last year, mainly for himself than anyone else. They searched the low cabinet and found plenty of sweet wrappers, suspecting Zac was the culprit, but little else apart from a dead spider and a DVD Zoe had forgotten they had. They went through the cupboard beneath the stairs, hauling out the vacuum and ironing board so they could get all the way to the back. They opened up the old suitcases stored at the side to check Zoe's dad wasn't hiding things in there.

'Sometimes it's as though she never existed.' Zoe slumped down on the floor in the hallway. Let's face it, their dad wanted his kids all to himself; whether it was selfishness or worry that they shouldn't see their mum sick, she had no idea, but he'd definitely cut the ties. She knew he loved them both but it was getting harder and harder to take his side when he was so unwilling to treat her and Zac with enough respect to share the information that she yearned to know, and that Zac would, sooner or later, want to know himself.

Ava emerged from the cupboard, her hair dishevelled and tugging at a cobweb from her face. 'Gross. Your dad needs to vacuum in there, big time.'

'I'll let him know.'

'Shame Mum didn't see it; she's a stickler for dust and dirt . . . hates it.'

'I'm not sure what's easier' – Zoe led the way to the kitchen and filled a glass of water for each of them at the tap – 'a parent who insists on everything being tidy, or one who isn't bothered. On the one hand you'd have an organised life; on the other, you'd be afraid to put anything down in case it got thrown away. At least Dad doesn't do that. I can leave piles of books lying around, or a collection of things I need to remember for school right by the front door so I don't forget.'

'And you're allowed to stick notes to the fridge.' Ava eyed the magnets pinning down a shopping list, a photo of Zoe and Zac with their dad in London, a picture Zac had drawn of the three of them, a picture her dad had drawn and Zac had coloured of a wizard she assumed must be Harry Potter, who Zac was obsessed with, another photograph of Zoe and Zac the morning of their first day of the school term, arms around one another, smiling at the camera, their lives a strange kind of normal now it was only the three of them.

'Aren't you allowed to?'

'It wouldn't be aesthetically pleasing,' Ava mimicked Viola's voice, getting it spot on. She undid the cutlery drawer, then the junk drawer, which was filling up nicely even though they hadn't actually lived here all that long. She even opened up the fridge.

'What . . . you think he's rolled up a load of documents and hidden them in the salad crisper?' She laughed as Ava pulled out the plastic section.

They scoured the rest of the kitchen, but nothing, and moved on to the utility room. As well as various bottles, there were matches and batteries, light bulbs in an assortment of shapes and sizes, old rags and fluffy dusters, something that Zoe knew fitted on the bottom of the floor mop, coloured blocks of liquid that hung from a plastic hook in the toilet bowl. 'I don't think Dad needs half this stuff.' She turned to find Ava had scaled the built-in shelving unit. 'What are you doing? You'll break your neck.' She stood behind her as she stepped from the last shelf she'd foraged in over to the worktop.

'I'll pick everything up.' She'd knocked out plenty as she was searching, a couple of oily rags, another pack of batteries that narrowly missed falling on Zoe's head.

'You will. Or Dad will know what we've been up to.'

'If he's anything like my dad, he won't notice; he shoves things in cupboards and can never find them again.' She pulled out a bottle of something. 'What the heck is sugar soap?'

'I think you use it to clean walls.' Zoe dodged a clothes peg that came in her direction.

'Oh, hello.' Ava's face, eyes wide, looked down at Zoe before she pulled something out from the topmost shelf.

She briefly looked inside and her mouth fell open some more. 'Bingo.'

'What?' Zoe shoved items back into shelves as, with what looked like a book of sorts in her arms, Ava negotiated getting down from the worktop in one piece.

On safe ground Ava blew her hair from her face and held up a notebook. 'It's a diary, with a photo inside.'

When Ava opened the front cover, Zoe lifted out a photo: a family shot of them all, Mum, Dad, her and Zac. Zoe couldn't stop staring at it. Suddenly this all seemed so real. 'What was that?' She'd heard a noise and she held her breath.

'I didn't hear anything but let me go to the door.' Ava thrust the diary at Zoe, but she was there and back in seconds. 'Just junk mail coming through the letter box. And I put the chain on the door. If your dad comes home unexpectedly, we'll tell him we did it as a security measure . . . you know, two young girls home alone.'

Zoe clasped the diary against her chest. She didn't want to open it. Against her body was safe, until she chose it not to be. 'What if this tells me things I don't want to know?'

'It might do.'

'I can't do it.'

'Do you want me to read?'

Zoe shook her head.

'Your choice. You can put it back.' Ava shrugged. 'Or you can put an end to the wondering. You can find out the truth. Maybe. It might not even tell us anything.'

'Let's go upstairs. I'd feel better in my bedroom. But first, put all this back as it was before, so if Dad does come home early he won't know we've been in here.'

'Right you are.' Ava did everything, Zoe couldn't move. Her past, her future, it could all be in this book still attached to her chest beneath a mighty grasp.

Upstairs, Ava lay tummy down on her bed and Zoe sat on the floor, back up against the wardrobe, the book on her knees.

'I can leave you to it if you like,' Ava suggested.

'Don't you dare. I need you here.'

'Remember when we found that love letter in your locker at the start of term?'

'You snatched it from my hand to read it.'

'I'm gonna do the same in a minute unless you get this over with.'

Zoe took a deep breath, opened the book to find dates heading each entry.

'Is there a name?'

'Not that I can see.' She'd flicked through a few pages, but no name had jumped out at her. 'Ready?'

Ava turned onto her back, looked up at the ceiling. 'Hit me with it.'

And Zoe began to read.

Date: July 2005

Our wedding in February of last year was nothing short of magical, much like our relationship had been up to that point. We had twinkly lights wound up the bark of trees, waiters floated around with glasses of champagne on silver trays, the room was filled with laughter and chatter and right then, I knew I couldn't have been happier.

Our daughter Zoe was born a few months later, one rainy morning in March, and, from the moment I saw her, I was in love. I was overwhelmed, infatuated, in awe of this tiny

human who depended solely on the grown-ups. From her deli-
cate fingers and toes to her tiny little nose and eyes that fixed
on mine from the start, she couldn't have been more perfect.

Zoe almost began to cry. This was her mum, talking
about her, and it made her desperate to see her again.

I'm starting this diary, because life has a funny way of
catching us off-guard, of changing when we least expect. I
don't mean the nice parts, like the first time you hear your
child laugh, or you pick them up when they fall over, the way
they take in the world around them. I mean the changes you
don't see coming, the ones that hit you at full speed.

Yesterday, our daughter turned one. We planned a party
with family and friends, or at least those who were close by
and could make it, but work that day had been hectic for
both of us and I wasn't able to pick our daughter up from
childcare on my designated day or make it home in time for
the party. I'd made a mistake and I knew it; I just didn't
expect the knock-on effects. As soon as I stepped through the
door I knew that I'd well and truly messed up. And only later
on that night – when all the guests had gone home, when
the remains of the cake were tucked inside their Tupperware
container and the lid clicked in place and our baby was safely
in her cot oblivious to everything else – did I pay the price.

What was that childhood saying? Sticks and stones may
break my bones, but names will never hurt me. That was it.
Well, it turned out that names could really hurt. I was called
everything under the sun, I was slapped around the head,
spat at for being such a useless parent. I went to bed that
night wondering whether those words were true. I should've
been on time for my own child's birthday, she only turns one

once, I was the bad person here. And I deserved the way I was treated.

Didn't I?

Zoe held the open book, aware of Ava looking at her.

'Jeez. I was expecting some diary about the weather, cheesy bands on the radio who we've never heard of. Not what those words are hinting at. They sound . . . sinister.'

'I don't know if I can read more.' She felt sick, numb.

'You could write and ask your mum what happened.'

'I don't want to scare her away. What if the truth makes her sink back into that dark place that made her have a breakdown?'

'Then keep reading. I'm here.'

Date: February 2006

A hug is supposed to release oxytocin, the love drug. Hugs calm your nervous system and are known to heal, relieve anxiety, feelings of isolation and stress.

But the only person hugging me right now is our daughter. And they're wonderful hugs. Unconditional cuddles with a power to calm me in the face of everything that's been going on in our family.

Zoe hadn't been aware she was crying, of how hard it was to read these words, until Ava came and sat beside her, urged her to go on. Instead of reading out loud, they both read in their heads, prompting the other when it was time to turn the page:

I never realised how damaging it could be to withdraw affection from a partner, what it could do to a person's well-being. But in a marriage, hugs are part of the deal, and I didn't know how much I needed them till they were gone. I can't remember the last time we had physical contact. Instead, I'm pushed aside or snapped at, ridiculed and made to feel about as big as an ant crawling beneath a rock for safety before it's trampled upon.

I'd hoped things could improve, but they seem to be going in the opposite direction and I feel I can no longer make the excuse of us both being tired from parenting and both working full-time. Yesterday I was apparently having an affair after I was forty-five minutes late home from work, the day before I was working too many hours, the day before that I wasn't loading the dishwasher correctly. I know all couples bicker, but these muttered tiny comments criticising me and the things I do grow to become great tidal waves and a torrent of abuse.

Growing up I was a happy child, I had parents who loved me, who showed each other affection, and I'd always thought that was what marriage was. But this depiction of marriage is far from what I ever imagined.

Today I am fed up, today I am upset, but today I am also hopeful things will improve, that we will be able to reconnect in some way.

I try to tell myself that things could be worse.

'Oh, Ava. This is too much.' Zoe clung to her friend, absorbing the dreadful truth, the realisation of what had gone on between her parents.

'You can stop, Zoe.' Ava's voice wobbled too. They were fourteen years old, too immature to take this in or to fully understand the adult behaviours at play.

'I can't. Not now I've found it. I need to read every

word, know how Mum felt. This *must* have been why she pushed me and Zac away. She had no choice. He was *cruel* to her. My own dad, he did all this. I want to know everything, then put it back, then I can decide what to do.'

'We might need to tell my mum.'

Zoe gripped her arm. 'Not yet.'

They read on. They read about the emotional abuse, alcohol usually to blame, the daily verbal explosions, how friends were driven away until there was nobody left. It was the sort of terror portrayed on TV, not in her own family.

Zoe wondered why her dad had taken the diary away, why he'd kept it; was it some perverse pleasure to relive what he'd done? What sort of person did that?

Ava read another entry out loud when Zoe curled up on the floor not wanting to look at the diary but desperate to learn what she could:

Date: New Year 2010

I was late home from work today and my punishment was being shut out of the house in a heatwave. My keys were no use; the chain had been drawn across. I was sweltering, nearly passing out. I had no water. I didn't want to knock at the neighbour's house because they'd know there was someone home. I could hear my kids' laughter from the upstairs window; it was bath time, I could tell.

I wandered down to the beach and found a café with air conditioning. I stayed for three hours, through a smoothie and two colas. And then I went home. I wished I had a friend to talk to but they've all stopped calling, stopped inviting me places.

When I finally got home I was shouted at for drinking, even though I hadn't been, I shouted back for shutting me out, and this time I felt like I was finally standing up for myself.

Until dinner time.

The kids had eaten earlier and I checked on them, wishing I'd been there to say goodnight and read them a story. I wondered had they asked where I was? Seen me out of the window?

Downstairs I filled a glass of water at the sink; I was in the firing line without realising. Instead of the boiling water from the pan of carrots being emptied into the sink, it came my way, covering my forearm, the skin exposed and vulnerable. The burns were so bad I had to go to the hospital. I told them it was an accident, I'd dropped the pan, I was clumsy.

I don't know what's worse, the physical pain I'm enduring or the emotional torment that this is the reality of our marriage.

Ava and Zoe struggled through the entire diary together, spent with emotion, wrung out from tears they shed freely.

'How could he do those things?' Zoe sobbed. The boiling water episode had only been the start. There'd been worse, much worse. 'She could've died.'

Ava's voice wobbled. 'Don't cry, Zoe. Please, don't cry.'

'I have to see her. I have to get me and Zac away.' She fell apart all over again. 'But I love Dad. I want to hate him, but I don't,' she cried.

'Nobody can ever understand this sort of thing.'

'Dad must have tricked her into letting us go, given her no option.'

'Maybe she thought it was safer to stay away and then

find you later . . . now, when you're old enough to have it explained.'

'I don't think I'll ever feel old enough to know those sorts of things.'

'No, I don't suppose anyone ever is.'

When Zoe picked up her phone at another text message from her dad, it took her a while to reply. 'How can I pretend everything is normal?' She tapped out a quick response and turned to her friend. 'I talked about cheese on toast, cleaning the grill, asked him when he'll be home. I don't care if he never comes back.' Except of course she did. She couldn't change her feelings overnight.

'What time is it in Australia now?'

'Middle of the night, I think.' But when she checked her phone her mum had replied.

'Come on, what does it say?' Ava was on her knees, trying to see for herself.

Zoe's eyes zoomed over the words and she gasped. 'She says she'll come.'

'Oh my God, Zo!' Ava gripped her arm tight.

'She's looking at flights. Right now.' A million butterflies fluttered around her tummy. This was real. It was going to happen.

'Ask her when!'

Zoe's hands shook as she sent another message and her mum wrote straight back. 'She's hoping a week Thursday.'

'Wait.' Ava pulled out her own phone and looked at the dates. 'That works out well. You have a long weekend from school, it's those two inset days. Where will you meet?'

'I don't know.'

'Here? Somewhere else?'

Head in her hands, Zoe reiterated, 'I don't know.'

'She's replied again.' Ava's eyes were trained on Zoe's phone.

'She's booked. Already!' Her eyes skimmed over the words, taking them all in. 'She arrives on the Thursday in the early hours . . . she's hiring a car . . . she'll drive to wherever I want.'

Ava squealed. 'She's so cool! I wish I was meeting her. OK, let's think. Not Cloverdale, it's too small, people will talk. How about a service station somewhere?'

Zoe turned her nose up. 'It's a bit seedy, I'm not sure.'

'What about London, you could get a train?'

As they were discussing locations, Susan sent through another message. 'She's asking if I remember the camping weekend she took Zac and me on.'

'I'm taking it you do, given your smile.' Ava hugged her tight. 'This is my Zoe, not the crying one, the one who doesn't know what to do.'

She texted back to say of course she did and told Ava, 'It was in a place called Hall's Gap. We toasted marshmallows, cooked all our food over the fire. Zac and I had a great time. She'd woken us up when Dad was asleep, he wasn't well, and she wanted to take us away to give him a break.' Her face changed. 'Thinking about it now, maybe she was so scared she wanted to get some distance. Maybe she was terrified. I can't imagine what it must've been like.' Would Zoe feel safe in her bed tonight? Her dad had never raised a hand to either of his kids, but perhaps neither of them had pushed him enough yet.

'How about meeting her at that camping place you went to in the Chilterns?' Ava suggested.

'I guess that could work.' She sent another message and

they waited for her reply. 'She wants to know if I have a tent.' Zoe giggled, she was excited. How on earth was she going to keep it together until her mum arrived?

With a thought in mind, Ava took out her own phone, tapped away and turned the device to face Zoe. 'They've got one at the Library of Shared Things. I remember it being donated. Erin's husband gave it away, knowing Erin would never go camping in her life. You can tell Jennifer or whoever else is on that day that you're surprising Zac and your dad so they have to keep it quiet.'

Zoe looked at the tent. A two-man, newish, everything in the kit, even two airbeds. 'Do you have sleeping bags I could borrow?'

'I do. If your mum arrives on the Thursday tell her you'll meet her on the Friday afternoon, at the entrance to the campsite. We'll send her the address and postcode. Say you'll bring everything. You can get a taxi. I have money to pay, don't worry about that.'

'And what am I supposed to tell my dad I'm doing? He's going to realise I'm not at home.'

'Haven't thought of that yet.'

'It'll never work.'

'We need a cover story.' She thought hard. 'You know Tatiana from school?'

'Yeah.'

'I covered for her last year. She had a huge fourteenth birthday party at her parents' mansion in the country and someone sneaked in a bottle of vodka, which they poured into Tatiana's glass of fruit punch for a laugh. She was wasted but her parents know me and didn't bat an eye lid when I went inside to ask if we could camp out in the garden for the night. Her dad helped me pitch the tent while Tatiana was supposedly saying goodbye to all her guests.'

'What was she really doing?'

'Sleeping it off at the back of the barn on a bale of hay.'

Zoe sniggered. 'And her parents never sussed what was happening?'

'No, or she would've been grounded for months. How about I ask Tatiana to help us out? It's the perfect cover. She could have us for a sleepover and the best part is that Mum has known the family for years; she'll happily drop us over there and not ask many questions.'

'Go for it.'

Ava tapped out a message for Tatiana and it didn't take long for her reply to say of course she'd do it.

'We'll say we're camping in the garden again,' said Ava, 'that'll explain to Mum why we need the camping gear. Tatiana's is only a two-man tent so not enough room for us three. We'll get you in a taxi and off to meet your mum, you come back the next day.'

'Won't it be obvious I'm not there?'

'Her garden is massive and her parents are super cool. They won't disturb us once they see us go out to the tent and they'll be off to work the morning after.'

And just like that Zoe began her countdown of days until she saw her mum for the first time in years.

She knew it was going to be the best thing ever.

20

Jennifer

'It's good to see you.' Isla stepped back to let Jennifer into the cottage.

'Here, I know you said not to bring anything, but I couldn't come empty-handed. Isaac chose it.' She handed her sister the bottle of wine.

'Well, I appreciate it. Would you rather I open this than the one already going?'

'Don't be silly. Put that in the kitchen, and if we need it, it's there.'

When Isla took her through to the kitchen, Jennifer ran a hand over the smoothly varnished bannisters. They looked stunning, the whole place had the cosy feel back again. It smelled of fresh paint and had that new carpet aroma, and it was still surreal to be inside these walls without either of their parents here. Jennifer had been here so little since their mum died that she almost expected to find her in the kitchen making a pot of tea, or in front of the television chuckling away at a favourite comedy show.

Isla's invite tonight for wine and cheese had come at the right time. After she'd talked with David and with Viola, Isla was the only person she still had to sort things out with. Jennifer wasn't quite sure how she'd become this person with so many things bottled up inside, so many strained relationships she hadn't known which way to turn. But she had, and she couldn't keep going in the same way.

'You've done an amazing job with this place.' She took the glass of wine that Isla proffered. 'I love the retro fridge.'

'Mum would hate it.'

'She really would. But it's very you, and I mean that in a nice way,' she added in case her sister thought she was being overly critical.

Isla gestured for her to follow her into the lounge where she'd already set up a cheese board on a low coffee table, with a selection of crackers in a contemporary white bowl. 'What do you think to this room?'

'It's brilliant; you've chosen such lovely colours.'

'Silver thaw on this wall,' said Isla, her fingers delicately touching the paint colour that made the background for the new wood burner which was already lit. 'Soft white on the others.'

'The furniture is beautiful.' The smell of leather lingered in the air, the sofa and chairs still in need of breaking in to give the material that welcoming feel.

'Sit, please.'

'Anywhere?'

'Of course. I'm not Dad who always had his favourite chair and got uppity if any of us sat in it.'

'He loved that chair.'

'I still have it.'

'Where?'

'It's in the dining room in the corner. I had it recovered in a lime green to brighten the place up.'

Jennifer laughed. 'Good job he can't see that.'

'Help yourself.' Isla knelt down on the rug in front of the coffee table and reeled off the list of cheese choices: brie, camembert, Roquefort, a mature cheddar, a creamy blue Stilton. 'There's apple and ale chutney, rosemary and gin jelly.' She turned the third pot round to check the label. 'And this one is fig chutney. I remembered you liked it.'

Jennifer helped herself, touched her sister had gone to so much effort. 'It's lovely and cosy in here with the wood burner.'

'And it's much warmer than it ever was with the old gas heater.'

'I'm so glad you got rid of it; it was an ugly old thing.'

'I kept telling Mum to do away with it, but she said anything else would be too much effort.'

'I guess they got set in their ways.'

'It was weird being here on my own at first.' Isla topped her cracker with the rosemary and gin jelly and added a piece of cheddar. 'Upsetting too. Kind of like I was rubbing my nose in the fact they'd gone and I'd never see either of them again. You'd think we'd be used to not having Dad around anymore, but some days it's as though he was here yesterday.'

'I know. Mum talked about him all the time; sometimes I'd worry she was losing her mind when she mentioned him as though he was still alive, but I suppose to her he'd never leave her, at least in her mind.'

'It'll be a shame to see it go but I guess we should start thinking about having the estate agents over to have the cottage valued. And probably best to do it sooner rather than later, seeing as it looks so good now. It looks like a show home.'

'You're right, it does. And thanks for sending me the costs; David will transfer my half of the money into your account later today.'

'I appreciate it.'

'About selling . . . I've been thinking, wondering really . . . are you sticking around?'

'You know I am, Jennifer. What do I need to do to convince you?'

'I'm not trying to start an argument, but what I was wondering was whether you would want to buy me out and keep this place for yourself.'

Isla put her half-eaten cracker down on her plate. 'You're serious?'

'Why not? You love it, don't you?'

'I don't know. I'd have to look into mortgages. They're not easy to come by when your chosen profession isn't that secure and income varies month by month.'

'Maybe we should sit down and go through your finances, work something out.'

'I mean, I'd love it if I could; I guess I never dared to dream it would be a reality. I always figured we'd sell the cottage and I'd use my half to put a huge down payment on a tiny flat somewhere close by. I found something last week that would've been ideal and leave me without a mortgage.'

'Wouldn't you rather be here?'

'Of course I would. I love Cloverdale; sometimes it's hard to believe I stayed away so long.'

'I was angry you weren't here much when Dad died, or when Mum was really sick.'

'I know you were, you still are.'

'Not true.'

'Isn't it?'

Jennifer went out to the kitchen to grab the wine and topped up both glasses. 'After all the trouble I brought Mum and Dad, I was never ever going to go anywhere else. I knew what they'd been through, I wanted to be close by. I suppose some of it was out of guilt, which I never admitted to them, but the rest was because I love the village. It seemed a no-brainer to me, to settle here and bring the kids up in Cloverdale. I was angry with you because I didn't want anything to hurt Mum and Dad the way I'd already hurt them. Having heavies round at your house is terrifying, and for two elderly people more so. I wanted to protect them from everything.'

'They never expected you to, you know.'

'I know they didn't, but I wouldn't have had it any other way.'

'There were reasons I didn't come back for long.' She hesitated, but then wound back the clock and told Jennifer everything she'd been keeping from her over the years. How she'd suffered injuries, been turned down at auditions, failed to dance as well as she once had, how she'd fallen pregnant and lost the baby she hadn't even realised she wanted. 'When I came back to Cloverdale each time, I didn't want to burden any of you with my crap. Mum and Dad had been through all that business with the loan shark, and in the same way you wanted to protect them from hurt, I did too. I didn't want Mum to worry about me. I wanted her to smile and laugh when I regaled her with my experiences across the globe. I know she always loved it; Dad, too. When Dad died and I came home, I almost confided in Mum and in you, but when I cried tears for our loss and both of you did too, I couldn't

305

add to that. I thought I could sort myself out, and for a while I did, but throwing myself off bridges and doing crazy things was my way of avoiding facing up to the fact I was lost and lonely.'

'I probably didn't make you feel all that welcome either.'

Isla smiled. 'You were in charge, that much was clear. You didn't let me help organise Dad's funeral, you said you had it all in hand. I know your intentions were good and to you I was the wayward sister who'd been away for a long time. You did it all, Jennifer, and I felt useless.'

'I never meant to make you feel that way.'

'It was worse when Mum was sick. Remember how I told you to have a day off and go and enjoy yourself.'

'I did; I went up to Buddleia Farm.'

Isla bristled. 'And what happened when you came home?'

'I don't really remember.'

'Everything I'd done was wrong. I hadn't given Mum the right food for lunch, she hadn't had her medication, her pillows weren't the right height, the temperature of the room was all wrong.'

Jennifer's face fell but she went and sat next to her little sister, gave her a nudge with her elbow. 'What a cow.'

At least Isla began to laugh. 'You bloody well were; I felt useless.'

'I'm sorry, I really am. I had a lot of stuff of my own going on while you were away.' She took a deep breath. 'I had three miscarriages, and never told Mum or Dad or you. For a while it was all I could focus on.'

'I get that,' said Isla, speaking from her own experience. 'I ended up pushing away the people who cared.'

'Exactly.' She let their similarities settle on the air

between them. 'I became horrible to be around. I was awful to David; I shut him out. To this day I don't know how he put up with me.'

'He loves you, that's why.'

She had more to explain. 'I didn't see it at the time, but lately I've been thinking a lot about why I can be so horrible and bossy where you're concerned.' She put out her hands as though making a big announcement. 'I wasn't only envious of you and your free lifestyle. I was downright jealous. You were spot on when you said that recently. You seemed to have so much fun, effortless fun without any of us. I always thought you did unconventional things, you did what you wanted, and sometimes I longed to do that myself and get away from my own life. After I couldn't carry another baby to term, and I felt I couldn't go back to work after the mess I'd made before, I think I've been too critical of others, worried I'm stuck in one place with no way out, taking out my frustrations on people who don't deserve it: you; Viola; David. I didn't mean to make you or anyone else suffer, but I know that's what has happened.' She covered her face. 'I'm a terrible person.'

'No, you're not; you're kind, you're responsible and you would do anything for anyone else. You know, I was always jealous of how together you were.'

'Uptight, you mean?'

'I don't actually. You and David, a match made in heaven, a family, a home, a life here in a beautiful English village. I was desperately trying to find my feet and no matter how far I travelled I never quite got there. I only wish it hadn't taken Mum dying for me to come home.'

'You know, in a way, you being free and adventurous

was a tonic for both Mum and Dad, particularly Mum once she was on her own. Her face lit up when she talked about you, the latest thing you'd done, how brave her young daughter was. Our parents were proud of both of us.'

'This was what they wanted, you know,' said Isla. 'Us, sitting here together, sisters.'

'I know. And I guess we're more similar than I thought.'

'How so?'

'We both keep things bottled up and don't talk to others enough. We could save ourselves a whole heap of heartache if we did.'

Isla clinked glasses with her sister. 'Amen to that. Come on, let me show you what I've done with the rest of this place.'

Jennifer followed her upstairs and as soon as she saw the bright orange colour on the wall of the main bedroom she began to laugh. 'Now Mum and Dad would totally hate that.' And she hugged her sister to her.

Isla was back in Cloverdale, they were together, just as their parents had always wanted.

21

Viola

Viola had finished Zoe's bedroom early last week and already she missed going round there, in part because it meant she could keep an eye on Zoe and Zac, make sure they hadn't come to any harm. She'd barely slept over the last few weeks, thoughts churning in her mind, worries waking her at all hours. And Isaac had noticed; he wouldn't be him if he hadn't, but she needed to wait to tell him, she had to tell Jennifer first, the woman who had got close to this man who was nothing like they imagined.

She stood at the kitchen sink in her own house after she'd finished washing up a cake tin. Staring out of the window her suds-covered Marigolds dangled in the water.

Isaac came into the kitchen and wrapped his arms around Viola's waist from behind. 'I wish you'd talk to me.'

She pulled out the plug and turned to face him. 'I will eventually, I need to sort something in my head first. Can you trust me on that?'

He looked about to say more, but he knew his wife well. 'I'm here if you need me.'

When Ava came downstairs and into the kitchen, Viola

took off her gloves. 'What's with the sleeping bags?'

'It's the sleepover tonight, remember? At Tatiana's.'

'Sorry, it totally slipped my mind.'

'You can still give me and Zoe a lift, right?'

'Of course.'

Ava dropped the sleeping bags on the floor where she stood. 'Mum . . . I've been keeping something from you.'

'Oh?' Viola's insides fluttered. More secrets.

With a deep breath, Ava came out with it. 'I sent my CV to a few people and I've found a week's work experience with a huge retail company, in their marketing department.' The words gushed out of her. 'And there's more. I applied for a Saturday job, had an interview last week and I start next month, as a waitress, serving in the café up at the farm.'

She looked so nervous and Viola wondered how she'd ever let that happen; it had never once been her intention.

'Mum? Aren't you going to say anything?'

Her voice caught. 'Of course I am. I'm going to tell you that I'm delighted.'

'You're not angry?'

'No. Proud, yes. But not angry.'

Before she could say anything else, Ava ran at her, into her arms.

'I love you, Mum.'

If the sink hadn't been behind her, Viola suspected she would've fallen over in a state of shock. Hearing those words, feeling her daughter in her arms, so close she could smell the lemon-scented shampoo she used and the new perfume that was sometimes overpowering yet felt a part of Ava . . . it was a gift she hadn't expected today, or any other day for that matter.

'I love you too.' She relished the closeness, her daughter telling her the words she loved to hear. And this hug, this display of affection told her all she needed to know. She'd done something right. A while back Ava had yelled at her, accused her of loving Zoe more than her own daughter, but somewhere along the line Ava must've seen Viola's love for what it was: real and unconditional.

'I'm glad you're my mum.' Ava was still clinging onto her, not the behaviour of a fourteen-year-old, at least, not hers.

'Me too.' This was the magical balance she'd strived to achieve. All she'd ever wanted was to push her kids in the right direction but have them see how much love was always behind it, even though she sometimes went a little over the top when it came to monitoring what they were up to.

'Mum?'

'Yes, darling.'

Ava lifted her head. 'When I've finished work experience, will you help me redo my CV, make it really professional?'

'I'd love to. I really would.'

Ava hugged her again as Isaac came into the room.

'What's going on?' He grabbed a piece of shortbread from the biscuit tin as Viola sniffed and turned away to hide her face.

'Can I?' Ava gestured to the tin and dived in the second Viola gave an over-enthusiastic nod to disguise her emotion. Ava had dumped the sleeping bags right in the way, something Viola would usually reprimand her about – what if someone tripped over, hurt themselves? – but she merely shifted them into the hall as Ava trotted back up-stairs to get her bag.

'What was that about?' Isaac asked.

'I couldn't tell you.' With a smile of contentedness, at least for now, Viola grabbed her car keys ready to take the girls to their sleepover. And then she was going straight to see Jennifer. It was time to tell her friend what she knew about Adam and make her listen.

In the hallway Ava had her jacket on, an overnight bag, and both sleeping bags.

'You look like you're leaving home.'

'You wish.'

She touched her daughter's hair lightly but not too much. 'Actually I really don't.'

'Me neither.' She smiled up at her mum. 'At least not yet.'

They drove over to Lilliput Cottage, and outside Viola kept the engine running while Ava knocked on the door. She didn't want to face Adam but when Zoe came out with her own overnight bag Adam came too and Viola had no choice but to open her window. 'Can't stop, I need to be back to meet Jennifer after I drop this pair off.'

'No worries. And you're OK with them camping?'

'Of course. I trust the parents, Alastair and Cammie; they're a lovely couple, and the girls are very sensible.' Viola glanced in her rear-view mirror and noticed Ava. If her mouth could've fallen open any more her jaw would've hit the floor. Perhaps it was time to give her daughter more leeway, and back off a little. Anything to have her be the way she was earlier at the house.

'And you have all your insulin and test kit, Zoe?' Adam peered into the back seat where their daughters were already whispering conspiratorially as only teens did.

'Yes, Dad.'

'I'll let you go then.'

'Tatiana's parents will bring them back some time tomorrow before dinner.' Viola called a goodbye and off they went.

The drive took less than an hour, and after she'd dropped the girls off, Viola made her way back to Cloverdale, with every mile adding to her trepidation about seeing Jennifer. When she arrived at the Library of Shared Things, Jennifer could only gush about her night with David and how appreciative she was. 'I should've talked to him sooner . . . but seriously, thank you.' She made two cups of peppermint tea and handed one to Viola. 'We needed the focus that night, the lack of intrusion, and I think the worry that it could be something terrible made David open to listening.'

'I'm really pleased. And Project Hairdresser is a go?'

'We're going to make up some flyers and distribute them around Cloverdale. Start small, going to people's homes, then see how that goes.'

'Book me in?'

'Of course I will, I used to cut your hair all the time if you remember.'

'I do.' Viola knew she was stalling for time as she asked, 'How was the rest of your talk with David? Did you sort everything out?'

'I didn't mention my feelings – or rather my confusion – about Adam. I read more into it than was really there, I turned to a friend for comfort but realise now that was all it was. And mentioning Adam . . . well, it would've made life messier than it needed to be. I don't want to lose his friendship; I value it. But I value my marriage even more.'

Interesting how Jennifer's choice of words fitted this situation perfectly because once she told her friend what she knew, it would all become one big mess, one catastrophic volcano about to unleash an eruption over an entire family.

They talked some more about David, about how he and Jennifer had walked home beneath the stars, talking about the past, looking forward to the future. 'I think I fell in love with him all over again that night,' Jennifer admitted. 'It sounds ridiculous, doesn't it?'

'Not at all.'

A little abashed, Jennifer went to pick up her handbag. 'Ready for lunch? I'm starving, I booked a table at the pub for us. We can gossip more there.'

'I thought we were getting sandwiches and soup from the bakery.' She couldn't do this in the pub with people all around them.

'The pub's nicer. Chicken stew and dumplings on today's menu.' She was standing unhooking her dark wavy hair from beneath her handbag strap, but when Viola didn't budge an inch she lowered back into her chair. 'What's wrong?'

'We need to talk.'

Jennifer kept quiet as Viola recounted what she'd found at Adam's house, the diary that said so much, that she knew the truth about the family, a man Jennifer liked and trusted and had almost been taken in by, a man who was romancing her sister and doing a good job of it. She told her of the violence, the emotional torture his wife had been put through. 'I've no idea why he'd keep the diary, he must be sick in the head. Perhaps he likes to remind himself of the things he did, the control he had, the fact he got the kids and she didn't. You know, it's good that Zoe and Ava are out for a couple of nights, away from Cloverdale. Perhaps you could take Zac for the night, then maybe . . . well, I don't know . . . do we confront him? Tell him we know? Guard the kids? Call the police? Jennifer?'

Her friend wasn't saying anything; she was staring out of the folded doors in the Library of Shared Things, at the leaves skittering past in winds that grew stronger by the second.

'Jennifer . . . talk to me. Are you OK? I know this is huge. I've kept it quiet for too long, I didn't know what to do, I—'

'I can't believe it.'

'You don't believe me?'

Jennifer looked at her then. 'Of course I do. But I can't get my head around him doing those things. I thought I knew enough about him, but I didn't. And what about Isla? She's involved with him, what if he hurts her?' She was starting to panic. 'Viola, what am I going to do? I need to get hold of my sister.' She grabbed her phone, dialled Isla's number, but there was no answer.

'Send her a text, tell her to meet us at my house. We're going to tell Isaac everything; he'll know what to do.'

Jennifer tapped out a text and sent it on its way. 'I've been sending Archie over to play with Zac all this time. I've had Adam in my house, sat and told him things about our family. It's like Gail all over again. She fooled me, and now Adam. I am so gullible.'

'Jennifer, this isn't the time to berate yourself for making a friend. He's the one in the wrong; you've done nothing to be ashamed of.'

When they stood up to go, Jennifer turned to Viola. 'I'm so glad I've got you in my corner again.'

Viola hugged her tight. 'Me too, now let's get going.'

'I need to head home, make sure the twins can mind Archie. Hopefully Isla will be in touch soon.'

Jennifer locked up, and the friends ventured outside into the brutal winds enveloping Cloverdale.

Both of them now knew Adam wasn't a man to be trusted. And they needed to stop him doing any more damage before it was too late.

'I don't believe it.' Isaac sat on the kitchen stool at the island bench after Viola came home and blurted everything. 'He seems so . . . normal.' He scraped a hand through his hair. 'I guess you can never know people completely.'

Hazel came downstairs as the sky outside turned sinister. 'Mummy, I've run out of toothpaste.'

'Disaster!' Viola mocked, scooping her up into her arms and cuddling her close.

'I can do this,' Isaac suggested, knowing how spent Viola was.

'No.' She looked over Hazel's shoulder at him. 'I need to do this tonight. Come on, Mummy will find you some more toothpaste and then we'll tuck you in.'

Viola made the most of her youngest daughter tonight and lay next to her, taking comfort in snuggle-time. She had lots of different books but loved to read *The Velveteen Rabbit* again and again. Viola supposed, like everyone, Hazel wanted to cling on to a little bit of who she once was. Usually Viola prompted her to read at least half of the book, but not tonight. Tonight she wanted to be near her daughter and enjoy the simplicity.

'I thought you'd fallen asleep with her.' Isaac put a glass of wine in Viola's hand the second she came back to the kitchen. 'I think you need it.'

She took a generous gulp of a smooth red but almost spilt it when the window pane in the kitchen rattled hard in the wind. Her mind went into overdrive. What if Adam came over, what if he knew? Would he come to get revenge for finding out his secret? Would he come to demonstrate how violent he could really be, show them all how he'd pulled the wool well and truly over their eyes?

Isaac stood behind her, his calming hands massaging the knots in her shoulders. 'Is Jennifer very upset?'

'She's worried about Isla but I know she's devastated that she's trusted someone with her child; she's talked to him like a good friend.'

'It's sickening when you think of trusting a man like that with your kids.'

Viola gasped. 'God, the kids! How's that going to work? Ava is close to Zoe; Archie is best friends with Zac. What happens now?'

'Let's not get ahead of ourselves; we need to think this through. The main thing is having all the kids safe. Zoe is tucked out of the way for the night, Archie is at home with his sisters and hopefully Jennifer has heard from Isla. Let's wait for them and then think about what to do next.'

Isaac reheated a portion of shepherd's pie, although neither of them were particularly hungry. And when there was a knock at the door, Isaac let Jennifer in. He gave her a hug, asked whether she'd heard from her sister.

'She's on her way over here.'

'Good.'

'You OK?' Viola asked.

'I will be.' It was obvious she'd been crying. 'I thought about going over to see him at Lilliput Cottage.'

Isaac spoke up. 'I don't think either of you should rush round there.'

'You're probably right,' said Jennifer, accepting Viola's offer of a strong coffee. The wine discarded, they all needed a shot of caffeine to kick-start their brains and think of where to go from here.

By now the rain had joined the wind outside. 'Blimey, I don't think the girls will stay out long in this.' Viola went to the window to see rain lashing at the glass, her lemon tree doing its best to put up a fight outside. She hoped it wouldn't be a casualty in the morning. 'They're camping at a friend's house.'

Jennifer pulled a face. She hoped the girls had been sensible enough to abandon the idea in this kind of weather.

Viola's phone rang as they were waiting for Isla. 'Alastair, is everything all right with the girls?' Isaac and Jennifer waited for her to finish the call, and she then explained, 'Ava has a migraine and Alastair's bringing her home. Let's keep this quiet when she gets here, I don't want her to know yet. And I don't want her messaging Zoe at Tatiana's only to have her panic.'

'Poor Ava.' Jennifer wrapped her hands around her coffee mug and savoured the warmth. 'If she has a migraine, all she'll want is peace and quiet in a dark room.'

Shortly after Ava came home and Viola settled her upstairs, Isla arrived at the house. Viola ushered her in out of the rain. 'You're soaking wet.' She pulled a towel from the linen cupboard in the hallway.

Isla rubbed the towel against her hair that she'd released from its topknot and when the worst was off she wound it up again. 'Is someone going to tell me what's going on?'

When they joined everyone else Viola took the lead and told Isla what they knew.

Isla was in shock, the tears flowed. Nobody said anything for a while. There really weren't any words of comfort they could offer.

When there was another knock at the door, Isaac made some joke about Piccadilly Circus and went to answer it and, from the deep voices, all three women knew it could only be one person.

'Hey, mate,' Isaac's voice got closer, shadows behind the glass doors that separated the enormous family room with its kitchen and lounge area from the hallway. 'You can't go in there.'

Adam came barging through, the glass doors trembling on their hinges.

Viola jumped and clung to Jennifer's arm.

'Adam, I need you to leave.' Isaac stood his ground. He'd got around Adam and stood between him and the women. 'Now.'

'I don't know what this is,' Adam began, 'but I'm here to find Zoe. Where is she?'

'She's safe,' Viola told him.

'She's not where she's supposed to be. She's not at Tatiana's house.'

'Adam, I dropped her there myself.' Viola stood, arms folded. She couldn't be sure but he had something tucked beneath the arm of his Barbour jacket and it looked very much like the diary that had told her everything she needed to know. 'It's probably best she's out of the way.'

He ignored her comment but looked her right in the eye. 'I went to the house, I took the girls a surprise food package, full of all the crap teenagers love, and I thought it would be nice for them. I also wanted to thank the parents for hosting three fourteen-year-old girls, so you can imagine how I felt when I was told that my daughter wasn't there.' He ran a hand across his jaw, the stress obvious to everyone. 'I'm going out of my mind with worry. And there are things you don't know; none of you do.' He looked from Viola to Jennifer, to Isaac, to Isla.

Jennifer and Isla stayed silent so Viola told him, 'We know, Adam.'

'I'm not sure what you think you know, but right now all I care about is keeping Zoe safe.'

'That's all we want too.'

He looked broken when he held out the diary. 'I found this on Zoe's bed. It wasn't for her eyes. I needed to tell her things myself. Please, Viola, I'm begging you, from one parent to another: if you know where she is, you have to tell me.'

If Viola didn't know the truth about him, she'd have a modicum of sympathy. But she did. And he deserved to be frightened. She bet his wife had been terrified of him. Maybe this was payback time. Perhaps Zoe was hiding from him now she'd found out the horrid truth.

Adam moved closer. 'I know you're close to Zoe. Please, tell me where she is.'

It was as though he hadn't registered anyone else in the room but her, the woman he thought had all the answers. Was this how his wife had felt, intimidated? Backed into a corner?

Isaac was about to step in but, before he could, Ava's

bleary-eyed form came into the room. 'What's all the yelling? I'm trying to sleep.'

'Sorry, Ava. Go back to bed.' Ava had had a few migraines on and off over the years, starting with an aura, progressing to a headache with vomiting, but this one had subsided quite a lot by the time she'd come home and all she needed to do was sleep away the leftover dull ache from behind her eyes.

Ava focused in on Adam before Viola could get her out of the way. 'What's he doing here?'

'Ava,' Isaac scolded. He wouldn't tolerate bad manners from his kids, under any circumstances.

'We know what you did!' Ava yelled, pointing at Adam.

Adam took in the faces: his friend Jennifer, his girlfriend Isla, Viola, Ava, Isaac. All accusing him. All with the truth at their disposal.

'Zoe knows everything,' Ava went on. 'She knows you bullied her mum, hit her, worse.' Tears were flowing down her cheeks.

Viola pulled herself together. It was one thing being defensive around Adam, but the real issue in hand was if Zoe wasn't at Tatiana's place, as he claimed, then where was she? Even if she was hiding, someone needed to know where she was. 'Ava . . . where is Zoe?'

'She's safe.'

'That wasn't what I asked. You need to tell me right now. Where is Zoe?'

Ava looked over at Adam with a kind of triumphant, I've-got-one-up-on-you look. 'She's with . . . a friend.'

'Ava, this isn't a game.' Viola had a bad feeling about this.

Adam stumbled backwards into the wall, defeated,

broken. 'She must hate me. But I need to see her. I need to make sure she knows the whole truth.' He turned, on the spot, as though searching for a way out of his own thoughts. He slumped down on the hearth by the fireplace, shaking his head. Everyone else stayed silent. The volume switch had been turned down on the shrieking, the truths spat into the air.

'Adam, mate.' Isaac's voice was soft, considering what he knew, as he moved towards the other man and crouched down on his haunches. 'You can't be here.'

Viola's heart betrayed her when it almost broke at the look in Adam's eyes, but she supposed he was the great pretender, making them believe him all this time. But those things he'd done . . . terrible things.

And then she realised he was crying. It left the room aghast. Isla was crying too; even Ava couldn't say anything now despite her accusations on behalf of her friend.

Adam looked at Isaac and at the rest of them.

'You've got it all wrong. All of you.'

22

Adam

'What do you mean we've got it all wrong?' Isaac's voice, measured, in control, didn't waver once as he asked the question.

'I've lied to you all for a very long time.' Adam had wiped his tears away now, tears of fear, pain, sorrow, who knew? He'd have to start from the beginning. If he didn't, they'd never tell him where Zoe was; he'd never find her and tell her the truth.

'Why don't you tell us.' Isaac's tone was better than Viola could've managed under the circumstances.

It took a few deep breaths for him to calm himself enough to reveal everything after all this time. He'd kept these secrets for so long, they'd almost broken him once. But all he cared about now was Zac and Zoe. He'd do anything for them.

'I met Susan, Zoe and Zac's mum, on the beach in Australia. She was this blonde beauty. I joked she was like a mermaid, there in a metallic silver bikini, her hair golden in the sun and curly from the salty ocean. We hit it off straight away; I loved how feisty she was, how she hated to sit still. She had a kind of energy behind her that I guess I admired.'

'I can't listen to this.' Isla began to walk away but Adam's voice stopped her.

'You need to listen to this, you all do. Please, if it's the last thing you ever do for me, for Zoe, for Zac . . . hear me out.'

'Adam, I read the diary,' Viola told him. 'I found it by mistake when I was looking for the sugar soap.'

'And you gave it to Zoe?'

'No! I promise I didn't; she must've found it herself.'

'I wish she'd come to me first.'

'What difference would that have made?'

'All the difference in the world. You all think you've got me worked out, but you're wrong.'

'How can we possibly be wrong?' Jennifer demanded.

He looked at the diary, all his secrets bundled between the sorry pages of a book that told about an abusive marriage. Yet he could remember every detail in there. Every smile, every scream, every laugh, every cry. 'It's a long time since I looked at this myself; I'd put that all behind me.'

'I'll bet you did,' Isla snapped, and when he looked at her, he saw the pain in her eyes and he wanted nothing more than to take it all away.

'It's my diary.' There, he'd said it. It was out in the open, his horrid secret.

He wasn't sure who it was who gasped or whether it was all of them, but Viola told Ava to go and wait upstairs. Ava told her she'd read the diary with Zoe, so instead, Viola held her daughter close. Something Adam wanted to do with Zoe, tell her the truth, keep her by his side. But he needed these people to know everything before they'd help him. He needed their trust and he should've gained it a long time ago by being honest. To them, to himself. But admitting he was a victim didn't come easy. It never had.

'I wrote every word in there.' His forearms rested along his thighs. He could smell soot from the fireplace next to him, shivered at the coolness of the raised stone surround he was sitting on. 'I didn't use names, I could barely admit to myself that I was the one who was bullied, tormented, beaten. I mean . . . what kind of man does that make me? Weak, pathetic?' Nobody answered, all faces stunned, as he told them about his painful past. A past that had held him captive with shame.

'It started more than a decade ago. Susan moaned about our lack of money but at the same time she complained I worked too many hours. She was paranoid, accused me of sleeping around. My punishment that time was a slap in the face, her contempt, and her spitting at me. Not long after that Susan started to drink. She'd returned to work as a teacher and told me I didn't understand the stress she was under. She'd insult me, tell me I was just a skivvy who worked with dirt all day in my job as a gardener. "What the fuck do you know?" she'd say to me. "You're a fucking gardener and a student, you're pathetic," she told me.'

When his voice caught, Isaac urged him to continue. 'She swore at me all the time, you know. I shrugged it off and she'd always be full of apologies after one of her rants, begging me to forgive her. She always said sorry, and I always gave her another chance.

'When Zoe turned one, we planned a big party for our little girl, but I'd been caught up at work, then stuck in traffic and I was late home. All the guests were there and Susan was livid. She punished me by hurling a pan of boiling water at me.' He had to keep talking despite Isla's look of horror. 'I went to the hospital, I told them I was clumsy. "What man knows how to work a kitchen?" I said to the nurse, to which she replied, "My husband wouldn't know one end of a frying pan from another." And we'd laughed as though I was completely hopeless.

'A few months after Zoe turned one, we decided she should start swimming lessons. I enrolled her, but she was petrified at first. Her little nails would dig into the skin of my shoulders every time. I'd laugh but Susan didn't. When Zoe did it to her one week, she went ballistic. I thought she was going to hit our daughter in front of the entire swimming school until she realised others were watching. And Susan didn't like an audience, not when she was being a bully. She preferred to do that behind closed doors.

'My parents visited one Easter, and Susan and I kept up the pretence that everything was fine, but Susan stayed out all night more than once, and it was hard to keep our troubles quiet; it was obvious something was up. And after they left I told Susan she could've been nicer to Mum and Dad who'd flown all that way to be with us. But I should've kept my big mouth shut.'

'What happened?' Viola prompted when his voice faltered and he wasn't sure he could do this.

'She shut my mouth for me with a swift knock from her elbow. I thought I'd lost a couple of teeth, but it was a split lip and a bloody nose. She settled down a bit after that; I don't really know why, but I thought perhaps we were through the worst of it. I studied hard and graduated, and I took Susan away for a weekend wine tasting in the Hunter Valley to celebrate. I'd told myself that every couple had their problems, this was clearly ours, and for Zoe's sake I wanted to work at it. I found a new graduate job not long after and we were invited by my boss to Melbourne Cup Day and when we both cheered at a good win on the horses and Susan told me she was pregnant again I couldn't have been happier.

'Susan had terrible morning sickness with Zac and at Christmas that year, I took charge of the dinner. We were having turkey, all the trimmings, but everything was wrong according to Susan who spent the day lying on the sofa. The turkey was too dry, the cauliflower overcooked, the gravy had lumps, she hated the sprouts. When she went for an afternoon nap that lasted long into the evening and beyond, I was thankful she'd left Zoe and me in peace, to be honest. We watched a movie, ate chocolate, and it was better that Susan was out of the way. I hoped her moods and criticisms were temporary.'

'And were they?' Isla sat beside him and took his hand but his look told her the answer to her question.

'The day Zac was born was as special as the day Zoe came into the world. A full head of hair, the same colour as mine, I couldn't take my eyes of him. And Susan seemed happy too; she hadn't moaned at me once, not even at Zoe who was over-excited about the new addition to our family. I thought I had the Susan I'd married back with me, and that day we were one big happy family.

'The happy family didn't last long. Susan was soon snapping at Zoe, even Zac who was still in nappies. And if he cried, I had to get there first because she had no patience. I suggested she see a doctor, get a prescription to help her out, and just when I thought I was getting through to her, she stomped outside and lit up a cigarette.' He harrumphed, shook his head. 'She'd never smoked before, as far as I knew. And when I went outside and tried to make a joke about her looking as sexy as Sandy from Grease, her response was to stub the cigarette out on my arm.'

Ava had begun to cry but he had to go on. All of it had to come out; he needed them to understand. 'I tried to tell a friend what was going on but the conversation was a non-starter. When I showed my mate the burn he laughed and joked that I must've forgotten her birthday or something. As though I deserved it. The only person who understood was my mum but she was all the way over in England. I broke down and told her everything on the phone one night; she'd cried and told me to leave, but I wanted to try harder, for the kids. Susan had been out that day at a spa being pampered. She came home in the hottest lingerie – any man would've struggled to resist her – but when she told me she wanted another baby I knew I couldn't do it. And when Zac started crying, and I saw a flash of anger in her eyes, I made a decision. I was going to get the snip as soon as I could; I couldn't put any of us through it all over again. I needed the family I already had to work better than it was.

'The next Christmas I treated Susan to a Thermomix. They were the latest thing; everyone raved about them, and I thought she'd love it. But she slung it at me, narrowly missing my head before it smashed to the floor. I had a text that night from my mate, Mal. Susan had been texting him, claiming I was shagging his wife. I confronted Susan and she told me I was overreacting; it was only a joke. But nobody apart from her saw the funny side. She'd been intercepting my texts too, replying on my behalf, making snide remarks to close friends, turning down nights out with the boys. My friendships fell away with my crazy wife playing games. Nobody wanted any trouble.'

'She sounds like she had some real mental health issues.' Viola didn't seem sure about saying anything, but she looked like she was finally realising how wrong she'd read this situation.

'She did, and when she found out I'd been googling depression and abusive behaviour, I paid for that with a huge belt across the head. She didn't talk to me for a month.' He managed a smile. 'I wasn't sure whether to be sorry about that or not. She carried on much in the same way. One day, after I'd been out on site all day, I managed to bring mud inside the house and it got all over the carpet. She shoved me out of the kitchen door and locked it. I ended up making faces at Zoe and Zac through the window to make them laugh and take away the fright that Mummy was being nasty to Daddy. It was lucky she did most things behind their backs, like the time she threw a knife at me. I almost called the police that time but assumed, like my mate, they'd laugh it off. I also wondered if Susan would turn it around and tell them I was abusing her, and no way did I want to lose my kids. I blamed myself then; I asked why I couldn't stand up for myself. What kind of man was I?'

His question had Jennifer at his side. 'A good one, one who very much did the best he could.'

'I was getting desperate by that point. I wanted to leave, I needed to get out, but I also knew the courts would probably side with Susan and she'd tell all sorts of lies to get herself out of it. I googled domestic violence to see if

I could find somewhere to call or email for help but she searched the history on my phone and told me that if I wanted violence I could have it.' He couldn't look at them when he said, 'She punched me, kneed me in the groin, kicked me, tried to gouge my eyes.'

He heard Isla crying, Viola comforting Ava, but still he pushed on. 'The thought of hitting her back crossed my mind, I'm ashamed to say. But I couldn't do it. And so the violence, verbal and physical, continued. She broke my little finger and I had to have it reset at hospital. She smacked me over the head with a mug of coffee when a woman from work left a message on my answer machine about a meeting I'd missed. And then, when she yelled at me to fix the smoke detector that wouldn't stop bleeping intermittently, I got an idea. I changed the battery but I remembered something I'd seen on TV. After a bit of online research – I deleted my search history that time – I found what I was looking for. A hidden camera that, to the untrained eye, looked like a smoke detector. Most of the abuse happened in the kitchen or the lounge when the kids were out of earshot and couldn't see. She was clever that way. The curtains were usually shut too, so there'd be no chance of a passer-by seeing anything. I told Susan I'd had to replace the faulty smoke detector with a new one and I bought one for the bedroom too as sometimes she'd turn on me the moment I woke or when I came to bed. I made sure I had a couple more working smoke detectors in the house – she never questioned why so many – and then I waited.

'I didn't have to wait long. One evening, Susan was in the lounge ironing a top, ready to go out with work colleagues, other teachers who knew nothing of her dark secret. I hadn't been well that day – the kids and I had stinking colds – and I came downstairs in my pyjama bottoms to get some paracetamol. I walked past her, and the pain that shot into me sent me careering into the wall.' If he looked at Isla now, he would start crying himself. He could hear how upset she was, and the others looked just as bad, but he couldn't stop now. 'Susan smirked, she turned around and looked at the iron she'd held against the bare skin of my back and tutted. "See what you made me do," she said. "I'll need to clean this now." And off she went to take care of it as though she hadn't done anything at all. I went upstairs to jump into a cold shower and take the heat out of the burn, but not before I turned and bent over near the hidden camera to make sure the evidence was there for the world to see what she was capable of, if that's what it came to.

'Every couple of days I tested the camera, removed its memory card and took it to a local shop to put the footage on CD. I felt blocked every way I turned though. I called a shelter for people being abused, only for them to try to put my call through to a line for male abusers to talk to someone about what they were doing. I went to a different hospital to have the burn treated and told them I'd tripped over the flex of the iron and the thing had fallen on me. It hurt for days. Susan apologised, she cried, but I didn't care. I waited for her to punch me, yell at me, but all she did was look me straight in the eye and tell me that if I ever told a soul she'd deny it, say I raped her night after night with a knife at her throat and it was self-defence on her part. She told me she'd make sure I never saw my kids again.

'I stood up to her a couple of times but after that Susan

became unpredictable, I couldn't trust her. I'd never questioned her love for the kids until then.'

He took a deep breath, unsurprised at how painful it was to dredge everything up again. He ploughed on.

'One day Susan slapped Zoe around the head for not doing her homework, the day before Zac had felt a sting on his legs for getting toothpaste on the bathroom sink, another time she shrieked at Zoe for being selfish when she finished the last of the milk on her morning cereal. Then one morning I went to collect Zoe and Zac from school only to have their teacher tell me Mummy had picked them up at lunchtime for their dentist appointments. I played the part of the forgetful dad but I drove home out of my mind. That time I really wondered if she'd hurt them. They appeared at ten o'clock at night. The kids looked exhausted but happy and I was so relieved that they were home in one piece. They'd been down the Great Ocean Road; they'd seen the Twelve Apostles, eaten fish and chips on the beach, built sandcastles even though it was wet. I was fuming, but I knew I'd pay for it if I spoke up. I told myself to hang in there.

'How the hell did you get away?' Jennifer asked.

'I was biding my time; I knew I had one chance to do it, to keep us all safe. Susan spiralled out of control all the more, as though she hated all of us. We couldn't do anything right. It all came to a head one beautiful spring day after I'd tucked Zac beneath the bedcovers and assured him there were no monsters, after I'd read Zoe a story. I went downstairs and, after Susan yelled the usual abuse at me, which had become white noise by then, she looked right at me and said, "You try to take my kids from me and I'll make sure you never see them again. You always loved them more than me. But if I can't have you, neither can they." I was shocked, I couldn't say a word and she yelled, "I'll kill them both before I see you three happy without me."'

"Fuck,' said Isaac. 'Sorry, Ava,' he said to his daughter, who looked almost as distraught as Adam felt.

'She told me I was weak, pathetic, I was nothing. I didn't sleep for weeks, I couldn't. Every time she gave me a sly glance there were words beneath those looks, the thought of what she might do. Getting myself and the kids far away from her was the only thing that kept me going, and I knew it would have to be soon. The hidden cameras were in place less than a month but already I had plenty of footage of her slapping me, sometimes it was the way I woke up. I'd stumble into the bathroom, lock the door, hear her muttering and only come out when she left. I'd been late into work so many times my boss had had a word and I blamed the kids for acting up in the mornings. I started to get up well before Susan's alarm went off. To hell with it if she got annoyed for waking her; she got annoyed anyway.'

He took a deep breath before he could even repeat the next part. 'One morning I didn't wake to my alarm, but to Zoe's screams. "Daddy! Daddy!" she was saying. I couldn't see anything, everything was muffled, I couldn't breathe. Something was over my face and Zoe was still screaming as I realised what was happening. Susan had a pillow over my face. I grabbed her wrists, threw her off me. I started to laugh and told Zoe we were messing around. But it put the fear of God into me. I don't know how far Susan would've gone had Zoe not found us, whether she was capable of doing it to them too.

'A few days later, Susan and I were called in to the kids' school. Zoe had slapped a girl during an argument and shoved her into the vegetable patch. The teacher had delved into problems at home; she asked whether there was something going on that she needed to know about? We insisted that of course there wasn't. Susan didn't say a word to Zoe in the car on the way home but when we got to the house she sent Zoe upstairs and called her a little bitch. She saved her violent rage for me once Zoe was out of the way, and I knew that had to be the end of it. The next day I called my parents; Mum got on a plane as soon as she could and two days later, after I'd rented a small house for me, Zoe and Zac, I picked her up from the airport. I dropped her at the rental property and she lay low. If my plan was going to work, Susan couldn't get wind of any of it. I called in sick to work after dropping Zoe and Zac at school the next morning, I got the memory cards and CDs I'd stored in the old shed at the foot of the garden, knowing Susan would never go in there with her dislike of spiders and cockroaches, both frequent visitors, and took them all to the new house along with the diary. I'd written that diary to process my thoughts; I'd written in it to remind me of the evil side Susan had, I recorded it all in case things went too far one night and I wound up dead.

'I picked the kids up from school, dropped them at the house with Mum. They didn't ask any questions; they were far too excited to see her. She showered them with love and kisses, as they deserved. I asked a security guard at work to do me a favour, no questions asked, cash in hand, and for five hundred dollars he'd kept his mouth shut and came with me. Frank probably looked more menacing than he really was, but he was a gym addict, with guns to make Arnold Schwarzenegger jealous. When Susan came home and asked what was going on, Frank didn't utter a word when she demanded to know why he was standing there. I wanted to get it over with as quickly as I could. I already felt completely emasculated, asking for another man's help to leave a woman. I told her I was going, I'd taken the kids, we were all moving out and she wouldn't see us for a while. But I was scared. She called me all the names I had got used to over time, she laughed, thinking I had no hope of carrying out my plans. She went to Frank and told him how I'd beaten her every night, she tried to goad him like she did with me, but he didn't flinch. He was probably thinking of his five hundred dollars just to watch a domestic.

'Susan started talking about how she was well respected as a teacher, she said no court would ever take my side, she told me to go for it if I really wanted to. I'd never wanted to wipe the smile off someone's face as much as I did right then. She was sitting on the sofa as though she didn't have a care in the world, as though she was socialising with friends. I went over to the TV where the DVD was ready and when she saw the footage on screen she called me a fucking bastard, said I'd tricked her. But when she got up to fly at me, Frank stood in the way. She begged me to stop playing it as though she couldn't believe this was her. I made her sit through all of it, the slapping, punching, kicking, and the grand finale, the pillow suffocating. I wanted her to see the things she'd done. I wanted her to know she was guilty.

'I showed her the diary, turned the pages in front of her so she could see how I'd written down an account

335

of all the times she'd threatened me, hurt me, yelled at me. It was my way of coping, but it was also evidence. It wasn't easy confronting her like that. I'd got one up on her, but it didn't make me feel in the least bit victorious. She pleaded with me, said how sorry she was, told me she'd get help, begged me not to leave. She was sitting on the sofa shaking as though she'd gone to a far-off place I could never reach, some kind of breakdown. I called my mum who brought the kids to the door and when I let them in Susan did exactly as I'd asked. I said I wouldn't show any of the evidence to anyone, she could keep her job and reputation, her freedom, but she had to say goodbye to her children. She didn't deserve them and I couldn't trust her. At first she refused to do it but she knew she had no choice. I knew I'd keep the kids from her for a long time, I'd tell them everything when they were older and it would be up to them to decide whether they wanted anything to do with her. The woman was evil. She said her goodbyes to the kids but she said hardly anything to them apart from that she wasn't well, she didn't know how to be a mum anymore, and the way she clenched her jaw told me she wanted to lash out at someone or something. I had to get the kids out of there and when they left Frank stayed to make sure Susan didn't come after them.

'When I came inside the house, Frank met me at the door and said, "Mate, I had no idea," and it was one of the first times I saw that with all the evidence laid out, nobody could ever doubt what I'd gone through, nobody would question my claims. It gave me the confidence to know I was doing exactly the right thing, and I wasn't a lesser man for what had happened. I wondered if Frank would go home that night and hug his own wife and kids close and realise how good he had it. Susan seemed to forget Frank was there; she came over to me, sobbed, wet my T-shirt with her tears. But I still left. Frank didn't even want paying.

'I don't know how Susan managed it but two days' later she found our rental property. She hammered on the door in the middle of the night. I told her to go away, and for once she did. We had a rock through the window the night after and the glazier came the next morning to fix it up. And when she threw another rock the night after that and the glass splintered all over the carpet inside, we'd already gone. For good.'

23

Adam

Isla had a tissue clasped in her palm, Viola was fighting tears as she hugged Jennifer and comforted Ava who was crying and couldn't get her words out as they asked her where Zoe had gone and who with. The kid was next to hysterical.

'Where is she, Ava?' Viola prompted again, pulling away from her sobbing child whose head had been buried against her chest. 'Just tell me and we'll go and get her.'

Ava looked at Adam. 'We thought it was you who did all those things. We thought . . .'

'I know.' Adam asked for a glass of water. His mouth was dry; he couldn't remember the last time he'd drunk anything and it was no good to anyone if he collapsed from dehydration. 'Ava, all I care about now is that Zoe is all right. She hasn't done anything silly and tried to fly to Australia on her own, has she?' He should've checked where he kept the passports, but he'd thought she'd be in Cloverdale hiding out somewhere. Please God don't let her have gone across the other side of the world.

Ava fell apart all over again. This was too much for a kid; he imagined the hell she and Zoe had been through reading those diary entries. He felt sick they'd thought it was him doing those things.

'How could she say she'd hurt Zoe and Zac?' Ava pleaded with her mum. 'What if she does something to her?'

Viola snapped to attention. 'Ava, where is she?'

'Susan came here to England; Zoe went to meet her.'

Adam's panic boiled over and it was only Isla who managed to keep him calm enough to listen.

'They were going camping in the Chilterns,' Ava continued. 'We borrowed a tent.'

Realisation dawned for Jennifer. 'The tent . . . it wasn't a surprise for her dad at all.'

Not a pleasant surprise at any rate.

The wind howled through any gap in the windows that it could find as Ava repeated the name of the campsite, and Isaac looked it up to find the postcode. Adam remembered how much Zoe had loved it there and wanted to show her mum. He should've listened to her, answered her questions. Perhaps he should've told his kids the whole truth from the start. But the shame. The utter shame of being the man who couldn't hold it together and whose wife beat him. Running away had been the answer, but at what cost now Zoe was missing?

He slumped onto the chair nearest to him. 'Zoe wanted to show her mum the Chilterns one day. She told me she would, when her mum was ready to love her again.'

Isla wrapped her arms around him as Viola asked how Susan had made contact after all this time.

'Instagram,' Ava told them.

'Oh my God, it was her. That woman.' Viola looked at Adam and told him how someone had liked Zoe's photograph and she thought it might be her mum. 'She didn't say anything since and I assumed it wasn't her or she would've told me. Why didn't she?'

Ava gripped her mum's arm. 'Zoe thought you'd feel like you had to tell her dad so she didn't say anything.'

'It's my fault,' Viola said. 'All my fault.'

'It's not, Mum. You read the diary.'

'She's right.' Tears stung Adam's eyes. 'You were never going to help someone you thought capable of all those things.'

'Where's Zac?' Isaac asked.

'He's at home with Charlotte. I gave her time and a half to be at the cottage for as long as I need her. For as long as it takes to get Zoe back,' he muttered, almost to himself.

Ava meanwhile was showing Jennifer, Viola and Isaac the profile on Instagram, although there wasn't a photograph of Susan against it and she'd set her account to private so they couldn't follow her unless she allowed them to.

'I should've had Zoe's account tagged onto mine.' Adam grasped at anything he could've done to stop this. Then again, perhaps this was always going to happen. It was what they'd been running from and now she'd caught them. It had only been a matter of time. He was naïve, stupid to think otherwise.

Viola took control. 'All that matters now is finding Zoe. Ava, have you heard from her since she met up with her mum?'

'No, nothing.'

'Send her a message, please. Don't alert her to the fact we know anything. Get a message to her, see if she replies and we'll know she's OK.'

'I'll get my phone.'

'You probably all think I'm stupid,' Adam said the second Ava left the room. 'What kind of a man puts up with that shit and doesn't do anything about it? You know, when I first thought about leaving, I decided I'd find help from someone professional. There are help groups for alcoholics, people with eating disorders, those who have depression, and I found endless information written about men who were abusive, intimidating and controlling. But I couldn't find much about women like Susan, women who do the same. I was at breaking point; I didn't know what I'd face when I came in the door after work, when I woke up in the morning. Had I spoken to her properly? Had I taken on my share of household chores? What price would I pay if I hadn't?'

'It sounds like you've been through hell.' Viola came over to him and held his hand, gave it a squeeze. 'I'm sorry I ever doubted you.'

Ava came in, bag in hand. 'This isn't mine.'

'What are you talking about?' Viola looked at the trendy Oxford rucksack in its taupe, pale blue and cream patched colours, the soft handles and buckles. She'd bought it in the sales after Christmas last year when she dragged Isaac around the shops. 'Oh no.'

'What is it?' Isla was onto Viola's fear.

Viola turned to them and explained how both girls had gone shopping in the sales, separately, yet come back with the same bag.

'You mean . . .' Isla looked at Adam, then back at Viola.

'No need to panic.' Viola fished in the bag. 'Her phone surely must be in here.' She rooted around but it wasn't.

'She usually puts it in her back pocket,' said Adam. 'I've told her not to; she'll get it nicked one of these days.'

'Call her on your phone, Ava.'

'Wait.' Adam took the bag, rifled through himself and, as his hand landed on something inside, his face paled. He pulled out her test kit. He didn't need to check inside to know that it had an insulin pen, cartridges of insulin, blood testing kit and machine, emergency lollipops and a packet of jelly babies in case she tested low.

'We must've been in such a rush we picked up the wrong bags,' Ava said. She was inconsolable.

Isaac saw Adam grab his car keys. 'The police are warning drivers to stay off the road in the storm.'

'I don't care.'

'Her mum won't be crazy enough to stay out all night tonight, surely.'

'You don't know Susan like I do.'

'I'm calling the police,' said Isla.

'To say what? No, I need to go and get her and take her diabetic kit with me.' He didn't even want to think about what would happen if she went too long without a dose of insulin.

Because her body needed it to survive.

24

Zoe

Seeing her mum after all this time had been like nothing she could ever have imagined. They hugged for the longest time, out here in the Chilterns in the beautiful spot Zoe had found with her dad and brother and vowed to show her mum one day.

It hadn't taken long for the storm to come in, causing Susan to make endless jokes about the British weather, which had Zoe laughing. Who'd have thought her mum was so funny? After the shitty time she must've had when their dad took them away, she still had this witty sense of positivity about her and she glowed with it. Zoe hoped she'd grow up to be just as beautiful one day.

They sheltered in Susan's car not long after Zoe arrived in a taxi and the heavens opened. And since then they'd both cried, they'd been talking at a hundred miles an hour, and now they were tucked up in the car again after a quick dash to the toilet block.

'Tell me about your friend.' Susan's curly hair hung cheekily across her shoulders and her blue eyes sparkled with mischief. 'Ava, was it?'

'We haven't known each other all that long, but she's my best friend.'

'I want to hear everything. About your school, your house, your friends, any boys in your life,' she added mischievously. 'And tell me all about your brother too. Oh, I do miss him so much; you've both grown up so fast.'

They gossiped as the windows steamed up from their breath, every now and then wiping the glass to see that there was a world outside of them, here, now, in this car. Zoe's voice carried on at a million miles an hour as she tried to cram in everything she and Zac had been up to over the last few years.

'This storm is mental!' Susan was next to wipe the back of her sleeve against the windscreen. Her eyes were alive when she looked to Zoe. 'Melbourne was sunny and thirty-four degrees when I left.'

'I bet you'd be at the beach if you weren't here.' Zoe remembered going as a kid, the huge waves thumping onto the shore, the flags you always had to swim between. There was a lot she could remember still, but a lot of confusion about their lives back in Australia. Seeing her mum now she could remember sometimes her mum would retreat into herself and not want anyone near, but now Zoe knew the truth, she could understand why.

'I go all the time.' Susan stared at the windscreen already beginning to mist up again. 'It's my happy place.'

Zoe still couldn't get her head around her dad doing those things to this beautiful woman. She watched the raindrops pooling on the windscreen, ganging up to make a deluge so torrential Zoe had visions of staying in the car all night. It certainly hadn't been like this when she was here with her dad in the holidays. The sun had been shining, a cool breeze was welcome with the humidity of an English summer.

'I've missed you.' Susan reached for Zoe's hand and Zoe clasped hers back. 'I know we've messaged each other, and I feel I've got to know you all over again, but there's nothing like seeing each other in person is there?'

Zoe leaned in for a cuddle and felt her mum nuzzle her hair, kiss the top of her head. Zoe remembered her doing that when she was little. Or had that been her dad? Or both of them? She was so confused.

'The photos you shared are amazing,' Susan told her. 'You look like you have a teenage girl's haven with that new bedroom of yours.'

'Zac will be asking for his to be done next.'

Her eyes held a sadness not many could reach. 'I'm sure he will. I really need to see him again.'

'Could you come to the house?'

'I'm here for three weeks, so why don't we have these two nights, then think about what to do next?'

'Dad will have to know you're here.'

Her face contorted with an emotion Zoe couldn't really read. 'I don't know why he brought you back to this hellhole.' A lightning bolt hit across the fields in the middle distance, lit up the trees and the fence in front where a stile would allow them access to a trail to the campsite. 'The weather is shit, the roads are cramped, and it's bloody cold!'

Her laughter soon had Zoe laughing too, but she told her mum, 'It's not so bad. Cloverdale is a nice village, we're settling in, and I like my school too.'

'You're Australian. Born and bred.'

'Half English though.'

'Yeah, well that's your dad's fault.'

Sometimes Zoe yearned for the blue skies, golden sands

and sunshine of Australia, but England had its charm and they'd found plenty since they moved in to Lilliput Cottage. She couldn't imagine leaving now. But how could she stay with her dad when he'd done those things?

Her tummy rumbled and she knew it was almost time to test her levels and have a snack. She'd packed a few in her bag. But her mum didn't know this part of her, and that felt weird. Like she'd be exposing something she wasn't quite ready to do when she was enjoying every second of being so near to the woman who'd nursed her as a baby, her mum, who'd missed so much of her life. When she'd started her periods she'd had her dad to talk to but that wasn't the same and instead she'd turned to her friends. When she had her first crush at twelve, she'd only confided in a girlfriend, wishing with all her heart she could've told her mum instead. When other girls moaned about their mothers, she laughed and kind of joined in but deep down she was jealous. They all had the one thing she wanted more than anything in the world.

All of a sudden Susan leapt out of the car, into the rain.

'Mum, what are you doing?'

'Something to remember!' Susan twirled around on the spot, the rain spattering her face. 'Life isn't about waiting for the rain to stop, it's about learning to dance in it,' she giggled. 'or something like that . . . can't remember the exact words.' She looked like she was in a trance. 'Come on, let's get the camping gear, setting it up in the British rain will be an adventure. We can put it on our Instagram stories. Get my photo, we'll post it. Go on, grab my phone!

'You're crazy!' But Zoe was giggling. She couldn't stop. Every time a doubt niggled at her, her mum said or did something to remind her of how amazing this was.

She tapped the phone screen, snapping away and capturing her mum, the essence of this woman who was the best surprise.

'Come out, come on, Zoe, don't be chicken!'

Zoe didn't need telling again. She climbed out of the car and they danced around in the rain, splashing each other, covered in mud, not caring at all that their footwear was sopping, their jeans wet through. They chased each other all the way over to the fence at the far end of the car park, they ran back again, the rain pelting harder and harder as their laughter mingled with the dusk.

'I need the loo,' Zoe called over the din of the storm, the rumble of thunder.

'Again?' Susan led the way, running over to the toilet block. She even managed a cartwheel, although fell on her bum. Zoe almost wet herself, she was laughing so much.

After she'd managed to make it to the toilets, Susan yelled, 'Race you to the car!' and she was off again.

Back inside the car, Susan started the engine up for warmth and climbed into the back to get out of her wet clothes. 'You need to change, Zo-Zo.'

She loved the way her mum used her childhood nickname but it was painful to realise how long it had been since she'd heard it. 'I will.' When Susan was finished and back in the driver's seat, Zoe clambered between the seats, into the back and opened up her own bag. She took out a pair of jeans, pulled them on but she was so cold and wet the material stuck to her and she struggled to do the zip up.

In the passenger seat again Zoe took the towel from Susan who had her entire suitcase in the back, and they sat looking out at a storm that wasn't going anywhere. Susan found music on the stereo system, news reports interrupting to tell them it was a wild night, safer to stay indoors.

'They're pathetic,' said Susan. 'Hey, we danced in it!' she yelled at the radio station. She made an 'L' shape with her thumb and forefinger against her head. 'Losers!'

Zoe could only grin and join in, making the same 'L' shape with her hand.

But she was beginning to feel a bit off. She needed to test her blood sugar soon. She'd begun to feel weak, tired. She hoped her mum wouldn't make a big thing about it when she saw her kit. She hoped it wouldn't cause a fuss, she didn't like fuss. She just wanted to get on with things and be normal. And she would, but first she wanted her Mum to know that she understood why she'd told her kids she couldn't be a mum anymore. 'Mum . . .'

'Zo-Zo.'

It made her smile every time. 'I . . . I know everything.'

'Nobody knows *everything*, Zo-Zo. I'm sure your school can't be that good.'

'It's really not. But I do know.' She thought of the diary, her mum's account of the terror she went through. Had she put the diary back where she found it? She couldn't remember.

'Zo-Zo, talk sense. What are you on about?'

'I found the diary.' She was so tired, she needed to get this out in the open and then reach for her test kit.

'What diary?'

'Your diary.' Oh crap, she was pretty sure she'd left it on her bed. Viola had been outside honking the horn and she'd panicked her dad would come up so she'd shoved it under some text books. Surely he wouldn't go through those, would he?

'Zo-Zo, diaries are for losers.' She checked her reflection in the flip-up mirror on the sun visor. 'Life is for living, not wasting your time with your nose in one of those things.'

'But you wrote one, maybe you've forgotten. It's old. It's from when we lived with you. When Dad and you were together. He must've kept it. I don't know why.'

Susan's hand left the eyebrow she'd been trying to smooth down. 'He still has that?'

'Dad took it from you?'

She pushed the visor up again, her lips twisted together. 'Not exactly.'

'I don't understand.'

Susan turned to her, took both of her hands in her own. 'I was unwell when you were little.' She hesitated. 'I wasn't right in the head; I had a lot of anger issues.'

'What are you talking about?'

'I liked to have a bit of fun, a laugh, but your dad, well, he was serious.'

Dad was a bully, let's face it.

'Your dad . . . he only had eyes for you and Zac. And I was jealous.'

'Jealous?' She felt shaky, hot and bothered. But she didn't understand what her mum was talking about.

Susan leaned her head back against the headrest of her seat. 'Crazy, isn't it? What kind of woman is jealous of her own kids? It was as though I couldn't see past it. It made me angry with Adam.'

Not Dad', but 'Adam'.

349

'I don't know what the diary said, Zo-Zo, but I imagine he embellished the events to his liking.'

Embellished. Zoe had had a spelling test last week, which she'd aced, and that had definitely been one of the words. It meant dressed up, to decorate or enhance.

'Adam set me up good and proper, took you and Zac away, set traps for me to fall into. He had it all planned, the two-faced bastard.'

The foul language hit Zoe as hard as the lightning outside struck the trees, trying to do its worst. 'I don't understand.' She was so tired; her head had started to hurt.

'He collected his evidence of how I'd bullied him. But I'm a woman, he should've stood up to me. God, I hated the way he let me push him around.' She looked at her nails and it was now Zoe noticed how chewed they were, not the elegant, painted nails she was sure her mum had once had. 'Like I said, I had a lot of problems, but I sorted through them. And your dad . . . well, he should've given me a chance to do that.'

Zoe wanted to cry. Realisation hit. She felt sick. 'You did all those things.'

Susan looked at her. 'You just said you knew.'

Zoe tried to focus on the blackness outside, still for a moment as the storm held back trying to decide what to do next. 'I thought it was him. Doing those things. To you.'

'Zo-Zo, I don't know what you're on about. And I can't believe he kept it.'

Her mum rambled on. But Zoe couldn't hear any of it. Because she knew now. The whole truth and nothing but the truth.

And one entry sprung to mind, the one where the diary's author panicked that the kids would come to harm if they stayed in the family home much longer. After reading that Zoe had barely slept. She'd become wary of her dad, distrusting the man who'd tried to protect her her whole life.

And now she was with the woman who'd done and said all those things. And all she could do was cry. She wanted to go home.

'Zo-Zo, pull yourself together and stop snivelling.'

She couldn't.

'I've come all this way, come on, let's put up the tent.'

'I don't want to.' She wanted her dad; she wanted Zac. She wanted their nice, safe home in Cloverdale.

'What do you mean you don't want to?'

'Please take me home. I want to go home.' She reached for her bag, her head lolling. She was weak; this had happened before. She needed something . . . juice, the jelly babies she'd packed . . . something. She'd left it too long. She'd let her mum's irresponsible behaviour rub off on her in seconds.

She opened her bag but she could barely see inside, her vision was beginning to blur.

'No.' Susan dug her heels in further. 'I want to spend time with you.'

Zoe pulled a purse from her bag but it wasn't hers. It was the purse Ava had pulled twenty quid from and given her to shove in her pocket in case she needed it.

She looked at her jeans. They weren't hers either. No wonder they'd felt odd and she'd struggled to do them up. These were Ava's jeans, her favourite pair, True Religion, she'd got them for her birthday and looked amazing in them, all legs and bum, making the boys ogle at her on dressdown days at school.

Ava, her best friend, who she desperately wanted to see. Right now.

'Zo-Zo, whatever is the matter with you?'

She knew she'd been talking but she wasn't sure she was making any sense. If this wasn't her bag, she had no test kit, no snacks.

'Zo-Zo, are you putting this on so I take you back to your dad? Because I won't fall for it . . . I've come all this way. Please . . . let me show you I've changed.'

'My kit . . .'

'What?'

'Need it . . .'

'Zoe, stop pissing about right now . . .'

But Zoe didn't hear the rest of her mum's rant. She was spiralling to a place of unconsciousness.

And then everything went dark.

Everything went quiet.

25

Adam

Sitting in the passenger seat of Jennifer's car, Adam dialled again. And again. And again.

'The weather's so bad they may not get a signal,' said Jennifer, her voice calm.

'It's ringing, finally.' His whole body tensed, but it rang out with no answer.

A few more rings dropped out through lack of signal, but almost at the same time as the rain stopped pummelling the windscreen, a voice croaked from the other end. 'Adam . . .' and he knew it was the woman he hadn't spoken to since the day he ran away.

He had all kinds of things to say to her, her anger flooded his psyche, but he had no room for anything but his daughter. 'Where's Zoe? Where have you taken her?'

Susan was hysterical, wailing into the phone; nothing she said made sense.

'Susan, put Zoe on the phone.'

'I can't,' she spluttered.

'Put her on now. Don't play games.'

More sobbing. 'She won't wake up.'

'What do you mean she won't wake up?' He heard Isla

swear from the back seat, saw Jennifer glance his way briefly.

'She's floppy. I don't know what's happening. It's like she's taken drugs. Sleeping pills, I don't know.'

He pushed a finger into his ear willing the phone signal to hold out as he tried to hear more over the sound of the car engine, the background noise as they hurtled along. His instructions now had to be concise, clear. There was no time to waste. 'You need to take her to a hospital. Right now! She's a diabetic, she doesn't have her kit with her.'

Susan wailed something about a kit, how Zoe had mentioned it, but she'd slipped into a state of semi-consciousness before Susan could ask more.

'Susan listen to me . . . go to the hospital.'

'I don't know where the hospital is!'

Susan was panicking, yelling. It reminded him of the rages she'd flown into back when they were together. It sent shivers up his spine. What if she put the phone down?

He calmed his voice but kept it firm. 'Where are you?'

'Middle of nowhere,' she wailed.

'You must've used a postcode to get there.' He kept talking. Had to keep her in the moment.

'Yes!' There was rustling and he thought she'd hung up but then she was back, reiterating the postcode Ava had given them, the place they were heading to.

Isla had already googled the nearest hospitals and handed him her phone with a postcode of one. He gave it to Susan. 'I'll meet you there. Go now, Susan. Susan . . .'

But the call had dropped out.

His fingers shook as he touched the redial icon, but nothing. He tried over and over but got nowhere. He sent her a text with the postcode just in case. Jennifer had already diverted off the main road to make their way to hospital. It was just as quick to do that than it would be to go to find Susan.

But was Susan on her way there?

Or had she done what she always swore she'd do. And hurt one of the kids, to get to him in a way that would be the ultimate revenge?

26

Jennifer

The second they pulled in to the ambulance bay at the front of the hospital it was as though they were part of a film set. Adam ran into A&E but by the time Jennifer parked up and ran back to the hospital entrance, Zoe still wasn't there. Everyone was standing around ready to play a part; it was as if they were all waiting for someone to say action and for the mayhem to begin again.

And then with a screech of tyres it did.

A car swung into the crescent lay-by in front of the hospital and a mane of dull blonde hair emerged. Adam ran over; Susan was trying to haul Zoe out of the passenger seat.

Isla jumped in to help and pulled Susan out of the way while Adam leaned in and scooped Zoe into his arms. He turned and two paramedics plus a doctor surrounded him. He talked at a rate of knots, his words tripping over themselves to get out. He told them she was diabetic, they assured him they had it from here. He tried to run after them, through the doors, Isla at his side. And when Jennifer went inside a nurse was telling Adam to let the doctors do their job, his daughter was in good hands.

He raked his own hands through his hair, he fell to

356

a crouched position in the corridor. Isla had her arms around him and he clung on for dear life.

'Adam, they've got her now,' said Jennifer. 'They know what they're doing, she'll get through this.'

'What if she doesn't?' He didn't even try to hold back the tears. 'If I lose her . . .'

'You won't,' Isla urged. 'Don't even think it.'

'She's right, Adam. Come on, let's go and sit down in the waiting area; we're in the way in the corridor.' Jennifer and Isla between them led him that way but he hovered near the front doors looking out for the other car that had arrived with so much drama.

'Susan might be moving her car,' Isla suggested. 'She can't leave it in the way of the ambulances.'

'I don't want her here. Don't let her come in. I don't want her anywhere near Zoe.'

Isla comforted him, told him not to worry about anything else for now. But Jennifer knew if she saw the woman first she'd have to stop her coming in. Because Adam was in no fit state to see the person who'd subjected him to a version of personal hell and who he probably saw as being the one responsible for Zoe being in hospital.

'I failed her,' Adam said over and over. 'All I had to do was keep her safe and I couldn't even do that.'

'She's in good hands,' said Isla.

Adam clasped his hands in his lap, the tension not even breaking with Isla's comforting touch, and his nerves made him begin to ramble. He needed to talk, and Isla and Jennifer listened. Jennifer wished he'd come to them and told them everything sooner, but hindsight was a wonderful thing.

'When Zoe was first diagnosed as a diabetic I thought

357

we'd never cope with it all. She was so ill, she'd lost all this weight and I was terrified it was an eating disorder that would take her from me.'

'You must've been terrified.' Jennifer had one eye on him, the other on the doors in case Susan appeared.

'Rushing her to hospital one night was something I'll never forget. It was a huge adjustment when she came home but she was stronger than I was. She had her ups and downs, went through the emotions after her diagnosis, but then she took control. She took all the information on board, she managed it herself.'

'She's a great kid,' Jennifer told him, gripping the top of his hand for reassurance. 'And you're an amazing dad.'

'I don't know why this happened.' He rubbed his eyes with the heels of his hands. 'She's usually so careful. I should've insisted on her wearing the medical alert bracelet I bought her, then Susan would've seen it.'

'It might not have changed anything in this situation. She was still in the middle of nowhere with no kit.' Jennifer wanted to stop him going down this road, the journey towards blaming himself. 'And getting teens to do anything is hard. My twins wouldn't even wear the shoes I chose for them let alone a medical bracelet.' She'd coaxed a smile and for that she was glad.

Jennifer and Isla looked at each other helplessly. What could they say? All they could do was pray Zoe was going to be fine. And when it came to blame Jennifer almost wondered whether it was partly her fault too. She'd been wrapped up in her own problems, petty squabbles with other people who were only trying to do their best. She could've carved out more time for Adam, or not made him and Isla so uncomfortable with their relationship, by the time morning came around, she had a message waiting for her.

Zoe wasn't daft. She'd asked for a photograph so she could know who this person really was, and she'd asked this Suzie to clarify her full name, Zoe's date of birth and Zac's.

And once Zoe knew it was her mum and the messages started coming, she'd devoured each and every one.

Suzie: My beautiful Zo-Zo. How are you?

Zoe: I can't believe it's really you! And you remembered my nickname!

She must've been seven or eight when she'd last heard her mum call her Zo-Zo. Since then, her dad had only once tried to use the nickname and she'd yelled at him not to, said she wasn't a baby and asked him to never say it again. But it wasn't because it was babyish; it was because it had been her mum's name for her and she missed her so much she thought her heart would break.

Suzie: Of course I do, I've never forgotten. You've been with me every single day, in my heart and my head. I miss you and Zac so much.

Zoe: We miss you too. I wondered if you'd try to find us.

Suzie: Are you glad I did?

Zoe: Very!

She added a couple of emojis to that message, amidst

and perhaps Adam would've confided in Isla instead. This whole situation could've been avoided.

And here was the doctor, coming to them with news. And she couldn't read the look on his face.

27

Adam

Without Zoe and Zac, Adam would've walked away from Susan a long time before he did, way before she could try to take something else from him.

His two wonderful kids had depended on him and he'd ended up needing them just as much to give him strength every day to go on as normal. Normal. What even was that? He looked at Zoe lying in the hospital bed and longed to be 'normal' again. Having Zoe biting his head off and stropping around like a true teen, him being embarrassing by talking to her in public or in front of her friends, he'd take every single thing she threw at him if only she'd wake up.

As he'd waited on that uncomfortable plastic chair, the smell of the hospital surrounding them, voices of calm passing by, others of urgency, scenarios had raced around his head. But he hadn't had to wait all that long before the doctor found him.

The doctors had carried out their tests and found that Zoe had had a severe hypo. Usually, with a hypo they could react quickly at home and it never got so bad they had to come to hospital, but for whatever reason Zoe hadn't acted at the first signs. She'd pushed and pushed it until she'd fallen unconscious. And he knew looking at her now, sitting by her bed holding her hand, she was lucky. If Susan hadn't answered his call or found the hospital and got Zoe here so quickly, the outcome could've been a hell of a lot worse. She might not still be with them. And that was something he couldn't fathom.

He looked at her, so much like her mum with her long hair, the same delicate nose and mouth, but none of the bad things he'd had to endure over the years. He hated to think of her stuck in a car, in a storm, probably scared out of her mind when she realised, too late, what was happening. When he'd picked her up in his arms she was sweaty, lifeless, all the colour had been drained out of her. And he'd feared the worst.

Susan hadn't hung around. Isla had been allowed to come in a minute ago and see him, tell him there was no sign of the woman who'd caused all of this to happen. Perhaps she'd got a flight home to Australia; he didn't really care, not now. All he cared about was Zoe and Zac. Charlotte had been the gold-starred babysitter and agreed to sleep over the night in the box room, she didn't want paying she'd told him, and he'd almost cried at her generosity. A stranger almost, trusting him, believing in their family unit. She didn't tell Zac there was an emergency; she told him that Daddy had been stuck at a friend's house in the storm so it was safer to come back in the morning. Adam wanted to tell Zac about this himself. Although quite how much he'd say, he had no idea.

'Dad . . .'

'You're awake.' He lifted his head, his eyes met hers. And he let out a sigh. 'You gave me a bloody good scare.'

Zoe's eyes filled with tears.

'No crying, you don't need to say anything. You're going to be fine, that's the main thing.'

'I'm sorry.'

'No need to be.'

'I had the wrong bag.'

'I know you did.' He held her as her tears fell gently.

'I'm sorry I read the diary. It was yours not hers. I should've recognised the writing. Although it did look too neat to be yours.'

He laughed, felt relief for the first time since he'd realised Zoe wasn't at Tatiana's as he'd thought.

'Am I in trouble?'

'Yes, but not right now.'

'She was horrible to you.' Zoe croaked out the words and he helped her with the cup near her bed, moving the straw so she could take a few sips.

'She was. And I should've told you. But I was scared.' It felt odd to say it out loud, to his daughter. 'I wondered if you remembered the time she held the pillow over my face.'

'I don't remember.'

She'd probably blocked it from her mind. 'Not even when you read the diary?'

'I don't remember, Dad, I don't. I'm sorry.'

'Shhh . . . shhh . . . no need for that now.' He kissed her forehead and sat back down. 'I was afraid that if I told you everything, you'd hate me for telling her to stay out of our lives. I kept you from her and maybe that was wrong but it was the only way I could get out at the time, or at least I thought it was.' He stroked her hair again, too emotional to talk for a minute. He just wanted to watch her, let her recover, get back his beautiful daughter.

After a while he told her, 'The diabetes nurse will be stopping by tomorrow to talk to you – well, us – about taking better care of you.'

She managed a grin. 'We're in trouble.'

'I think we might be.' He grasped her hand, smiled at her. She said nothing else, shut her eyes and fell asleep.

The diabetes nurse would have no idea why Zoe had been so distracted she hadn't taken care of herself the way she should. She'd probably think Zoe was another teen who felt invincible, trying to defy the illness.

But Zoe and Adam knew the truth. Everyone in Cloverdale did now. And it was a relief rather than a burden.

Zac ran straight for them when they came through the door the next day. He'd been told his sister was in hospital but was going to be fine; he'd been allowed the day off school and he'd been able to choose anything he wanted for breakfast and lunch, watch whatever he wanted on television.

'Careful, Zac,' Adam pleaded. 'Your sister isn't a bean-bag you go running for.' He did that often enough in his bedroom, jumping onto the thing the second he raced up there.

Zoe was hugging Zac. She agreed to watch *Karate Kid* with him, the film Adam had bought on DVD last week for his son, who was itching to try out martial arts properly next year. Adam doubted Zoe would sit and watch television with her baby brother after today, or maybe like him she'd have more of an appreciation of their history and what had led them to where they were now and she'd make the most of her sibling. He could live in hope.

Isla had borrowed a heart-shaped tin from the Library of Shared Things to make Zoe a welcome home cake that strictly followed the recipe Isla had found online in a diabetic forum. With winter coming this way and a frost on the ground most mornings, the smell of a beef hotpot drew Adam into the kitchen where Isla had left the meal in the oven for tonight's dinner, plus a note welcoming them home and telling them the cake was in the Tupperware container in the cupboard. She'd had to put it out of sight because Zac kept looking at it and she was pretty sure he'd run his finger along the icing to steal a quick taste. She'd added a few kisses on the bottom of the note, and Adam couldn't wait to collect them in person.

Adam was about to boil some potatoes to eat with the casserole when there was a knock at the door.

He ran, expecting Isla.

What he wasn't expecting was to see a policeman. Neither was he expecting to hear the news about Susan.

28

Adam

The residents of Cloverdale rallied around over the next few weeks following the Parker family emergency, and Adam got to see first-hand what it was like to be part of a community with strong ties. Elaine had been over with endless meals – casseroles, stew, beef and Guinness pie – until he'd finally pointed out they were getting back to normal and he could take it from here. Wesley the local carpenter had fixed his front gate that had finally given up and fallen off its hinges, Harrison had supplied them with so much fruit and veg that Adam was in no doubt he was getting the recommended daily intake and then some. Adam had been able to focus solely on Zoe and Zac, and he'd never forget the kindness of these strangers who'd become friends.

And here they were yet again, supporting him today. The kids were both at home, they'd offered to come, they both knew what he would be talking about, but he hadn't wanted to put them through it. Instead he'd borrowed the ice cream maker from the Library of Shared Things, and promised they'd make maple honeycomb ice cream from Isla's recipe later even though the season had well and truly turned to winter.

Things with Isla were going smoothly. She'd kept her distance after what had happened, but only to give him space, and when he'd turned up at her cottage and taken her in his arms she'd been a part of his new beginning. He wasn't sure they'd spent much longer than twenty-four hours apart since. And the kids loved her. Isla had enrolled Zac and herself into local karate lessons together, which his son thought was the most awesome thing in the world, and she'd bought Zoe a trendy shocking pink medical alert bracelet that Zoe hadn't taken off since.

After the truth had come out, and Zoe had given him the biggest scare of his life, Adam had worked from home for a while so he could be there for his kids, so they could all get their lives well and truly on track. He'd managed to find a charity organisation set up to support victims of domestic abuse, and, through them, got to talk about his experiences and receive counselling. The charity had published several articles about domestic abuse against men – he wasn't alone, far from it – and when they first asked him whether he'd be interested in talking to others about what he'd been through, he'd refused. But then he'd got to thinking, how grateful he would've been if there'd been someone like him who got it, when he was going through the nightmare that Susan brought to their marriage. The statistics spoke for themselves. Domestic violence against men was more common than most people probably realised; only a small percentage of men spoke up or filed a report, and some men lost their lives because of it. And so standing here today, in this room, Adam realised that if he could change the life of one person here, then he'd count that as a win.

That day he brought Zoe home safe and sound from the hospital to Lilliput Cottage, the police had shown up at his door. Susan had been in a road traffic accident. She'd driven into a tree, on purpose as it turned out, and it was a miracle she was alive. The police had found Ava's bag in her car, Zoe's phone and his details and made contact that way.

Adam hadn't gone to see her in hospital, he hadn't wanted to, but three months later a man called Stuey, who was Susan's counsellor in Australia, made contact with him and he'd eventually agreed to let Susan speak with her children on the phone. He'd used speakerphone each and every time, in case she tried to set something up behind his back, but it also gave him a sense of the woman she was now, and even without seeing her, he knew something had changed for the better. He couldn't trust her completely, that would take a hell of a long time, but he'd listened to his children regale their tales of school, Zoe's make-up crazes, Zac's passion for football. And Susan in turn told them all about the beach, her part-time teaching role at a different school to before, even her visits with Stuey and the brightly coloured fish in the tank she could watch for hours.

Zoe and Zac seemed more content after everything that had happened. Something had shifted and as a family unit the three of them were closer than ever before. And Zoe was making a real effort to keep the lines of communication open. She didn't share everything, not by a long shot, but she made an effort to keep him more informed, to not shut herself away so much. And he knew it was her way of saying sorry for ever doubting him.

Now, Adam moved a little more to the left to avoid the

winter sun coming through the frost-edged windows as he addressed his audience here in the library with its surrounding book shelves and from where he could see the bright yellow doors across the car park in the Library of Shared Things, the place where he'd really started to make friends when it opened up in Cloverdale.

The charity he'd contacted had advertised the talk and were responsible for filling the room and now, it was time to share his story. As he talked he tried not to gauge reactions but it was hard. He saw people wince at the details he shared, he saw one person wipe away a tear; whether in sympathy or because their own journey was just as bad, he had no idea. His voice wobbled as he shared details of the emotional and physical abuse he'd endured, the terror, the upset, the being stuck in a life he couldn't claw his way out of. His voice caught as he told them what his marriage had been like, how his friends had fallen away, how he'd fled to another country to keep his kids safe. He hadn't needed props, visuals or diagrams like he did when he presented ideas at work. All the evidence was there in his voice, with his words, on his face as he conveyed the feelings he'd kept so well hidden.

'I'd read something once about how a diary can help our mental wellbeing. I thought it was a load of rubbish,' he told his audience, enjoying the laugh he got in return. 'But I did it because I was desperate. If anything could take away a tiny bit of my pain and my feelings of isolation, give me a little bit of self-worth and realisation that it was someone else doing these things, not me, then it would be worth it. And once I started writing it, I couldn't stop.'

His diary was still there beneath his hand on the lectern.

It was a real thing, a solid part of his experience, part of his journey from then to now.

'Diarising my thoughts, my fears, everything that happened, it was someone to talk to. I'm not suggesting I talk to a book.' Another laugh. 'But when your spouse alienates your friends and relations until you literally have no place left to turn, I'd suggest giving it a go.' Nobody laughed now.

'For a long time I felt I was doing something wrong. I suppose that's how I maintained my distance, by not putting names in my diary. The writing it down helped, but there was still an element of denial.' He sipped from a glass of water again. Much more and he'd need to pee. 'I admit I talked to myself. I'd stand in front of the mirror sometimes and say, "Adam, get a grip. This is your marriage. Make it work." It's advice I assumed my parents would give to me. But they saw what I couldn't. That it wasn't my fault. I didn't ask for it, and I didn't deserve it.'

As the crowds clapped him after this part of his talk, his eyes met his father's, then his mother's, both here to support him. When they'd hugged him this morning at Lilliput Cottage, the physical gesture had spoken more than a thousand words; it showed him their relief that their son and grandchildren were happy and safe and had a sense of peace they'd struggled to find for so long. They also wanted to check out the Library of Shared Things. Since Jennifer had roped him in to help that day, and he'd been brave enough to mingle with new people who knew nothing of his pain, he'd talked to his family about the library and how it worked and his mum had had the urge to start up a similar venture where they lived.

He cleared his throat, ready to sum up. 'I thank you

all for coming here today, to listen to me, to find hope if you need it, to know how important it is to reach out, to someone, anyone, to know that you're not alone. Abuse, whether physical or psychological, is real. It's a social problem affecting both sexes, and accepting that is the first step.

'I now think of myself as lucky. A few years ago, I never would've said that. But I came here to Cloverdale and found my home. The Library of Shared Things offered me a new start. They've given me vacuums, a waffle maker, a lawnmower . . .' his voice trailed off to more laughter from his audience. His eyes met those of a man in the front row who'd talked confidentially with him when he arrived and who he could see had been affected by the presentation today. The man had been in an abusive marriage for a decade and like many others, like Adam once, couldn't bear the thought of losing his kids. Adam hoped he found his own way out soon.

Adam met Jennifer's glance across the room. She was standing encased in David's arms, happy albeit busy with her home hairdressing that had taken off in a whirlwind. She and Isla were getting back on track these days, Jennifer's doubts about her sister cast aside now Isla had told her everything about her reasons for leaving in the first place, and what had kept her away. He guessed Jennifer would always watch over her younger sister and mother her, at least a little; it was the way she was and he knew if Zoe and Zac could stay as close as those two throughout life, he'd be pretty happy.

His gaze moved to Viola who stood linking arms with Ava, her daughter who had been there for Zoe through everything. Viola had been over to the cottage many a time, apologised for her involvement and her doubts, and the only way he'd been able to stop the apologies had been to let her decorate Zac's room for free.

His eyes met with Isla's, this woman he hoped to spend his future with, and she smiled back at him. She'd been almost as nervous as he was today, but seeing her watching him, believing in him, along with all their friends, he knew he'd reached a new phase in his life, one he didn't want to run from.

'All jokes aside,' he said, as he came to the end of his talk, 'Cloverdale and the Library of Shared Things gave me a sense of place, of belonging. I've found friends who believe in me, people I can trust, I've come to realise I'm still me and not this person who was so unhappy, running scared. I have people in my life who care and who've given me a sense of self-worth I hadn't felt in a very long time.'

And more than that, he'd found Cloverdale, with its mishmash of cottages, its windy roads, the way the street dipped outside the bakery and created a huge puddle of water every time it rained. A village, a home, and people who cared. Adam had found the missing pieces of him.

He'd found a place to call home.

Acknowledgements

When I proposed my idea for this book to Clare Hey, Publishing Director at Orion, I was thrilled she loved it. So a big thank you once again to Clare for believing in me enough to present me with another publishing contract. I still have to pinch myself sometimes!

I had some serious themes in this book and so needed a setting that would enable me to tell the story but leave my readers uplifted. And so, after investigating how communities can help one another, the idea of the Library of Shared Things in a small fictitious village called Cloverdale was born. I fell in love with the setting and hope my readers have done the same.

Thank you to Rebecca Trevalyan, founder of The Library of Things who ran a presentation on the idea that she, along with friends, had introduced to West Norwood. She'd always been passionate about bringing people in the community together and hoped that rather than dying out, libraries could become thriving community hubs. I hope I have done the concept justice by representing Cloverdale's Library of Shared Things.

A big thank you goes to my older brother, Matthew, for answering my many questions about diabetes and patiently letting me run through scenarios I had come up with to make my characters' experiences true to life. I still owe you that coffee, Matthew!

Thank you to Olivia Barber who has done much of the editing on *The Little Village Library*. We had versions going back and forth until we were both happy and she's a pleasure to work with as well as an amazing editor. I can't wait to work with you again, Olivia.

Many thanks to Britt at Orion for constant supplies of promotion graphics when it comes to announcements, reveals and the build-up to publication day. And a big thank you to the Orion cover designers for coming up with a cover that I'm sure you'll all agree is beautiful.

I'm especially grateful to every single one of my readers who have picked up a copy of this book and trusted me to take them into another fictious world and tell a brand new story. I hope you enjoyed the book! And I love hearing from readers on Facebook, Twitter or Instagram, so please feel free to get in touch any time.

And finally, my biggest thanks goes to my husband and children for being there at my side always. I couldn't do it without your support. Love you all!

Credits

Helen Rolfe and Orion Fiction would like to thank everyone at Orion who worked on the publication of *The Little Village Library* in the UK.

Editorial
Clare Hey
Olivia Barber

Copy editor
Donna Hillyer

Proof reader
Jane Howard

Audio
Paul Stark
Amber Bates

Contracts
Anne Goddard
Paul Bulos
Jake Alderson

Design
Rabab Adams
Tomas Almeida
Joanna Ridley

Editorial Management
Charlie Panayiotou
Jane Hughes
Alice Davis

Finance
Jasdip Nandra
Afeera Ahmed
Elizabeth Beaumont
Sue Baker

Production
Ruth Sharvell

Marketing
Brittany Sankey

Frances Doyle
Georgina Cutler

Sales
Jen Wilson
Esther Waters
Victoria Laws
Rachael Hum
Ellie Kyrke-Smith

Operations
Jo Jacobs
Sharon Willis
Lisa Pryde
Lucy Brem

If you enjoyed *The Little Village Library*, you'll love Helen Rolfe's heartwarming story of romance, friendship and second chances . . .

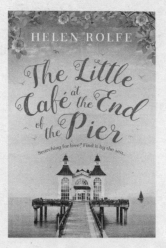

Searching for love? You'll find it at the little café at the end of the pier . . .

When Jo's beloved grandparents ask for her help in running their little café at the end of the pier in Salthaven-on-Sea, she jumps at the chance.

The café is a hub for many people: the single dad who brings his little boy in on a Saturday morning; the lady who sits alone and stares out to sea; the woman who pops in after her morning run.

Jo soon realises that each of her customers is looking for love - and she knows just the way to find it for them. She goes about setting each of them up on blind dates - each date is held in the café, with a special menu she has designed for the occasion.

But Jo has never found love herself. She always held her grandparents' marriage up as her ideal and she hasn't found anything close to that. But could it be that love is right under her nose . . . ?

Escape to the countryside with Helen Rolfe's
charming story of new beginnings and
second chances . . .

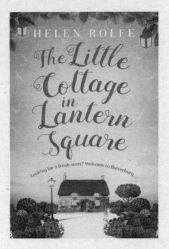

Step into the enchanting world of Lantern Square . . .

Hannah went from high-flyer in the city to business owner and has
never looked back. In the cosy Cotswold village of Butterbury she
runs Tied up with String, sending handmade gifts and care packages
across the miles, as well as delivering them to people she thinks
need them the most.

But when her ex best-friend Georgia turns up and wants in on the
action, will Hannah be willing to forgive and forget? With her
business in jeopardy she needs to maintain the reputation she's
established, and discover who she can trust . . .

Meanwhile, mysterious acts of kindness keep springing up around
Butterbury, including a care package on Hannah's own doorstep.
Who is trying to win her heart – and will she ever be willing to give
it away?

Available in paperback and ebook from June 2020